TEN
BELLS STREET

Mary Collins

piatkus

PIATKUS

First published in Great Britain in 2018 by Piatkus
This paperback edition published in 2019 by Piatkus

1 3 5 7 9 10 8 6 4 2

A CIP catalogue record for this book
is available from the British Library.

ISBN 978-0-349-41616-8

Typeset in Palatino by M Rules
Printed and bound in Great Britain by
Clays Ltd, Elcograf S.p.A.

Papers used by Piatkus are from well-managed forests
and other responsible sources.

MIX
Paper from
responsible sources
FSC® C104740

Piatkus
An imprint of
Little, Brown Book Group
Carmelite House
50 Victoria Embankment
London EC4Y 0DZ

An Hachette UK Company
www.hachette.co.uk

www.littlebrown.co.uk

To my family, especially my father,
whose streets these were and who
always walked them with pride.

Chapter One

1 August 1930
Spitalfields, London

Bernie knew that her grotto was the best. Marie's had been a pile of mud with some leaves and a shell on top. The boys' effort was even worse. Of course Mammy had said they were all nice, but then Mammy wanted them out of the way so she could work. By the time they got in for their tea, the whole flat would be wreathed in steam and the lines in the yard would be full of other people's washing. Mammy would be worn out but she'd still have to cook for them all and then she had a sewing job on for Mr Sassoon.

'Remember the grotto!' Bernie said to a passer-by.

The old Jewish man looked at her, shook his head and walked on. Her daddy had told her the Jews didn't believe in grottos. Bernie didn't understand it. You didn't have to believe in grottos to like them. Grottos were beautiful. Well, Bernie's was.

She'd taken a board from the yard and covered it in moss to

start with. A bit of broken mirror became a pond, then she'd put a Holy Card she'd got for good attendance at school on the edge of the glass. It showed her namesake, St Bernadette, praying to Our Lady of Lourdes, to thank her for all the miracles of healing she'd performed. Bernie had surrounded this with flowers 'borrowed' from Christ Church graveyard. Mammy would've killed her if she'd found out. She would've double killed her if she'd known that the little sparkles glittering between the flowers were the hatpins she'd inherited from Great-nanny Burke. One of them was a proper stone, which went into Uncle's every time the rent was due. To prop up the picture, Bernie had used one of Aggie's dolls' chairs. Bernadette had asked her little sister. Aggie was too young to answer, but Bernie had asked.

Her brothers and Dermot's pal little Chrissy Dolan had taken their grotto up the pub. That was the best pitch. People didn't know what money they had left when they came out, and cared even less. The odd farthing might even fall from a limp, tipsy hand by mistake. The boys'd be on it like starving rats. Marie and her friend Doris had disappeared down towards Liverpool Street Station with their messy old wreck.

Bernie pressed herself up against the wall next to Kipper's Bananas. The fruit and veg market was also a good pitch for a skinny kid with a pretty grotto. Flat-cap-wearing costers with fags hanging out of their mouths could be good for a farthing or two – or else a few cauliflower leaves. The old girls with their headscarves and mourning jewellery might tell her to 'Get out of it!', but Bernie knew to ignore them. They didn't like 'Irish'. Her mammy always said to turn her nose up at such ignorant women.

But on this bright morning in August, even the blokes were ignoring her. Maybe her grotto just wasn't big or good enough?

Or maybe it was as her daddy kept saying and no one had any money? Bernie wished she was with the boys. Seven-year-old Paddy had nicked a handful of bread and dripping from underneath their mammy's nose and Bernie's stomach was rumbling at the thought of it.

'What's that you have there?'

When she looked up to see where the voice had come from, Bernie expected its owner to be a grown-up woman – and a posh one at that. But it was a girl who had spoken to her.

'What?'

In fact it was the girl who lived across the road. Her dad was rich, so Bernie's mammy said. A tailor by trade, he wore a little cap like a bishop's and a thick overcoat even in the summer. Like most people on Fournier Street, this family were Jews and worshipped at the big Synagogue there. Bernie and the rest of her family had to drag themselves all the way almost to the Tower of London to go to Mass. Them Jews, her mammy said, had it easy.

'What is it?' asked the girl again.

She pointed at the grotto. It was then that Bernie saw the Jewish girl wasn't alone. Two massive green eyes, set deep in the tiniest, dirtiest face in Spitalfields, peeped over the tailor's daughter's smartly dressed shoulder.

'It's a grotto,' the green-eyed child whispered.

Smelly Ellie. Now Bernie knew *her*.

'How'd you know that?' she said, curious. 'You don't go to school or nuffing.'

'Me dad told me. And I *do* go to school. Sometimes.'

'Don't lie! You ain't got no dad, Ellie.'

'Me name's not Ellie.'

The child's name was Rose and she too lived on Fournier Street. But not in a house like the Jewish girl or even in a small flat like the one Bernie lived in with her family. Rose and her mother and a revolving selection of men lived in two basement box rooms.

'Anyway, that's a grotto,' Rose said to the Jewish girl. 'You make 'em new every year and ask people to "remember" them. Then they give you money.'

'What for?'

'To remember the grotto!' Bernie said. 'It's like a saint's miracle or the Virgin Mary, me daddy said.'

'So did me mum,' Rose agreed.

Bernie's patience snapped then. Everyone knew what Smelly Ellie's mum was. She wouldn't have that old brass compared to her daddy!

'Shut up, Ellie,' she said. 'Your mum don't know nuffing. Anyway, thought your "dad" told ya?'

'He did.'

Bernie looked at the tailor's daughter. 'What you doing going about with Smelly Ellie? You know she don't wear knickers, don't ya?'

The girl put a hand in the pocket of her smart blue dress and took out a ha'penny.

'That for the grotto?' Bernie asked, quick as a flash.

'You can have it if you don't call my friend here rude names,' the Jewish girl replied.

Bernie didn't like being told what to do even by her mammy. She said, 'Well, what do you call her then?'

'Rose. And I'm Rebekah,' the girl said. 'Rose is my friend.'

'Since when?'

'Since she taught me how to swing off lamp-posts.'

'Anyone can do that.'

Bernie had been hooking old bits of rope around the tops of lamp-posts and making swings all her life.

No one said anything. Bernie looked at the coin in Rebekah's hand. Eventually Rose said, 'How old are you?'

Bernie didn't know whether she or Rebekah was being addressed but said, 'I'm ten. You're younger though, ain't ya? You're the same age as our Marie.'

'Eight.'

'I'm ten,' Rebekah said.

Bernie wanted to ask her what she was doing playing with a kid two years younger, but she didn't. She wanted that ha'penny and she was going to get it. She already had sixpence from when she'd found old Peg-leg Dooley's dog down by Wapping Stairs back in June. Her brother Joey had taken the mutt for a laugh, but Peg-leg didn't know that. It was then, just after the old man had given her the tanner, that Bernie had seen The Photographs.

Old Mr Katz had run the paper and string shop on Brick Lane for donkey's years. But no one had known he had a brother until he had turned up and started working in the shop at the beginning of the year. People said he came from Germany. Bernie didn't know. In fact, she didn't know anything about this man, Walter Katz, until her mammy sent her into the shop to buy some string.

The usual Mr Katz had been out and so his brother had served her. While he cut the string to the length she needed, Walter Katz said that if she wanted, she could look at some photographs of his country. They lay on the counter and they were beautiful. There were pictures of castles that looked like they came from fairy tales, of pretty, clean little villages, the houses covered in flowers, and of men and boys proudly wearing very smart uniforms and shiny boots. Bernie asked Walter Katz how he'd got the photographs and he said that he had taken them himself. 'That was my job, being a photographer,' he'd told her, 'until those men with the shiny boots told me to stop.'

He'd not told her why they'd asked him to stop and Bernie hadn't enquired. It was rude to ask grown-ups too many questions, so her mammy said. But then he'd shown her his camera and she'd asked more questions than her mother could have imagined. A sleek black-and-chrome Leica, it was nothing like the huge camera that Mr Cohen the photographer had in his studio. It took both Mr Cohen and his wife to move that. But Mr Katz's camera was so small, it could go anywhere. Even, Bernie had daydreamed, to Egypt where the Pyramids were, which was where she was going to become an explorer when she grew up. She knew all there was to know about the Pyramids because Sister Joan at school had let her read about them in a book.

Then Mr Katz had told her what his camera would cost. He'd said, 'Maybe one day when you're older you can have one.' Bernie had run home then and cried. Ten pounds was an impossible amount! But then she'd remembered her tanner and thought, Well, it's a start!

And now here was a rich girl who had made friends with Smelly Ellie. If this Rebekah could make friends with someone like Ellie, she could make friends with anyone!

'Well, if you're ten then and you can swing on lamp-posts, you should learn to ride a bike,' Bernie told her.

'A bike? Papa wouldn't like that,' Rebekah said immediately.

'Does he like you swinging on lamp-posts?'

'He doesn't know about it. Anyway I couldn't ride a bike because I don't know how.'

'Me brother Dermot made himself one,' Bernie told her. 'He lets me ride it. I can teach you.'

'Can you teach me too?' Rose asked.

'That would be nice. If we could all ride the bike,' Rebekah said. 'I see people on them all the time. I've always wanted to try.'

Bernie looked at Smelly Ellie's ragged clothes and tangled,

filthy black hair. Mammy said that Rose and her mum were gypsies. She always said that her own kids should keep away from that family in case they got cursed. But then if Smelly Ellie was with this Rebekah, she'd make sure she didn't do anything magic, wouldn't she?

'I seen your Dermot's bike,' Rose said. 'I won't bust it. Honest.'

Bernie pretended to think for a moment and then she said, 'You can if you put on knickers.'

Rose trembled with excitement. 'I will!'

Rebekah put her ha'penny down in front of the grotto.

It took every ounce of self-control Bernie had not to snatch it up immediately and put it in her pocket. Instead she said, 'Daddy says that if you remember the grotto you'll be happy all year.'

'Because it's magic,' Rose said.

Just very quickly, Bernie shuddered.

A farthing a lesson seemed about right – except that Rebekah learned fast and anyway Dermot nicked the coin off Bernie when he found it. Well, it was his bike.

As it happened he did his sister a favour because as the long hot days of the summer holidays passed, Bernie began to like 'Becky' more and more. She was even able to put up with Rose, provided she didn't pick her nose too much and kept the smell down. But Bernie continued to steer clear of Rose's mother, Nell.

The latest man in Nell Larkin's life was, like the one before him, a drunken bully. When he wasn't in the Ten Bells at the bottom of the road, boozing, he was lying drunk in those tiny stinking rooms they all shared, or smacking Nell about. Not that she couldn't give as good as she got. One afternoon when Bernie and Becky went to meet Rose they heard her mother yell, 'Next time I'll fuckin' kill ya!'

Rose had said, 'Me dad's had a skinful again.' And then laughed nervously.

But to tell the truth Bernie was actually more afraid of Becky's dad than she was of Rose's mum. Nell Larkin was a mad gypsy woman and so of course she was scary. Becky's dad was just odd.

One day when they were all out in Bernie's mammy and daddy's back yard, skipping, Bernie said to Becky, 'Why don't your dad go out?'

Moritz Shapiro, Rebekah's father, was always busy. But so were all the tailors in Spitalfields. In spite of this, they were seen on the streets most days, with the exception of Moritz. He went to the Great Synagogue and came home and that was it. Occasionally his elderly, disapproving face would be seen at one of the windows of his dark, ancient house on Fournier Street, but he would never utter a word to his gentile neighbours.

All Becky ever said about him was, 'He's been like that since my mama died.'

But that had been years ago. Becky had been five at the time. Since then the only women who ever went into the Shapiros' house were Moritz's maiden sister Rivka, who came to prepare and share the *Shabbos* meal with her brother and his daughter every Friday night, and a woman who came to do the washing and cleaning on a Monday.

After they'd all first met at the fruit and veg market, Bernie had heaved her grotto about for a while and made another tuppence. She'd told her daddy, because unlike most daddies she knew, she could tell him anything. But she didn't tell her mammy. Money had a way of disappearing Mammy's way if she knew about it.

As Patrick Lynch had taken his boots off that night he had

whispered to his daughter, 'Not bad for the first day of the oyster season.'

'The oyster season?'

'Yes,' he'd said. 'That's what grotto day's about, my little duck, to celebrate the first oysters of the year.'

'Not about the saints?'

'Not really, no. I just say that so your mum won't tell you off.' Then he'd coughed. He'd started to make an awful hacking noise in recent times that made her mammy frown.

He'd tucked Bernie up in bed and kissed her. And she'd said, 'Daddy, what's oysters?'

Patrick Lynch laughed softly so as not to wake his other five children or his exhausted wife.

'Oh, they're sort of fish,' he'd said. 'Used to be poor men's food, did oysters. When me granddad Lynch first arrived in England, everybody ate 'em. But now only the rich can afford them. Maybe one day, when you grow up, you can go to a nice, posh restaurant up the West End and try some.'

'When I'm an explorer with a camera?' Bernie had said then.

Patrick smiled. 'When you're famous all round the world, including Egypt,' he'd said.

Then he'd coughed his way off to bed, leaving Bernie and all the other Lynch children to try and get some rest. It wasn't easy. Little Aggie's hair was full of nits again and so she scratched and cried for much of the night. Marie had a cough like her daddy's and the boys groaned in their sleep because they were hungry. Dermot in particular was growing fast. Bernie hoped that she'd be tall too when she got older. She didn't want to be a shrimp like Smelly Ellie. But then her mammy said that the poor girl didn't eat. Any money her mum got went on the drink. Bernie was really lucky compared with her. But not with her new friend, Becky.

9

Becky had nice clothes and clean hair and her face was pleasantly plump – not all greasy and fat like that of old Mrs Healey, Father Reynolds' housekeeper. Becky's cheeks were smooth and red and made her look like a pretty china doll. She was clever too. When she grew up she wanted to be a doctor. Bernie had no doubt she'd do it too. That was, unless her scary 'papa' stopped her.

Like the fog that came off the Thames in thin grey rolls, thick yellow sheets and wisps of white like ghosts, Spitalfields was about layers. Layers of people and layers of time. Just beyond the walls of the ancient City of London, the area had been home to outsiders for centuries.

In the eighteenth century Huguenot refugees from France had settled there. Silk weavers by trade, they hadn't been allowed to work inside the City, where local British weavers lived and did business, and so had created an industrious and, at the time, elegant quarter of their own in Spitalfields. They built tall, handsome houses, vast airy churches and, it was said, made the best silk clothing in the world. As they became wealthy and established in England, though, they moved out to other, more rural parts of the country where they integrated with the local population. Their formerly fine East End houses and public buildings emptied out, only to be rapidly colonised by the families of Irish immigrants, refugees from the potato famine in the mid-nineteenth century.

By this time the Industrial Revolution was in full swing and the Irish were soon joined by people from all over the British Isles, attracted to London by the prospect of work in the flour-ishing docks, which handled departing goods and cargoes arriving from every part of the globe. But the docks could employ only so many. In London, some unfortunate newcomers discovered further grinding poverty instead of higher wages. The old Huguenot houses became rat-infested slums where upwards of twenty people would live to a room. And the overcrowding kept getting worse.

In the 1880s another group of immigrants arrived. These were Jews escaping the persecution imposed on them by the Russian Tsar. They came from Poland, Hungary and Ukraine, bringing with them their strange, to British eyes, religion and customs. They brought few possessions and very little money, but in time established themselves. They worked for their community as kosher butchers, bakers or in Yiddish theatre, and for the wider population as tailors, jewellers and cabinet-makers. In 1898 what had once been a Huguenot church at the end of Fournier Street became the Great Synagogue where, amongst others, Moritz Shapiro would go to pray.

The evening light was fading as he looked through the cracked window of his house onto the filthy street beyond. At one end stood the Synagogue, at the other a church and the Ten Bells public house. His gentile neighbours went there to drink and have fights. He even knew of a few Jews who slipped in from time to time – those so-called actors at the Yiddish theatre. No one he associated with would stoop so low. Acting was lying and Moritz had no time for that, or for any other sinful pursuit.

The sounds of glass breaking and intoxicated laughter rang out in the street and Moritz went up to his daughter's bedroom to make sure she wasn't frightened. But Rebekah was asleep. She'd grown accustomed to such sounds, unlike her mother.

When she was alive, Moritz's wife, Chani, had always been afraid of the pub. She'd told him, 'You know, I've heard the *goyim* say it's cursed. That a long time ago a terrible killer called Jack took women from that pub and cut them to pieces! And, Moritz, he has never been caught.'

To which he'd replied soothingly, 'And yet the gentiles still go there, Chani. There's nothing to fear.'

When he'd first arrived in Spitalfields with his parents and sisters, Moritz had heard all about Jack the Ripper. He had to have died a long time ago now. What a pity others like him hadn't perished too. If only they had, his Chani would not have been stabbed to death in their own home while he had been out taking Rebekah to see his sister on Hanbury Street.

But then Moritz knew that it wasn't really a man or men who had killed his wife, so much as the poverty that surrounded them. Spitalfields had that in abundance. Whoever had killed Chani had also taken all the money they'd had in the house at that time. All ten shillings of it . . .

Fog took hold of Fournier Street then and obscured even the filth in the gutter from Moritz's view.

Chapter Two

Winter 1934

'Oi! Leave him alone!'

Dermot Lynch pulled the bigger lad off his puny mate and pushed him to the ground.

The boy, who was twice the size of Dermot's friend Chrissy Dolan, promptly got up and punched Dermot in the face.

'He's my bruvver so you can keep out of it, Lynch, you bastard!'

Dermot punched him back. This time, Chrissy's brother Ernie stayed down.

Wiping his bloodied nose on his shirt-sleeve, Dermot grabbed hold of Chrissy's arm and pulled him along Fournier Street towards the Lynches' two-roomed flat.

'I never done nothing, Der,' Chrissy said. 'He just started on me!'

Dermot believed him. Poor Chrissy, who was in the same class as him at school, was always getting beaten up by some-one. And that included his six brothers and even his dad.

Dermot dragged his friend down the steps that led to the Lynches' basement flat, yanked him through the open door then locked it behind them.

'Ernie'll get me when I go 'ome,' Chrissy said as he stood in the middle of the crowded room, looking pitiful in his ragged shorts and filthy shirt.

All the Lynch kids as well as their dad, Pat, were at home. Bernie, the eldest girl, ran over to Chrissy and brought him to the range to warm himself. She sat him down on an old cushion and said, 'You wanna thump him back, Chrissy.'

The boy, though two years older than Bernie, was a good head shorter. Like her brother Dermot, Bernie Lynch was tall.

'Ah, they all gang up on him. It's because he always gets the girls.' Dermot was smiling as he teased his red-haired friend.

Chrissy looked down at the floor in embarrassment.

'They're just jealous, boy,' Pat Lynch joshed him. 'I was a bit of a devil for the girls meself before I met my Kitty. Had to fight me corner more than once, I can tell you.'

Bernie looked up at her dad and smiled. He coughed, bending almost double under the onslaught, his face turning purple. Bernie shuddered. Her daddy was more off work than he was on, now he had that cough all the time. She'd heard one of her mammy's sisters say she thought it might be consumption, the disease so many here had and died from.

'I like girls and they like me,' Chrissy said miserably. 'What can I do about it?'

'You can punch them jealous little blighters back!' Pat said. 'Because that's all it is, Chrissy, jealousy.'

Dermot agreed. 'Yeah,' he said. 'They're just jealous.'

But he saw his elder brother Joey's smirk. He wasn't going to help boost Chrissy's damaged confidence. Like Chrissy's own brothers, Joey gave the little boy constant grief about always hanging around with the girls at school. Called him a 'poof'; said that if Dermot carried on being pals with Chrissy, people'd think he was queer too. Dermot ignored him. Ever since he'd left school and gone to work in the docks, like their dad, Joey had become arrogant and hard in a way Pat Lynch had never been. But then a lot of the blokes who worked in the docks were like that. Sometimes Dermot wondered how his gentle father had survived there.

Chrissy stayed with the Lynches for the rest of the day, joining the family, along with little Rosie from next door, for tea. Dermot's mammy had been able to get hold of some meat from somewhere and so they'd all shared a big stew that was, in reality, more spuds and onions than lamb. But no one complained. Out on the streets of Spitalfields, those his dad called 'the poor' sat in gutters and shop doorways without so much as a crust to keep them going. To be without work was to die and Dermot knew that if his dad got much sicker he'd have to give up his docker's hook and pass it on to his second son. Then Dermot would have to leave school and assume a man's responsibilities. Just the thought of it made him sad. He promised himself he'd go to Mass in the morning and pray it didn't happen any time soon.

There were two of them: one a great big lump of a young man, and the other slim, dark and with the look of an Arabian hero about him. Just like Rudolph Valentino.

'What's that say?' Rose asked, pointing to some words scrawled on the wall of the pie shop.

Becky pulled her coat close around her freezing body and answered, 'It says: "Yids go home".'

'Does that mean you? But you *are* home,' Rose answered in bewilderment.

15

The handsome young man who, Becky now noticed, had a long Roman nose and full red lips, said, 'Work of the fascists, darling. They want us out.'

'Us?'

'Jewish people, Rosie,' Becky said. 'Not you.'

'Oh, they won't stop at us Jews,' the young man said. 'They'll go after anyone who's not like them.' His name was Solomon Adler and he was one of the Young Communists Becky's papa described as 'atheist scum'. Becky herself saw them as heroes, the only people willing to stand up to the increasing numbers of rich men coming into the East End expressly to cause trouble. Although they had money themselves, they seemed to believe that in the slums the Jews were taking jobs away from 'ordinary folk' – whoever they were.

The big bloke, who by now had managed to scrub away the 'Y' from 'Yids' using a wire brush, turned to the girls and said, 'What they don't understand is, there's no work here for Jews either.' Then he squinted at something across Brick Lane. 'What's she doing?'

'Oh, that's just Bernie,' Rose said. 'She's an artist.'

'What's she drawing?'

Bernie didn't look up from her sketch pad but said, 'I'm drawing life round here. And, Rosie, I'm not an artist.'

'Give us a look and we'll decide,' said Solomon Adler.

Becky saw fear in her friend's eyes. She was a good artist but she had to know a person really well before she'd let them look at her work. Rose and Becky had only ever seen fragments of it.

As the handsome young man walked towards her, Bernie closed her book. 'No,' she said.

'Oh, come on!'

She looked him in the eye and repeated, eyes blazing, 'No.'

Adler raised his hands in surrender. But then Bernie could

be quite scary. Sometimes when she fought with her siblings she was like a tigress.

She smiled then and said, 'Come on, girls, let's get to Auntie Bridget's, it's brass monkeys out here.'

And it was. So far the winter had been wet and warm, but on this Sunday morning in December it had turned cold.

Leaving the two 'Commie boys' behind, the girls made their way down Brick Lane to Fashion Street and knocked on the door of the house where Bernie's Auntie Bridget lived with her three kids, all under the age of five, in two rooms on the top floor.

Pregnant again, Auntie Bridget had asked Bernie and her sister Marie to come and help her clean the flat. She had swollen legs and the twins and her Peter, who was a lively three year old, were driving her mad. Her husband, Uncle Kevin, was away to Mass and then the pub.

As Bridget led the girls upstairs she said, 'So, Bernie, it's very nice of your friends to come with you, but where's little Marie?'

'Oh, she decided to go to Mass with Mammy.'

Marie, though only twelve, was already an expert at getting out of anything she didn't want to do, even if it meant going to Church instead.

'These are my best friends, Rebekah and Rose.'

'Oh.' Bernie saw her aunt look at Rose and knew what she was thinking. Everyone in Spitalfields knew the Larkins.

But Auntie Bridget smiled, with some difficulty after climbing four flights of stairs.

Although the one-year-old twins, Rita and Edna, and their brother Peter were as clean as whistles, Bridget's flat was a total mess. Clothes and bedding, much of it soiled, were slung everywhere, the sink in the corner was jammed with crockery and beer bottles, and the slop bucket looked ready to explode. The smell made Becky avert her head.

17

'I know it's terrible,' Bridget said. 'But the little ones won't stop crying and I've not been able to get downstairs to wash anything for weeks. Kevin's at his wits' end.'

Bernie knew enough about the lives of women in the East End to know that this was code for the fact that Uncle Kevin spent most of his time down the pub. A stevedore by trade, her dad's youngest brother had been sacked from his last job over a month before, for the 'usual'. This too was code for Kevin's excessive love of the drink.

While Becky loaded the three children up into Bridget's ancient pram, Bernie and Rose set to washing the laundry in a tin bath out in the back yard while Bridget took the opportunity to lie down with a cup of tea and a fag.

Becky had never seen anything like it. When she returned from taking the kids for a stroll down to Petticoat Lane Market, she found Rose sitting on the ground all covered in suds, laughing fit to burst while Bernie scrubbed stains off a sheet with a bar of Sunlight soap. She was rubbing so hard her face was purple.

Becky, who'd finally managed to get all three kids off to sleep in their pram, left them in the hall and went out to join the others in the back yard.

'Thought I might take a bath while I'm here,' Rose said when she saw Becky arrive.

'It looks like it!'

Bernie glared at the slacker. Becky asked, 'Do you want me to help?'

'Last sheet,' Bernie said, panting. 'Where're the kids?'

'Asleep in the hall.'

'Well done. They're little devils. You must have the touch.'

Becky laughed. 'They're just a little bit lively. It can't be a

18

lot of fun for them, crammed into two rooms.' Then, realising what she'd said, she added, 'What with your auntie expecting ...'

But Bernie and Rose knew Becky. They understood how much better off she was than they were. They knew her occasional, to them strange, assumptions, didn't mean she felt they were beneath her in any way.

Bernie hung the last sheet out on a bowed washing line. Pushing her long blonde hair off her face, she said, 'At least Auntie Bridget's managed to have a bit of a rest. 'Course, I think Uncle Kevin should be doing this really, but then that's just me.'

She rested her aching back against the dustbins. Becky joined her, while Rose sat in the washing suds, staring into space.

'Men don't do housework,' Becky explained. 'When my mum died, Papa got Mrs Michael to come in every Monday to do our washing and cleaning.'

'To be fair, my dad does his share at home,' Bernie said, 'when he's well enough.' She lowered her voice. 'But then, he's not a drunk like his brother.'

Rose, only vaguely aware of what was being talked about, said, 'Len don't do nothing indoors. But then Mum don't do much either.'

Len Tobin was Nell Larkin's latest 'bloke'.

Becky and Bernie looked at their friend, but said nothing. Rarely at school, Rose was used as little more than a slave by her mum and whichever bloke was in residence. But what could her friends do about it? That was life for lots of girls in the East End. Rose was in no way exceptional.

Becky said, 'The twins and Peter are sweet. Noisy, bless them, but sweet.'

Bernie shook her head. 'Don't want no babies meself,' she said. 'I've spent too much time looking after little Paddy and Aggie. All she ever done was cry for the first year of her life. It was like living with a scream in your head all the time.'

'I'd like a little girl,' Rose said. 'But not a boy. Don't know what I'd do with one of them.'

'I expect you want kids, don't you, Becky?' Bernie said.

She smiled. 'Yes. But first I have to have a husband and that'll be up to Papa.'

Bernie frowned. 'Why?'

'A lot of Jewish marriages are arranged,' Becky explained.

'Arranged? By who?'

'A matchmaker,' she said. 'A woman who finds suitable husbands for young girls ... makes sure the young men come from good families.' She looked down at the ground. 'But that's a long way off still. I don't want to think about it now.'

'I wouldn't do it!' Bernie said.

'You don't have to.'

'I would,' Rose said, 'but only if my mum and dad was nice. I'd like to have a baby, though.'

The others ignored that.

'Anyway I don't want to get married,' Bernie said. 'I want to go out and see the world.'

'I'd like to be a doctor before I get married,' Becky said. 'But I don't suppose I will.'

'Why not?'

'Same reason why you've never been able to buy a camera.'

'But your dad's rich!'

Becky smiled, sadly. 'No, he's not,' she said. 'Not enough for that. I'd like to be a nurse though.'

'Then you should do that and not get married at all,' Bernie told her. 'I mean, do you want to end up like me Auntie Bridget?'

And then, as if to underline her point, Peter and the twins started crying.

The hatred in the slogans that men in smart black suits daubed on the walls of Spitalfields made Moritz Shapiro feel sick. But there was no way the local Communists in their shabby coats, dutifully carrying their copies of *Das Kapital*, were going to be able to do anything about it. The Jewish Board of Guardians, the highest Judaic authority in the land, had said they were not to provoke the fascists, but to keep their heads down. It would pass, they said. And they were right. To anger such people was dangerous. The whole reason Moritz Shapiro and his family had left what had then been the Russian Empire was because hot-heads among their fellow Jews had had decided to provoke the Tsar's Cossacks. Or so it was said.

Moritz Shapiro marched past the two young men busy removing anti-Semitic slogans from the walls of Spitalfields without saying a word. Fools! They even thought the *goyim* would help them! But if and when a crisis point came and violence broke out in the streets, they wouldn't. His Rebekah was friends with the Irish family over the road whose father was a Communist, but Moritz didn't like it. What would that Irishman and his family care if the men in black clothes came for the Jews? They'd hide themselves away and wait for the trouble to pass, and who could blame them? That or else join in like the Poles and the Ukrainians had done, as his father had told him. The youngest Lynch boy was playing cricket in the street with a gang of other local urchins. He didn't even have a proper bat, just an offcut from a plank of wood that left splinters stuck in his fingers. These people had nothing. And those who had nothing were ripe for ideas pedalled by those who promised them everything. People like Oswald Mosley and his British Union of Fascists.

21

The little gypsy girl Rebekah had taken to, however, she was another matter. The gypsies, like the Jews, always got swept up in any trouble when times were hard. It was said the settled *goyim* hated them because it had been the gypsies who had made the nails that crucified their Christ: a terrible legend that still made men kill one another. As a Jew, Moritz knew such stories only too well. But he also had eyes in his head, which showed him how much worse the poverty in the East End had become in the past few years. Men and women were hungry for bread, thirsty for clean water and craved some warmth and comfort. Such people were also in need of hope and that could come from many directions, including from the men in their smart black suits with their loud, posh voices. And if those men blamed the Jews loudly and often enough, they would become convenient scapegoats for the hungry and the homeless.

Moritz would see what happened. But if things got much worse round here he'd have to bend his mind to how he might make Rebekah safe. Now that his poor wife was dead, his daughter was all he cared about.

Chapter Three

1936

'Come on, Rosie! Keep up!'

They'd promised Becky and Bernie's dad that they'd meet up on Princes Street. But Rosie was limping and kept on looking at the ground as if in a dream.

'Don't you want to come?' Bernie asked her.

'Yeah, it's just that . . . '

Bernie stood still. Few people could keep up with her while she was walking at full pelt, much less Rosie whose bare, skinny legs were like twigs. She stopped outside the vapour baths and caught her breath. Usually a crowd of Jewish men stood outside, waiting to go in and steam themselves, but Bernie reckoned most of them had to be going to the meeting too. It was, after all, mainly Jews who were involved.

'What's the matter?' she asked Rosie.

'I'm tired.'

'What? Doing too much at school, are you?'

'No.'

Rose limped up to her and then glanced away. The poor kid rarely made it to school these days.

'Is he hitting you again?' Bernie asked.

She'd always been bigger than Rose and Becky, her two best friends, but now she towered over them. At sixteen Bernie Lynch was a striking girl: six foot tall with masses of curly blonde hair.

'Who?'

Bernie slid an arm around Rose's slight shoulders. 'You know who,' she said. 'Ruddy Len!'

Rose's mother still lived with Len Tobin who was still a hopeless drunk. Bernie's mum called him a 'pimp'. Everyone knew Nell Larkin had been on the streets for years. Men she'd lived with in the past had sponged off her earnings, but Len Tobin did more than that. He pushed her out the door and took the money from the hands of her customers himself. It was also obvious from the bruises on their arms and faces that he knocked Nell and her daughter about. In the two years since he had been on the scene, Rose had gone to school even less than she had before.

The smaller girl looked up at Bernie. 'I'm all right,' she insisted.

She was just a kid. Fourteen, still scrawny, unable to read or write properly ... Bernie hugged her and then quickly let her go. Rose didn't like to be touched too much these days. Bernie's brother Dermot said he'd heard whispers about Len Tobin. Long ago Len had been a docker like Bernie's dad and two of her brothers, but he was too full of drink to keep his docker's hook for long and the guv'nors began to ignore him at the morning call-ons when work for the day was allocated. But it wasn't drink that was the main problem with Tobin. Dark

24

stories went around about his liking for little street girls. Very little street girls.

"'Cause if he's touching you ... you know, like he shouldn't ...'

'He ain't,' Rose said. But she wouldn't meet Bernie's eyes when she said so.

Bernie shook her head. There was no point arguing. Both she and Becky knew that Rose's life with her mum and Len was brutal and grim. But neither of them knew what to do about it. They had problems of their own. Everyone did. Work was hard to come by and these days nobody had any money, not even Becky's dad.

'Well, come on then.'

Bernie began walking, more slowly this time.

Rose, following her, said, 'Bernie, who we going to see?'

She had a memory like a bloody goldfish.

'I told you, Rose,' Bernie said, 'it's a meeting about the fascists. Mosley and his Blackshirts want to march through the East End and start trouble here, and we have to stop them. It's Mosley and his oiks who've been beating people up and writing all them bad things about the Jews on people's walls.'

'Oh. So if this Mosley's a fascist then who're we?' Rose asked.

'We're the good ones,' Bernie said.

Pat Lynch's cough was getting worse by the day.

'This bleedin' smog don't help,' he said as he held the clean handkerchief Becky had given him up to his mouth. 'Thanks, love.'

Bernie's dad had always been kind to her. Ever since the girls had first become friends, when they were ten years old, she'd been welcome in the Lynches' overcrowded flat. Bernie's mum, Auntie Kitty, could be a bit frosty when she chose, and was really rather more fond of Rose these days. But at least

Becky could visit freely. Neither Bernie nor Rose could come to Becky's own house unless her papa was out. He didn't like her having friends who weren't Jewish. Whenever the subject came up he'd say, 'If I'd wanted you to have friends amongst the *goyim*, I would have sent you to a *goyische* school!'

Goys were non-Jews and so they didn't go to the Jews' Free School on Bell Lane, which Becky had recently left. She'd made a few friends there whom she had been able to bring home, but they weren't the sort of friends that Bernie and Rose were. The three of them were close as sisters.

'Has Mr Piratin gone inside yet?' Becky asked when Mr Lynch had stopped coughing.

They were waiting outside the Synagogue on Princes Street where Phil Piratin, firebrand leader of the Communist Party of Great Britain, was about to convene a meeting in the basement. 'Commies' like Mr Piratin and Mr Lynch used the Synagogue's social room to hold their meetings.

'I think so,' Patrick Lynch said. Then he looked up the road towards Brick Lane. It was difficult to see anything much through the early-autumn fog. 'I wonder where me girl's got to?'

'Rose was going to meet her outside her work,' Becky said. 'Maybe she was late.'

'Yeah, and maybe that pig her mother lives with was knocking her about,' Patrick said.

Becky didn't know what to say to this. She was aware that Len Tobin treated her friend badly, but the direct way that Mr Lynch always spoke about things like violence and injustice made her uncomfortable. It was one of the reasons why her papa hated Communists: because they 'said things'. If people did that often enough, it could only bring trouble, in his opinion. But then Bernie's mother spoke out too and she was no Communist. Like a lot of East End Irishwomen, Kitty wasn't overtly political unless it concerned women and children. That was the reason why she raged against Tobin.

'Because he's an ungodly, wife- and child-beating bastard!' Kitty would say.

'Comrade Piratin'll have a plan,' Patrick said. 'We'll stop Mosley, if we all stick together.'

Becky smiled. When Papa had heard the fascists were planning to march through the East End, he'd said, 'He's coming for the Jews. The *goyim* blame us for the fact there's no work, that millions go hungry every day. Nobody'll help us. They never have.' His proposed solution was for them to 'stay indoors, like we did when the Cossacks came for us'.

Her papa had come from Russia where Jews had regularly been attacked by Cossacks sent by the Tsar to hound them out of the country. But this time it would be different because this time everyone was against the oppressors, Jews and Gentiles alike. Because even a young girl like Becky knew that this was really about mass unemployment, and how the rich were blaming the poor for not being able to get jobs that didn't exist.

'I just wish I was the man I once was,' Patrick sighed.

Again, Becky said nothing. Bernie's dad was ill with what her papa called 'the consumption', which meant he coughed all the time and couldn't work any more. She knew he hated being reliant on his two eldest sons, Dermot and Joe, who now laboured on the docks to keep the family. She also knew that her father's illness was what had forced Bernie to leave school and go and work for Mr Sassoon, the man her mum did home sewing for. Becky worked in his garment factory though. She'd never been able to buy herself a camera and it didn't look as if she'd ever get to Egypt. Instead, she carried on sketching on paper she bought from old Mr Katz. She could've used any old paper but she went to Katz's shop because she wanted to see

27

his cameras and photographs. Becky thought Bernie's drawings were amazing. She liked to draw ordinary street scenes, which, somehow, under her scrutiny, became magical.

'Dad!'

Bernie's legs were so long, it took less than a second for her to reach them from the bottom of the road.

'Bernie girl!'

She ran up to Pat and kissed him. 'Sorry we're late!' she said. Becky looked around for their other friend. 'Where's Rosie?'

'Coming.'

And then there she was, her ancient over-sized boots clanking against the cobbles, legs bare in the evening chill, hair like a tangle of black eels.

Becky took her scarf off and wrapped it around the smaller girl's neck.

'Oh, Rosie,' she said. 'You look perished!'

Rose smiled.

'Sorry,' she said. 'Had to come out before me stockings was dry.'

They all knew she was lying. Rose didn't have any stockings unless someone gave her a pair. Not even in the depths of winter.

'Mosley and his Blackshirts are planning to speak on four platforms, one at Shoreditch, another at Bethnal Green, one at Bow and the last one at Limehouse.'

Phil Piratin was a dark, intense young man. When he spoke, people listened. And the social room underneath the Synagogue was packed with people who wanted to hear him.

'He's gonna blame Jews for the failure of the capitalist government to build a fair society. Blaming the working classes for their own poverty, brought about by people like him!'

Oswald Mosley, leader of the British Union of Fascists, was a baronet and a respected member of the establishment. He was also an admirer of foreign fascists like Mussolini in Italy and Adolf Hitler in Germany.

It was hot in the basement and the room was full of smoke from all the dockers' and the Commie boys' fags. There was a smell of beer from the many Irish stevedores who lined the walls as well as the reek of the cheap perfumes worn by the sweat-shop girls. People looked at the three young women and the thin, coughing docker when they arrived. But mainly they looked at Rose.

She'd not even had time to wash her face before she'd run out into the street after Len had done what he'd done to her. Whenever her mum was out or unconscious, he threw Rose on the bed, smacked her about and then had his way with her. Rose knew she could've fought him harder and so she felt guilty. But she also knew that if she did resist him, he'd kill her. Her mum had fought him off once when she'd not been in the mood, and he'd broken her nose. Both Rose and Nell knew what he could do.

But she'd had to attend this meeting. She'd promised Becky she would. It was about people coming and causing trouble for the Jews. Len had said they deserved it, but he was a pig. And anyway Rose liked Jews, even if a lot of them were looking at her funny now. But then, why wouldn't they? Her face was all dirty and she smelled of *him*.

'I say, they shall not pass, comrades!' Phil Piratin declared. 'They're coming here to crush us and we won't let them!'

'Bloody right!' a man in the audience said.

'We'll die before we let 'em come through!'

'We'll need to build and man barricades at Gardiner's Corner,' Piratin continued. 'We'll cut the bastards off before they can even start!'

People cheered. Mr Lynch coughed but managed to shout his two penn'orth as well. 'Yes!'

Piratin said, 'Who's with me?'

The whole room erupted with cries of one word: 'Me!'

Bernie and Becky sprang to their feet.

'We'll need every one of you!' Piratin said. 'And don't misunderstand me, comrades, we'll need every one of you prepared to *fight* these fascists!'

Everyone cheered.

'Because Mosley and his thugs are here to destroy us. They're here to take what's ours, and if we let 'em, the working classes in the East End'll be finished.'

A man even younger than Piratin sprang up onto the platform in front of the leader.

Becky clasped her hands together and whispered, 'Comrade Adler!'

He seemed to be everywhere these days, he and his great friend Wolfie Silverman: cleaning filthy slogans off Synagogue walls, recruiting new members for the party, chasing the fascists out of Spitalfields.

'This is how Hitler started in Germany in 1933,' he said. 'Now Jews and Communists are beaten up every day in Berlin! Some are deported! People have been killed!'

If anything Comrade Adler was more of a rabble-rouser than Phil Piratin. He was certainly more handsome. Tall, dark and intense, he had a face that reminded Rose of a picture of Jesus she'd once seen in Bernie's home. Or was it John the Baptist? Whoever he was, he had been good-looking. It was said that all the sweat-shop girls were in love with Adler.

'Comrade Adler's right,' Piratin said. 'And look at Spain! The fascist forces of the Falange have taken Spain to Civil War. Do we want that here?'

'No!'

Through the smoke and the steam coming off the damp coats and hats of hundreds of people, Rose saw Becky's face. She was looking at Comrade Adler with an expression that Rose had only seen on her friend's face once before. Becky had been telling them about when her Auntie Yentl had taken her to the new Troxy Cinema on the Commercial Road for her fifteenth birthday. They'd gone to see the film *Devil-May-Care*, which had starred someone called Ramon Novarro. When Becky spoke about Novarro her eyes shone and her cheeks became red. She looked like that again tonight. She was smitten.

'Then we have to fight!' Adler raised one fist high in the air. 'And we have to win!'

The room erupted. But above the mayhem, Piratin yelled, 'And we must organise!'

People signed up to build barricades and provide weapons in the form of broom handles, coshes and cricket bats. A group of old Jewish women said they'd keep cups of tea coming and Mr Miller the tobacconist said he'd make sure no one fighting the fascists had to do so without a fag. Mr Lynch was very grateful for that.

'I can't fight fascism without a good smoke.'

Becky volunteered to man the barricades and Mr Piratin seemed impressed by her enthusiasm.

'We need as many young comrades as we can get,' he told her when he took her name. 'You'll be an example to others.'

Comrade Adler had been by his side at the time, but he'd said nothing. Rose wondered whether Becky was disappointed.

But then she heard Piratin shout, 'Oh, and we'll need someone to take photographs. We need a record of this. Can anyone help?'

The only photographer round the Lane was Mr Cohen on

Hanbury Street but he didn't approve of Communists and so he wasn't at the meeting. For a while, no one said anything. Cameras were expensive and so even if someone had one, they'd hardly own up to it. No one wanted to be robbed.

'Anyone?'

Rose looked at Bernie. She'd wanted a camera for years but never got one. If she had, Rose was sure she would have volunteered.

Then a man's voice, heavily accented, said, 'I have a camera, though my eyesight is poor.'

He walked through the audience and up to the platform. It was the younger of the Katz brothers, Mr Walter. He shook Piratin's hand.

'You are welcome to use my camera,' Walter Katz offered the spokesman.

'Well, thank you very . . .'

'Oi!' Bernie shot her hand up in the air. 'I'll use it,' she said. 'I'll take as many photographs as you want, Mr Piratin! I'll take a photograph of Mosley's ugly mug for you!'

Rose saw Walter Katz smile. 'You know, I think this young lady will do a good job,' he said.

Becky shook her head.

'What are you going to do with that?' she said to Bernie.

Her friend didn't remember seeing this particular camera in Katz's shop. It was smaller than the others.

'I dunno,' she said.

'Why did you volunteer like that?'

She shrugged. 'It just come to me.' She'd never stopped dreaming about buying herself a camera ever since she was a kid. All that drawing had been a poor substitute. Once her dad had got sick, any money she'd had was needed by the family.

She and her siblings had gone out and got jobs and it was all hands to the pump.

'I'm not daft,' she said. 'I can work it out.'

Becky didn't doubt it. Bernie was probably the cleverest girl she'd ever met. But she was still worried, not wanting her friend to make a fool of herself.

Rose, who was also sitting on Bernie's bed, took the camera and held it up to her eye.

'It's heavy,' she said.

'So put it down,' Becky snapped.

Rose wasn't exactly clumsy but she did have 'accidents' with things. Mainly, Becky suspected, because she'd sometimes had a nip or two of her mum's beer. The Larkins' home was always cold, and with that Len always sprawled over Nell's bed it wasn't the sort of place to be restful on the nerves.

Rose put the camera down beside Bernie, who tucked it under her pillow.

'So why didn't you volunteer to nurse the sick then, Becky?' Bernie asked.

'Because I'm not a nurse ...'

'Yes, you are!'

'I've told you I don't know how many times!' Becky said impatiently. She loved Bernie with all her heart but had to admit that her friend wasn't the world's best listener.

'I'm a mother's help,' Becky said. 'I wish I were a proper nurse.'

'Up old Mother Levy's,' Rose put in.

'I work out of the Jewish Maternity Home that some call Mother Levy's, yes,' Becky said. 'But I'm not a nurse, Bern. I'm a mother's help. I go into the homes of women who are expecting or have new babies and help them with their chores.'

'Yeah, but you must know a bit,' Bernie said. 'I mean, I know a bit because I was at home when Mammy had our Aggie.'

'I've never been around for a confinement,' Becky said.

'You ain't seen a baby being born?'

'No! Papa wouldn't allow that,' she said. 'It's not decent for an unmarried girl to see such things.'

Bernie said, 'But you want to be a doctor!'

'Well, yes ... But ... ' Becky shook her head. 'It's all a bit more complicated than I thought. You need a lot of money to study medicine.'

'Your dad's rich,' Rose put in.

Whenever the subject of her father came up, Becky felt embarrassed. Compared to her friends' fathers, Moritz Shapiro was rich. He had his own business, owned his own house ...

Only Becky knew how tough the world of high-class tailoring had become in the past few years. A combination of cheap foreign imports and a faltering economy had conspired to render a lot of East End bespoke tailors almost redundant. The best that Becky could hope for, if things continued to deteriorate, was eventually to train as a nurse. If her papa would let her. The worst ... Well, the worst didn't bear thinking about.

She said, 'If I'm lucky, I'll become a nurse one day and then I can see about being a doctor.'

Bernie looked at her a bit funny for a moment, as if she didn't quite believe her, then said, 'Well, at least you get to talk to people ... can't hear meself think where I work. And when we are allowed a tea break, all the other girls do is gossip about film stars or boys they fancy.'

She was the only non-Jewish girl working at Sassoon's and, although she understood Yiddish, often felt a bit left out of the loop, especially when she and her fellow machinists took breaks. It didn't help that sometimes her mammy gave her bacon rinds in her sandwiches. She had to find a corner on her own when she wanted to eat those.

'Wish I was at work,' Rose said.

'You should be at school,' Becky told her. 'Your writing gets a lot better when you go.'

Rose glanced away. 'Yeah, but me mum needs me.'

Becky looked at Bernie, who raised her eyebrows. Nell Larkin was very rarely conscious these days. It was that Len who needed Rose, and Bernie, at least, knew why.

Kitty Lynch yelled out then for the girls to come into the kitchen for some bread and dripping. Rose, as usual, was the first to sit down in front of the kitchen range, eating her gooey, beef-fat-slathered bread greedily. Becky, on the other hand, said she had somewhere else she needed to be.

'I'll have to go home right away or Papa'll worry,' she said.

'All right, love,' Kitty Lynch told her. Then, when she'd gone, said to Bernie, 'She too grand to eat here or something?'

'No!'

'Well, she never does.' Kitty looked down at Rose, busy munching her way through bread, fat and the ever-present snot from her own nose. 'Not like some.'

But when Becky left the Lynches' flat, she didn't go over the road to her own house. Instead, she turned right onto Brick Lane. If Bernie was going to take pictures of the fascists she was going to need some help. Also, Becky wanted some time on her own to think her own thoughts without the sound of her father continually kvetching in her ear as soon as she got in. He hated the Commie boys and said no good could come of challenging the fascists. All he ever did was hide away.

Well, Becky wasn't going to hide. She was going to be like Comrade Adler and take the fight to the fascists!

Also, if she was lucky, she might actually get to talk to Comrade Adler on the barricades ... Her Auntie Rivka knew the comrade's mother and said she was 'no better than she

35

should be.' When she thought about that, Becky laughed. She'd always liked people who were no better than they should be – whatever that actually meant.

'Oi, Kitty Lynch! You got my daughter in there?'

Nell Larkin's voice was unmistakable: loud, rough and slurred from the booze she'd just necked.

Kitty looked down at Rose who was already trembling. What went on in that flat with Nell and her bloke wasn't right. Kitty put her finger to her lips and nodded to the girl. She opened the door and walked up the area stairs to street-level.

'I ain't got your girl,' she said.

Nobody's coward, Kitty was nevertheless always wary of Nell Larkin. Thin but muscular, she had black hair down to her waist, dark eyes that could pierce armour-plating and a temper worthy of a drunken sailor.

'So where is she?' Nell demanded. 'She over the road with that Jewess?'

'I ain't seen her,' Kitty said. Then, noticing that Nell's blouse had come open, said, 'Oh, for Gawd's sake, make yourself decent, Nell.'

'What?'

Kitty pulled the woman's blouse over her exposed breasts and said, 'Get home, girl. It's a rotten cold night!'

Just then a man appeared by Nell's side.

'What you talking about, missus?' he said.

Nobody knew where Leonard Tobin had sprung from originally, but most people who met him wanted him to go back there.

Kitty looked down her nose at him. 'I'm talking to the organ grinder, not the monkey,' she retorted.

She saw him swing back his fist just as Patrick came out of the flat behind her.

'What's all this?' he said. Even walking up the area steps wore him out these days. 'Oi, you!' he gasped.

His fist still raised, Tobin said, 'You wanna keep your missus' mouth shut for her!'

Patrick Lynch knew his wife had a temper, but he still didn't appreciate being told what to do when it came to his own family.

'What's your problem, mate?' he asked Tobin.

'Your woman's lying!' he said. 'You've got our Rosie and we want her back.'

Patrick looked at his wife then back at the street slut and her pimp. 'Your Rosie?' he said. 'We ain't seen her.'

'Yes, you have! I saw her go down your gaff with me own eyes!' Tobin yelled. 'She's got fucking work to do!'

'Well, she ain't . . .'

'Mum . . . Len . . .'

Rose had crept up the stairs after Patrick, alarmed by the kerfuffle outside. Eyes downcast, Rose still knew they were all looking at her and she had to say something fast to stop what could become a fight.

'I hid in Auntie Kitty's,' she said. 'It's warm there. She never knew, nor Uncle Pat . . .'

'I let her in,' Bernie said.

Towering over everyone, she stood behind Rose with her hands on her friend's shoulders.

'Rosie . . .'

Nell had tears in her eyes. She grabbed her daughter's thin arm and hugged her to her chest. 'I needed you home, babe,' she said. 'You know I always need ya, don't ya?'

The girl said nothing.

Patrick Lynch glared at Len Tobin. 'So there's your explanation then, mate. Kid was being hidden by our Bernie.'

'Who you wanna give a good hiding to!'

'Yeah, but then she's my girl so that's up to me, ain't it?' Patrick said. 'I suggest, pal, you get your facts straight in future. Coming here and making accusations against my missus ...'

'She was fucking lying and you know it!'

Patrick stepped forward. 'Oh, yeah?'

Tobin squared up to him. 'Yeah. And what you gonna do about it?'

Kitty wanted to stop what she could see would soon develop into a fight. But she also knew her husband was a proud man who would always defend his family. Even if it meant getting beaten up by a stronger man.

Patrick raised his fists just as his son Dermot came down the road.

'Here!' the young man yelled as he broke into a run. 'What's going on?'

Mr Herman Katz was almost as reclusive as her papa, and so Becky was surprised that he answered the door when she knocked on it.

'Oh,' she said. 'I was looking for Mr Walter ...'

Herman Katz, fingers gripping tightly to the splintered edge of his front door, peered at her from underneath bushy white eyebrows. 'Who you ...What you want?'

'I'm Rebekah Shapiro,' she said. 'Moritz Shapiro's daughter, sir.'

'At *shul*?'

'Yes, my father is always *at shul*. Can I speak to ...'

'Wait here.'

He shut the door, leaving her outside in the cold as well as the gathering darkness. She assumed he'd gone to get his brother, though she didn't know for sure. The Katz brothers, like a lot of local people, were more fluent in Yiddish than in English.

Becky's own language skills were the reverse. Where she'd been educated, the Jews' Free School, English and only English was spoken, the whole point of the word 'Free' being to integrate the sons and daughters of immigrants and teach them how to be 'English'.

The front door opened again and Mr Walter Katz looked at her through bottle-bottom glasses. '*Jah*?'

'Mr Katz, my name is . . . '

'Rebekah Shapiro, I know,' he said. 'What you want?'

He wasn't going to ask her in. The Katz brothers were known to be observant, like her father, and so it was unlikely they'd let themselves be alone in a room with a woman who wasn't a relative. Not outside business transactions anyway.

'Earlier tonight, you lent a camera to the campaign to stop the fascists.'

'Yes, that friend of yours, the Irish girl who is always coming here to buy paper and look at my cameras , she will use it. I see her drawing sometimes. She has a good eye, I think.'

'Yes, and it's really very generous of you, Mr Katz . . . '

'Mmm.'

'But the fact is,' Becky said, 'she, my friend Bernadette Lynch, doesn't know how to use it.'

'Then why she say she'll take photographs? She'll break it!'

'No . . . no, she won't,' Becky said. 'She'll be really, really careful with it, I promise! But, Mr Katz, she needs some help. If you could . . . '

'Me? I do what?'

He was alarmed by the idea that Bernie might break his camera and with good reason, but he was also hard work. Becky breathed in and made her voice sound soothing and calm.

'Could you show her?' she said. 'She's a really clever girl, Mr Katz, and so she'll learn quickly.'

'Show her?'

Why did he keep on repeating everything Becky said?

'Yes, show her,' she said. 'So she can take pictures of all the brave Jews stopping the fascists. That's why you were at Mr Piratin's meeting wasn't it? To help?' And then she remembered something he had once said to her friend. 'You know, fascists – like the men and boys in shiny shoes and smart clothes back in your country.'

His eyes narrowed. 'Who told you about such things?'

'Bernie ... Bernadette,' she said quickly. 'You showed her your photographs from Germany. A long time ago.'

He thought for a moment, then said, 'This girl only buys bits of paper from me. If she really wants to be a photographer ...'

'She's poor!' Becky said. 'Her dad's ill and she has to work to put food on the table.'

'The world is poor, young lady. Why is this a problem for me?'

Becky was furious. How could he be so hard-hearted? Everyone knew the Katz brothers had money. But then maybe that was why he didn't care.

'Mr Katz,' she said, 'you were at Comrade Piratin's meeting and so you have to care about stopping this fascist march. You very kindly offered your camera so that someone can record what's going to happen because you can't any more. Bernie will do it and she'll do it well. She's a terrific artist, as you know. But first she needs help!'

'Why she volunteer if she needs help?'

Becky threw her arms up in exasperation. 'I don't know!' she said. 'She's always wanted to draw ... take photographs ... explore ... for as long as I've known her. But now her dad's sick she can't do any of that. Please help her, Mr Katz. Please.'

The old man stared into her eyes. It made Becky feel uncomfortable but she stuck with it for Bernie's sake. Then he shut the door in her face. It was only after she'd turned to leave that she heard him say, 'I'll think about it.'

Tobin hit Patrick so hard he fell down the area steps and ended up crumpled against the front door.

'Pat!'

Kitty ran to him just as Dermot threw three punches in quick succession at Len Tobin's head. He dropped to the pavement like a sack of spuds.

Leaning over his victim, Dermot said, 'You so much as touch my old man again and I'll put you in the hospital!'

'You fucking skinny . . .'

Dermot hit him again. Nell Larkin screamed.

'You stay down, you pissed-up bastard!' Dermot ordered. 'Or I'll fucking kill you!'

But Tobin had never been strong on common sense. He began to stumble to his feet.

Nell ran towards him but he knocked her to the ground.

'Fucking bitch!'

Dermot hit him again and, this time, he stayed down.

'I don't know what this is about,' said the young man. 'But you don't touch my family, get it?'

Then he walked down the steps to see if his father was all right.

Nell put her arms around her battered man and said, 'Come on, Len, let's get you home.' Then she yelled, 'And in future, you Lynches can mind your own business! Leave us alone!'

Only Bernie noticed Rose: shivering in her thin clothes, staring at Dermot Lynch, all wiry muscles and thick, curly black hair, as he helped his father to his feet and led him back into the flat.

Chapter Four

4 October 1936

'Rebekah!'

She'd thought her father was still asleep. But he was sitting at the kitchen table, listening out for her.

'Papa?'

Already wearing her overcoat and her blue felt hat, Becky sat down.

'If you're going where I think you're going, then I forbid it,' he said.

Dermot Lynch hadn't even knocked on the front door because Becky had seen him walking towards the house and gone out to meet him. Maybe her father had heard her open the door? Whatever the reason, there was no point in lying.

'Dermot came to tell me the Young Communists are going to occupy Victoria Park,' she said. 'He's going to help.'

'And he wanted you to go?'

'No!' she said. 'Well, I could've gone, but I promised Bernie

42

I'd go with her. They've got barricades up everywhere to stop the fascists ...'

She didn't tell him she'd volunteered to man one.

'Who have? The Communists?'

'It's not just Communists ...'

'So it's all *frummers*, eh?'

'Papa, this is everyone's fight, not just the Jews'!'

'Not ours,' he said. 'You want to get yourself killed? Because that was what happened when the Yiddisher folk tried to take on the Cossacks.'

'These are not Cossacks,' Becky said.

Her father looked old that morning. Grey and lined and thin, his gnarled tailor's hands resting shakily in his lap. Becky didn't want to hurt him, but she couldn't stay home when possibly the biggest fight of her young life was on the horizon. When Comrade Adler would be there ...

'I lost your mother to hatred,' he said. 'I can't lose you too, Rebekah-*leh*.'

Becky looked down at her hands. She didn't know what to say. Whether her mother had been killed because she was Jewish had always been open to doubt. But the fact remained that she had been murdered and, if anything happened to Becky, her father would be left alone.

'Papa ...'

'If you go there will be consequences.'

'I know. It could be dangerous, but ...'

'No. I mean for you, and for your future,' he said. 'Reputations. Yours and mine. This is not what we do, Rebekah-*leh*, not people like us!'

Rose looked round the room with nervous eyes. But hard as she peered into the darkness, she couldn't see Tobin. Only her mum, half-asleep in the chair by the range, one fist wrapped around a bottle of brown ale.

When she saw the girl, Nell said, 'He ain't here.'

But Rose knew not to trust her mother. She lied for him all the time, mainly so she didn't get a beating. Rose didn't step over the threshold.

'Where's he gone?'

'I dunno. Out. You in now, are ya?'

'Nah.'

'Where you off to then?'

She didn't dare tell her mum that she was going to meet Bernie Lynch. Ever since Len had thumped Bernie's dad and then been thumped by their Dermot, even the name 'Lynch' was forbidden in this household. Not that Rose had always done what she was told. She'd still been eating round at the Lynches' whenever she could, as she had been doing for years. She loved it down at Auntie Kitty's with Bernie and the kids – and Dermot. Especially, just recently, Dermot.

'Rosie?'

'Eh?'

'Where you off to, I said, Dolly Daydream?'

She had to think fast. She looked at the mean stack of sticks her mother would burn on the range, if and when she could be bothered.

'Thought I'd get us some wood,' she said.

Her mother nodded. Kids were forever picking up sticks in the street, especially round the markets – Spitalfields, Club Row, Petticoat Lane – which they'd either bring home to burn or else sell.

'Good girl. Bring me back a bottle of stout, if you make a few bob,' Nell said as Rose was shutting the door behind her. 'An' bring me one back if you don't.'

'Yes, Mum.'

Rose knew the barmaid down at the Ten Bells who always gave her mother beer on tick. And she knew why. Nell had helped out a few women in the past who'd found themselves in the family way. Women who came in the dead of night and left clutching their bellies. Rose had no idea what happened, but what she did know was that those women never had kids after that.

Rose ran up the area stairs and onto Fournier Street where Bernie stood waiting for her. She looked like a film star with her long blonde hair down, wearing the slim black trousers and jacket she'd made for herself. Both girls looked up at Becky's house.

'Do you think her old man's stopping her coming out?' Bernie said.

Rose shrugged.

Bernie shook her head. 'We'd better go and get Mr Katz,' she said. 'Our Joey's just come back from the Whitechapel Road where there's all sorts happening.'

Rose looked confused. Bernie knew that the fact the fascists were trying to march through the East End didn't mean anything much to her. The poor kid could barely read or write. But her ignorance still grated.

'The Jewish Ex-Servicemen's March is being attacked by the police,' she said. 'They're going to be protecting the fascists! This is really serious!'

'Why we got to get Mr Katz then?' Rose asked.

'Because he wants to make sure I don't drop his camera! And he showed me how to use it so I owe him.'

Walter Katz had just turned up at the Lynches' flat uninvited one evening and given Bernie a photography lesson. She knew that it hadn't been his idea because he'd told her so, but she was grateful nevertheless.

'Oi, Bernie Lynch!'

A boy with flaming red hair ran past carrying an equally red-headed baby in one hand and a dog on a piece of string in the other.

'What?' Bernie said.

The lad, Lionel Weiss, said, 'Everyone's going down Gardiner's Corner. Commies have a massive barricade down there. They say that bastard Mosley's arrived with an army!'

Bernie looked at Rosie. 'Jesus, Mary and Joseph, it's all kicking off!' Then she looked up at Becky's house and called out, 'Becky! There's a fight on! We need you!'

The bright early-autumn sun brought out the shine on the fascists' black jackboots a treat.

'Look at that.'

There were so many people massed at the Corner that Solly Adler had to get up on his best friend Wolfie Silverman's shoulders to see Sir Oswald Mosley and his British Union of Fascist supporters, the Blackshirts, marching smartly towards the East End.

A roar went up from the massed observers: *'No pasarán!'* The words were borrowed from the Republican side in the Spanish Civil War: 'They shall not pass!'

Solly, fag in one hand, cricket bat in the other, let out a wild whoop of anger. Finally, after months of sporadic attacks on Jews and threats to come and 'clear them out' of the East End, the fascists had arrived. And Solly wanted to get stuck in.

Looking over big Wolfie's head at the approaching Blackshirts, he said, 'Well, there's more of us than there are of them.'

'Well, maybe,' his friend said said. 'But what about the coppers?'

Technically Mosley's march was legal and so he was entitled

to police protection. Also it was well known that he had sympathisers in the police. So there were a lot of men in police uniforms in front of the Blackshirts, protecting them.

Solly murmured, 'Bastards.'

But further anti-fascists were arriving all the time.

'We must outnumber them,' Wolfie said.

'We do,' Solly said. 'But we'll still need more than a few old armchairs and a couple of cracked chamber pots to keep them out.'

The barricade built in front of Gardiner's Department Store had taken every spare stick and stone in the East End, but how it, and the people manning it, were going to stand up to charges from policemen, on horseback as well as on foot, Solly wasn't sure.

'Blimey, I'm hot!' Wolfie said.

An old woman standing beside him said, 'You should be glad it ain't raining. Imagine this, in the rain.'

'At least I wouldn't be burning up.'

She looked him up and down and said to his face, 'Shouldn't be so fat then.'

Solly was just about to get down off his friend's shoulders when he saw a tram stop in front of the barricade. At first he thought it was bringing reinforcements, but then he saw the driver get out and run off into the crowd. The police tried to pursue him but he disappeared.

'Christ!' Solly yelled. 'Some bloke's just given us his tram to reinforce the barricade! What a *mensch*!'

The crowd roared in appreciation and Solly began to sing: 'One, two, three, four, five, we want Mosley dead or alive!'

Becky's eyes were still wet from crying. She hadn't wanted to leave her papa in such a state, but when she'd heard Bernie calling, she knew she'd have to go. She'd also known that, at some point, she would be punished for her defiance.

The three girls joined the crowd at Gardiner's Corner, slotting themselves in behind a group of boys holding bags of marbles.

'What're they for?' Bernie asked the tallest of the lads.

He smirked. 'You'll see.'

Bernie took her camera out. She still felt a bit guilty about leaving Mr Katz behind but by the time Becky had managed to get away from her dad, Fournier Street had been jammed with people on their way to Gardiner's Corner. It had taken them almost an hour to reach this point and now, it seemed, something really bad was about to happen.

Infuriated by the arrival of the tram, it seemed the police were getting ready to charge the barricade – on horseback.

Bernie heard Becky whisper, 'We could die!'

In order to take her mind off her own fear, Bernie looked through the viewfinder of the camera and took a picture just as the horses began to advance.

It was then that the boys threw down their marbles.

'Christ!'

Suddenly, out of control horse-flesh was everywhere. Marbles thrown under the horses' hoofs made them skid and fall, tossing their riders down on the hard pavement.

'Those kids are fucking heroes!' Solly said as he watched a group of boys at the front of the crowd throw down another hail of ammunition. 'Keep it going, lads!'

Solly's brother Ben, who'd been at the front of the crowd but had now scrambled his way back to his sibling, said, 'The ruddy ingenuity of it! Some of those kids have got bags of pepper too!'

And when the police charged the crowd again, the boys used them: opening them in front of the horses' muzzles so that the poor beasts were temporarily blinded.

Other children ran home to get their marbles and beg their mothers for pepper as charge after charge failed to break the barricade or the will of those behind it.

Down at the front Solly even saw what looked like a girl, taking photos.

Then he tried to see where the fascists were and realised that they had gone.

Rose and Becky couldn't stop sneezing. Everyone around them sneezed, including the kids who'd thrown the pepper at the horses. Only one person managed to control the reflex: Bernie. Now sitting on the shoulders of a massive Irish docker, she was busy capturing every detail she could with Walter Katz's camera. She'd even, to her friends' amazement, managed to take out one film and replace it with another.

'You learn fast,' Becky said, battling streaming eyes and a sore nose.

'Mr Katz is a good teacher,' Bernie said. 'But then you knew that, didn't you?'

Bernie smiled. One of the first things old Katz had told her was that Rebekah Shapiro had asked him to help her. He'd said he hadn't wanted to, although secretly Bernie had doubted that. Katz had turned out to be a grumpy old sod but she felt his heart was in the right place.

Another charge brought more marbles, more falling horses and yet more screams of terror from both demonstrators and coppers. However Becky, in spite of the fact that her eyes felt as if they were on fire, now had other concerns.

'Where's Rosie?' she shouted up at Bernie.

The kid had been by her side only a moment ago but now she'd gone.

Bernie looked around and then shrugged. 'Dunno.'

Rosie's space had been taken up by a fat woman shoving a *beigel* into her face. Becky asked her if she'd seen Rosie but all the woman did was tip her head backwards. This had to mean Rosie had gone to the back of the crowd. She had been sneezing like mad and had maybe wanted to go to the toilet too, knowing her. A lot of the kids were pissing up against Gardiner's wall.

Becky shook one of Bernie's legs. 'I'm going to go and see if I can find her,' she yelled.

'All right!'

It was hard work pushing her way through crowds of thin, worn-out dockers smoking fags, women clutching babies while trying to cling onto toddlers, gangs of firebrand Commies and the odd rabbi here and there. She even, at one point, came across a nun. The smell of warm, unwashed bodies mixed with cigarette smoke, pepper and salt beef was almost overpowering. Becky felt herself gag.

Still upset about her papa, who had told her to 'go, kill yourself, dishonour me and break my heart' as she'd left the house, she hadn't eaten since the previous evening and was beginning to feel faint. Pushing forwards became stumbling forwards. Whether she would eventually have collapsed had she gone any further, Becky would never know.

Suddenly, there was Rose.

'Becky!'

She put a hand on her friend's shoulder. 'Rosie! Where were you?'

'I couldn't breathe down the front.'

'She's all right now,' a deep voice said.

Becky looked up and saw a tall, heavily bearded man who seemed familiar.

A sound, shrill and piercing, ripped across the crowd and made everybody cringe. The girls put their hands over their ears. Becky noticed that the bearded man was carrying another man on his shoulders.

Then the sound stopped and a loud voice that sounded as if it was coming from inside a tin shouted, 'The fascists are going through Cable Street! Get down there now!'

The man on his friend's shoulders jumped down and Becky found herself face to face with Comrade Adler.

Cable Street was an Irish area, full of dockers and their families. Bernie knew it well. She'd lost Becky and Rose at Gardiner's Corner but had no doubt they weren't far behind. When she got there she put her camera away for a while so that she could help build a barricade out of old prams, furniture and mattresses inside an upturned lorry. If the fascists managed to enter the East End and march through its streets, Bernie knew that she and her friends would be done for. They'd be just like the poor who'd been ruthlessly subdued by fascist forces abroad, so her dad said, in cities like Berlin and Madrid. In those places people who protested had died.

Behind the barricade, Bernie got out her camera and tried to find the best place from which to take pictures. She needed somewhere suitable to be what Mr Katz had called a 'vantage point'. Kids had scattered marbles and broken glass in front of the barricade to unseat mounted police officers and, if she looked up, Bernie could see the good Irish wives of Cable Street, their hair neatly tied back in buns, shoulders covered with knitted shawls, ready at their windows with full chamber pots to chuck down on their enemies' heads.

Unlike Gardiner's Corner, Cable Street was much easier to defend because it was narrow. It was also full of tough Irish families, who'd come out in support of the Jews. One of these families belonged to another of her father's brothers, Uncle Connor. Patrick Lynch himself was probably somewhere on Cable Street, though Bernie couldn't see him. What she could see, however, was the police. And the fascists. And there were thousands of them.

'I lost my friend because I went off to find Rosie,' Becky gabbled. 'Do you know my friend, Comrade Adler? Bernadette Lynch?'

They were on their way to Cable Street, together with what seemed like the whole population of the East End. Becky held Rose's hand while Solly Adler and Wolfie Silverman walked behind. Becky knew that she was blushing furiously and hoped Comrade Adler hadn't noticed.

'That's one of Pat Lynch's girls, isn't it?' he said. And then he smiled.

'She's the eldest,' Becky said.

'Good comrade, Pat Lynch. I heard he's not been well.'

'Yes. He's got the consumption,' Becky said. 'But he's out today. Dermot, that's his son, he told me that his dad was going on the ex-servicemen's march down the Whitechapel Road.'

'There was violence down there,' Wolfie said. 'Started by the fascists . . .'

Getting down Leman Street wasn't easy. The defenders had already built one blockade and they had to climb over what Wolfie described as 'some poor sod's worldly goods' to get into Cable Street. The noise was deafening.

'They shall not pass! They shall not pass!'

'Listen to it!' Adler said, his face shining with joy. 'Just bloody listen to that passion!'

But when they turned into Cable Street they saw what they were up against: what looked like millions of police, many of them on horses.

'Christ!'

The fascists were massing in Royal Mint Street, behind them. But nobody looked that way. If the Blackshirts came for them, after the coppers had had a go, they'd be warmed up and ready. But Solly Adler, for one, didn't believe they would. People like Mosley and his toff mates were cowards who disliked getting their shiny boots dirty and preferred to put up anti-Semitic posters on Brick Lane rather than fray their kid gloves with outright confrontation. It was the mindless thugs who followed them that were the real threat.

The huge Cable Street barricade came into view then. It was built around an upturned truck in the middle of the road.

Pointing, Rose said, 'Bernie!'

And there was Bernadette Lynch, sitting on top of the truck, camera in hand, like a great big blonde avenger.

Becky heard the two men draw in their breath sharply and Comrade Adler said: 'Bloody hell, look at her! Christ, she's like a goddess!'

When the Irishwomen hurled rotten vegetables, old chicken heads and stinking rabbit skins, plus the contents of their chamber pots, down on the police, they were called all the names under the sun.

'Fenian whores!'

'Dirty, bog-trotting Paddies!'

The women laughed raucously and some of them yelled back, 'Ah, look at them, the piss-faced coppers!'

The police came at the barricade again and again, with and without horses, but they didn't make a dent in it.

'They'll have to try something else soon,' Wolfie said as he sucked on a fag.

'Like what?' asked Solly.

'I dunno.'

The two men had ended up sticking with Becky and Rose, more to stop the girls being crushed than for any other reason. Solly knew of Becky's father, Moritz, even though they moved in very different circles. For Solly, Judaism as a religion was unimportant; it was the fact of being a Jew and the inequalities that went with it that motivated him. But Solly also saw the Jewish struggle as part of a greater movement of working-class people, irrespective of race or religion. For him Communism was the only solution to the class struggle. Moritz Shapiro, on the other hand, took his religion very seriously. He was widely known as a very pious man, a *frummer*. Solly knew that it was the *frummers* who had heeded the call of the Jewish Board of Guardians not to protest against the fascists. So he was surprised to see that Moritz's daughter had come out.

'What does your father think of you being here?' he asked her.

Becky tossed her head. 'I'm sixteen, I do what I like.'

Solly smiled. Sixteen! He could remember when he'd been that age and believed he could do what he wanted.

'I've been a Communist for over a year now,' she continued.

'Have you?'

'Yes, I have. I just made up my mind one day.'

He couldn't remember seeing her at any of the meetings he attended, but then he couldn't remember seeing Pat Lynch's daughter either and she was a girl it was impossible to ignore. She had to be six foot tall, he reckoned as he watched her bend down to take a picture of a kid carrying a kitten. All that blonde hair plus the fact that she wore trousers (trousers!) made her a real sight for sore eyes. He remembered seeing her with the other two girls in the street once a couple of years back. But she hadn't looked so, well, gorgeous, then ...

'And me,' a small voice said. 'I'm a Communist too.'

Solly smiled. He had no idea who this little girl was. Rose something or other. She looked as if she hadn't eaten for a while and, by the smell of her, was in serious need of a good scrub.

Then, suddenly, she said, 'It's all gone quiet, hasn't it?'

And she was right. Solly looked at Wolfie who said, 'I don't like the look of this, mate.'

From where she was standing, Bernie could see that the police were getting ready to charge the barricade again. Even covered in piss from a poorly aimed chamber pot, she didn't care. The woman who'd thrown it had apologised to her.

'Sorry, love,' she'd said, shame-faced. 'I never could aim straight!'

Bernie looked back at the crowd behind her and saw that they were bracing themselves for another assault. But she saw something else too. A group of men at the back were pushing their way to the front. Well dressed and armed with what looked like truncheons, Bernie knew coppers when she saw them.

'Oi!' she yelled. 'There's coppers over there!'

But the wind carried her voice the wrong way. What were the coppers doing? Then she saw one of them grab hold of Phil Piratin.

They were trying to arrest the ringleaders.

All hell broke loose. Solly turned to face the man who had just grabbed his arm.

'What's your problem, pal?' he said.

The bloke tried to yank him backwards.

'Oi!'

'Come with me, Adler,' he said. 'Come quietly and you won't get hurt.'

Suddenly Solly realised what this meant.

'The coppers are here!' he yelled.

He felt Wolfie try to pull him out of the copper's grip, then another bloke struck his mate on the head with a truncheon and he fell to the ground.

Becky screamed. Solly kicked and punched, but the bloke wouldn't let go.

'Fucking bastard!'

But then suddenly the copper roared. He also let go and Solly pitched forward and collided with Becky as they both watched Rose sink her teeth into the copper's arm and then hang on for dear life.

People around them pitched in to punch and stamp the coppers to the floor. And by the time Wolfie regained consciousness a few minutes later, the police had all gone.

When he sat up, he said, 'What the flamin' fuck was that?'

Chapter Five

A warm day had turned into a chilly night and so, when he left the house, Moritz Shapiro turned up the collar of his coat. Even by normal standards the pub at the end of the street was sending out a terrible racket and he'd come to see what was happening.

Ever since Rebekah had defied him and gone to take part in that wretched demonstration, Moritz had listened to the wireless while he worked. There had been terrible scenes at Gardiner's Corner and later on Cable Street where the demonstrators had built a huge barricade, which had been charged by police for hours, it seemed.

Halfway through the afternoon he'd heard the Salzedos' son, Hyman, singing tunelessly outside his window. The simpleton wandered the East End like a lost soul, which was strange given that his father was a respected *mohel*. Reuben Salzedo was a man of faith and learning, but Hyman . . .

Moritz had gone out to tell the boy to stop making a noise. With so many defying the Board of Guardians, the streets were almost empty. It was something Moritz wanted to enjoy while he could.

'Hyman, you're shredding my nerves!' he'd protested. 'Softer, if you please, or move away. I don't care which.'

Hyman Salzedo wasn't really a boy. He'd seen his fortieth birthday some years ago. But people still treated him as if he were a child. However, Hyman knew about people and the bad things they sometimes did to each other. He knew, for instance, that his father went to see a woman in Stepney every Thursday evening – and that she wasn't even Jewish. Hyman picked up all sorts of whispers.

And so when he told Moritz Shapiro that he'd heard the Jews and their allies were winning in Cable Street, Moritz was inclined to believe him. Since then he'd heard other snippets from Cohen the poulterer, who was a known Communist and had come to tell Moritz the 'comrades' were winning because he knew it would upset him.

But Hyman Salzedo had also told Moritz that people had been injured. He couldn't shake the conviction that one of them might be his daughter. In spite of her running wild with that Irish family and the mad girl with the gypsy mother, Moritz knew that his daughter Becky was essentially naive. She'd grown from a bookish child into a red-haired beauty with all sorts of high-flown ideas about social justice. None of them would ever come to anything, of course. They were plain wrong. They were the delusions of Communism and that was a philosophy developed by a man at odds with his god. Even if Karl Marx had been born Jewish.

Now it was almost eleven o'clock and Rebekah still had not come home. She needed to be curbed. It broke Moritz's heart but he knew he had to do it. He looked down the street towards the Ten Bells and saw an unsteady figure walking down the middle of the road. Abuse from a drunk was the last thing he needed. Moritz shook his head and began to walk back to his house.

'Oi! You!'

If it hadn't been a woman's voice he heard he wouldn't have stopped. Moritz turned and found himself face to face with the gypsy mother of his daughter's scrawny friend.

'Mrs ... Can I help you?' he said.

She stank of beer. She was usually drunk, she and that thug she lived with, but he'd never been close enough actually to smell her before. The stench almost made him gag.

'Your daughter still out, is she?' the woman asked.

'Sadly, yes,' Moritz told her. 'How did you know Rebekah was out?'

'Her and my Rosie and that Bernadette Lynch are always hopping off together,' Nell Larkin said. 'Rosie told me she was going out collecting wood but she ain't come back and now the East End's having a massive great party.'

'A party?'

'The Commies,' she said. 'They stopped them Blackshirts marching through. Turned them back at Cable Street.' Nell laughed aloud. 'I reckon them girls was there.'

So did Moritz, although he didn't say so.

'Mind you, I'd rather Rose was home now,' the woman continued.

'Mmm.'

Her face was flushed with booze and she had deep lines etched around her eyes and mouth. But underneath all that Moritz could see she was a handsome woman. Tall and statuesque, with long black hair that seemed to glow in the light thrown by the street lamps.

'I worry about my Rosie ... ' she said.

Were those tears in her eyes? Possibly, but she glanced away.

She had a reputation as a hard woman, which probably didn't sit well with crying in public.

'Mrs . . .'

'So, you seen my Len?'

She turned back to look at Moritz and he saw that her eyes were dry.

'Have you?' she urged him.

'No,' he said. He didn't add his thanks to the Almighty that the creature she lived with was nowhere to be seen. A bullying drunk like that was trouble. Moritz was always glad to see the back of Len Tobin.

Nell shrugged and walked on towards her rooms.

It was strange the way that Rebekah and Bernadette had made friends with that woman's child. Moritz had always thought the girl was simple, like Hyman Salzedo. What did the other girls see in her?

He walked up to his own front door and went inside. There'd be no sleep for him until Rebekah was home again.

They danced. It wasn't ballroom or Latin or anything like that, they just moved their feet and shook their arms. It felt wonderful.

'Here, you wanna be careful! I'm covered in wee!'

Bernie tried to make him hear her over the din of all the other revellers, but it was impossible. Solly Adler put an arm around her waist and whirled her round and round until she was dizzy.

'Hey! Watch it!'

Solly was drunk – on beer and success – AND he was dancing with a girl who was filthy dirty and totally beautiful. As soon as he'd seen her climb down off that Cable Street barricade, he'd made straight for her. A girl with hair like sunshine – and wearing trousers!

'I don't care!' he said. It was as if a huge weight had been lifted from his shoulders, as if he'd fallen in love with life all over again. Mosley had been defeated and he wasn't coming back. There was hope once again. The old British Isles were not going to go like Germany or Italy and now that the fascists had been pushed out of the East End Solly could concentrate on Spain.

He took Bernie's hand and led her over to the kerb.

'Gotta sit down!'

As he collapsed onto the pavement, someone put a pint in his hand, which he drank in one go.

'Easy does it!' Bernie said as she sat down beside him. 'You'll get pie-eyed at this rate!'

She'd had the odd taste of port and lemon herself and wasn't exactly sober. But Solly was steaming.

He laughed and then he slung his arm around her shoulders.

'Well, comrade,' he said, 'how does it feel to defeat fascism?'

'I just hope that the photos I took come out all right,' Bernie said.

'They will.'

'I hope so.'

He squeezed her arm. 'Couldn't take my eyes off you when you were standing up on top of that barricade,' he said. 'Anything could've happened to you. You could've fallen and broken your neck, you could've been beaten by the coppers ... Well, done, comrade. You're a credit to us all. A great big beautiful credit to us all.'

Bernie felt embarrassed. Here she was, slightly drunk, with a man's arm around her . It felt weird and, if she was honest, a bit uncomfortable. She hoped he didn't try and kiss her or anything. Or maybe she did? Apart from anything else, Rose was watching.

'Yeah, well . . .'

'But we mustn't rest on our laurels,' Solly said. 'Not while Spain's under threat.'

Bernie's dad had talked about Spain a lot in recent months. Back in July, the left-wing government there had been over-thrown by a group of fascists known as the Falangists. Led by a general called Franco, they had plunged the country into a state of civil war. It was said that other fascists, like Hitler, were supporting Franco while the Communist Soviet Union was backing the left-wing Republicans.

'Moscow's setting up an International Brigade to go and fight for the Republicans,' Solly said. 'A lot of the East End comrades are joining up.'

'Yes, me dad said.'

Solly lit a cigarette and told her, 'I'm going.'

Bernie didn't know how to respond. Fighting fascism was a good thing, but if he was going to war he could get him-self killed. Eventually she said, 'Is your mum all right with you going?'

While she didn't know Solly's mum, Bernie knew of her. Dolly Adler had been an actress in her youth but now she worked as a 'Nippy' waitress in Lyons Corner House on Coventry Street. It was said that other Jewish women didn't approve of her, even though many of them enjoyed looking at her handsome son. Still very glamorous, Dolly, like her son, was a committed Communist.

'My mum? Are you joking?' he asked. 'She's all for it.'

There was no Mr Adler as far as anyone seemed to know and Solly only had one brother. Surely Dolly had to be worried about him going to war? Bernie knew that, committed though he was to the cause, her dad would hate it if any of her broth-ers went. In common with most families, the Lynches had lost many relatives in the Great War. Nobody wanted to go back to that, not unless they had to.

'Becky!'

She was almost home when she heard Rose running up behind her. Becky turned.

'I thought you were staying on with Bernie.'

'No. She was with ...' Rose stopped abruptly. She didn't want to say Solly Adler's name in case it upset Becky. Even if Bernie didn't know, Rose understood how Becky felt about him.

'Solly Adler, yes,' Becky said. 'They get on really well.'

'Yeah, but she's not Jewish and so it won't ...'

Rose stopped talking. Becky was looking at her in 'that' way, as in pitying her.

'Oh, Rosie,' she said, 'religion doesn't matter if people like each other enough.'

The poor kid could be such a dunce sometimes. Becky had seen the way Solly had looked at Bernie. She knew what that meant. She'd seen them dance together too, their bodies entwined in a crazy, drunken victory spin. Solly had barely spoken to Becky, which was why she'd left. It was one thing to see the only real man she'd ever felt anything for with her best friend in his arms; it was quite another to hang around and see what happened next. Not that she blamed either of them. When they looked in each other's eyes there was a spark between them that just wasn't there when Solly looked at Becky – or anyone else.

'Anyway, what are you doing here, Rosie?' Becky asked. 'Why aren't you back at the pub?'

'I was worried about you,' she said.

Becky put her arm around her friend's narrow shoulders. 'Oh, Rosie,' she said, 'you are a mate.'

'Rebekah-*leh*!'

Her father's voice was unmistakable. Hanging out of his bedroom window dressed in an old grey nightshirt, Moritz Shapiro looked like a ghost.

'Papa!'

'You must come inside,' he said. 'Wandering the streets in the middle of the night! It's not decent! Who's that with you?'

Her father couldn't see very well these days but wouldn't get glasses.

'It's just Rosie,' Becky said. 'From across the . . .'

'Her mother is looking for her!' Moritz said. 'Her mother and I, out on the street like poor people, we were, both looking for our children!'

Rose shrugged. No, she couldn't see her mother out on the street looking for her either.

Becky said, 'I'd best go in.'

'All right.'

But Rose didn't move.

'Rosie?'

'Rebekah-*leh*! In!'

The rotted sash window Moritz hung through shuddered with the force of his order. Like every other house in the street, the Shapiros' place was slowly falling apart.

Rose whispered to Becky. '*He*'ll be there. Len. He's always home at night. He'll go potty.'

'What? About you being out?'

'I'm not supposed to be out when he's in,' Rose said.

It was cold, but Becky knew that wasn't the only reason her friend was trembling. Although Rose never told either of her friends what Len Tobin did to her, dark rumours about them persisted. Becky could barely believe them. But what was undeniable was that Rose was always covered in cuts and bruises. Of course her mum could have hurt her although not many people seemed to believe that.

'Rebekah!'

Becky grabbed Rose's hand and opened her front door.

'I'm bringing Rosie in with me, Papa,' she said. 'I think her mum's gone to bed.'

Royal Mint Street was still covered in marbles. A lot of them had been crushed underfoot – or hoof – but there were still enough whole examples to make staying upright a problem. Bernie tried to steer Solly towards the pavement, but he wanted to process down the middle of the road, like the cock of the walk.

'I'm gonna miss all this!' he said, spreading his arms wide, as if walking on a tight-rope. 'The old East End! My home! I've never lived anywhere else. Don't think I'd want to.'

He was steaming drunk but he'd insisted on walking Bernie home. She was glad in a way because he'd be there to take some of the flak when Mammy told her off for being out so late. And she liked him. But she was also nervous about being on her own with him. Blokes only ever wanted one thing and Bernie definitely didn't want *that*.

Mammy had been in the family way when she'd got married and it had meant that, from the age of sixteen, Bernie's age now, life for her had been hard. One pregnancy had followed another with three babies dying to Bernie's knowledge. She wanted her life to be more than just endlessly producing kids. It wore women out. Her mammy was still beautiful but looked much older than her thirty-five years.

'I want to travel,' Bernie said. 'I want to see the châteaux of France, the Mediterranean Sea ... and most of all I want to see the Pyramids of Egypt.'

'Blimey! Egypt!'

'Yes. Why not?'

'Why not? Well, yes, why not indeed, comrade,' he said. 'I . . .'

Seeing that he was about to step on a marble, Bernie pulled Solly out of the road.

'Oh, the girl saved my life!' he said as he stumbled against her. 'That's handsome!'

She saw a twinkle in his eye that she liked but also found a bit frightening.

She wagged her finger at him. 'Yeah, so behave yourself!'

He laughed. 'Christ, and you're sensible too, Bernadette Lynch!' he said. 'Blimey, is there anything you can't do?'

Bernie shook her head. 'You are very drunk. In fact I think that maybe *I* should take *you* home.'

In one smooth movement, Solly took her in his arms.

'I'd like that,' he said. 'Take me home and make love to me!'

For a moment, she didn't know what to do. Their lips were almost touching and she could feel his warm, beery breath on her face. Handsome and clearly eager for her, Solly was the sort of man a lot of girls dreamed about. But did Bernie Lynch?

She pushed him away.

'Oi!'

'Oi, nothing,' she said. 'If I'm so sensible, I won't want to get in the family way, will I?'

'Family way? I just wanted a little kiss.'

'Is that right?'

Solly flung himself down in front of her, begging on his knees, hands raised as if in prayer.

'Beautiful, darling sweetheart . . .'

In spite of herself, Bernie laughed. 'You are so drunk!'

Big brown eyes looked into hers and she was tempted. Men had started to show an interest in her about a year ago, but none of them looked, or spoke, like Solly Adler. He was special.

But then, according to Mammy, her dad had been special too. Handsome, kind, clever in his own way, besotted with her . . .

'I'm going home now, Solly,' Bernie said.

'Yes, I'll take you and . . .'

'On my own,' she said. And then she ran.

She heard him still calling after her three streets away.

'Bernadette Lynch! Come to me, Bernadette! I need you!'

And in spite of herself, Bernie smiled.

Chapter Six

Rose had long gone by the time Becky got up to go to work. But when she walked into the kitchen to make herself some tea, she found that her father had other plans.

'No work for you today,' Moritz said. 'We have to go somewhere.'

Becky shook her head. 'Papa, Mrs Rosenberg is expecting me,' she said. 'She's eight months. She can't manage the washing on her own.'

Most people did their washing on a Monday morning and Mrs Rosenberg would be mortified if she couldn't. Even old Mrs Michael, who did the Shapiros' washing for them, always did it on a Monday. She'd already made a start before Becky even got up.

'You're not going,' her father said. 'In fact, after yesterday, you're not leaving this house.'

'Papa!'

'Last night you were out drinking like a common tart,' he said.

'No, I wasn't!'

She'd seen Bernie and Rose have a drink but she herself hadn't touched a drop.

'I went out so I could be part of the action against fascism!'

'Yes, in contravention of what the Board of Guardians instructed.' Her father shook his head at her sternly. 'Such wickedness! And what will happen now? I'll tell you. The British will come for us, that's what will happen! I told you there would be consequences.'

'You didn't stop me!'

'No,' he said. 'Because I am a silly old *amoretz*. Tired to my bones, trying to look after a girl on my own! Is it any wonder you're running wild!' He wagged a finger at her. 'But not any more. Gone are the days when I let you roam at will just because your poor mother is no longer living. Now you must do what I say. Now you must behave like a decent girl. No more going out, no more *goyim* ...'

'Papa, I've done nothing wrong!' Becky sank down at the table. 'What I did, what we all did yesterday, was the best thing that's ever happened here. Now we've run Mosley and his fascists out ...'

'The police will be back to send us to some other place! Maybe to Ireland where your friend comes from. That's a place with no food and no work!'

'It won't happen!'

'It will!' Moritz stood. 'Drink your tea then go to your room. Put on your best dress and tidy your hair.'

'Yes, but ...'

'No buts!' He leaned down and said, close to her face, 'No buts or I will do what I have never done before and beat you.'

Becky gasped. This wasn't like her father. He was different from other men. Most of them did beat their children, but not Moritz Shapiro who had always prided himself on his humanity. What had happened to make him behave like this? Was it simply because she'd gone to fight the fascists? Or had something else taken place that she didn't know about?

Bertha Fischer was full of it; leaning on her sewing machine, fag in one hand, big mug of tea in the other.

'Ronnie Blackman kissed me in front of everyone!' she half whispered as soon as Mr Sassoon left the girls to finish their tea break. 'And then Frankie Salmon had a go!'

'He never!'

'He did!'

Bernie felt herself cringe. What if someone had seen Solly Adler going in for a kiss from her? Jewish boys with Jewish girls was one thing, but she was Irish. And every one of these girls fancied Solly. Bernie stared into her teacup and kept her head down.

As soon as she'd got home last night, Mammy had gone potty. She'd smelled the drink on Bernie right away and shouted the odds at Daddy about being a bad example to his children. He had just laughed and coughed, coughed and laughed. Until he'd seen her shoes. Bernie hadn't realised she'd got so much glass embedded in the soles. It would take months to save up for another pair. In the meantime she'd just have to put up with the holes.

'My Monty's better looking than Frankie Salmon,' Brenda Green said.

'Yeah, proper bloody *sheyn mensch*, him!'

All the girls turned and looked at Sharon Begleiter. Older than all the others, she was some sort of relative of Mr Sassoon's, although nobody knew the details. What was unmistakable however was that he allowed her to do what she liked, when she liked, and what Sharon liked to do most was gossip.

'Oh, come on, Brenda,' Sharon said, 'your Monty ain't no oil painting, is he?'

'He's . . .'

'He's a tanner short of two bob, and you know it,' Sharon said.

It was true Brenda's fiancé wasn't the brightest star in the sky, but he was a decent bloke as far as Bernie could tell. Not that decency was anything Sharon Begleiter would find interesting. Still unmarried at almost thirty, she fed on the frailties of others, probably as a way of distracting people from her own faults. She was a born bully.

'Not like Solly Adler,' Sharon continued.

Bernie felt her face flush. Did Sharon know? Oh, please God, don't let her know!

'Now that's a *sheyn mensch*,' Bertha Fischer agreed.

Sharon laughed. 'You wouldn't stand a chance of *shtupping* that one!'

'And you think you would?'

Silence clamped down like a vice. Questioning or insinuating anything about Sharon wasn't done. Even if it was meant to be a joke. And in the case of Hessy Winter, it probably was a lame joke. Not that Sharon took it that way.

She turned her pale blue eyes on Hessy and said, 'Yeah, but at least I ain't got a leg as looks like a wooden walking stick, do I?'

All the girls, including Bernie, looked away as Hessy cried. She was only fifteen, the youngest girl in the workroom. And she had a clubfoot.

'You stand about as much chance of *schtupping* Solly Adler as you do of going to the moon,' Sharon said. Then, with a sickening prod to Bernie's ribs, she said, 'Ain't that right Bernadette Lynch?'

He'd gone out – somewhere. Not that she cared where. As far as Rose was concerned, Len Tobin could go anywhere he wanted, just as long as he went. Because once he was out of the flat, she could, if she was lucky, forget what had just happened.

Nell hadn't so much as moved since Rose got home. The girl only knew she was alive because she could hear her snoring. Len, on the other hand, had gone berserk.

He'd accused Rose of everything he could dream up. Of drinking, which she hadn't, of stealing from him, which she would never dare do, and, most seriously, of going with men. Len didn't like the idea of that because that was his privilege.

'Like Commie cock inside you, do you?' he'd yelled at her as he'd pushed her down on the bed he shared with her mother.

Rose had looked at the wall, as she usually did. Then, when it was over, she'd run into the corner beside the range and bitten her nails. Once he'd run out of drink, Len had left.

Still shaking, Rose went out the back and filled a bowl with water from the tap. Then she came back in and washed herself. She hated the stink of him on her. When she'd finished she threw the water down the drain and sat on the steps outside.

Her mum had never told her who her dad was but Rose was pretty sure that if he knew what Len did to her, he'd have something to say about it. Whoever he was. Although she never said, Rose envied Bernie and Becky their families. Even though Becky's mum was dead, at least she knew who she had been. At least she had photographs. Not that Becky was happy at the moment. Rose had seen the way Solly Adler had looked at Bernie and she'd noticed when they'd gone off together. Becky had almost cried then. Luckily Bernie's brother Dermot didn't seem to have a girlfriend, but when he did get one, Rose knew she'd be upset just the same as Becky was now. And he was going to get one, some day. Dermot was handsome and brave and kind. Any girl would be lucky to get him. Any girl except her ...

'Men are all shits!' was what her mum always said. And in

the case of Len Tobin and all the other men she 'saw', she was right. No doubt Len would return at some point with a couple of boozed-up blokes from off the ships all eager to 'see' her mum. Money would change hands and afterwards her mum and Len would go down the Ten Bells and get rat-arsed. But not all men were like Len and the others he knew. The Lynch boys, Joey and Dermot, liked a drink but weren't brutal and didn't behave badly. Their parents would never have put up with that. Even Becky's dad, although he was a weird old thing who always dressed in black and spoke with a funny accent, was decent enough. But how could Rose ever even pretend to be that?

Decent girls didn't do what she did. They didn't look like her or even smell like she did. She couldn't read or write properly, although she was one up on her mum who couldn't attempt to do either. She'd heard people say it was because her mum was a gypsy that she was ignorant. But Rose knew that wasn't the whole truth.

Once, when Rose was a little 'un, an old man and a woman had come to visit them, riding on a horse. Her mum had told the child that they were her grandparents. The woman, the image of her mother and covered in elaborate gold chains and earrings, had smiled at her and given her sweets. She'd also, Rose remembered, read to her.

Why her mum couldn't read too remained a mystery. If Rose ever asked about her family, all Nell ever said was, 'I fell out with them thieving gypsies!' But they'd come to see her once and, as Rose remembered them, they'd been kind. The old man had even brought food. What had happened between her mum and her family? If she'd known where they lived, Rose would have gone to see them. But she didn't and, if they really were gypsies, they probably moved around.

'Hello, Rosie. You all right, love?'

Rose looked up. It was Auntie Kitty, Bernie's mum.

Rose smiled. 'Yeah.'

But Auntie Kitty wasn't a woman who was easily fooled.

'Well, come and have a cuppa and help me with the washing,' she said. 'I've got bread pudding if you're hungry.'

Rose didn't have to be asked twice.

Mr Sassoon had come and told them all to get back to work before Bernie could find out what, if anything, Sharon knew about Solly and her. Not that there was a 'Solly and her' as far as Bernie was concerned. All that had happened was that he'd tried to kiss her. Boys did that to girls, it didn't mean anything. Not usually.

But still Sharon kept looking at her over the top of her machine and smirking. Bernie wanted to punch the meddling cow. She wanted to tell her, 'Solly's going to Spain to fight – and anyway I don't want a bloke!'

However, she knew that the bit about not wanting a man wasn't true. She'd thought of nothing else but Solly Adler ever since he'd tried to kiss her. It made her cross. Jews and gentiles didn't mix, not romantically. Well, only sometimes, like Mr and Mrs Simon in the tobacconist's shop. But it was said that Mrs Mary O'Brien, as Mrs Simon was, had been forced to convert to Judaism so she could marry her present husband. Bernie knew she could never do that. Church didn't mean a whole lot to her, but if she gave it up, she knew her mammy would be upset. Anyway she had other things to do. She'd told Solly that she wanted to travel and he'd been quite shocked. Probably once he'd sobered up, he'd thought how barmy the idea was. When she'd got out of bed this morning, she'd wondered why she'd even told him. How was she ever going to travel further than Southend?

Before work, she'd taken the camera and the films she'd shot back to Mr Katz who'd said he'd start developing them straight away. Bernie still didn't know whether what she'd photographed was any good, and the thought that maybe it wasn't, made her feel anxious. Mr Piratin had said he wanted to use those pictures and she didn't want to let him down. She saw Sharon wrinkle her nose at her and laugh. Bernie knew she should have it out with her. But she was also hoping to get back to Mr Katz after work and that was far more important than sorting out some gossipy old bag from Flower and Dean Street. Everyone knew that where Sharon Begleiter lived was little better than a knocking shop.

Not everyone knew who lived in the sombre blackened house on Folgate Street, opposite the Pewter Platter pub. But most Jews did. Even the most ardent Commie knew where Auntie Ada lived – and what she did. What few people knew was who Ada Rabinowicz really was.

There were rumours. Some said she owned and lived in her great big Huguenot house all on her own because she'd once been married to a rich furrier who had made a coat for King Edward VII. Others said her mother had been a big star of the stage back in her native Kiev and had even had an affair with the last Tsar of Russia. Ada herself neither confirmed nor denied any of it. She didn't need to. What she did gave her power amongst certain sections of the Jewish community. While those it didn't touch, she didn't care about.

Ada Rabinowicz had been a *shadchan*, a matchmaker, for at least four decades. How old she was when she began wasn't known, just as how she'd got started was a mystery. But some-how Ada Rabinowicz had got herself into a position where she and she alone arranged matches between the more Orthodox young Jews from Spitalfields, via Whitechapel, right out to Stepney.

As soon as Becky saw her father walk across the cobblestones up to the *shadchan*'s front door and ring the bell, she knew what was coming.

'Oh, Papa, I don't want to get married!'

'I told you there'd be consequences,' he said. 'Hush now!'

Becky knew Mrs Rabinowicz by sight. In spite of her reputed wealth she could usually be seen bustling around Petticoat Lane Market on a Sunday looking for bargains, haggling over pennies with sellers who could hardly afford to eat. Always dressed as if she was just about to go to dinner at a high-class West End restaurant in company with a very low-class actor, Mrs Rabinowicz's Californian Poppy perfume did some violence to Becky's nose when the *shadchan* opened the door.

'Oh, Mr Shapiro,' she said as she patted her elaborate ginger wig with one heavily ringed hand. 'Ah, and this must be Rebekah. Lovely.' She smiled, revealing brown teeth. 'Come in! Come in!'

Becky had always known that her father would want to arrange her marriage one day. But so soon? She was only just sixteen, which was young even for a girl from a very *frum* family. This had to be in reaction to her staying out with the protesters – and her friends. Papa didn't like Rosie or Bernie and he hated the Commies. He told stories about how, back in 1930, a load of Jewish anarchists had thrown bacon slices at a group of rabbis coming out of the Great Synagogue. She'd tried to argue, saying that Communists and Anarchists were different, but he hadn't listened. He'd just gone on and on about how he'd heard about it from Manny Schiff who was the most honest man on Brick Lane, blah, blah, blah …

Becky had given up trying to tell him that the story was

probably a lie made up expressly to frighten *frummers* like him. He didn't understand because he didn't want to understand.

And now he was going to arrange for her to marry a stranger who would, most certainly, not be Solly Adler or any other kind of Commie boy. Not that Solly would have wanted her anyway. On last night's showing, he only had eyes for Bernie.

'This I like so much.'

Walter Katz handed Bernie a black-and-white photograph of one of the Irishwomen who'd hung out of the windows above Cable Street. Chamber pot in hand, long grey hair flying in the wind, she looked like an ancient witch from the wild coast of County Clare.

'You see,' he said, 'you've managed to catch the lines on her face, the bags under her eyes. It's a very interesting photograph.'

'I just pointed the camera and snapped,' Bernie said.

He handed her another print. She remembered taking this shot very well. Covered in piss, she'd been dripping wet and feeling precarious on top of that rickety barricade, when she caught a copper whacking a demonstrator on the bum with his truncheon. The victim, a blond lad, was turning round in fury and looked as if he was about to bite the copper's face.

'You have natural talent,' the old man said. 'Whether Mr Piratin wants to use these photographs to help his cause or not, you must not stop now. You must build a portfolio of work and take it around.'

'Take it around where?'

'To photographers!' he said. 'So you can get a job.'

'I have a job,' Bernie said. God, what had she been thinking when she took that camera? And telling Solly that she wanted to travel! How silly was she? When Daddy had got sick, all her dreams seemed selfish and impractical. The prospect of the

77

whole family being unemployed was too terrible to imagine. And yet all over the East End there were families who had to live like that. They were the ones Bernie sometimes saw sleeping under railway arches or lining up outside the doss house in hopes of a bed for the night. She'd been really lucky to get the job at Sassoon's even if it had been because Mammy had home-worked for him for years. And if she kept her nose clean, she might even be able to get her little sisters in too when the time came.

'I mean a job where you can use your talent,' Mr Katz said. 'You're always sketching. I've seen you. You have a painter's eye, Bernadette, and that is rare.'

'Thank you.' She felt herself blush. What he was saying was very nice even if it was a load of old tosh.

'Now,' he said, 'I will make a set of prints for Mr Piratin and a set for your portfolio.'

'Well, that's very kind of you but I have to give all me money to Mammy ...'

'No charge!' he said. 'No charge. And also I will make a gift to you as well.'

'Oh, no!'

That had come out more forcefully than she had meant it to. But then Mammy had always told her never to take presents from men. She said they always wanted something in return and Bernie knew what that was! Surely not Mr Katz, though ...

'Yes! Yes!' he said. He put the camera he'd lent her back in her hands. 'You must have this.'

Bernie nearly dropped it. 'But it's yours,' she said. 'Your camera.'

'It is one of my cameras, Bernadette,' he said. 'One of them. I have many. And besides, as I told you at the meeting, my eyes are going now, it ...'

'Mr Katz ...'

His eyes weren't going. He could see perfectly well as far as Bernie could tell. The reason why he'd offered his camera to the East End defenders had to be more to do with the possibility that he doubted his own strength to work while thrown about by a crowd. That or he'd simply wanted a younger person to do it.

'And you will owe me nothing,' he said as he closed her fingers around the camera. 'Only that you don't give up.'

Bernie wanted the camera. But could she promise Mr Katz that she'd carry on taking photographs? How would she even be able to afford the film?

'Times are hard,' the *shadchan* said as she lifted her delicate teacup to her ruby-painted lips. 'But, thanks be, most of our young men have employment.'

'I do not want a lazy boy, I want someone who will be able to keep my daughter in a decent fashion,' Moritz Shapiro said. 'A boy with prospects, from a good family.'

Becky had to say something. 'Papa, people here aren't lazy, they're poor!'

But the adults ignored her.

'Of course. Of course,' Ada Rabinowicz said.

'And with skills. A trade.'

She raised a hand. 'There's no *dreck* on my books Mr Shapiro, I won't contemplate it. Decent families, like yours, want decent *chossens* for their daughters. Only thing I will say to you is that, at sixteen, the girl is a little young.'

'Times, as you say, Mrs Rabinowicz, are hard,' Moritz said. 'So much trouble ... demonstrations on the streets! People with no jobs!'

'So you want to get Rebekah settled because you care for her?'

'My wife is gone and I am old . . . '

'And if you spend time on this . . . and with her only sixteen you have time . . . you can be sure you find the right man for your daughter.'

He smiled. 'You understand me.'

Becky thought, *But neither of you understand me!*

She didn't say it, though. Her father seemed to have changed before her eyes and, for the first time in her life, she was afraid of him.

Mr Lynch, or Uncle Pat as she called him, was sitting smoking on a chair in the back yard when Rose arrived.

Auntie Kitty, who'd already put out one line of shirts and jumpers to dry, shouted at him.

'Oh, blimey, Pat, can't you at least smoke away from the clean washing?'

He coughed. 'What for?'

'So the bleedin' clothes smell nice!'

Once he'd stopped coughing, Patrick Lynch said, 'What . . . here?'

And he had a point. Although it was still only early October, there was already a winter chill in the air and, even in the day-time, a lot of people were lighting fires.

Auntie Kitty ignored him. She said to Rose, 'You hang out the girls' dresses and I'll go and put the kettle on.'

'Ta.'

Rose was thirsty and hungry and, as usual, her mum had nothing indoors. She took a handful of dolly pegs out of a box on the ground and hung up what she recognised as Marie's best dress. Unlike Bernie, fourteen-year-old Marie liked as many frills and flounces as her mother was prepared to sew on her clothes. Little Aggie was the same, another properly 'girly' girl. Why was Bernie so different? Maybe it was because she had been born directly after two boys, Dermot and the eldest Lynch brother, Joey. Maybe because of them, she'd taken on a boy's way of thinking? In some respects at least.

'Not at school today, Rosie?' Uncle Pat asked. The Lynches were much keener on their kids going to school than her mum was. Even Aggie was better at reading than Rose.

'I think I've probably done with school now,' she said.

Patrick Lynch shrugged. His own older kids had left school before he'd wanted them to because of his health. Very few people in the East End had the luxury of a long period of education.

'So you looking for work, are you?'

Rose had seen the look of joy on Patrick Lynch's face when he'd met up with his old docker mates while they'd all defended Cable Street. Work and education – they meant so much to this family! Her mum worked too, of course, but that was different...

'I help me mum,' she said.

She watched Patrick Lynch's face darken. Rose let men into the flat and then gave them water to wash themselves afterwards, if they wanted it. Len took the money. Some days, the 'work' never stopped.

Auntie Kitty returned with a cup of tea and a lump of bread pudding complete with currants.

'Here you go,' she said.

Rose knew that whenever she did eat, she gobbled her food. She always tried not to, but she usually failed. As she sat down on the ground between the hanging dresses, she wedged half the pudding into her mouth all in one go.

'Oi! Gannet!'

But Auntie Kitty was smiling when she said it.

Uncle Pat coughed until his face turned purple. Whether

he was laughing or not was difficult to tell. Whatever he did seemed to make him cough now.

Rose had just started her tea when the sound of someone hammering on the Lynches' street door made her blood turn cold. Even though Len was out, she knew that she was expected to stay at home with her mum in case anyone came. It was her job to wake her up.

Auntie Kitty went indoors and then Rose heard Len's furious voice.

'Where is she? Rose? Get over here, you little scrubber!'

It was dark outside, but her father was still hard at work. Sitting out in the glass-covered area that had once been the Huguenots' weaving shed, he worked under both moon and gaslight. He looked, Becky sometimes thought, like a gnome from one of her fairy-tale books, sewing wings for elves and pixies. Except the material he was using was dark blue and he was making a suit for a lawyer.

She took him Russian tea. Black with lemon. She put the cup and saucer down on the fabric cutting table and said, 'I'm going to work tomorrow, Papa.'

He said nothing, which she took for, if not approval, lack of opposition.

As soon as they'd got home, Becky had gone out to see the lady she was supposed to have been working for, Mrs Rosenberg, and explained why she hadn't come to visit her. Not much older than Becky, Mrs Rosenberg had understood.

'Mrs Rabinowicz got me together with my old man,' she'd said when Becky told her. 'My dad paid a fortune.'

She'd looked sad. But then Becky knew that Mrs Rabinowicz had only one thing on her mind when she put a man and a woman together and that was money.

She didn't know anything about Mr Rosenberg except that he had a business in Black Lion Yard, where all the local jewellers had shops – and he was a lot older than his wife. Becky had never seen him when she'd gone round to help Mrs Rosenberg.

'I won't tell Mrs Levy you never come this morning,' Mrs Rosenberg said when Becky left. Then she'd smiled and put a hand on her shoulder. Becky had wanted to cry.

Yesterday she'd been on the barricades with every other freedom-loving man and woman in the East End. Now she was facing a forced marriage to someone she didn't even know. It was as if she'd gone back a hundred years in one night. If only she'd gone straight home when it had got dark! Maybe, if she had, Papa wouldn't have contacted the *shadchan*.

When they'd got home, she'd asked him again why he'd done it. But he didn't answer and he wasn't going to. All he'd said was that she was free to reject any potential husband she didn't like. Becky was inclined to think she'd reject them all whether she liked them or not. And she knew she wouldn't like them. Not unless one of them was Solly Adler. But then he wasn't going to be presented to her because he and his family were nobodies. His mother worked as a waitress and nobody knew who his father was.

And he was a Communist.

Becky went to bed, but she didn't sleep. In the end she got up and looked out of her window at the dark street in front of the house and she cried. Not even the jaunty piano music belting out from the Ten Bells on the corner could make her feel any better.

Chapter Seven

'Oi! Blondie!'

Bernie looked across the road where she saw Solly Adler. Wearing a greatcoat several sizes too big for him, a pair of brown boots that had seen better days and a trilby hat at a cheeky angle, he smiled at her through the smoke from the fag at the corner of his mouth.

'I'm on me way to work,' she said. She knew she looked a sight in that horrible brown dress she wore for work! Why did he have to see her in that?

Bernie hadn't slept much, mainly because she'd spent a lot of the night thinking about the rumours that cow Sharon Begleiter might be spreading about her and Solly. What did Sharon think she knew about it anyway?

'I'm off to fight more fascists,' Solly said.

Was he off to Spain? Already? Bernie shook her head to wake herself up. Something else that had kept her and her dad awake had been all the noise coming from Rosie's flat. So much screaming and shouting that in the end her dad had got Dermot and Joey up to go round and bang on the door. But no one had answered and, after that, the place had gone quiet. Probably her mum having yet another barney with 'her' Len. The pig.

'In Spain?' Bernadette asked, forcing herself to concentrate on the here and now.

'Yeah,' said Solly. 'Liverpool Street Station today, France tomorrow, if I'm lucky, then ...'

'You saw off Mosley's Blackshirts,' Bernie said. 'Don't we have enough fascists for you here?'

Then she felt embarrassed. Why had she said that? It sounded as if she wanted him to stay. But then ... she did.

Solly's eyes twinkled and he said, 'Why? Want me to stay?'

'No!' She turned her head away so he wouldn't see her blush.

Solly laughed. 'You're a strange one, Bernadette Lynch,' he said. 'But I like you. When I get back from Spain, I'll take you up West and show you the time of your life.'

In spite of herself, Bernie smiled. She turned her head to look at him again and said, 'The conquering hero, eh?'

'That's the ticket!'

He picked up the canvas pack at his feet and shouldered it.

'Makes a difference to a bloke, knowing he's got a smashing girl waiting at home for him when he goes off to fight, you know.'

'Oh, yeah? Pity I'm not smashing then, ain't it?'

Solly, laughing, shook his head. 'When they made you, they broke the mould.'

He began to walk away, down towards the Ten Bells and then across Commercial Street to the Market and Liverpool Street Station.

Bernie began walking in the opposite direction, but stopped. Then she turned and ran towards his retreating back. When she caught up with him, flustered and out of breath, she didn't have a thing to say because she really didn't know what she was doing. She just stood in front of him, her eyes suddenly full of tears.

Quick as lightning, he took her in his arms and this time she let him. What she was feeling was unfamiliar, exciting and also very frightening. Bernie heard her breath catch in her throat. Solly pulled her closer so that their lips almost touched. For just a second neither of them moved. And then he kissed her.

It seemed to last both forever and for just a moment. His mouth on hers, his arms pulling her in close, so close . . .

Only when, finally, their lips parted, did she manage to say, 'Don't die, Solly. Please, please, don't die.'

Again, he laughed, and then he said, 'With you back here, waiting for me? No chance. I've never met a girl like you before. I won't let go of you easy. I'll write. Will you write back to me?'

'Of course,' she said. 'Of course I will!'

They kissed again and this time Bernie didn't want to let him go – ever. But in the end she had to and it was then she saw Sharon Begleiter, staring at her with bitterness in her eyes.

Nell was still lying where Len had thrown her, out in the yard beside the khazi.

Rose shook her. 'Mum!'

Len and the men he'd brought home had only just gone. Even though she'd fought and screamed, Rose hadn't been able to get out until now. Covered in blood and filth, her whole body shaking with fear and disgust, she slapped her mother's face, willing her still to be alive.

One swollen eye opened first. 'Mum!'

'Rosie?'

She spoke funny, her jaw moving sideways. She dribbled. 'Mum, what . . . '

Nell opened her other, blood-crusted eye.

'Did they ...'

Rose knew what her mum wanted to ask, but couldn't say. She didn't answer. Of course they had! Len had brought three of them home from the pub, all drunk. She didn't know who they were and suspected he didn't either. But they'd had money.

Rose helped her mother sit up. As she moved she clutched her ribs. It wouldn't be the first time Len had broken one or two of them.

'Dermot Lynch knocked,' Rose said. 'Wanting to know what all the racket was about.'

'You never let him in, did ya?'

'No.'

She'd wanted to. In a way. She knew that Dermot would have fought to save her. But she also knew that Len and the three drunks would probably have killed him. One of them, the one who had taken her first, had been built like a bull. A huge, filthy, sweating bull.

Nell looked at her daughter and cried. 'Oh, my chick,' she said, 'what have they done to you?'

Len had brought his new 'best mates' home to see Nell. And at first they'd seemed to be impressed. But then the smallest of the trio, an ancient bald character, had seen Rose, crouching in the corner by the range.

She had seen his eyes widen.

'I fancy some of that,' he'd said.

And so had his mates. Not even Len saying that they'd have to pay extra for her put them off.

Rose had never seen her mum fight like that. Standing in front of her daughter, she'd taken them all on, Len included. She'd never done that before. They'd beaten her to what Rose saw now, a broken, bleeding ghost of herself.

'Oh, my little chavvie!'

Rose wanted to hug her mother, but Nell held her away so that she could look at her.

'What did they do?'

One after the other, with Len looking on, counting his tanners and ha'pennies. She'd never stopped fighting, even when they'd put their hands over her mouth. Bitten, punched, her skin ripped and bruised, they'd all used her and then, when they'd collapsed drunk on floor, so had Len.

And that had been the worst of it. That had been the point at which she'd wanted to die. Only the thought that her mum might need her had kept Rose going. And Nell did need her.

Becky left Mrs Rosenberg lying down while she went off to do her shopping. Mr Rosenberg had told his wife he wanted grilled chicken livers for his dinner that night and so Becky was on her way to the kosher butcher's shop on Hanbury Street when she saw Bernie. It was almost eleven o' clock. Why wasn't she at work? And why was she sitting on the ground?

It took Becky a little while to spot Bernie's black eye. Almost hidden by an endless stream of people in winter blacks and browns, she sat outside Truman's Brewery just as she had the first time Becky had spoken to her. As she crossed Brick Lane to go and see her friend, Becky wondered what Bernie's mum would make of the fact that she was smoking a fag in the street.

Becky put Mrs Rosenberg's shopping bag down on the pavement and then sat beside her friend. Bernie had to know she was there, but she didn't look at her. Or speak. In the end it was Becky who broke the silence. People were beginning to look at the two girls with disapproval. Only kids sat on the ground, kids and dodgy boys. Something was wrong.

'What happened to you?' Becky said.

Bernie shrugged.

'You look like you've been in a fight.'

Bernie looked at her for the first time. 'I have.'

Becky put a hand up to her mouth. 'Oh, Bern! Why?'

'Sharon Begleiter,' Bernie said. 'I had to stop the old cow's mouth.'

'Sharon Begleiter's a trouble-maker, everyone knows that,' Becky said. 'You want to ignore her.'

'I couldn't!'

'Why not?'

'Because she saw me with Solly Adler,' Bernie said.

Becky felt herself go cold. She'd seen her friend with Solly after Cable Street, she'd noticed the way he'd looked at her. He hadn't been able to take his eyes off her and when they'd danced they'd looked like a couple in love.

'Yes, well, everyone was really excited on Sunday . . . '

'Weren't Sunday, it was this morning.'

Becky felt her heart pinch.

'He's gone off to Spain,' Bernie said. 'To fight. I wished him well and we kissed. You always give a man going for a soldier a kiss on the cheek, don't you? And that's all it was, a peck. But *she* made something out of it, something that it wasn't.'

'She saw you?'

'I never knew she was there.'

'So why aren't you at work?' Becky said.

Bernie put her head down. 'Because I got the sack,' she said. 'The old bitch kept on and on about it, wouldn't stop, and so I hit her. Then Mr Sassoon came and, well, I ended up hitting him too. It was an accident, but . . . '

Becky both did and didn't want to comfort her. Bernie was lying. It hadn't been just a peck she'd had with Solly. No one lost their job over just a peck. And Becky had seen them after Cable Street. She knew and it broke her heart. Solly was in love with Bernie and she wished them happiness, but only because Bernie was her friend.

Her mum took a sip from the last unbroken cup in the place and closed her eyes.

'Tea.'

'It'll do you good,' Rose said.

'Be better with a bit of gin ... '

'They drank it, Mum,' Rose said.

The men had drunk all the booze. Then they'd smashed everything, then they'd left. Len included. Not only didn't he care about her mum, Rose realised he didn't even care about himself. Only the drink mattered and anything could and would be done to get it.

Sometimes she wondered whether Len even knew what he did to her when her mum was too drunk to accommodate him. Did her mum know? Other people seemed to. Bernie's parents ... How?

'We'll have to get some gin somehow,' Nell said.

Rose shook her head. 'I ain't got no money.'

Her mother swore.

Rose looked away. Even now when what her mum probably needed most was a doctor, all she could think about was drink. 'Oh, Mum ... '

'Not for me, you soft bleeder!' Nell said. 'For you!'

Rose sat down. She didn't want gin. She didn't want anything except to be somewhere else. She said, 'I don't like gin.'

'That's as may be, but you'll have to get some down you,' Nell said.

Rose shook her head.

'Oh, yes, you will, Rosie,' her mum said. 'Because that's one of the nicer ways of making sure you're not up the stick. If them three blokes had their way with you ... '

And Len, she wanted to say, but didn't. Len had been doing it for two years but she'd not got in trouble so far. Why should this be any different? But she said, 'Yes, Mum.'

Once Nell had finished her tea, she fell asleep. Usually she couldn't without a drink, but she'd just spent a night out in the cold yard, and she was badly hurt. Rose watched her. She wanted to go and get Bernie's mum so she could help look after Nell, but she knew her mum wouldn't like that. If Len found out he'd go bonkers. He hated the Lynches, called them 'interfering cunts'. Of course he was jealous really. The Lynches, for all their troubles, always stuck together. They loved each other while nobody loved Len. Nobody, probably, ever had.

When Nell woke up, she told Rose to light the range. The previous night's visitors had broken most of the chairs and a couple of shelves, which could at least provide some warmth even if they were useless for anything else. Rose took the bigger sticks of wood out into the yard to break them up and it was while she was doing that, her mum apparently found something.

It was a brooch and, when held up to the light, the big stone in the middle shone with all the colours of the rainbow.

'Where'd you get that?' Rose asked.

Nell said, 'See that big stone there? That's an opal, that is. Rest of it's gold.'

'Mum, where ... '

'Take it down Uncle Pinchas' and tell him your mum says if he don't give a good price for it, his old girl could get the fright of her life. Then come straight back here. No sodding off round the Lynches'. You got that?'

Rose took the brooch. To her it looked like something the

91

rich Jewish ladies would wear. People like Bernie's employer's wife, Mrs Sassoon.

'Shall I finish making up the range first, Mum?' Rose said.

Nell shook her head. 'No. More important we deal with you first. Get back here quick as you can and I'll go down the Ten Bells. Oh, and if Pinchas gives you any old flannel, tell him if he don't give me at least two guineas, I'll put a curse on him. *And* I'll tell his missus what he likes to do with me when he's drunk.'

Becky had pushed her friend in through the door of Katz's paper and string shop.

'Mr Walter will know what to do,' she'd said. 'And if all else fails maybe you can ask him if you can pawn the camera.'

Selling or pawning the camera had been the first thing that had come to Bernie's mind. But Becky had told her that had to be a last resort.

'The camera is your way out of here,' she'd said. 'You can't give that up.'

Then she'd left.

As soon as she'd arrived at the paper and string shop, Bernie had realised that both of the old men were looking at her. But only Mr Walter spoke.

'Bernadette,' he said. 'I'm glad you're here. I have some news for you.'

A customer came in and so Mr Herman went over to help him.

Noting her pallor, as well as her black eye, Mr Walter said, 'Are you all right, my dear?'

Bernie cried then for the first time since Mr Sassoon had sacked her. Mr Walter took her into the small kitchen at the back of the shop and made her a cup of tea. In return, she told him everything.

'I knew she'd seen us and I knew she'd run off and tell all the girls at work and she did,' Bernie said. 'She can't keep nothing to herself!'

'This Sharon Begleiter?'

'Yes. And so I hit her,' Bernie said. 'I didn't stop hitting her even when Mr Sassoon come in and tried to break us up. In fact, Mr Walter, I'm ashamed to say I hit him too. By accident, like. But that's why I got the sack. I hit Mr Sassoon and I think I might have broke his nose.'

She began to cry again. 'Mammy's gonna go raving mad when she finds out!'

He put a hand on her shoulder. But it didn't make Bernie feel any better. How could she have been so stupid as to let her emotions run away with her like that? And with her dad out of work ...

'Even if I went crawling on me hands and knees, I know Mr Sassoon'd never have me back after what I done to him!'

'It seems unlikely,' Mr Walter said. 'You know, Bernadette, that Mr Solomon Adler is a very greatly desired young man amongst the young Jewish women here?'

She looked up at him. 'I know,' she said. 'Solly's, well ...'

'Handsome and passionate is what he is, and that is very attractive,' Mr Katz said. 'And yet he only has eyes for you, a *shiksa*. And that is why they laugh, those girls. From jealousy.'

'That's as maybe, but that won't get me my job back!'

She knew Solly was handsome and charming and dangerous. Those were all the things she found irresistible about him. But ...

'You know in this country you have a saying that: *Every cloud has a silver lining,*' he said.

'Yes, it's c— it's rubbish. Things go wrong and then they keep on going wrong.'

'In many cases that is true,' Mr Walter said. 'But, in this instance, maybe not. You know I told you I have some news for you, Bernadette?'

'Do you?'

When she'd first arrived she'd hadn't paid too much attention.

'I do,' he said. 'And it concerns a man I know who is looking for a member of staff.'

'What, in schmatte?'

'No,' he said.

'But that's all I can do!'

'Ah, but that isn't true, now is it, Bernadette?'

Becky dawdled on her way back to the Rosenbergs' house. At once sorry for and angry with Bernie, she didn't know how she felt now about her friend. Solly Adler was the first boy Becky had ever come across that she actually liked. Apart from Bernie's brothers. But they were like family. Bernie and Rose were the sisters she'd never had. Or they had been. Not that she thought that Bernie had 'stolen' Solly from her. She hadn't. Bernie didn't know how Becky felt about Solly. Nobody did.

She'd put Mr Rosenberg's chicken livers at the bottom of the larder and made herself a cup of tea before she realised that the house was unusually quiet. She'd left Mrs Rosenberg lying down on her bed and so maybe she was still asleep. She had high blood pressure and had been ordered by Dr Klein to rest as much as possible before the baby was born. Becky called out her name a couple of times and then went up to her bedroom.

The Rosenbergs' house in Elder Street was almost identical to Becky's home in that it was an old Huguenot building. Until she'd died the previous April, Mr Rosenberg's mother had lived on the top floor in what had once been the weaving loft. But now the couple lived in that vast four-storey house alone, just like Becky and her father.

Even as she walked up the dark, creaking staircase, Becky had a sense that something wasn't right. And when she stood outside the Rosenbergs' bedroom, she felt her heart begin to race. Mrs Rosenberg was a chatty young woman even when she was really tired.

Becky pushed the bedroom door open and saw her lying on her bed, underneath a blue counterpane, a smile on her face. At first, she felt a sense of relief. But as she drew closer and saw that Mrs Rosenberg wasn't breathing, Becky began to panic.

'Oh, God.'

Trembling, Becky put a hand on the young woman's arm and then drew it away again as if it had burned her. She was cold. Stone cold. And if Mrs Rosenberg was stone cold then so was her baby.

Becky ran. Out of the bedroom, down the stairs and into the street. Screaming.

Rosie Larkin was a funny little thing. Skinny and wild, she was nevertheless a pretty kid underneath all the dirt. Without work that day, Dermot Lynch was at a loose end. He'd been 'on the stones' outside the West India Docks waiting to be chosen, all morning, but he'd got nothing. Unlike his dad, Dermot was green, and unlike his older brother Joey he didn't have shoulders like a wrestler. Also, and more worryingly, his face didn't fit. He didn't know why but whenever foreman Artie Cross was making his pick, his eyes always passed automatically over Dermot. And so he'd walked home, only to find little Rose Larkin sitting on the steps down to her mum's rooms, staring into space like a nutter.

'Rosie?'

She didn't seem to hear him and so Dermot went down and sat next to her.

'Here,' he said, 'move over a bit.'

When he shoved her, she looked shocked.

'You all right, Rosie?' Dermot said. 'You look a bit, well ...'

'Mum's gone down the Ten Bells,' she said, as if this was news.

'Oh.'

Did that mean Nell had gone with Tobin or was he in the flat on his own? Dermot knew that Rose didn't like to be alone with her 'step-father'. He also knew that she didn't often get a choice. Perhaps the old bastard had passed out? Whatever was going on, Rose didn't look well and Dermot noticed that she had blood on her dress.

'Have you hurt ...'

'No,' she cut him off.

Dermot wondered why he'd even mentioned it. Rose was always covered in bruises and cuts. He'd just never seen her look as bad as this before. And she was shaking. He'd have to see whether his sister could get anything out of her, although he doubted it. Bernie was just as helpless around Rosie as he was.

'Tell you what,' Dermot said after a minute of watching the girl stare at nothing, 'why don't I roll you a fag?'

'I don't smoke.'

'I never did either until last year,' he said. 'Me brother taught me. And I tell you what, Rosie, it don't half perk you up.'

She didn't answer. But he took his tobacco tin out and began to roll anyway. Even if she didn't want to smoke, he could do with a fag.

Then out of the blue, the kid said, 'You should tell Bernie to leave Solly Adler alone.'

'Solly Adler? What ... Comrade Adler? What you talking about?' Dermot said. 'Bernie don't know him, does she?'

'They met on Cable Street,' Rose said.

Dermot and his brother Joey had started out in Victoria Park with the Young Communists. But then Joey had gone off with his mates from the docks. Dermot had only reached the Cable Street barricades much later. He'd seen his sister with that camera old Katz had lent her, but he hadn't noticed her hanging about with Adler.

'She danced with him outside the Ship.'

'On Cable Street?' Dermot asked.

'Yeah. Twirling her around he was, both of them lookin' into each other's eyes.'

Dermot hadn't seen any of that. If he had, he would have put a stop to it. His sister was only sixteen! Comrade Adler was twenty-four, it wasn't right. And, although he was almost ashamed to think it, Comrade Adler was Jewish. There was no place for Bernie in his life.

'And there's something else,' Rose said.

'What?'

She looked at him with her great, sad green eyes and said, 'Becky's in love with Comrade Adler.'

'What, Becky Shapiro? She knows him?'

'No, but she's seen him and I see the way she looks at him,' Rose said. 'Love at first sight, I suppose you'd say.'

Dermot shook his head. 'You don't believe that load of old pony, do you? Love at first sight? Blimey!'

Rose didn't say anything. The kid was, so Dermot's mum always said, a bit simple. What did she know? But what he could believe was that Bernie had caught the eye of Solly Adler. A handsome bloke like him had the pick of all the girls and his sister was one of the best-looking girls around – if not *the* best..

'Rosie . . . '

'What's he doing here?'

Dermot looked up into the fierce eyes of Nell Larkin and got to his feet smartish.

'Sorry, Mrs . . . '

'I should fucking think so!'

God, but she looked rougher than ever! Two black eyes and what looked like a mouth full of broken teeth. Her face wasn't even the same shape any more. Tobin must've been beating her to a pulp when he and Joey had gone round in the middle of last night. Dermot began to wish they'd broken the door down.

'Don't want you round here, you're not welcome!' Nell said.

'Oh, Mum, don't have a go at Dermot!'

But Nell was adamant. 'Go on your way, boy,' she said. 'This ain't no place for you.'

Dermot left. But as he walked back up the steps and into the street he heard Nell say to her daughter, 'Come on, let's get this gin down your neck.'

And he thought about telling the woman not to make her daughter just like her. But stopped himself. Rose, sadly, was none of his business. Bernie, on the other hand, was.

Chapter Eight

Becky heard Dr Klein talking to her father.

'I've told Mrs Levy that I think Rebekah should have a week at home to recover,' he said. 'She understands completely. A lot of very young ladies work as mother's helps so this is not the first time an incident like this has occurred.'

He was right. Becky had heard stories about women dying unexpectedly when they were pregnant. But she'd never seen it herself. Why hadn't she been there for Mrs Rosenberg? She couldn't help thinking it was because she'd been too busy talking to Bernie about Solly.

'You must reassure Rebekah that there was nothing she could have done,' the doctor continued. 'Mrs Rosenberg had a weak heart and with late-pregnancy high blood pressure, it was too much for her. These things happen.'

Becky heard her father say, '*Neh.*'

'I told her to rest and she rested. What more can a doctor do?'

People said that Dr Klein drank. Apparently there were stories about him and another doctor, O'Dwyer, going on pub-crawls. And Klein did look old for a man of forty. But Becky had always found him kind and caring and knew that he had probably done his best for Mrs Rosenberg. But had she?

When she'd told Becky to go shopping, Mrs Rosenberg had been lying down. But had she looked ill? Becky couldn't remember. Had she, perhaps, been pale? Probably. She was often a little pale, although she sometimes went a very strange grey colour when she felt a bit wobbly, and she hadn't looked like that this morning. But then, how much attention had Becky paid to her?

Still so cross, if that was even the right word, with her father for taking her to the *shadchan* and with Bernie for dancing with Solly Adler, she had been floating about in a dream that morning. Mostly feeling sorry for herself.

She heard her father see Dr Klein out and begin to walk up the stairs towards her bedroom. Becky snuggled down under her bedclothes and pulled the sheet over her head. She didn't want to talk to him, or to anyone. Of the three friends, she was supposed to be the one who had the best chance in life. But so far all she could see in front of her was an endless desert.

Old Mrs Green's idiot daughter Esther from upstairs kept banging on the khazi door.

'I need to go! I need to go *now*!' she keened.

But Nell wasn't taking her Rose anywhere any time soon.

'There's a lavvy on your floor. Use that! What's the matter with ya?'

'It's all blocked up,' Esther said.

'So shit on the floor,' Nell replied. What did she care? Her daughter had her head down the toilet, bringing up all the gin Nell had poured inside her. And she was still bleeding from her privates. If she ever saw those blokes who'd ripped her girl's insides so cruelly again, Nell'd kill them.

Rose lifted her head out of the pan, while Nell pushed her hair behind her ears.

'Mum . . .'

Outside Esther said, 'I want to go!'

Ignoring her, Nell passed over the bottle of gin she'd bought from the Ten Bells, and which was only just a quarter drunk, to her daughter. 'Sup up.'

'Oh, Mum, I . . .'

'You gotta keep some of it down, girl,' Nell said. 'Let the gin do its work.'

Nell had been, probably, younger than Rosie when she'd first got up the stick. People had called her the 'idiot' chavvie when she was a kid, the only one in her family who couldn't read or write, and so no one was very surprised. But her ma and pa were shamed when she gave birth to that poor, dead thing in a pile of autumn leaves on the edge of the camp. Ma had buried it and no more had been said – until black-eyed Nelson the basket-weaver's son got at her again. Then they'd told her to leave. Four months later, Rosie had been born in a brothel in Canning Town. The other girls had helped Nell look after her and Nell really wished that she was still there in many ways. But then she'd met a man who'd brought her to Ten Bells Street and who'd used her until another man came along, and another and another, until one day, Len Tobin had arrived. Dark, dangerous and handsome, once Len had loved her, or so he said. He'd also got drunk with her. Now he just used her and, latterly, her daughter too.

Rose drank some gin and pulled a face.

'You'll get used to it,' Nell said.

She had. She'd hated booze at the start. But now it was all that kept her going.

'You can't be up the stick, Rosie,' Nell said. 'We ain't got no money. And I can't be rid of it for you, I'm your mother. The one thing a woman can never do is be rid of her own flesh. I'd be cursed forever.'

Rose knew she shouldn't because they never talked about such things, but she said, 'Len could get a job.'

'Len!' Nell shook her head. 'Who'd have him?'

'Yes, but you . . . '

'I do what I do and you don't gab about it,' her mother said. 'Len protects us.'

'He never protected us last night,' Rose said.

Nell looked away. 'Yeah, well . . . '

A tiny voice from outside whispered, 'Now I've done it in me knickers.'

Her mother knew. Bernie could see it in her eyes and hear it in the silence that greeted her when she finally arrived home. Her dad and the rest of the kids sat stony-faced around the kitchen table, waiting for the explosion.

'Lost your job, then,' Kitty said.

Bernie's head went down. 'I'm sorry.'

'Sorry? Mr Sassoon only kept me on because I begged him,' Kitty said. 'And now the chances of his taking on our Marie are out the window. What was you thinking of, fighting? That's not you! And over a boy!'

'Who told you?'

'Never mind who told me, I know!' Kitty roared.

Bernie's dad said, 'Kit . . . '

'Shut up, Pat!' She put her hands on her hips and thrust her face into Bernie's. 'And a Yiddisher boy at that! You shouldn't even have been looking at one of them!'

'Nothing happened!'

'Yes, it did, you got the sack!'

Bernie began to feel tears sting her eyes.

'Your dad can't work because he's too sick, we're already on bread and scrape most of the time, Dermot can't get chose more'n twice in a row! We can't get by on just Joey's wages . . . '

'I know!' She sat down and put her head in her hands. 'It was that Begleiter cow! Making things up about me and Solly!'

'What things?' her mum said. 'That you kissed him? Well, she never made *that* up because Mrs Smith saw you with him in the middle of the road this morning! And Ikey Nathan did, and *he* can't usually see a plank in front of his face, he's so bloody soft! Almost having it off, the pair of you, according to him!'

She shouldn't have done it. She shouldn't have run to him and she should have pushed him away. But he was going off to *fight*. And of course, she'd felt something, something new and exciting . . .

'Mum . . . '

'Tomorrow you'll get yourself out and get another job,' Kitty said. 'I don't care what it is! You'll sweep the bloody streets if you have to!'

Bernie wanted to tell her mammy what Mr Katz had told her about the man in Black Lion Yard, but she knew that, for the moment, it would only make things worse.

'Yes, Mammy.'

'And if you can't find nothing, you can pick up after the market,' Kitty ordered.

Vegetables dropped from costers' carts at the various markets in the area were already on a lot of people's minds and competition for them was fierce. Little kids, quick as whippets, were the main competition. And cats.

'There's soup on the range, if there's any left,' Kitty said. 'I'm off to work.'

She had a pile of shirts for button-sewing stacked a mile high in the bedroom. When she departed, Kitty slammed the door behind her.

Bernie looked at the rest of her family and they looked at her. In the end it was her dad who broke the silence. He said, 'Don't worry, girl, we'll manage somehow. We always do.'

Marie hugged her. 'I don't want to work for Mr Sassoon anyway,' she said. 'He's a miserable old sod.'

Little Paddy kissed her while Aggie spooned some carrot and barley soup into a bowl and put it on the table. Only Joey and Dermot remained stony-faced. This wasn't lost on Bernie and, once she'd eaten, she followed Dermot out into the yard.

He gave her a fag and then said, 'You can't be courted by Solly Adler.'

'I'm not being,' she said.

Inside, their dad was putting the younger kids to bed while coughing his guts up. They heard Kitty shout, 'For Gawd's sake, Pat, will you take that medicine my mam give ya!'

'Makes me drowsy, Kit!'

'So sleep!'

'Solly's gone to Spain,' Bernie said. 'To fight with the International Brigade.'

'Oh, and he ain't coming back?'

'I hope so,' Bernie said. 'But it's got nothing to do with me. I give him a kiss because he was going to fight. That's all.'

But she felt her face go hot and could see that Dermot had spotted it.

''Cause us and the Jews, we can't be together,' he said. 'Or only as comrades.'

'I didn't think that Communists bothered about religion?'

'We don't,' Dermot said. 'But the Jews are different, and anyway it'd make Mammy ill if you went off with a Yiddisher. And Becky.'

'Becky? What – my Becky? What's she got to do with it?' Bernie said.

Dermot lowered his voice. 'She loves him,' he said.

'What . . . Solly?'

'Yeah.'

'How'd you know that?'

'Because little Rose told me.'

Bernie sat down on the bricks outside the khazi. It was cold and she was upset and her legs felt wobbly. 'How'd she know about us?'

Her brother sat down beside her. 'Rose saw how she looked at him. And that Becky was upset when you was with him after Cable Street. She ain't as dozy as she looks, that Rose.'

And if Bernie really thought about it, she could see the signs had been there. At the meeting before Cable Street, Becky had been like a girl in a frenzy. Bernie had thought it was because she had been all caught up in the passion of the protest. But then maybe that hadn't been the only passion she'd been experiencing. Bernie felt cold. Poor Becky. And of course Dermot was right about the fact that Solly could never be for her anyway, so why stand in her friend's way?

'There is no me and Solly so Becky needn't be worried,' Bernie said as she stubbed her cigarette out on the ground. 'Not because he's a Jew and I'm not but just because there is no him and me. It was only a bit of fun.'

'So why'd you get so out your pram with Sharon Begleiter?' Dermot asked. 'Even if she did see you, you could've denied it. You know what a liar she is.'

'I saw red,' Bernie said.

Dermot smiled. He was the same. That was probably one of the reasons he wasn't always chosen when he was on the stones. Or so he reckoned. That hot Lynch temper.

105

'Where you gonna look for a job?' he asked once he'd put his fag out.

And then, finally, Bernie smiled.

'Mr Katz has a friend who is a photographer in Black Lion Yard,' she said. 'He wants someone to train up to do wedding photos ...'

'Oh, blimey, that's bloody brilliant!' Dermot said. 'Couple of months' time, you could be keeping the lot us if you get that!'

Chapter Nine

Christmas 1936

The limp was the least of his worries. The fact that the sodding wound kept on getting infected made him weak and Solly couldn't have that. He had to be able to fight and, sometimes, run, especially now the bastards were bombing the city.

Solly had crossed the border from France into Spain on 2 November 1936. It had been harder than he'd thought. The French were not amenable to foreign volunteers making for Spain and so he'd had to hide out in the Pyrenees for a couple of weeks before it was safe to cross. Inducted into the XI International Brigade, he'd joined up with a comrade from Birmingham called Nobby Clarke. He'd died on the first day of fighting in Madrid. On the second, Solly had broken his leg. Pinned down by General Kléber's Nationalist forces in Casa de Campo, Solly hadn't been injured in combat, but as he was running to get out of the line of fire of a Moroccan Regular soldier. That had been six weeks ago and the damn' thing still hadn't healed in spite of the fact they'd got a doctor, a Russian, to set it almost immediately.

Solly pulled the bandage down around his ankle and looked at the wound. Swollen again. He'd be lucky if he didn't get gangrene.

'Christmas pud, kiddo?'

Roy Oberman had turned up in Madrid a week ago and already he and Solly had become firm friends. He was another Jewish comrade from the East End, Stratford in this case. Roy pushed a piece of gritty Spanish bread into Solly's hand and then laughed.

'Is it Christmas?' he asked.

'Yeah. If you like that sort of thing,' Roy said.

Solly's mum had always done Christmas for her boys. A lot of Dolly Adler's neighbours had disapproved. But she hadn't cared. The *frummers* could think what they liked but she'd given up all that 'Jewish stuff' when her parents had thrown her out for being pregnant with Ben. Then Solly had come along. What neither her parents nor her boys knew was that her son's father was a *shochet*, a pious kosher animal slaughterer who, though married with six kids at the time, liked teenage girls. He liked having sex with them and being so violent towards them they were too afraid to grass him up.

'Mum always got hold of some meat,' Solly said. 'And me and my brother had a stocking.'

'Each or between you?' Roy asked.

'Each.'

'Blimey, you're posh.'

Solly smiled. Now at an apparent impasse with their enemies, the fascist Nationalists, Solly and the other forces of the Spanish Republic were trapped in Madrid in a district called Carabanchel. Holed up in what remained of what had once, probably, been a very nice apartment building, Solly's contingent of the XI International Brigade had chosen this place to hunker down and treat its wounded. That was provided they didn't get bombed by the planes the Nationalist General Franco kept on sending over the city.

'What happened to the doctor who sorted your leg out? I've not seen him,' Roy asked as he lit up a fag and then passed it on to Solly.

'Copped it,' Solly said. 'There's only that Belgian left. There he is.'

He pointed. Both men looked down from their position on the half-ruined first floor of what had been someone's home into something that was probably a kitchen. A man lay unconscious on a table while another man took out a saw and checked the blade.

'That'll be me, if this leg don't heal soon,' Solly said as the doctor began his work.

And then he wondered what Bernie Lynch would make of him if he couldn't dance with her any more? He'd written to Bernie, and his mum, while he'd been holed up in France. He just hoped they'd got his letters.

Nell Larkin knew the signs. She also knew she couldn't help Rosie herself. If she tried, Nell knew she'd only mess it up because Rose was her daughter. And then she'd be cursed for killing her own flesh. So on Christmas Eve she'd gone to visit Mrs Swan in Canning Town and given her a shilling up-front while she still had it.

Mrs Swan had always done for the girls Nell had worked with when she'd first come to London and none of them had ever had any complaints. She'd said she'd see Rosie on Boxing Day.

'My gentleman friend's coming over for Christmas dinner,' she'd told Nell when she'd shown her out of the parlour. 'You understand.'

Rose had begged to go round to the bloody Lynches' place for Christmas dinner. And this time Nell had said that she could. Len had lost his temper over it – until Nell had explained. The stupid bastard hadn't even noticed that Rose wasn't as skinny as a rake any more.

Alone on Christmas Day, Nell was glad that Len had gone out. She had no idea where and even less interest. But she had gin and tobacco and it was nice watching those who felt the need walk down to Christ Church in all their Sunday best. If she looked hard, she could just see the face of old Moritz Shapiro opposite, looking out of his window too. When he saw her, or so Nell felt, he turned away.

'So? What did you think?'

Becky's father looked at her over the rim of his teacup.

'I think he had a face like red porridge,' Becky said, and sat down feeling dispirited.

It wasn't often that Becky wanted to be anything other than what she was, but Christmas Day was one of those occasions. Even the poorest Christians received some sort of gift. Her papa hadn't even lit the fire. And, the previous day, she'd been subjected to the latest of Mrs Rabinowicz, the *shadchan*'s, potential 'matches'. This one had been pathetic.

'The boy was shy is all,' her papa said.

The 'boy', Manny Kahn, had been forty if he was a day. The youngest son of an ancient pair of milliners who lived on Artillery Row, he was fat, withdrawn and could only speak in whispers. He made the most beautiful hats with those sausage-like fingers of his, which was why he was such a 'catch'. Manny had money. But Becky didn't care. He was peculiar and he smelled of moth-balls and, worst of all, he wasn't Solly Adler.

'He has his own house and a maid,' Moritz continued. 'You'd be well provided for and you wouldn't have to do anything.'

Becky poured herself some tea. 'I don't like him,' she said.

Her father said nothing, but he scowled.

She knew why he wanted her to marry someone like Manny. He wanted her to be safe. And she would be with someone like the milliner. But she'd also be bored and, if he ever tried to make love to her, she'd die. She was young and pretty and so she wanted a young, handsome man to love her. Not some strange, bloated bachelor. She wanted Solly Adler. And, somehow, her father knew it.

'So you'd rather waste your life on that boy your *shiksa* friend kissed in the street, out in the open like a bad woman,' her papa said.

Although Becky was upset about what had happened between Bernie and Solly, she wouldn't condemn her friend.

'Bernie isn't a "bad" woman, Papa,' she said. 'You know that. Solly was on his way to Spain. Now he's gone and we'll probably never hear from him again. Anyway, what do you mean? Solly Adler's nothing to me!'

'You think? That's not what I see when I watch the stars in your eyes whenever you talk about him. He's a good-looking boy. But he has nothing. And he's a Communist.'

Her heart hurt. There had been a big battle in the Spanish capital, Madrid. A lot of people had died, including foreigners. Anything could have happened to him. And because neither Becky nor Bernie knew Solly's mother or brother, they weren't going to find out anything in the near future.

'Anyway this has nothing to do with the milliner,' Becky said. 'Who I don't like and who I will not marry.'

Moritz shrugged. 'You've already rejected two ...'

The sulky boy her own age, son of a rabbi, had been bad, but her second suitor had been old enough to be her father's father.

'Papa, they were both terrible.'

'Raymond Berkowicz owns twenty properties just in this area. He's a rich man. I've known him all my life.'

'*You've* known him all your life, Papa, yes,' she said. 'Which means he is very old.'

Her father leaned across the table, his eyes fixed on her face. 'Rebekah-*leh*, you know that people believe something bad is coming.'

'The fascists left, Papa,' she said. 'We drove them out ... well, I did.'

'No! No! From abroad,' he said. 'This war your Solomon Adler fights in Spain is really between Germany and Russia. This is what people say.'

'So how does that have anything to do with us?'

'Because it always does!' he said. 'Jews are dying in Germany. In Europe! This man Hitler in Germany, he blames the Jews for everything! And he wants war. If he comes here ...' Moritz shrugged again. 'Only those with money will get out.'

'Get out? Get out where?'

'America, Canada, anywhere!' he said. 'But only for those who can pay. Like Berkowicz and the milliner boy ...'

'Papa,' Becky said, 'I'm not marrying either of them. I don't like them. You said yourself that I didn't have to marry anyone I didn't like. I want someone my own age! I want a man I can love! If I want anyone at all.'

'Yes, yes! But you also want a man who will make sure that you are safe!'

'I am safe!' Becky stood up. 'We got rid of the fascists, Solly and all the rest of us. We are safe, Papa. Stop listening to those mad old men from the Board of Guardians. They don't know what they're talking about.'

'And you, a girl, do?'

Becky shook her head and then left the room. Her father was obsessed with a danger that had passed and was using it as an excuse to marry her off to some rich man she couldn't and wouldn't love. She walked over to the front parlour window and watched the Christian children playing in the street. Then she called out to her father: 'If Mrs Rabinowicz can find me a young man, not an old relic or a child, I will consider it. If not, well, I will take my chances, Papa. I will stay with you and take my chances.'

Kitty put the unopened envelope back in the pocket of her apron and then took the roast potatoes out of the range. They were starting to go brown, but they'd still need another good hour.

'I've told you, I haven't been to any weddings yet,' Bernie said to her sister Marie as the girl twirled around in her new Christmas dress complete with bows and ruffles. 'I've been learning how to develop film and so I've been in a dark room most of the time.'

The whole Lynch tribe had been to Midnight Mass and so the older kids were still tired while the younger ones were over-excited. Kitty had got up early to put the chicken Joey had managed to liberate from somewhere in the oven and she was ready to drop. But her mind was troubled. Not only did she feel guilty about that letter in her pocket, she was disturbed by the sight of little Rosie Larkin. The kids thought she looked a lot better with some extra weight on her bones, but Kitty knew better. That child was pregnant. She'd lay money on it.

Kitty put the greens on and then went into the bedroom and closed the door. Until she served up dinner she had work

113

to do. She looked at the pile of shirts beside her bed and went to pick one up, but then stopped. She hadn't opened the letter that had come for Bernie at the beginning of the week. She hadn't invaded the girl's privacy – yet. She looked at the envelope again.

Spain. It had come from Spain, which meant it had come from that Adler man. What had made him take such a shine to her daughter when, apparently, every girl on the manor wanted to walk out with him? Bernadette was a handsome girl, but she could be reckless and had a temper on her like a devil. But then maybe that was the attraction. Why had he written to her? What did he have to say? If it was some sort of declaration of love, then surely Kitty should know about it? And was she even going to let Bernadette have the letter?

It was cold in the bedroom. She wished she was with everyone else around the nice warm range. But in a two-room flat, where else was there to go?

In one quick movement, Kitty opened the envelope and took out the contents. The kids were singing carols now and she could hear Pat coughing his guts up, no doubt while smoking a fag or two. They'd all think that she was working and so no one would come in and disturb her. Kitty looked at the letter and, even by the end of the first sentence, she knew what she had to do.

Rose ate her Christmas present slowly. An orange. It smelled fresh and sharp and every segment tasted like sugar. It was a good orange. Auntie Kitty had chosen it well. It had been nice of her to get it. It couldn't have been cheap. But Rose knew that what her mum had bought her was going to be much more useful and expensive.

When she'd told Len, there'd been a row and her mum had

lost another tooth when he'd punched her. But even he knew it had to be done. There wasn't money for another mouth even with Rose herself working as well as her mum. Also, men wouldn't pay much for a girl who was up the stick. They didn't like it.

Little Paddy Lynch pinched her cheek affectionately as he made his way out the back to go to the khazi. Rose wished it could have been Dermot but she smiled at Little Paddy anyway. He had told her that his big brother, Joey, had nicked the chicken they were all going to have for Christmas dinner. She didn't know whether that was quite right though. As far as Rose was concerned, men who worked in the docks just got stuff. Whether they nicked it or not, she didn't know.

A hand landed on her arm and she looked up to see that Bernie was sitting beside her. Uncle Pat had started singing 'Hark, the herald angels sing!' and Bernie, Dermot and the kids were all joining in. Rose didn't know the words, so she just hummed. But that was all right. That it was Christmas and they were all together was enough – even though Rose really wanted her mum to be with them too, and Becky. But, as she knew only too well, in life you could never have it all.

So please don't worry about me, Mum, and tell Ben to keep the Red Flag flying. Your loving son, Solomon.

It didn't matter how many times Dolly read Solly's letter, it didn't make up for his not being home for Christmas. Ben and old Mrs Llewellyn pulled the only cracker Dolly had been able to find time to make and she heard the old woman cackle with delight when a walnut fell out onto the table.

Dolly put the letter away and smiled at Mr Green – Stanley. What, she wondered, would her Solly make of him? Mrs

Llewellyn had been coming to the Adlers' for Christmas ever since Solly was a baby, but Stanley was new. A widower, Dolly had met him at work. She watched him light his pipe and then lean back into what was usually Ben's chair. She knew her eldest son was happy to give up his chair to a guest, but she was also aware of the fact that Ben frowned whenever Mr Green wasn't looking. What would Solly make of her new beau? Dolly wondered.

That Mr Green had his own business and his own house, in Ilford, wouldn't, she knew, impress her absent son. Ben, who shared most of his brother's views on things, had said, 'You be careful he just don't want someone to wait on him in his old age, Mum.'

But Dolly was no fool. When the boys were young she'd worked the halls as a magician's assistant and so she knew all about men. And if Mr Green wanted a housekeeper in exchange for a wedding ring, that was all right by her. Twenty years her senior, he was Jewish, well-heeled, and kind. All the trouble that Moseley and his Blackshirts had brought to the streets of the East End had made a lot of people, particularly the Jews, think about their future. Unemployment was high and many people were worried about what was happening in Europe. Solly had always said that Spain was going to be just the start of a great struggle between the forces of socialism and fascism. That was why he'd wanted to go over there so much and why Dolly hadn't even tried to stop him. Unlike Ben, who had a good job in *schmatte*, Solly had never been able to settle to any one job. The only constant in his life had been The Party.

'Lovely plum puddin', Dolly love,' Mrs Llewellyn said. 'Evaporated milk too! You done us proud. Proper treat.'

The old girl had come from Wales with her husband Wyre back in the 1900s and yet her accent was still as thick as

Swansea mud. Dolly had met the couple on the halls. They'd performed a Sand Dance act until Wyre had died just before Solly was born. The two women had lived together for a while, until Sylvia Llewellyn had got a job with Jones the milkman. She'd never had any kids and so she looked upon Dolly's boys as surrogate grandsons.

'If only Solly could be with us, God love him,' the old woman said.

'Solly's always been a lucky little bleeder,' Ben said as he put a hand on her shoulder. 'He'll be fine, Auntie Sylvia. Bet he's having a right old slap-up Christmas with a load of Spanish señoritas even as we speak. Wine and goose and all sorts.'

They all laughed. Even Mr Green who'd never met Solly. But Dolly wasn't so sure her youngest son was with a group of Spanish girls even if he was all right. She'd heard the rumours about Solly and that Irish girl with the long blonde hair, Bernadette Lynch. A bit on the wild side that one, by all accounts, wearing trousers and taking photographs. Dolly rather admired her. If only the girl wasn't so poor. God knew the Adlers weren't rich. But the little flat Dolly shared with her boys on Commercial Street was clean and smart and they only had to share the privy with one other family. The Lynches lived in a two-room basement and shared their khazi with a cast of thousands. And there were who knew how many kids in that family.

'Do you want me to go and fill up the coal scuttle, Dol?' Mr Green asked.

The fire was a bit low and so she said, 'Yes, thank you, Mr Green, that's very kind of you.'

After he'd gone, Mrs Llewellyn said, 'You should hang on to him, Dolly love. A man who gets the coal in is hard to find.'

Dolly smiled. The old girl was right. But did she love him?

Dolly knew the answer to that and it made her feel sad. She'd never loved anyone romantically. Apart from her boys, men had just used her. Love had never come her way and that was that. It made her wonder about Solly and whether she had the right to deny him the love he might be able to find with Bernadette Lynch.

As God was her witness, her son Solly had never been smitten before even though every girl in the East End wanted him.

It was gone midnight when Becky went outside. The street was dark and empty and everywhere smelled of shit because the drains were blocked. Luckily, for most of the Christians, they wouldn't even notice because they were drunk. That's what they did on Christmas Day, they went to church, they ate meat if they could afford it and they got drunk. But come Boxing Day they were still poor. What was the point? In the morning they'd all get up and be overwhelmed by the smell of their own waste and their women would have to scrub their privies until their hands were raw. And even then the smell would persist, because in reality it was nothing anyone could do anything about. Only the government. But they didn't care.

'Becky?'

It took a moment for Becky to see who was talking to her through the gloom. But when she saw a tall figure leaning on the Lynches' railings she knew who it was. Becky walked across the road and gave Bernie a hug.

'Merry Christmas.'

Bernie laughed. 'Well, me daddy's drunk and so it must've been. You should've come over. Rosie's with us. There's still a couple of Mammy's mince pies left ...'

'I'd've liked to,' Becky said, 'but Papa ...' She shook her head.

The two girls hadn't spent much time together since Cable Street. Mr Devenish the photographer worked Bernie hard in his studio in Black Lion Yard. First she'd had to learn how to develop film then he'd put her to work doing that all day long. Every night she came home dog-tired, red-eyed and stinking of developing fluid.

'How's the job going?' Becky asked.

'It's not much fun being in the dark all day and old Devenish is a bit odd ...'

'In what way?'

'Dunno. Maybe it's me but I thought that working for someone who knows Mr Katz would be different. More sort of nice, I suppose.'

'He isn't nice?'

'Not that,' Bernie said, 'but he's often grumpy and if customers complain, it's always my fault even though I don't take the photographs – yet.' She laughed. 'Do you feel better now after ...'

Bernie and Rose had gone to see Becky as soon as they'd learned that Mrs Rosenberg had died. But she hadn't talked about it, not to them or to anyone.

'I've been working for Doctor Klein's sister, Mrs Gold,' Becky said. 'She had a lovely baby boy day before yesterday.

'Good-oh.'

There'd been some upset after Mrs Rosenberg died. Her husband had accused Dr Klein of being a drunk and had said that Becky had been too young to be a mother's help. Luckily, Mrs Levy had stood up for Becky and had showed her confidence by getting her back to work as soon as she was able. But Bernie knew that Becky still hurt. She could see it in her face. And that wasn't the only reason for her misery either.

'Becky ...' she began. 'About Solly ...'

'You looked so happy when you were dancing together that night!'

Her smile was just too wide and Becky knew it.

'It didn't mean anything,' Bernie said. 'Just a bit of fun.'

Becky looked confused. 'You lost your old job . . .'

'Oh, I lost me temper with that old cow Sharon Begleiter,' Bernie said. 'Always making things up about people, she'd had it coming for a long time.'

'So you and Solly . . .'

She should've heard from him by now. He'd said he'd write. But men were, as her mammy always said, 'full of nothing' and so Bernie had, she told herself, moved on.

She forced a smile. 'We're mates, but that's all,' she said. 'That's all we ever were. It's all we're ever going to be.'

'Oh.'

It wasn't difficult to see the relief on Becky's face even though she clearly didn't want it to show. What Rose had told Dermot was true and, although Bernie hurt at the thought of it, she knew that she and Solly would never work. And, because she'd not heard from him, he'd either moved on or . . . She only hoped he hadn't died. Because other men who'd gone to Spain had.

'Do you think he's all right over there?' Becky asked as she chewed nervously on her bottom lip.

Bernie smiled. 'I think if anyone can survive, it's Solly Adler.'

Becky smiled.

They both heard the Lynches' front door open and saw Rose appear at the top of the area steps. When she saw that Bernie was with Becky, she ran across the road and hugged them both.

'Merry Christmas, Becky!' she said.

'And to you too,' Becky said. 'Did you have a good time at Bernie's?'

'Oh, it was amazing,' she said. 'I got an orange, all to meself, and we had chicken and sausages and roast potatoes, mince pies, and then there was marzipan what Joey had got, and bread and butter . . . and I'm stuffed!'

Becky laughed. 'My goodness, with all that inside you, you'll be the fattest of all of us!'

Rose until recently had always looked half-starved and so it was good to see that she had a bit more meat on her bones. But Becky noticed that Bernie didn't smile at her comment. And neither, oddly, did Rose.

'Oh, I didn't mean to say that you're fat,' Becky said. 'I just . . . '

'A joke,' Rose said, and then smiled. There was an awkward moment of silence and she added, 'Better get home now.'

The three girls exchanged kisses and Rose left. Unusually, when she went into her mum's flat no one shouted.

Alone, Becky and Bernie linked arms and then Bernie said, 'Merry Christmas, Becky. I don't care whether you believe in it or not. And may all your dreams come true.'

Chapter Ten

Boxing Day 1936

Pat and the nippers were still rotting in their pits when Kitty got up to take her jerry out to the stinking khazi. As she poured the piss down the bunged-up hole, she gagged at the smell of it.

'Jesus, Mary and Joseph!'

Why did the drains get full so quickly? Probably because people had too many kids. Not that she'd ever say that in public. Kitty put the jerry back under her bed and then went out the front door and up the area steps into the street. The bent back of Alf the hot chestnut man from Wentworth Street was just disappearing towards Commercial Street when Kitty saw Nell Larkin and little Rosie come out of their flat. The nipper's face was white and Nell, unusually, had a coat on and looked as if she might be sober.

The two women shared a look, which revealed that each of them knew what was going to happen. Then Kitty said, 'If you need any help – after – you just have to ask.'

Nell said nothing, but she nodded.

Then as Nell and Rosie made their way up towards Brick Lane, Kitty asked the Holy Virgin to forgive her for approving of something so unnatural.

Victoria Dock Road exhibited another face of London immigrant life. Whereas Spitalfields and Stepney were Jewish and Irish, the outer docklands of Canning Town and Custom House were home to the families of sailors from India and Africa. Many had married local women and the streets were full of their mixed-race kids and the smells of cooking spices and garlic.

Strangely, to Rose, the kids all looked happy even though most of them were dressed in hand-me-downs even she would have looked at with horror. One little boy with the thickest, curliest black hair she'd ever seen in her life, ran up to her and said, 'Merry Christmas, lady!'

Lady. That was a funny word to use about her, Rose thought.

Her mum led her into a shop that sold old clothes and then up some stairs to a flat where she was introduced to a fat old woman with long, grey hair and another, small woman whose skin was the colour of tea. The fat one greeted her mum as an old friend and then asked whether she had the 'ten bob'. Nell took a crumpled note out of her pocket and handed it over. Then the woman looked at Rose.

'You're a little 'un, ain't you?'

Rose didn't know what to say to that.

The woman continued, 'Well, I'm Mrs Swan and this here's Mrs Chaudhuri.'

The brown-skinned woman didn't even look at her. Completely absorbed in knitting something, she didn't so much as grunt in acknowledgement.

The flat seemed depressingly familiar. One room containing some hard, wooden chairs, a frowzy bed covered in dirty blankets, a cracked sink and a tiny, useless fire in the grate.

This was the place where Rose was going to have her baby taken away from her.

How he'd got back home so quickly, Solly Adler didn't know. But there was his mum and there was Ben and they were smiling and it was summer. He knew it was summer because he was so bleeding hot he had to throw his blankets off the bed onto the floor. His mum, silly old mare, pulled them back on, which made him angry but she insisted.

'You'll catch your death, you daft bastard!'

Solly said, 'Can I have a fag?'

'Only if you have some water first.'

Ben poured water into his mouth. It tasted stale. Something wasn't right and Solly suddenly felt afraid. But then Ben said, 'It's all right kiddo. Everything's gonna be all right now.'

Kiddo? Ben had never called him kiddo in his life. 'Bruv' and 'nipper', yes, but never 'kiddo'.

Solly began to shake. He was as hot as hell and his whole body screamed in pain. Something strange was happening. What was it?

'How far gone is she?' Mrs Swan asked Nell.

'Seven weeks.'

'Should be easy then,' the old woman said.

Rose was already lying down on the bed, her eyes round with fear. The kid didn't even know what was coming and already she was terrified. Nell put a hand on her forehead, which was clammy with sweat. Nell had done this to other girls and herself, many times, but this was her daughter. This was different. There was a moment when she wanted to grab hold of Rosie and run, but she held herself together. This baby couldn't be born, not where it had come from. Poor little soul.

Mrs Swan went over to the sink and picked up the familiar equipment. A length of rubber tubing, a straightened-out coat-hanger. Nell needed a drink.

As if reading her mind, Mrs Swan said, 'Gin's beside the bed.'

Nell took a swig. Mrs Swan had performed her first abortion. It had hurt, but she'd lived. She'd also been drunk at the time.

'For your daughter!' Mrs Swan said. 'Gawd help us, Nelly, you don't improve, do ya?'

Of course it was for Rosie! Of course!

Nell raised the bottle to her daughter's lips and said, 'Here you are, chavvie darling. Drink. Drink!'

The weird Indian woman in the corner with her knitting made some sort of noise in her throat and Nell was tempted to tell Mrs Swan to chuck her out. But the two of them had been together for longer than Nell had known them and she knew that they always came as a pair. The girls she used to work with used to say that the two old women were lovers. But she'd never believed that. Mrs Swan at least, was always on about blokes.

'Mum . . .'

Nell sat on the bed beside Rose and took her hand. 'It won't take long, Rosie, and then you'll be back to normal,' she said.

'Will it hurt much?'

'No,' Nell lied. 'Just for a little bit.'

Nell looked behind her and saw the old woman lift Rosie's skirt up.

Dropped waistlines hadn't been fashionable for years, but then the dress had probably belonged to an older sister or cousin. Or even the girl's mum. Bernie didn't often look too hard at

125

the dresses the brides wore in Mr Devenish's photos. She was more interested in how the couple or group were arranged and from which angle the picture had been taken. But the pictures of Florence Palmer and Sidney Rolfe's wedding had caught her attention. On the face of it, theirs was not unlike many of the other weddings Mr Devenish photographed. The venue, Victoria Park Baptist Church in Bow, was a handsome building and, although not decorated and dressed like a Catholic church, it was quite dignified. It could not have been a cheap option for the father of the bride. Neither were the very elaborate bouquets of flowers that the bride and five bridesmaids held or, indeed, the number of photographs they'd had Mr Devenish take. But this had come at more than just a monetary cost.

A closer look at the photos revealed the reality of what unemployment and poverty were doing to even apparently 'respectable' families like the Palmers and the Rolfes. The tired, unfashionable wedding and bridesmaids' dresses, the broken shoes and dusty suits worn by men made thin and pale by lack of food and warmth. Even in the eyes of the bride, Bernie could see want and a sadness that belied the small smile on her lips. Bernie shuddered. Now she had a job, she had to hang onto it for dear life. Even if that did mean Mr Devenish used her as his cleaner.

She was sweeping the floor behind the counter when one of the jewellers came in. All the Black Lion Yard jewellers were Jewish and, like Becky's father, were pious and always wore skullcaps on the backs of their heads. Bernie recognised a couple of them from her journey to work, but this one was new to her. Tall, dressed in black, of course, he was blond and young and, when he approached Mr Devenish, he smiled.

'Mr Devenish, a very good morning to you.'

Devenish, a thin, dry man in his fifties, said, 'Ah, Chaim, my lad. What can I do for you, eh?'

'It's about the gems Father wanted you to photograph . . .'

'Ah, yes,' he said, and smiled. 'If it's convenient for Mr Suss then tomorrow evening . . . shall we say about nine?'

'That should be acceptable.' Chaim smiled. Then he nodded his head slightly in Bernie's direction and left.

When he'd gone, Mr Devenish pulled a face. But he said nothing. Bernie carried on sweeping.

Mr Devenish didn't like Jews, she felt, and wondered how and why he had become involved with Mr Katz. Probably just through business. Mr Devenish bought all his paper bags from the Katz brothers and clearly he worked for some of the jewellers too. She'd never thought about photographing jewels before but obviously that was something people wanted. Why, she couldn't imagine so she asked.

'Mr Devenish,' she said, 'do you take photographs of jewels often?'

'No,' he said.

Then she said, 'I'd like to see how you do that one day.'

Mr Devenish stopped cleaning his lenses and looked at her with, Bernie felt, some distaste.

'Well Miss Lynch,' he said. 'I'll have you know that such photography is very specialised and so it's not something that a trainee will be able to do for many, many years.'

'Oh, I didn't mean to be forward . . .'

'Yes, but you were,' he said. 'Please do not be.'

'I'm sorry.'

'The time will come when you'll be able to be a photographic artist, just like myself,' he said. 'But that time is a long way off, young lady. You're learning how to develop and that, for the moment, is all you can be trusted with. Are we clear?'

Bernie said that 'they' were 'clear'. Then Mr Devenish left to go and prepare his studio for a portraiture session. Bernie felt

127

put down and a bit crushed. How long would he keep her in the bloody dark room on her own? She could develop pictures standing on her head. She should have made a bit of a stand at the very least. But then she knew that she couldn't if she wanted to keep her job. And even working in the dark room was better than being back at Sassoon's.

She was just about to go back to the dark room when Bernie saw the young Jewish man who'd been in earlier looking through the window at her. He smiled, but she didn't smile back. Blond and a bit pampered-looking, he wasn't her type at all.

The man was a foreigner of some sort. But then this was Spain. Solly had to bear that in mind because sometimes he felt as if he was back home in London.

He was ever so cold.

The man said something but Solly didn't know what it was. He said, 'Can't understand you, mate!'

Then the ground shook and the man who had been speaking to him shook his head.

'What the fuck is going on?' Solly said.

And then a familiar face replaced the foreigner's and Roy Oberman said, 'Now listen Solly mate, the doctor here is gonna sort you out but for the moment we have to move out of here because they're bombing us again.'

When whoever it was lifted him up to take him who knew where, Solly did feel a bit of pain in his leg, but not nearly as much as he'd experienced in the night. He didn't understand why he needed a doctor.

He even sat up with the intention of telling everyone so but then suddenly everything went black.

*

Rose shook.

It hadn't taken long, but it had hurt and now she felt sick.

She'd seen the thing the old woman had put up inside her when she'd thrown it into the sink. It had dripped with blood. Ashamed that her dress was still pushed up around her middle, Rose wanted to cover herself up, but not even her mum would let her.

'Just lay still and let the air get to you, chavvie,' she said.

But the air smelled bad. Not of shit and urine so much as it did at home but of other things she couldn't imagine. Things probably produced by all the factories around the Royal Docks – Tate and Lyle's sugar works, Cape Asbestos, the Primrose Soap Works.

The Indian woman, still knitting, beckoned Mrs Swan to her and whispered something in her ear.

'Mrs Chaudhuri's just reminded me we got another appointment in a half-hour,' the old woman said. She looked down at Rose. 'You'll do. Go home and the rest'll come away in the next couple of days.'

Her mum put a hand on Rose's head and said, 'She's hot.'

'Get her outside and she'll cool down,' Mrs Swan said.

The old woman and her mum heaved her to her feet. For a moment Rose felt as if she might faint. But then her head seemed to clear and she just felt weak – and sick. Her mum pulled her dress down and put Rose's knickers in her coat pocket.

'Thank you, Mrs Swan,' she said as she supported Rose down the steep stairs leading down to the second-hand clothes shop.

'It was short notice, Nelly, I hope you appreciate that,' the old woman said.

'Yes, yes.'

As her mum attempted to hold her up, Rose nearly slipped down the stairs. 'Shit!'

'Give her castor oil,' Mrs Swan said.

She heard her mum say, 'I ain't got none!'

'So get some!' the old woman said and then shut her door behind her.

Even with her mum's help, Rose didn't know how she got out into the street. Her legs felt like rubber and, although she'd had nothing to eat since Christmas Day, she kept on heaving as if she wanted to be sick. But at least she didn't feel quite so hot anymore.

Her mum dragged her over to a low wall outside an ironmonger's shop and made her sit down.

'I'm sorry, Rosie girl, I ain't got no money for a bus.'

They'd walked all the way to Canning Town but Rose, at least, hadn't given a thought to how they might get back.

'Rest up for a mo' and get your strength,' her mum said.

Rose wanted to curl over and lie down on the ground.

'Mum . . .'

And then it suddenly hurt so much . . .

'Mum!' She dug her fingernails into Nell's arm and then she screamed.

Dolly Adler wasn't someone the *shadchan* saw very often – thanks be! Always looking down her nose when she was no better than she should be, that one!

Mrs Rabinowicz remembered Dolly as a child. From a nice *frum* family in Hanbury Street, as she recalled. But the girl had gone to the bad when she'd been little more than a child. First one bastard child and then a second. There was no hope for some. Although, it had to be said, Dolly Adler had taken nothing from anyone and had always supported herself – even if half the time that had been on the stage. Which was little better than being on the streets. And now here she was, looking in jeweller's windows on Black Lion Square!

Had she, perhaps, reason to believe that someone might

finally put a ring on her finger? Mrs Rabinowicz's cousin Raymond, who was into everyone else's business, like an old woman, had told her that Dolly had been seen out with a man.

'Old as Time, so I heard,' Raymond had said. 'Mind you, dapper too. A man of means . . .'

But was this man Jewish? And did Dolly Adler even care? Mrs Rabinowicz shook her head and walked on by. She wasn't in the Yard to see Dolly Adler or even to drool over all the jewellery she could but shouldn't buy. No, she was here to see a client and, if he was the young man she thought he was, she had a girl in mind for him already.

'I've had enough of this!' the ironmonger said. He picked up a stone and threw it at Mrs Swan's window. 'Oi, you old cow!' he yelled. 'Stop bringing whores here! Do your butchering elsewhere!'

Rose had bled down the wall and across the pavement. Nell, beside herself, walked up and down the pavement, whimpering. Every time she tried to move Rose, the girl howled in pain. Nell needed some help and she needed a drink! But people were just watching her and doing nothing, except for the ironmonger who wanted her to pick her daughter up and go. She knew he wouldn't call the coppers, people didn't. But if she didn't do something soon, he could get violent. Also Rosie, God love her, was bleeding like a pig.

'Missus, where is it that you live?'

Nell had never seen such a tall man. In spite of the cold, wearing only trousers and a vest, the man was black and spoke in what Nell imagined was the accent of Africa.

The crowd around Nell parted to let him through. He knelt down in front of Rose and looked into her face. Then he looked up at Nell.

'Missus?'

'Ten Bells Street,' she said. 'That's Spitalfields.'

Rose groaned. 'No, no,' she said, 'it's called Fournier Street, Mum. I told you before.'

'I know Fournier Street,' the man said. 'There is a market there. My wife will take you, but you must get a doctor for this child, missus.'

An old woman who'd come to see what all the commotion was about said, 'She can't do that, you daft ha'porth! The girl's been caught out and they've tried to do something.'

'I can deal with her,' Nell said to the man, 'I just need to get her home.'

The man stood up. He was so tall he seemed to fill the cold, grey winter sky.

'I will go to get my wife,' he said.

Nell was about to say no, but she was so exhausted she just sat down next to Rose and put an arm around her shoulders. 'All right,' she said, 'if you think she can help.'

The girls met, purely by accident, on Brick Lane outside the Russian Vapour Baths. Both on their way home after work, they walked arm in arm through the crowds out shopping, going to see relatives or, like them, coming home from work.

'You know what tonight is?' Bernie said to Becky.

'Boxing Day.'

'No!' Bernie slapped her playfully on the shoulder. 'Not if you're Irish.'

'Oh!' Becky remembered, Bernie had told her about this years ago. 'St Stephen's.'

'That's right,' Bernie said. 'Which means that Nanny and Grandpa Lynch'll be round and all Mammy's brothers and sisters. Oh, and me daddy and me brothers will all be drunk.

Just like Christmas really but without the presents. I wish you could come.'

'Me too,' Becky said. 'But Papa . . . ' Then her eyes widened and she pushed her friend into a shop doorway. 'Oh, no, the *shadchan*!'

'The what?'

People, including a large women dressed in fur, passed them by and then Becky said, 'Mrs Rabinowicz. You know, the matchmaker.'

Becky had told Bernie that her father was trying to marry her off through the rich old woman on Folgate Street. But they hadn't talked about it much, mainly because Bernie could hardly believe it.

'Oh, blimey, is your dad really . . . '

'He won't give up,' Becky said. She looked so miserable. 'It's what we do.'

Bernie put an arm around her friend's shoulders. 'How can some old woman choose who you marry?' she said. 'That can't be right.'

'I wish it wasn't this way,' Becky said. 'I can say no and Papa will listen . . . '

'So just keep saying no until he gives up.'

'I don't know whether I can.'

'What about Solly Adler?' Bernie said. 'You're sweet on him, aren't you?'

Becky pulled away from her. 'He doesn't know me,' she said. 'Whenever he did speak to me, he treated me like a stupid kid.'

'I'm sure he didn't,' Bernie said.

'He did. You weren't there. Anyway he loves you.'

'Loves me?' Bernie laughed. 'We danced once and we kissed once and he said he'd write to me and he ain't. All a lot of nothing.'

'I'm sure it wasn't,' Becky said.

Bernie shrugged. 'I dunno,' she said. 'Got other things to worry about. Dad don't get no better and Dermot can't seem to get called on. Mammy's taken every penny I have for the rent. How can you work so hard and still be skint?'

'I don't know,' Becky sympathised, even though she didn't know what the kind of hardship Bernie was talking about was like. But then she returned to the subject of Solly again. It was as if she couldn't let it go.

'It's so bad in Spain now,' she said. 'I do hope that Solly will be all right.'

Bernie just smiled.

Patience McLaren took one look at Len Tobin, laid out on the filthy bed, drunk as a sack, and threw him out into the street.

'You can't have this sort of behaviour around your girl when she's so sick,' she told Nell.

'Yeah, but ...'

'Men don't belong around women at times like this,' Patience said. 'And, missus, if he come back, he will have me to deal with.'

Like her husband, Patience was tall, muscular and black. As she'd walked back to Spitalfields with Nell, pushing Rose in the old pram Patience had once used for her own children, she'd spoken of the hot island in the Caribbean where she had been born.

'Trinidad, where the sun shines every day but nobody have nothing.'

Patience put a blanket from the pram down on the bed and lifted Rose onto it. Nell, still terrified that a furious Len might come back any minute, kept looking at the front door. She was amazed by how easily Patience had got rid of him. When she'd woken him up, it was as if he'd seen a ghost. Maybe he hadn't seen any black people before?

'Main thing is to keep everything clean,' Patience said. 'Now I have here some salt. Put it in any water you use to wash her. Make the water hot.' Then she lifted Rose's dress up and parted her legs. The girl, half-asleep, groaned.

'Ah, most of what she had is come away now. Early like this, it's just blood, you know?'

Nell felt she wanted to ask whether Patience did abortions too, but the woman had been so kind that she didn't want to offend her. She certainly knew a lot.

'I'll put the kettle on,' Nell said.

'Yes, let's get your lady here clean and smart.' Patience smiled.

According to this woman who may well have saved Rosie's life, she'd come to England with her husband who had been a sailor. Maurice, the husband, had white grandparents who lived in Silvertown when the couple came into the country. His grandfather had got him a job in the Royal Docks and then the children, four of them, all grown up by now, had come along.

Nell boiled a kettle and then poured the water into a bowl. Patience threw in a handful of salt from a hessian bag. Then as she gently bathed Rose, she said, 'You know, darlin', that man of yours is no good. The smell of booze on him . . . Terrible. You are a strong-looking lady, you don't need him.'

And yet Nell knew that she did. She needed him to get the punters she couldn't stand going out on the streets to get for herself. She needed him to protect her and Rose from all the other, worse men who would move in on her as soon as he had gone. And she needed someone to drink with. That last was the thing of which she was most ashamed.

'Back in Trinidad, you know, before I met my Maurice, I worked as a nurse,' Patience said. 'And you know, darling, I see so many women just like you. Good women with bad men they too afraid to leave.'

Nell wanted to cry, but instead she said, 'You don't know him, Patience.'

'And that is what they all say.'

Nell turned away.

Chapter Eleven

1 March 1937

Dear Mrs Adler

I'm sorry to write to you out of the blue. My name is Roy
Oberman and I am a friend of your son Solomon. Both in
the XI International Brigade, we fought as comrades and
brothers at the Battle for Madrid. Solomon was very brave
and you should be proud of him. But he did get wounded
and on Boxing Day 1936 he had to go through an operation to
remove one of his legs. He bore this bravely too. But we were
being bombed by the fascists all the time by that point and so
we had to move out of the city. This was when I lost contact
with Solomon who, I was told by the doctor who operated
on him, was going to be sent back to the French border. But
before I left him, he gave me your name and address and I
promised him that I would write to you, in case he couldn't.
Hopefully, he's back home again with you safe and sound
by this time. I'm still fighting, this time on the banks of a

river called the Jarama. I wish I could tell you, Mrs Adler, that I could see an end in sight to this terrible situation, but at the moment I can't. All I can do is wish you and Solomon and all of your family well. I live in Stratford, which isn't far from you. Here's hoping we can all meet up under happier circumstances one day.

Kindest regards,

Roy Oberman

Dolly Adler passed the letter to her son Ben. When he'd read it he said, 'Well, he's alive.'

'He was,' Dolly said. 'At Christmas.'

Ben took her hand. 'And he probably is now, Mum,' he said. 'Just 'cause he ain't made it back yet, don't mean he's dead. It's a long way from Spain.'

'A country soaked in blood if the papers are to be believed,' she said.

Mr Green, who was now a very regular visitor to the Adler flat, said, 'No need to mention the red stuff, love.'

'What – blood?' Ben said. 'Why not?'

'Well, it's not nice . . .'

'War ain't nice. My brother's gone to fight a war. He's not on some beano down to Southend!'

'Ben . . .'

'I'm sorry, Mum,' Ben said, 'but ever since he's been coming here, I've had to listen to his stupid opinions on everything, from politics to how to do the washing-up properly. I've had enough!'

Mr Green stood up. 'Well, if I'm not wanted . . .'

Dolly went to him. 'Oh, no, Stan love, that's not what Ben means . . .'

'I bloody do!'

'Language!'

'See!' Ben yelled. 'That's what I mean, Mum! I'm twenty-six years old and he tells me what I can and can't say! For your information, Mr Green, this is a Socialist household and so the beliefs we have about liberty . . . '

'Are Bolshevik,' Mr Green said.

Ben stood and squared up to the older man. 'Well, if you don't like it . . . '

'Oh, stop it, will you, stupid bleeders!'

Dolly pushed the two men apart and then stood between them. 'There's room for all in my flat,' she said. 'So I won't have no arguments! Anyway, main thing now is that we find out what's happened to our Solly.'

'Yes, Mum.' Ben sat down. Of course that had to be the priority now. But because the British Government didn't recognise the volunteers for Spain, it wasn't going to be easy. 'I'll go and see Phil, I've got a meeting after work. See if the comrades have heard anything. Although if they had, they would've told us by now surely.'

'What, that Phil Piratin?' Mr Green said. 'He's as dodgy as a wagonload of monkeys that one.'

Dolly, finally exasperated with him, said, 'Oh, Stan, just button it, will you, love? Phil Piratin's a good boy. I've known him all his life. What do you know about the working class out in Ilford with your stair carpets and your pianos?'

Old Mr Taylor, the bride's father – who was paying the bill – had been very specific about a group photograph. He wanted the whole family involved. The trouble was, there were what looked like bloody millions of them.

Bernie knew the bride, Elsie Taylor, through her brother Joey who had once walked out with her. But Elsie, who was the

Taylors' youngest, was one of eleven and all her siblings, plus their kids, had come to the wedding. Even the large churchyard of St George-in-the-East, could barely cope with all of them. Bernie tried to control it.

'Budge up, will you!' she yelled at the hordes assembled around the bride and groom. 'I can't get you all in!'

'We are budged up!' old Mr Taylor said.

'Well, you'll have to budge up some more then!'

It was Bernie's first wedding without Mr Devenish. Not that he'd planned to leave her on her own so early in her apprenticeship but he'd needed to be elsewhere. Bernie didn't know why, but then she didn't care. This was her first solo photography outing and she was going to make the most of it.

Elsie and her groom Billy Smith were a good-looking pair. The bride, so Bernie thought, looked a bit like the American film star Mary Pickford while the groom was a dark, slightly mysterious-looking boy. His family, which was almost as big as Elsie's, were very like him. Slightly brooding, they never smiled, no matter what Bernie said or did. In fact they looked downright miserable.

Later, when she was packing her camera equipment away, Bernie wondered whether the Smith family disapproved of the wedding between their boy and Elsie. As far as she knew, the Taylors and the Smiths were both Church of England. Maybe Elsie was up the stick?

Ever since that night she'd danced with Solly, Bernie had wondered what would have happened if she'd let him kiss her then. Would it have been as passionate as the kiss he'd given her when he left for Spain? And if it had been, would she have let him go further?

It was so easy for a girl to take a wrong turn with men. It was also all too easy to regret what might have been. Not that Solly was her concern. All talk, like most blokes, he hadn't written to her once since he'd been in Spain.

Bernie thought it best to concentrate on her work. If these photographs came out well perhaps old man Devenish would let her do some more jobs on her own.

Her mum had come up with the story.

'You have to have a good story or people'll know and then you could get in bother with the law,' Nell had told Rose.

They'd settled on kidney stones, mainly because Nell had known quite a few girls use that excuse in the past. Pain from stones was bad and would also explain all the yelling that had gone on when Rose had been really ill. And she had been. She'd lost a lot of blood and then she'd had an infection for four weeks straight. Her mum said that if it hadn't been for the black lady, Patience, she would have died. Somehow, Patience had got hold of some cream which she'd used to pack out what Rose called her 'insides'. That, after a lot more pain, had worked.

'That's the beauty of poisons for you,' Patience had said the last time she'd come to see Rose. 'If it don't kill you, it will kill what ails you.'

What the 'poison' in the cream had been, Patience had never said.

That had been almost a month ago and, although still weak, Rose was feeling a lot better. She missed seeing Patience though. But Len hated her and so once Rose had begun to improve, she'd stopped coming. Her mum wasn't going to leave Len. That didn't mean, though, that Rose couldn't go and see Patience in Canning Town once she was up to it.

Becky and Bernie and Bernie's mum had all been kind. When Len was out, they'd come round when they could and some-times brought food with them. Rose's mum hadn't been keen on this but she'd allowed it, probably because she was always hungry too.

And now that she was able to do more, Rose was determined to find a job. She knew that Len wanted her to go with men as soon as she was able, but if she got a job and gave him money, maybe she wouldn't have to. She knew her mum would never stop, but she also knew her mum didn't want her to do the same.

One afternoon when it had just been the two of them, Nell had said, 'You need to get out of here, Rosie. Get a job and find a place of your own.'

She'd argued that she was too frightened to leave her mum alone with that man, but Nell had said, 'On our own, he'll be better. It's the extra mouth to feed he sees when he looks at you. Once you're gone, he'll calm down.'

Rose knew she was lying. Someone like Len was never going to calm down. One day, he was going to kill somebody, maybe her mum. So Rose knew she couldn't leave. She could get a job, although what she didn't know. Becky had been able to work as a mother's help because she was educated and because, one day, she wanted to be a nurse. Like Bernie, she could read and write and do sums. Bernie had talent too, with her photographs and her sketching. But what could Rose do? As far as she was concerned she couldn't do anything.

Washing day at Mrs Blum's wasn't as bad as it was in some other households. This was because Mrs Blum always sorted her own washing the night before and put heavily soiled items into cold soak overnight. And because the Blums had electricity, Becky didn't need to light a coal fire underneath the copper to boil the washing water. All she did was switch on the electric copper, which got going in a few short minutes.

Mrs Blum, who already had three kids, all at school, lived in a big flat crammed with heavy furniture above her husband's corset shop on Fashion Street. Older than most of the women Becky went out to help, Mrs Blum had a bad back, which meant that doing her own housework while pregnant was a problem. Not that she was one of those women who just let the mother's help do everything while she sat down and drank cups of tea; Mrs Blum helped when she could. She was in the process of lifting wet underwear from the cold soak into the copper when there was a knock on the scullery door.

'Can you get that for me, Rebekah love?'

Becky put down the washing basket she was about to take outside and opened the door. Although the Blums lived above the shop, the scullery was behind Mr Blum's business on the ground floor. Visitors usually came to this door. Although she didn't know her, she recognised Mrs Adler.

'Oh.'

'Is Evelyn there?' Mrs Adler asked. She looked flustered and her hair, usually very neat, was really very messy.

'Yes,' Becky said. 'Mrs . . . '

'Oh, hello, Dolly,' Mrs Blum greeted her friend then. 'Come in.'

Tall and slim like her son, Mrs Adler wasn't dark like Solly even if she did have very black eyes. She looked at Becky.

'Hello, Miss . . . '

'Oh, this is Rebekah, my mother's help from Mrs Levy,' Mrs Blum said.

'Hello, love.'

Becky smiled. 'Hello.'

'Becky's Mr Shapiro's daughter, from Fournier Street,' Mrs Blum said.

143

Mrs Adler looked at Becky, impulsively took her hand and said, 'Oh, darling, you was the one who lost your mum!'

'Yes.' Becky looked down. Although she often found *frummers* like her papa cold and difficult to talk to, the more free and easy, non-religious Jews were often too demonstrative for her taste. They touched you all the time and, when they were selling you something, they stood far too close. But then just as quickly as she'd grabbed Becky's hand, Mrs Adler let it go.

'I've heard about Solly, Evelyn.'

Mrs Blum sat down at the kitchen table. 'Oh, my Gawd,' she said. 'Put the kettle on will ya, Rebekah?'

'Yes.'

And although her heart was hammering and her hands shaking, Becky managed to fill the kettle and lift it onto the range. What about Solly?

'So, Dolly, what?' Mrs Blum said.

Dolly Adler offered her a fag and they both lit up.

'I got a letter this morning,' she said. 'From some bloke called Roy Oberman, a mate of Solly's in the Brigade.'

Becky took a pair of cups and saucers out of the cupboard above the sink.

'I don't know when it was written, but this Roy says my Solly got wounded in all the fighting in Madrid. He wrote that, on Boxing Day, Solly had to have a leg taken off.'

Only just managing to hang on to the crockery, Becky leaned against the sink.

'Oh, Dolly!'

Becky didn't look at the women; instead she concentrated on placing the cups in front of the teapot and finding the tea-cosy.

'I'm trying not to get meself in a state, but it's hard,' Dolly continued. 'Roy reckoned Solly was going to be sent home, but he hasn't been, has he? Ben's got a CPGB meeting after work and so he's going to see if they know anything. Although they would've told us, wouldn't they?'

'Probably. What about the War Office?'

'They won't know nothing! Government won't get involved in Spain, will they? Don't want to upset that Hitler and his ruddy Germans!'

The kettle boiled and Becky poured a small amount of water into the teapot to warm it. But she missed and splashed boiling water on the draining board. Was Solly dead? Had he had his leg off and then bled to death?

'You all right, Rebekah?'

Mrs Blum looked round at her.

'Yes . . .'

Becky spooned tealeaves into the pot and then poured on hot water from the kettle. This time she didn't miss. When she'd finished she saw that Mrs Adler was frowning at her.

'Here,' she said, 'don't you go round with that Irish girl with all the blonde hair?'

'Bernadette Lynch, yes,' Becky said. 'Her father's in the Party, with your sons.'

'Yeah.'

Dolly looked grave. Did she know about Solly and Bernie? But she said no more about it and instead talked about someone called Stan who had, apparently, been upset by her son Ben.

Once she'd made the tea, Becky went out into the yard to hang out the clean washing. But halfway through she felt dizzy and sat down on the ground. What were these terrible, fierce feelings she had about a man she didn't know? Mrs Rabinowicz had introduced her to a nice enough boy just after the New Year. He had a good business, he was young and he wasn't bad-looking. But she'd not said whether she wanted to see him again. What was wrong with her?

And what, if anything, was she going to tell Bernie about Solly?

The river stank. Even with the windows closed a miasma hung over the entire district, made up of sewage, dead fish, coal and rotten wood.

Menachim Suss didn't go to pubs in the normal course of events. Except this one. Sometimes. Normally it happened when he was waiting for Devenish. Like now.

Limehouse had once been a Chinese area. Before all the slums around the Causeway had been knocked down to widen the road back in 1934, the streets had teemed with pony-tailed Chinese sailors and their, very often half-white, children. Now while a few Chinese laundries, the odd caff and some restaurants remained, Limehouse was predominantly white. What remained the same as it always had been, however, was the cheapness of the property. Limehouse was still a slum in every sense of the word. It reeked, it bristled with activity, noise and dodgy dealings, and many of its inhabitants were drunks.

The Bunch of Grapes on Narrow Street wasn't the worst pub in Limehouse but it wasn't the best either. What it did have going for it, as far as Menachim was concerned, was the fact that it was almost opposite a property he had bought five years earlier. It also, at the back, had an uninterrupted view of the Thames that was useful when the place got a bit lairy and Menachim wanted to tuck himself away in a corner with a port and lemon and look at the water that had once carried him into this huge, bad city.

He always used to tell his three sons that if they thought their business in Black Lion Yard was good, they should've seen the shop his father had once owned in Vienna. Menachim's father Rudolf had counted the cream of Austrian society amongst his customers. Even the Emperor himself, before the Great War. After that tragedy, life became hard for Jews in what had been the Austro-Hungarian Empire and the Suss family had left Vienna with only the clothes on their backs. Menachim didn't often dwell on the fact that he was now reduced to making ugly engagement rings for people with no taste, but what had become his position in life irked him. As did Michael Devenish.

'You could've got me a pint,' the photographer said as he set his camera and tripod down in the dim corner beside Menachim. The whole place had mellowed into different shades of brown over hundreds of years of boozing, smoking and fighting. Charles Dickens had known the Bunch of Grapes from his night-time meanderings in the seedier parts of London. In 1864 he'd described the appearance of the pub as 'dropsical'.

The photographer went up to the bar and got himself a drink. Menachim noticed that he had a little chat with the barmaid, who was small and pretty.

When he rejoined Menachim he said, 'I think that went well, Mr Suss.'

He didn't reply. What did Devenish want? Approval? Agreement?

The photographer drank a liquid that was so dark it looked like molasses. Menachim had never understood the appeal of British beer.

When he did speak, Menachim said, 'Everyone happy?'

'Why shouldn't they be?'

He looked at the photographer and felt his skin crawl.

But Devenish was no one's fool and the look on Menachim's face made him frown.

'It's all right for you,' he said. 'You've got God to forgive you. I'm on my own.'

Menachim sighed. Even living amongst Jews all his life, Devenish clearly didn't understand them.

'You're confusing us with the Catholics,' he said. 'If we break the rules then there's nothing but the displeasure of the Almighty waiting for us. Judaism is about observing the law.'

'So why'd you do it then?' Devenish asked. 'And, if you do do it, why'd you keep wearing all the Jewish clobber and going to synagogue?'

'I do everything for my family,' Menachim said. 'I've a son to marry off. I need money. To be poor is death. That's all. As for why I remain outwardly a pious Jew ...' He shrugged. Then he said, 'If I'm not that, then what am I, eh?' He changed the subject. 'So when next?'

Devenish supped his beer.

'We need new blood,' he said. 'You know how it is.'

Menachim nodded his head. Yes, he did.

Chapter Twelve

Pat had gone to see his dad. The old man was sick with his ulcerated legs again. All the kids were out, at work or playing in the street, so Kitty was home alone. A rumour was going round that Solly Adler had been wounded out in Spain and she felt terrible. Poor boy. And what was worse was that he'd written to Bernadette and Kitty had thrown his letter away.

What he'd said had frightened her. He'd said how much he admired her daughter, how he thought she was the best girl he'd ever met and that he thought he was in love with her. All rubbish, of course. How could he be in love with her based on one night dancing outside a pub and a kiss in the middle of Fournier Street? But then hadn't Kitty fallen for Pat as soon as she saw him? She knew she had and she also knew that the feeling had been mutual. The difference was that she and Pat were the same sort. Solly Adler was a Jew.

Kitty sat down on the area steps and wondered what Pat would say about what she'd done. That didn't take a lot of working out. The old man'd go garrity. In her mind she could hear him.

'What you thinking, reading the girl's post?' he'd say. 'So what if the boy's Jewish? He's a good comrade!'

What she'd done had been wrong – and selfish. Ever since she'd had Bernadette, Kitty had dreamed of the lovely white church wedding she'd some day have for her. But of all her girls, Bernie was the one least likely to want something like that. In spite of everything, she was making a career for herself. Kitty didn't like it, but Pat was all for it. A photographer, for God's sake! And the girl was a Socialist. What did it matter to her if the man she ended up with was a Jew? It would certainly mean very little to Pat or the rest of the kids. It mattered to Kitty and only to her, and as she sat pondering what she'd done, she wondered why she was the exception.

She wasn't religious. Not really. Not in the way her mother and her Auntie Nula were. They rarely missed Mass and went to Confession all the bloody time – although God alone knew why. The two of them never did anything 'bad' – except for the gossip, of course. They loved that and, if Bernadette did end up with Solly Adler, they'd do it all the more – and viciously. Mam would probably never speak to any of them ever again.

Oh, Jesus, Mary and Joseph, it was all about Kitty, wasn't it? Solly Adler, it was said, had been wounded and had a leg taken off. The poor boy could be dead and here she was, wondering how she'd cope with her mother and her aunt if Bernadette decided to be with him!

Unusually for her, Kitty began to cry.

'Dermot!'

If Dermot Lynch could be said to have a best friend it was little Chrissy Dolan. They'd been to school together, played and fought together, and had stayed fast friends when Dermot had gone to the docks and Chrissy had taken a job in a shop up West.

'Hello, Chrissy mate,' Dermot said. 'What you doin' here?'

'I could say the same to you,' the little lad said. 'You not been called on?'

They'd come across each other in Limehouse, outside the Bunch of Grapes. It was a place neither of them belonged.

Dermot shook his head. 'Hardly get a look in these days,' he said. 'What about you?'

'Laid off,' Chrissy said.

'What, from that posh place?'

'Swan and Edgar, yes.'

Chrissy had always been good at art and so Dermot had imagined that when he'd been taken on as a window dresser in one of the West End's most prestigious department stores, he was probably going to do really well for himself. The previous Christmas he'd even been allowed to work on the store's famous festive window. Dermot had gone to see it. 'Dancing Christmas Trees' it had been called, and it had been like a fairy tale come to life. How could anyone with talent like that be laid off?

'What happened?'

Chrissy looked down at the ground. 'Mr Bolton, he's the floor manager, he's never liked me. Well ...' He sucked on his fag and then breathed out before he said, 'There was a complaint.'

'About you?'

'Yes.'

'But you're really good at all that artistic stuff,' Dermot said.

'Not good enough apparently.'

'I'm sorry.' Dermot rolled himself a cigarette and said, 'You want a pint?'

'I'm skint.'

'Yeah, but I'm not.'

'Oh, Dermot Lynch, don't be such a fool!' Chrissy said. 'If you're not getting called on, you're skint too!'

They stood in silence for a moment, both smoking. Then Dermot said, 'What you doing down here then? Not trying your hand on the stones, are you?'

Chrissy snorted. 'You having a laugh? I've not grown since I was twelve.'

Even at school Chrissy hadn't been the kind of boy who enjoyed games like football or spent his time boxing other boys to impress the girls. He hadn't needed to. Girls went to him as if drawn by some invisible magnet. And that was because he talked to them, he drew pictures, told stories and he liked to read. Dermot had always thought that, had Chrissy been from a rich family instead of from a vast tribe of boys headed by a father who was always drunk, he would probably have gone to art school.

'I don't know what I'll do,' his friend said. 'I come down here on the off-chance the Chinese might want someone to wait in their restaurants, but they don't. What are you gonna do?'

'I don't know,' Dermot said. 'I keep on giving it another week, but I can't go on like that forever. Artie Cross just looks over the top of me head every time he calls blokes on. Our Joey always gets picked and ...'

Chrissy looked suddenly very grey in the face and so Dermot helped him sit down on the pavement. Right from a kid he'd had a weak heart.

'Here ...'

'Sorry, mate,' Chrissy said. 'Just a turn, you know.'

'Sit quiet and breathe slowly,' Dermot said.

If Chrissy hadn't had a weak heart, would he have played more sport and even grown bigger? Dermot didn't know. That Chrissy had always been a good mate was all he concerned himself with. Now his friend had lost his job, Dermot was worried for him. There wasn't a great need for window dressers in the East End and Chrissy was too weak for hard labour.

Black Lion Yard wasn't on her route to work. In fact it wasn't on a route to anywhere Sharon Begleiter usually went. And that was what upset Bernie the most. The cow had gone out of her way to hurt her.

"Course, Solly'll still have all the girls falling over themselves for him even if he has only got one leg,' Sharon had said when she'd found Bernie alone behind the shop counter. Mr Devenish had only just gone out on a job. Had she been waiting for him to go? Bernie wondered.

'Although what work he'd do, I don't know,' Sharon continued. 'Fit, active man like him ... '

But Bernie had kept her temper. She'd asked Miss Begleiter what she could do to help and, when she said 'nothing', Bernie had let her stay inside the shop until she got bored. Only after she'd gone had Bernie allowed herself to shed a tear. Then she'd had a fag and pulled herself together.

If Solly was hurt she was really sorry. She was more than sorry, she was beside herself. How he was feeling, she couldn't imagine, but she knew that if she could be by his side she would be. Not that he'd want her. He'd never written to her.

Then she remembered Becky and wondered whether she knew. That blond boy, Chaim Suss, was the latest bloke the old matchmaker had lined up for her friend. But Bernie knew Becky didn't like him. She wasn't going to like anyone except Solly. And she wasn't alone. The thought of Solly suffering, in some foreign place, made Bernie's heart ache. Then she cried. How, she wondered, did someone stop loving?

*

Patience and Maurice McLaren lived in an upstairs flat on Victoria Dock Road. Like the abortionist's place it was small and the couple and their son Robert had to share a toilet and a sink with the people downstairs. But unlike Mrs Swan's place, the McLarens' flat was clean and bright and Patience made tea in a shiny white teapot.

Rose wasn't proud of the fact that she'd stolen the flowers she'd taken Patience from Christ Church graveyard. But she was glad she'd taken something.

'You drink your tea while I put these lovely flowers in water,' Patience said as she handed Rose a delicate cup of steaming tea. 'It's lovely of you to think of me.'

'You saved my life,' Rose said.

Patience smiled. Then she went out back to the sink and returned with the flowers neatly arranged in an old jam jar.

'You needed help and God arranged that I was the one who gave it to you,' she said. 'You owe your life to Him.'

Rose looked down at her tea. She didn't know much about God, but she did know that Patience was one of the kindest people she had ever met.

The woman sat down. 'So now you're better, Rose, what you going to do? You going back to school?'

'Mum wants me to get a job.'

Most girls of her age were either working or trying to get jobs. A large number of them were doing what Rose's mum did. But Nell didn't want that for her – and neither did Rose.

'Jobs are not easy to get these days,' Patience said. 'Lucky for me, my Maurice has always had work. And Robert, he work at the sugar factory, but they have no place for me.'

'You work?'

'Not enough but I mustn't complain,' Patience said. 'I do some cleaning in a big house in Forest Gate.'

'But you're a nurse.'

'In Trinidad, not here.' Patience smiled at her. 'You have to be white to be a nurse here.'

Rose frowned. 'But that's wrong,' she said.

Patience shook her head. 'A lot of things wrong, girl. People sin. Only God is perfect.'

Apart from Bernie and Becky and Bernie's mum, Auntie Kitty, Patience was the nicest lady Rose had ever met. Why did her colour make people not like her?

'You don't go to church, Rosie?'

Rose shook her head. She'd only ever been to church on the odd occasion. Her mum had never even talked about it. She'd heard Len say once that God hated 'gyppos'.

'You should,' Patience said. 'What you did that day at Mrs Swan's was a sin. You have to make up with God now, you know that?'

Rose nodded. But she didn't know it. What had God got to do with her having an abortion? What she did know, however, was that she wanted nothing to do with men ever again.

'If you came to church that would be a start,' Patience said.

'I s'pose I could go with Bernie . . . '

'The Irish girl you friends with? Mmm. She Catholic, I think.'

'She sometimes has to go to Mass with her mum,' Rose said. 'She don't like it.'

Patience smiled. 'Oh, dear,' she said. 'Maybe it's best you go somewhere else, Rose. Maybe you come with Maurice and Robert and me.'

'Yeah, but what if I get a job where I work Sundays?'

Patience put a hand on her knee. 'Then we have to make sure you don't have to do that,' she said. 'Work is hard to get, but maybe if we pray hard enough the Good Lord will find a solution.'

Rose hoped so. But in the meantime she wondered whether stealing more flowers to sell might not be a good idea. Patience had really loved the ones she'd been given and Rose had always liked making people happy.

'Who told you that you had consumption?'

Pat's head was still spinning from the fall he'd just suffered.

'Me Uncle Connor died of it,' he said.

'Did any other members of his immediate family have it?' Dr Klein asked.

Pat breathed in as deeply as he could and then replied, 'No. They were lucky.'

'And none of your children have it?'

'No. But I try to kip out in the yard as much as I can, doctor. Can't afford to go to one of them places in the country.'

'A sanatorium. No, I don't suppose you can.' Dr Klein frowned. 'You know, Patrick,' he said, 'I think that what you have, bad as it is, is not tuberculosis.'

'But me breath's gone.'

'That's as may be.' Dr Klein clasped his hands. 'But there are other diseases of the lungs that afflict many people round here. All to do with the bad air from the factories and the docks. Bronchitis is a big one of course and also emphysema, which is what I think you have.'

'Is there anything you can do, doctor?' Moritz Shapiro asked.

Pat Lynch had collapsed outside the Shapiros' front door while he'd been chatting with Becky, who had brought him inside. Because Pat was struggling to breathe, Moritz had called the doctor. As yet, Kitty Lynch and her kids were in blissful ignorance.

'In common with the treatment of TB, fresh air is what's really needed. Days by the sea ... '

Pat laughed. 'Dr Klein,' he said, 'I may as well wish for a crock of gold.'

The doctor shook his head. 'I'm sorry.'

'Don't know how I'll pay you for today ...'

'I will,' Moritz interrupted. 'You can pay me back. Pat. I couldn't leave you to die outside.'

Becky said, 'But what about treatment? Medicine?'

The doctor shrugged. He'd been in the Ten Bells, getting started on his evening drinking, when Becky had run in to fetch him. He stank of beer and smoke and his face was the colour of ash.

'I ain't dyin',' Pat said.

'No,' the doctor said. 'But you must rest and, yes, Miss Shapiro, medicine exists, but it has to be paid for.'

'Of course, as does everything,' Moritz said.

Becky asked, 'What is it, doctor, and what does it do?'

She kept one arm supportively around her 'Uncle' Pat in a way that she almost never did with her father. This was not lost on Moritz, who was at the same time jealous and anxious about how his soft-hearted daughter would feel if Pat Lynch did die.

'It's called ephedrine sulphate,' Dr Klein said. 'It helps to open up the airways and make breathing more comfortable.'

'Do you have some?'

'At the surgery, yes,' he said.

'So you could give him an injection right now?' Becky said.

'I could. But he would have to have regular injections for the drug to make a difference.'

'Please do that then,' Becky said. 'I will pay.'

'Becky, love ...'

'Uncle Pat, you'll never find work feeling like this,' she said.

'My boys ...'

'Dermot doesn't always get called on,' Becky said. 'And

157

Auntie Kitty works all the time. And, most important of all, Bernie must carry on at Mr Devenish's studio even though it pays really badly when she's got so much talent and ought to be ... '

She ran out of breath.

Pat squeezed her shoulder. 'Which is why ... ' He struggled to breathe. 'Which is why, no medicine for me, love. Doctor, would this effy-stuff get me back to full-time work?'

'Realistically, no,' Dr Klein said. 'But it would mean you could lead a more comfortable life.'

'So that's worth it then!'

'Becky, love ... '

Moritz put a hand on his daughter's shoulder. 'Rebekah-*leh*, Mr Lynch has said no. Please do not insist. Do not embarrass yourself in this way.'

Becky looked at her father with hatred in her eyes. Her Uncle Pat, her friend Bernie's father, needed help and her father wouldn't let her even try to do her bit.

But then she felt Uncle Pat's hand on hers. He said, 'Your father's right, Becky. I am so touched you want to help, but there really is no need. We can manage.'

Becky knew that was a lie. But she knew why he was telling it. Uncle Pat and Auntie Kitty didn't have much, but they did have their dignity.

Joey ignored his brother. It wasn't that he didn't see Dermot, he deliberately overlooked him. Strutting through the dock gates with a load of hard old bastards Dermot recognised from when his dad was down the West India, Joey behaved as if his own brother didn't exist.

In the distance, Dermot saw foreman Artie Cross and the mob of favourites he always had round him. Artie, unlike

Joey, was looking at Dermot. And he was smirking. Dermot instinctively clenched his fists, but then unclenched them. Cross already hated him for some reason, why make him angry too?

With his hands in his pockets and his head bowed under one of his dad's old caps, Dermot followed Joey until his mates had all peeled off and his elder brother was finally on his own.

In spite of his superior build, Dermot swung Joey round to face him.

'What's all this about then, bruv?'

Joey, a roll-up stuck in one corner of his mouth said, 'What?'

'You fucking ignoring me!'

'I'm not.'

'Yes, you are! You and all them hard nuts, you behave as if I don't exist!'

Joey looked down at him and shook his head. 'You ain't worked it out yet then?'

'Worked what out?'

Joey shrugged. 'If you don't know ... '

'Don't know what?'

Dermot pulled his brother by his collar into an alleyway that smelled of foreign spices and piss.

'You and that fucking iron!' Joey said. 'You've been seen! Why else d'you think Artie never calls you on when he knows our dad's out of work?'

'I've been asking meself that for weeks,' Dermot said. 'What iron? I don't know no poofs! What you talking about?'

'Chrissy Dolan,' Joey said. 'Your bum chum.'

Dermot stood there in silence. Chrissy had always been good at drawing pictures, he'd always liked to look nice and was no fighter – unless he had to be. The kid wasn't well! And Joey had been his friend too ... once.

'Why'd'ya think he worked up West in a shop like a girl?' Joey said. 'Why'd'ya think his dad chucked him out on the street?'

Chrissy had told him he'd lost his job, but Dermot didn't know anything about his friend being thrown out of home.

'He never said ... I ain't seen Chrissy for months until we bumped into each other yesterday!'

'Yeah, but you was like little sisters at school, weren't you?' Joey sneered. 'Helping him make pretty pictures out of tissue paper!'

'Because he was ill ...'

'Too bloody right!' Joey said. 'Sick in the head! Anyway you was seen ...'

'He's got a bad heart. What do you mean, we was seen?'

'Artie saw you and him round the back of Schwartz's, touching each other ...'

Dermot felt his face burn. He and Chrissy hugged sometimes, they always had. But there was no way they'd done anything like *that*. Why was the foreman making up lies?

'When?'

'I dunno,' Joey said. 'But he saw you. Fucking disgusting!'

Dermot shook his head. His brother was looking at him as if he was a piece of dirt on his shoe and Dermot didn't understand. He wasn't queer and neither was Chrissy. And why would they have been doing unmentionable things round the back of Schwartz's bakery? They might both have been there to get bread at the same time. But he couldn't remember any such occasion.

'It's a crime, what you do,' Joey said. 'And Artie can't have criminals ...'

Dermot wanted to say that if Artie didn't want any criminals in the West India, he'd better start by sacking himself and all his mob – and Joey. They all walked out of those dock gates with

160

things that weren't theirs and everybody knew it. But then that wasn't like . . . unnatural practices.

'Stop seeing the queer and you'll get called on,' Joey spelled it out.

Dermot exploded. 'But I'm a good worker!' he said. 'What's it matter . . .'

'Oh, so it's true!' Joey laughed. He'd become a nasty bastard in the last few months. Maybe it was the company he was keeping now he was clearly one of Artie's favourites.

'No, it ain't!'

'Then stop seeing . . .'

'I hardly see him as it is!'

Joey grabbed his brother by the throat. 'Don't see him at all then,' he said through clenched teeth. 'If you want to do that sort of thing then do it off the manor, do you hear me? I won't have no brother of mine being one of *them*!'

'But you will have me out of work when our dad's ill!'

Joey said nothing, but gradually slackened his grip.

'Why didn't you tell me?' Dermot said. 'We need my money!'

Joey smoked the last inch of his roll-up and then threw it on the ground.

'Because,' he said, 'what you do disgusts me so much, I don't wanna talk to you about anything.'

And then he walked away. Dermot, alone in the stinking alley, wondered what the hell had just hit him. He wasn't queer and neither was Chrissy! Or even if Chrissy was, surely that was his business? Joey had become someone he couldn't recognise but if Dermot wanted to survive in the docks, and help to support his family, he'd have to do as his bigoted brother said. He'd heard stories about queers being beaten up, thrown down into ships' holds, pissed on . . . Would Artie's mob do that to him unless he convinced them he was a regular bloke like they were?

161

Chapter Thirteen

1 May 1937

As Bernie drew level with her, Mrs Adler turned her head away. But then why wouldn't she? The woman didn't know her.

Bernie took the shop keys out of her handbag and was opening up when she felt someone tap her shoulder. She turned and looked into the smiling face of Solly's mate, Wolfie Silverman. It seemed it was her day for coming across people connected to Solomon Adler.

'Hello, Miss Lynch,' he said. 'I'm . . . '

'Wolfie, yes,' she said.

She'd only ever seen him from a distance – mainly at Party meetings – since Cable Street. But Bernie had his image tucked away in her memory alongside that of Solly.

'Are you well?' Wolfie asked.

She opened the shop door, but didn't go inside.

'Yes,' she said.

'I've not seen your dad . . . '

'Well, no. He's not so good.'

Although it was a secret and she was sworn never to tell her father that she knew, Bernie had been told about his collapse back in March by Becky. In one way it was good to know that Dr Klein had finally seen him and told him he didn't have consumption. But that he had emphysema was almost as bad. It had been kind of Becky's dad to pay for the doctor to come out, but Pat Lynch was a proud man and the fact that so far he'd only been able to repay Mr Shapiro half of what he owed him was making him miserable. Thank God Dermot finally seemed to be getting called on more often now.

Wolfie held out a brown envelope. 'I wanna have this framed,' he said. 'It's a portrait photograph. Me uncle Jacky used to do a bit of photography back before he got his heart trouble. He took it two years ago.'

Bernie opened the envelope. The photograph was postcard-sized and was a head and shoulders portrait. It showed Solly looking almost heartbreakingly handsome.

'Oh.'

'I thought I'd do it for his mum,' Wolfie said.

'I just saw her ...'

'Yeah, I did too, but she finds it hard to talk to anyone, what with her not knowing where Solly is. You been following things in Spain, Miss Lynch?'

'Off and on.'

That wasn't the truth. She read everything about the Spanish war she could get her hands on. She knew that Becky did too. Even the bad news made you feel closer somehow.

'I'd like a nice frame if Mr Devenish can do one,' Wolfie said.

'Of course.' She smiled. 'Although I won't be able to get you a price until Monday. Mr D's out today.'

'Price don't matter,' Wolfie said. 'Just so long as it's nice. For Mrs Adler.'

And then he walked away.

A lot of the Commie boys like Wolfie had gone to support the omnibus drivers who were currently on strike for shorter hours and better working conditions. May Day was International Workers' Day and, even if the government didn't acknowledge it existed, a strike tended to bring the plight of the poor to their attention – albeit briefly.

It was still less than a year since first Cable Street and then the short colonisation of the East End by starving workers from the North East who'd come through on what had been called a 'Hunger March'. The Commie boys had put those workers up and fed them even though they'd barely had enough for themselves. Bernie knew that what she should really do was close the shop and go and support the omnibus drivers. It was what Solly would have done. Even if he did lose his job.

But Bernie couldn't take that risk. Her dad, so Becky had told her, needed expensive injections to help him breathe. Bernie was going to make sure he got them. She'd already saved a pound. Solly, from his photograph, smiled approval. Bernie had to hold back tears.. Where was he? And why did just looking at his picture make her heart beat so quickly?

Mrs Rabinowicz the *shadchan* looked up at the onyx clock on the mantelpiece. It was running slow and needed adjusting. Was even *that* work?

Keeping *Shabbos* was a nightmare without help in the house. How was she supposed to know whether she could move a chair or put her feet up on a stool? Edith, her maid of all work, had also acted as her *Shabbos goy* – before Mrs Rabinowicz sacked her on Thursday. But the girl had stolen from her! A yard of green satin ribbon and a pair of white lace gloves. Apparently her sister was to be married this very day and, according to Edith, she'd just wanted to make her bridesmaid's costume a little bit more special. Because her family was poor. The usual nonsense.

But now without a *Shabbos goy*, a gentile employed by religious Jews to do things like lighting fires and cooking on the Jewish Sabbath, she was stymied. Her legs, already swollen and ulcerated, were cold, in spite of the warm weather, and she yearned for a fire. But if she did that and someone who knew Edith had left saw the smoke . . .

Mrs Rabinowicz had never been religious. That had been the province of her husband Saul. And of course religious was what each and every customer for her services as a *shadchan* was – and in the quest for a match with a suitably religious partner, paid her well for it. And so she was stuck here, still in her night attire, hungry and thirsty and cold. She'd have to get another maid of all work or at least a *Shabbos goy* before next weekend. Another carry-on like this would kill her.

But at least it would end well before she was due at the Suss family's house in Stamford Hill. That was Sunday's task. The jeweller and his wife were to welcome (again!) that miserable little madam their Chaim wanted to make his *kallah*. Completely taken with the girl, they were. Why?

The *shadchan* didn't know, unless it was because the boy believed the girl's father to be rich. Moritz Shapiro may or may not have money, the miserable old bastard always kvetched about his business declining. But one thing Mrs Rabinowicz did know was that his Rebekah didn't have any feelings for Chaim Suss. That had been apparent since the first, embarrassing meeting she'd arranged back in March when Rebekah Shapiro barely looked at the boy. Still mooning over that Solomon

Adler, so people said. Some people ... she couldn't remember who. But they probably knew what they were talking about. Gossip didn't just spring up from nowhere. Adler, though, was probably lying in a Spanish grave by this time. And good riddance to him.

'Penny for 'em.'

Mrs Michael, who wasn't in any way an observant Jewish woman, had opened the parlour window so that Becky could get some air. It was a warm day. She was wondering whether it was also warm in Spain, when her friend Rose and Dermot Lynch turned up outside in the street and glanced in at the window.

Becky ran to the back of the parlour as if scalded. She couldn't talk to them! Not on *Shabbos*!

She heard Rose say, 'What's wrong with Becky?' And then Dermot reply, 'Oh, it's their Sunday, ain't it?'

'What? Jewish Sunday? What's that then?'

'I dunno,' Dermot said. 'But they ain't allowed out and they can't talk to no one.'

They moved away.

Alone again, Becky felt bereft. Not only couldn't she talk to friends, she wasn't sure if she could even think about them. Was that work, or wasn't it? She didn't care. She'd already decided that when she had a home of her own, she wouldn't observe *Shabbos* like her father did. She'd be much more liberal. Unless of course she married a *frummer*. Like Chaim Suss.

She'd met him twice now, in company with her father and the *shadchan*. And while Becky didn't dislike Chaim, she knew she couldn't love him. It wasn't that he was unattractive. He was in fact quite handsome. But, like her father, there was a dustiness to him. A dreary, black severity that manifested itself not just in his tired, *frummer's* clothes, but also in the way he carefully counted coins out from a small purse he kept in his pocket and in the manner in which he deferred so completely to his father. But then really Orthodox men were like that. They also required their wives to wear wigs. Chaim's mother's was piled up on top of her head like a wedding cake.

Could Becky marry this man? The thought of him touching her with his pale, flabby hands was too horrible to think about.

She sat in what had once been her mother's chair. The three friends – Bernie, Rose and Becky – had all been so happy when they were children. Now Bernie, though she had a job that she wanted, didn't and couldn't have the man that she loved. The same man who had captured Becky's soul even though she didn't even know him. And then there was Rose. Bernie said that Auntie Kitty had intimated to her that Rose hadn't been ill just after Christmas. She'd had an abortion. Whose child had the poor thing been? It was almost too terrible to think about and neither Bernie nor Becky could ask Rose about it for fear of upsetting her. And it got worse.

Because she couldn't read and write properly, it was difficult for Rose to find a job. But she needed one. Her vile 'stepfather' had refused to feed her now she'd left school, and her mother was drunk all the time. So Rose found odd jobs where she could. Which wasn't many places. For a while she'd done some cleaning at Mr Sassoon's *schmatte* shop but then he'd got rid of her because she was, as he'd put it, a *nebbuch* – or poor fool. A lot of people didn't want her because they knew what her mother was. But if she didn't get something soon, she'd end up just like Nell.

If she wasn't already doing what her mum did.

'Seems as if Captain Cortes is managing to hold out against the fascists at that shrine I can't pronounce,' Patrick Lynch said from behind his newspaper.

His wife said, 'Oh, blimey, Pat, you still on about Spain? We've got the Coronation in just over a week and all you can do is talk about Spain!'

Pat put down his copy of the *Daily Worker*. 'If Spain falls to the fascists we're all up the creek,' he said. 'The Germans are behind Franco and his mob. On our side we've got Comrade Stalin and the might of the Soviet Union, but we ain't doing so well at the moment. If Cortes falls then Gawd knows what will happen. I tell you, Kitty, if that Hitler manages to manoeuvre things in Spain, he'll flex his muscles all over Europe.'

Kitty rolled her eyes. 'Oh, I can't think about all that!' She was hand sewing silk flowers onto hats for Mr Sassoon's brother the milliner. She'd taken on more work lately. Just because Dermot seemed to be getting regular shifts now, there was no need to be complacent.

'I'm more worried about our Joey,' Kitty said.

Pat disappeared behind his newspaper again. 'What about him?'

'He's throwing his weight about,' Kitty said. 'If you notice, Dermot and Little Paddy only speak to him when they have to. And the way he talks to the girls . . .'

Pat laughed. 'He don't get no change out of our Bernie!'

'No, but he shouldn't talk to her like that.' Kitty said. 'I heard him call her a slut the other day. I told him if he did it again, I'd give him a clip round the ear.'

Pat looked up from his paper again. 'What did he say?'

'He laughed at me! Drunk again.'

'I'll have a word,' Pat said. 'Won't have our girls spoke to like that.'

He stopped speaking and coughed. His chest seemed to get worse when he became agitated. But Kitty knew better than to comment on it. There was nothing anyone could do so what was the point?

'Boy deserves a good pint after work,' Pat said once he'd recovered. 'But, yeah, drunk ain't no good. 'Cept at Christmas, weddings ...'

'Yes, Patrick,' Kitty said, 'and all the saints' days in between. I know you. But Joey ain't good with drink.'

'I'll speak to him,' Pat said. 'But you know how dockers are, Kitty. You know how I had to toe the line. You know what them foremen are like.'

Kitty put her needlework down and pointed at her husband. 'Now you listen to me Pat Lynch,' she said. 'A dodgy cut of meat at Christmas or something for the kids is one thing, but I don't want Joey getting on that Artie Cross's mob.'

'Oh, Kit ...'

'No, I'm telling you,' she said. 'That man was a crook when you was down the docks and he's a crook now. And I know he let you off of taking part in his scrapes because of the kids, but you was forever turning a blind eye to all sorts. Joey's too full of himself, believes he can do what he likes. I don't want him in trouble with the law.'

'Joey's not in Artie's mob,' Pat said.

'Not yet. But I've seen him with some types I don't like,' Kitty said. 'Lads with things in their hands that should've never left the docks.'

'Kit ...'

'Boozed up,' she said. 'And our boy with them. I don't like it, Pat. I don't like what Joey's turning into.'

Dermot saw Chrissy standing outside the Ten Bells, but the little lad didn't see him. They hadn't spoken for months. Not that Dermot had ever explained why. In the main he'd just avoided his childhood friend. One time he had actually snubbed him and after that, Dermot imagined, Chrissy had probably made sure he kept out of the way. Rumour had it he was living down Limehouse now, but nobody knew where. He didn't look himself. Scruffy and dark around the eyes, he was with a woman who was already so pissed she could hardly stand. And it was only eight o'clock.

Dermot heard the woman yell, 'I'll fucking go back inside if I want to!'

Chrissy grabbed her arm. 'Landlord's banned ya, Trisha!'

'Yeah, but I wanna drink!'

Dermot looked down at Rose who, he noticed, had turned her face away from the scene. The woman with Chrissy was behaving just like Nell Larkin did. In fact, she was probably in the same line of work.

Whatever and whoever she was, this Trisha pushed Chrissy away and flung herself through the doors back into the pub. A burst of piano music blasted out into the night.

'A Little of What You Fancy Does You Good'.

Dermot had taken Rose to the pictures that afternoon. The kid was always round their place whether Bernie was at work or not, usually being fed by Dermot's mum. He'd needed to do something to take his mind off things and the pictures, though expensive, had seemed like a good idea.

'Trisha!'

Chrissy ran into the pub after the woman as a great roar welled up from the drinking punters inside.

Dermot took Rose's arm. 'Best get you home.'

They'd dawdled until they'd got to the pub, happy to be chatting about whatever took their fancy. But now Dermot looked tense, which was odd, Rose thought, seeing as the boy outside the pub had been his best friend. Although what Chrissy had been doing hanging about with that old brass was anyone's guess. Rose didn't say anything, though. She didn't want to spoil what had been a perfect day.

As she often did, Rose had shared breakfast with the Lynches and then, once Bernie had gone to work, Dermot had asked her if she'd like to go for a walk. Rose had always liked Dermot but had almost blushed purple when he'd asked. She'd wanted Becky to come along too, which was why they'd stood under her parlour window that morning. Then they'd remembered it was her Sabbath. But by that time Rose had said she'd go anyway. She'd never stepped out with a boy before and for a long time they walked in shy silence. It was only when they reached Gardiner's Corner that Dermot had the idea they might go to the pictures.

'There's a huge great modern picture house called the Troxy,' he'd said. 'You heard of it, Rosie?'

She hadn't. But now she'd been there, she'd never forget it. Quite apart from the pictures they'd seen, it was the most glamorous place she'd ever been. It had wide, elegant staircases, thick carpets you could lose your feet in and even chandeliers! Outside it was all white with columns and sculptures on the front of it. Rose had thought it a palace – a massive place full of people dressed up as if they were going to a posh dance. And Dermot had paid for them both.

She'd been sweet on him since last year and now he'd taken her to see *King Kong*!

'Here we are, miss,' he said as he walked her to the area stairs.

'Thank you, Dermot,' she said. 'I've had a smashing time.'

'Me too.'

He squeezed her hand and then he left. She watched him go into his own home and then sat down on the stairs. Horribly, she could hear her mum was busy and didn't want to go in until she'd finished. And Rose wanted to think. Dermot was getting shifts down the docks regularly now so he and his family had money. But he wasn't happy.

He'd told her that he'd had a falling-out with his brother. Joey had got in with some bad men at work, but Dermot hadn't said how or why they were bad. And, although he'd enjoyed *King Kong* as much as she had, he'd not been able to concentrate on the second feature, the newsreel or even the cartoon. He'd just smoked. Looked down at the floor, smiled at her when she looked at him, and smoked.

Then he'd seen Chrissy, said nothing and hurried on. Had it been because of who Chrissy was with? Rose didn't know the boy except by sight, but she did know what Dermot had said about him in the past. A smart, clever boy like Chrissy wasn't the sort of person Rose could imagine hanging around with a drunken old brass. Perhaps that was why the two lads had fallen out?

Chapter Fourteen

Sunday 2 May 1937

Only Aggie and Little Paddy went to Mass with Kitty on Sundays now. Her other children, like their father, always seemed to have other, more important things to do. If she was honest, Kitty Lynch wasn't a religious woman herself, but she liked to go because it was comforting and familiar and because it meant she could catch up with her sister Assumpta who lived just around the corner from St Anne's.

On this occasion she also saw someone she'd not come across for a while.

'Hello, Chrissy,' she said to Dermot's little mate from school.

Standing outside the church on Underwood Road, Chrissy Dolan looked drawn and lonely and Kitty noticed that he smelled of stale beer. He was also not with his dad or his brothers who had all left immediately after Mass had finished. They hadn't even looked at Chrissy.

Chrissy Dolan politely took his cap off, revealing his shock of bright red hair, and shook Kitty's hand. 'Mrs Lynch.'

For years he'd called her Auntie Kitty like most of the kids who came to play with her nippers. But then Kitty had heard a few rumours about little Chrissy Dolan lately and so she wasn't entirely surprised he was keeping his distance. Poor lad.

'I hear you have a place of your own now, Chrissy,' she said.

'Yes.' He blushed. 'I've a position down Limehouse. Companion to a lady of mature years.'

Dear Chrissy, he'd always had the knack of dressing things up – and that had included himself when he'd worked up West. Kitty didn't know exactly why he'd lost his prized job at Swan and Edgar, but she could guess. Boys like him were always harmless, in her opinion, even if the priests saw them as committing the most terrible sins. But society too viewed them as a threat – even when some in society used such boys for their own pleasure. Chrissy Dolan, God love him, was working as a 'maid' in a brothel.

'Well, even if you've moved to Limehouse, you're still welcome on Fournier Street,' she said. 'You always liked my kidney pudd'ns, didn't ya?'

Chrissy smiled. 'Yes.' Then he replaced his cap and said, 'Nice to see you, Auntie Kitty.'

He went on his way.

Assumpta joined her sister. 'They say Chrissy Dolan's a poof,' she weighed in.

Kitty shook her head. 'Ah, he's a nice lad. I used to love it when he came round to play with our Dermot.'

'Don't s'pose your Dermot wants to be seen with him now,' her sister said with a sniff.

It seemed he didn't. But then he wasn't getting on with Joey either, probably for a very different reason.

Kitty took her sister's arm. 'Come on,' she said, 'we'd best get round to Mam's before she starts thinking we've been picked up by the army on suspicion of being Fenians.'

'If only the old moo'd leave the flat,' her sister said. 'I swear to God, she still thinks King Teddy's on the throne!'

Len Tobin kicked Rose up the bum and sent her sprawling out into the area.

'Pictures? Fucking pictures!' he yelled. 'So you can go to the fucking flicks, but you can't buy food to put on the table here, can you? Where'd you get the money from to go to the fucking pictures?'

Rose picked herself up. 'Dermot paid,' she said.

She'd been telling her mum about *King Kong* when Tobin had come back from wherever he'd been the previous night. Even though Nell said he protected them, he was hardly ever in the flat these days unless it was to deliver customers to his common-law wife. Nell was like an imprisoned slave, working simply to get drunk and fed occasionally.

One of the old maids on the top floor opened her window and called out, 'Stop swearing, Mr Tobin!'

Len looked up and yelled, 'Fuck off!' Then he glared down at Rose. 'And you can fuck off too,' he said. 'I'm sick of feeding you when you don't do nothing!'

'It's not you as feeds me, it's Mum! And Auntie Kitty!'

He slapped her face so hard it made her ears ring. Rose put a hand up to her cheek, which was bleeding.

'Then you fuck off over to your Fenian pals,' he said. 'Move in with your boyfriend's mum ...'

'Dermot isn't my boyfriend!'

Len laughed. 'No, you're probably right there,' he said. 'From what I've heard he ain't too fond of girls!'

She was expected to look modest but pretty. The first bit she could do, but the pretty bit was hard with these clothes. Becky

175

didn't care on her own account. But her father appeared to be so taken with Chaim Suss, she didn't want to disappoint him. She looked at herself in the mirror and sighed. Even if he was still alive there was no way she was ever going to marry Solly Adler. Other girls married Socialist heroes, not her. Not a girl dressed all in brown wearing a cardigan buttoned up to her neck. Even her shoes were horrible. Dark brown flats with laces. And she wasn't 'allowed' to wear nylons. Long grey socks was what her papa had instructed. Just like those worn by the *frummer* women with the wigs. Everything about the way she looked was hateful.

Down in the workroom her father was doing a fitting for a man he'd told her was an actor. Well-spoken and blond, he had a name she recognised from the West End stage. Why was such a person having a suit made in Fournier Street? She'd asked her father who had told her the man had actually been born in Fashion Street – and then he'd told her his real name.

If you wanted to get on in the world of the *goy*, you had to be like them. You had to pretend. But then wasn't Becky pretending too by trying to enter the world of the *frummers*? In spite of the fact that Moritz was religious, her mother had never worn a wig. She'd had a job, as a seamstress, and she'd liked a good laugh – or so Becky recalled. Chani Shapiro hadn't led the life of a *frummer* woman and, Becky suspected, would be horrified to learn that her daughter was contemplating such a thing. But then the match with Chaim Suss wasn't her idea, was it?

'He'll not come and get me on account of his work, and I can't go all that way on the bus on me own.'

Kitty and her sister knew what was coming. Their mother wanted one of them to take her to their brother's house on William Street, Stratford.

'If I go now, I can stay with our Derek until after the party and then he can bring me home.'

Kitty looked at Assumpta and knew she was thinking the same thing, *What did Derek and his missus have to say about that?*

Ever since her mother had had a fall two months before, Kitty had found her impossible. She just wouldn't go anywhere. Not even to Confession.

'Mam, the party's not until Coronation Day. That's ten days off.'

'I know,' Theresa Burke said. 'I can count. You're here now, so you can take me.'

The old woman had spent all but the first year of her life in London, but she still spoke as if she'd just got off the boat from Cork. Pat Lynch, whose family had left Ireland during the Great Hunger of the 1840s, disparagingly called his mother-in-law a 'bog-trotting Paddy' on account of both her accent and her dark Catholicism. When he'd first met Kitty, Theresa had been almost permanently at Mass. But now, since her fall, she lived trapped in her flat, waited on hand and foot by her youngest child, Maeve, a woman of thirty with the mental age of a twelve year old.

'I want to go to a street party and that's that,' Theresa said.

'Mam, you don't even like the King.'

'Maybe not, but I can drink his health the same as anyone,' she said. 'Our Derek's going. That Sandra's cooking some Italian cake ... '

Kitty and Assumpta's eldest brother, Derek, had made the mistake of marrying an Italian woman. And in spite of the fact that Sandra was a good Catholic who had given him six children, his mother still couldn't bring herself to approve. All her other children, except Maeve, had married Irishmen or women.

'I've my boys to see to, and Pat,' Kitty said, 'and you know our Assumpta's Mary's about to drop her little 'un any minute.'

'So take me to Stratford and get it over with!' the old woman said.

Assumpta opened her mouth to speak, but Kitty stopped her. Mam could wind Assumpta around her little finger and she wasn't having it. Her sister had enough to worry about.

'Mam, I will take you on Coronation Day and not before,' Kitty said. 'Our Bernie won't be working that day, so she can come with us. Marie'll look after Aggie and Paddy. Then Derek can bring you home.'

'I want to go now!'

In spite of his poverty, Theresa's late husband, Ed, had always spoiled her. As soon as her kids could stand they'd been made to work so that their mother didn't have to. Kitty, almost alone in the family, had taken a stand against Theresa's selfish ways years ago. She had enough on her plate.

'Well, you can't,' Kitty said as her sister Maeve came in from the scullery bringing a cup of tea for their mother.

Theresa looked at Kitty and said, 'You're a hard woman, Kitty Lynch.'

'Yes, Mam, I am,' Kitty said. 'Take it or leave it.'

Black-leading the range was a dirty job. First Bernie had to mix the powder with paraffin and then apply it to the doors, shelves and body of the kitchen range. That was messy but it wasn't as bad as wiping the horrible gunk off, which was what she was doing when Rose appeared at the door.

'I hope you've come to give me a hand with this,' Bernie said when she saw her friend. 'Mammy likes it perfect and I'm making a bit of a pig's ear of it.'

'You got lead on your nose and down your pinny,' Rose said.

Bernie looked down at her apron. 'Jesus!'

Rose helped herself to some rags off the pile Bernie was

using and began to rub away at the cooker. After a moment, she noticed that Bernie was looking at her and frowning.

'What you done to your face, Rosie?'

'Oh.' She put a blackened finger up to her cheek and said, 'I . . .'

'Don't bother to make nothing up, I know he hit you,' Bernie said. 'What was it this time?'

Rose didn't know what to say and so she shrugged.

Bernie shook her head. 'You need to get a proper job and get out of there,' she said. 'I realise you don't want to talk about it, but I know what happened to you last Christmas. Weren't hard to work out. Stay with him and you'll get up the stick again.'

Rose turned her head away. She'd never talked to either of her friends about her abortion. She didn't have a clue how Bernie knew. But then Bernie was clever.

Eventually she said, 'I'd like to live here.'

'You almost do.'

'Yeah, but prop'ly. Like you do.'

Bernie knew that Rose just said the first thing that came into her head with no malice intended, but that irked her. There had been times when her parents had struggled to feed their own brood let alone the girl next door.

'Well then, you'd best marry me brother then, hadn't you?' Bernie said. 'Now you're stepping out to the pictures together.'

She'd said it as a joke, but Rose looked upset.

Bernie said, 'Oh, I was only pulling your leg!'

Even though she knew that Rose had taken a fancy to Dermot, Bernie saw them both as just bits of kids.

She said, 'Oh, Rosie! Buck up!'

But Rose put her cloth down and sat on the floor.

'Rosie!'

'Bernie, you know I do like Dermot, don't you?'

179

'You've never hid it from me,' she said. 'Oh, sod it!' She threw down her own cloth and sat next to her friend. 'What's the matter? You look as if you've lost a tanner and found fourpence.'

'It's not nothing.'

Bernie put one stained hand on Rose's crossed knee. 'Come on,' she said, 'you're upset and if you don't tell me why I'm just gonna sit here until you open your gob. Then if Mammy comes in and finds the range like this, we'll both be for it. And it'll be your fault!'

She knew that Rose would sit in silence for a few more moments and then she'd come clean. Only the abortion had ever shut her up like a clam. Bernie knew her well.

Rose said, 'Bernie, you know your Dermot ...'

'A bit. He is me brother.'

Rose swallowed. 'Well,' she said, 'I heard he don't like girls.'

'Don't like girls? Who told you that?'

Rose didn't answer. But Bernie knew. Bloody Len Tobin, doing everything he could to make Rose's life a misery – as usual. He had to know how she felt about Dermot. Pig!

"Cause if it's your Len telling you this then you know it's Tommy-rot,' Bernie said. 'Dermot likes girls and he's always been very popular with them. He likes you.'

'He's not tried to kiss me,' Rose said.

'Be grateful for that!' Bernie said. 'He's a good Catholic boy!'

'Mmm.'

She didn't look convinced and, to be fair, Bernie could understand that. Dermot wasn't queer, of course he wasn't, but his best mate was, or so it was said. And Dermot had stopped hanging about with Chrissy Dolan ever since his dad had chucked him out for reasons he wouldn't talk about. Joey in particular found the whole situation with Chrissy both disgusting and funny, which, Bernie believed, had caused her brothers to fall out. Not that Joey was being nice to anyone now he thought he was a big man down the dock.

Bernie picked up a rag. 'If you're saying you think Dermot's an iron . . . '

'I'm not.'

'Well, he ain't,' Bernie said. 'Len Tobin tells lies and that's the end of it. Now come on, let's finish this range and make Mammy happy when she gets in.'

'All right,' Rose said, and started cleaning again. But then she stopped and stared into space.

Bernie looked at her and shook her head. 'Buck up, Rosie! Come on! What now?'

'I was just thinking how complicated all this liking and loving thing is,' she said. 'I mean, you like Solly and so does Becky and how do you work all that out? And then there's Dermot and me and, though it's nice he's a good boy, I do feel a bit sad he didn't try to kiss me at the pictures.'

Bernie, cleaning furiously now, said, 'Welcome to the world of being grown up, Rosie.'

And then, suddenly, she burst into tears. Rose, without a word, put her arms around her.

Her poor papa. He wasn't listening because he really didn't want to.

'Edith, you see, was Irish, Mr Shapiro,' Mrs Rabinowicz said. 'They're wild. So now I have to find not just another maid but a new *Shabbos goy* too. It's unbearable.'

Talking at the top of her voice and dressed as if she was on her way to the opera – in a mink coat and a midnight blue evening gown – Mrs Rabinowicz was not the sort of woman anyone could ignore. Especially not on a trolley-bus. Becky, and she suspected her father too, wanted the earth to swallow her up.

'I just can't go through what I went through yesterday next *Shabbos*,' the *shadchan* continued. Then, with a sudden change of subject that was typical of her, said, 'So, Rebekah, now listen: the boy Chaim is keen, very keen. You've impressed him. But he won't wait forever, so . . .'

Becky had told the *shadchan* that she'd give her an answer after this meeting. But she knew she was only putting off the inevitable. Her papa liked the boy – or rather he desired a match with what was a very well-off and respected family. He wanted to make her safe.

'You will have my answer today, Mrs Rabinowicz.'

'Good. So now, look,' she said as she flashed her heavily beringed hands in front of Becky's face, 'the Coronation. Are you going to join the crowds at Westminster? Or is there going to be a street party? I think I may treat myself to a taxi and go and watch. I mean, I know the new King isn't as glamorous as the old one . . .'

'George V? Glamorous?' Papa said, looking puzzled.

Mrs Rabinowicz huffed. 'Ach! No,' she said. 'No, this one's brother, Edward. The one who married the American woman.'

King Edward VIII had abdicated the previous December in favour of his brother Albert who, when crowned on 12 May, was to become known as King George VI.

'A slut, that Wallis Simpson,' Mrs Rabinowicz continued. 'Just like my maid.'

'Wallis Simpson isn't Irish,' Becky's papa said.

'No, but I am,' said a grimy-looking geezer on the seat in front of them. 'So stop saying bad things about us, if you please, missus.'

Mrs Rabinowicz said nothing and there was an awkward

silence. However, it did give Becky a chance to think and to come up with a possible solution to Mrs Rabinowicz's maid problem.

All the men looked older than they were. Someone had told him that Artie Cross wasn't even forty. But he looked twenty years older than that. Like a lot of the docklands foremen, he came from one of those families based around Watney Market who'd been dockers for generations. Everyone he favoured, those on his 'royalty' list, were men to whom he was related or blokes who'd done him favours.

Dermot's dad had been on Artie's dad's 'royalty' list once, which was why his son had taken a shine to Joey. What Pat Senior had done for old man Cross, Dermot didn't know or want to know. Cross's dad had been easily as crooked as his son, but Dermot didn't have any problem with him. Not that there was a problem with Artie now that Dermot had stopped associating with his old mate Chrissy.

He'd never said anything, but Chrissy had seemed to know he shouldn't talk to Dermot any more. Whenever Dermot saw the little lad, Chrissy turned away and often ran in the opposite direction. Dermot knew he was living in a brothel just off Narrow Street in Limehouse. It was a poor place for poor men, full of old, sick, unhappy women who'd do almost anything for the price of a beer.

It was run by a woman who grandly called herself Mrs Smith-Brown; she was actually originally from Amsterdam and, people said, her real name was unpronounceable. A madam, a landlady, and some believed a murderer of girls who wouldn't do what she wanted, Mrs Smith-Brown was now Chrissy's employer. It was a right come-down from Swan and Edgar's and Dermot couldn't help wondering what he had done that had been so bad as to lead him into the fleshpots of Limehouse.

'Bruv.'

Joey was drunk. Not roaring, but he smelled of beer.

Dermot looked up. He no longer recognised this red-faced bully boy as the loving brother he'd once been.

'Come on then – Mary,' Joey sneered.

The two boys walked towards the small group of men standing under the railway bridge and everyone shook hands. Artie Cross and his 'royalty', all boozed up after a session in the Railway Tavern, greeted Joey with something Dermot recognised as respect. By contrast, they hardly looked at him.

But at least they weren't lairy, and when Artie addressed them all it was in a conversational tone. 'So, brothers, we have an order. No names, no pack drill. But it'll be worth your labour, of that you can rest assured. Could all go on a right old beano after this one if we play our cards right.'

Everyone knew that goods coming into the docks sometimes went 'for a walk'. Joey had 'liberated' a chicken for their table the previous Christmas. Pat Lynch had done similar things when he'd been in work. But Dermot and Joey's dad had always steered clear of anything 'big'. And he'd told his boys to do so too.

'There's blokes'll take orders for hooky goods from people you don't want to get involved with,' he had warned them. 'Be careful of the foremen in particular. Some of them bastards'll get you in bother.'

'I'm talking Tom Thumb,' Artie said.

Rum. It came into the dock in great wooden barrels. Stored in vast five-storeyed warehouses, it was the West India's most valuable cargo.

'Fucking hell, Artie,' one of the blokes, an old geezer called Ron Kettle, said, 'how much we talking here?'

Artie looked around the group and then said, 'Two barrels.'

'Two barrels!'

'How we s'posed to do that?'

Dermot had seen those barrels. He'd rolled a few into the warehouses himself – with another bloke. It took two men to roll each of them. They were massive.

'It's all worked out, you don't have nothing to worry about,' Artie said. 'Suffice to say, it's all set up. I'll give you the nod when we're ready to go. But be ready.' Then he looked at Dermot. 'Good little introduction to the brotherhood for young san fairy ann here.'

Joey had made him come to this meet-up. Dermot could've killed him. This wasn't 'knocking off' a few bags of sugar! This was the kind of theft their father had warned them about. Carried out not on behalf of impoverished family and neighbours but for a 'customer' somewhere, an undeserving rich bastard who wanted cheap booze. It was also by way of being some sort of initiation too for 'san fairy ann'. Artie Cross was using Dermot's friendship with Chrissy to make him do things he didn't want to do. And with Joey, his own brother, in tow as well, how could Dermot refuse?

Nothing would be decided until Moritz Shapiro and Mr and Mrs Suss had spoken separately to their children and then to the *shadchan*. As far as Becky could see, this dinner she was trying to eat was simply a chance for Mrs Suss to show off her skills in the kitchen.

Their hostess wore a lot of jewellery. Diamonds, emeralds, pearls. All the glass and silverware on the table shone in the light from three huge candlesticks, and yet Becky couldn't help but be struck by how ragged the carpets and curtains in that big dining room were. Clean, but ragged. A bit like Mrs Suss's long

185

dark blue knit dress. Why didn't rich people like these replace things? They had the money, what was wrong with them?

Mrs Rabinowicz praised every dish that was presented to her. The *challah* bread was 'just perfect', the *gefilte* fish 'a joy', and the chicken was, apparently, 'like butter'. The *shadchan* also complimented their hosts on having such a lovely maid who was clearly a 'treasure' and a 'darling', unlike the awful girl she herself had employed. In fact she went on about it to such an extent that the *shadchan*'s staff problems entirely overtook the conversation.

'She stole from me, I'm sure,' Mrs Rabinowicz said. 'Of course I can't prove it ...'

Mr Suss shook his head. Chaim Suss looked at Becky almost without blinking. It made her uncomfortable. His eyes bulged a bit, she noticed, making him look a bit like a very pale fish.

Her papa, probably overwhelmed by Mrs Suss's jewellery, was almost completely silent. He had been when they'd visited before. He'd looked sad then. But it had been he who had wanted this match.

Becky felt Mrs Suss's food turn to cardboard in her mouth. She'd have to say yes to this match. She really didn't have a choice. But every time she thought about being married to the jeweller's son, she felt sick. What was it about him that put her off? Was it simply because he wasn't Solly Adler? Or because he looked like a fish?

'Ideally I'd like a girl who would live in,' Mrs Rabinowicz continued her monologue. 'The last one wouldn't. But that would be my ideal. Clean, honest, quiet. I mean people need jobs now, there aren't enough apparently, you'd think someone would jump at the chance ...'

'People are greedy,' Menachim Suss said. 'Venal and greedy and immoral, these days.'

'I know a girl,' Becky said.

It had just come out before she'd properly considered whether this was the best place to mention it. Had it been because she'd been going out of her mind with boredom and indecision? She didn't know. But now it was out, she had to justify it and suddenly she didn't know that she could. Rose was hardly honest, and cleanliness was a bit of a movable feast with her. Becky fell quiet.

'Do you?' Mrs Rabinowicz said. 'Tell me all about her, dear.'

Becky saw her father look at her and scowl.

Chapter Fifteen

12 May 1937 – Coronation Day

The three girls walked arm-in-arm down Commercial Street towards Aldgate East Tube station. Dressed in their best clothes they looked as if they were going to a party – which they were.

Becky, all in red, with white gloves and matching hat, wore the highest heels she knew her papa would tolerate, while Bernie looked sharp in a bottle-green trouser-suit she'd made for herself. Rose ... Well, Rose was clean and even though her mum's best dress did swamp her, she walked with her head held high, just like her friends.

'Do you think we should've brought something?' Becky asked as the girls walked past Toynbee Hall.

'No. Me mum and me aunties have got loads of stuff,' Bernie said. 'There'll be jam tarts, cheese sandwiches and sausage rolls as far as the eye can see.'

Rose looked up at the gothic towers of Toynbee Hall, covered in red, white and blue bunting for the Coronation, and said, 'Is that where them students live?'

'Yes,' Bernie said. 'Oxford and Cambridge boys coming down here to help us out.' She shook her head. 'No, I dunno why either.'

'They help in the soup kitchens, I heard,' Becky said. 'Papa said they're here to learn about how poor people live.'

Bernie snorted. 'Bloody waste of time,' she said. 'What they gonna do? Check our hair for nits?'

Becky looked at the new white gloves her papa had bought for her and tried to imagine what would happen if she took them off. She dismissed it from her mind. She was going to a street party with her friends, that was all that mattered.

'Is Dermot coming?' Rose asked Bernie.

'I think all the family'll be there,' Bernie said. 'Everyone except me nan likes me Auntie Sandra. She's just had another little 'un, they've called him Mario.'

'Why doesn't your nan like her?' Becky asked.

'Oh, 'cause me auntie's Italian not Irish,' said Bernie. 'Nanny Burke's a miserable old cow, don't like anyone different from her. But at least there'll be lots of other family about to keep her occupied. And Auntie Sandra's cooking some Italian cakes, which'll make a change from cheese sandwiches and jam tarts.'

'Is that what your mum's bringing?'

'I expect so,' Bernie said. 'And I saw her cooking a sponge cake last night. I expect that'll come out too.'

'I don't think I've ever been Stratford before,' Rose said. 'I've been to Canning Town . . . '

'Well, don't get too excited,' Bernie told her.

'What do you mean?'

'Stratford, Spitalfields, Whitechapel . . . all the same really, ain't it?'

Becky frowned. 'No. Different people live in different parts of the East End. You can get different types of food depending on where you are, for instance.'

'If you can afford it.' Bernie shrugged. 'I just mean that wherever you go round here, people are poor. Everyone's poor. Even people you think are rich, aren't. I mean, look at that Mrs Rabinowicz of yours ...'

'She's not mine!' Becky said.

'Yeah, but she's Jewish.'

'So?'

'Got her own house, her own business, but she's still not like the people who live up West, is she? Even she don't drive around in a Rolls-Royce and go to posh restaurants with the la-di-dahs. There's them and there's us,' Bernie said, 'and *they* don't want *us*.'

'I 'spect the King does,' Rose said. 'He's la-di-dah but he has to like us.'

'Does he?'

'Yeah,' she said. ''Cause if he don't we might chop his head off like they done in France.'

'Who told you about the French Revolution, Rosie?' Becky asked.

Rose had rarely been to school and yet, just occasionally, she showed that somewhere along the line, she'd picked up information.

'Me mum,' Rose said. 'Told me all about some French queen who made people eat cake and then they chopped her head off. The poor people did it.' Then she looked up and smiled. 'Me mum might not be able to read and write, but she ain't silly.'

The wireless wasn't something that Mrs Rabinowicz actually used and so she had to call her neighbour, Mr Berger, to come and make it work. As he struggled to tune the thing in – or whatever they called it – she looked contentedly at the lovely 'spread' her new girl had organised for her guests. It was a pity that young Rose had insisted upon honouring an invitation she'd been given to some street party because now Mr Berger's wife Milly would have to be paid a few coppers to make tea, but there it was.

Mrs Rabinowicz had wanted to go to Westminster to watch the Coronation procession, but then her legs had let her down. Standing, even for a few minutes, was agony and so she'd opted for a Coronation tea party at home with her friends – and a few clients. These included the widowed Rebbetzin Cohen, whose son she'd married to a very nice girl from Poplar, and the widower Shapiro whose lovely daughter had recently agreed to wed the very eligible Chaim Suss.

It would have been nice if the newly engaged couple had agreed to come to her little Coronation affair, but the girl, Rebekah, had insisted upon going to the same street party as the *shadchan*'s new maid. Such a strange girl for Rebekah to be close to! Funny, scrawny little thing with a gypsy for a mother and who knew who for a father. But she could shop – she could keep an entire list of groceries in her head – clean quickly and efficiently, and she was living in.

The girl she'd employed before, Edith, had lived in too. But she'd done nothing but complain about her room. It was too cold in the winter, too hot in the summer, there were mice, it was haunted ... But not a word from Rose. In fact, she had actually seemed grateful for it.

Some crackling noises came out of the wireless. Mr Berger said, 'Be all right in a mo'.'

It had better be! Her sister-in-law was coming from Enfield and she always had her snout out sniffing around for any faults. Anything that wasn't *kosher* ...

Mrs Rabinowicz went through a mental list in her head to make sure that everything was covered. Food and drink, provided Mrs Berger didn't make a mess of the tea, was taken care of, the wireless was in the pipeline, as it were, and the house was clean and decent. And she'd had a pre-emptive word with Rose before she'd left. 'Now don't get involved with any young men at this street party you're going to. Keep your eyes down at all times and don't let them take any liberties.'

It was said that old Charlie Brown, late publican of the Railway Tavern, Poplar had cultivated friends from all over the globe. And if the strange collection of articles that lined the walls of his pub were anything to go by, that wasn't just a myth. As soon as he'd arrived, Dermot Lynch had seen two Chinese vases almost as tall as he was, and a stuffed brown bear. Now he found himself looking at something he couldn't identify suspended in some sort of fluid in a jam jar. It looked vaguely like a fish.

He hadn't wanted to go to the pub with Joey. The pair of them were supposed to be at Uncle Derek's street party in Stratford, but apparently Joey had received a message from Artie Cross. The day had finally come and they were 'on'. The meet was at the Railway Tavern, which was hopping with happy revellers getting well oiled in time for the Coronation.

'I don't see as how getting pissed is a good idea, given what we've got to do,' Dermot said to Joey.

'You dunno what we've got to do. Anyway, ain't until tonight.'

His brother supped his pint and then went over to join Artie and his mates.

Dermot heard one of them shout, 'Oi! San fairy ann!'

He went outside. It was a dull, dreary day for a Coronation. Some kids were messing about with a cart made out of old orange boxes, and laughing. Their high spirits spooked him. Were they laughing at him? Did they know about him, something he didn't even know about himself?

Inside the pub, Artie, Joey and the other men would be talking about what they were going to do that night. Dermot didn't want to knock off a load of rum for some dodgy bastard who could probably afford to buy it. If their dad knew, he'd lose his mind. But what choice was there? If he didn't join in then he'd never work on the docks again. Not just in the West India, but anywhere. And he couldn't and wouldn't grass them up. Grasses had a habit of dying in mysterious circumstances and he didn't want to do that.

Dermot sat down on the pavement. Had there been a reason he'd always been friends with Chrissy Dolan? At school he had been Dermot's one and only male friend. Him, a boy who liked football and skiving off school. Chrissy liked to draw, read and wear his best clothes all the time. He'd never talked about girls . . . Not like *that*.

Of course, Dermot must have known all along what Chrissy was. He'd tried to fool himself it wasn't so, he'd even had fights to protect Chrissy's 'good name'. But what did that actually mean? And why had he felt he had to do that?

Bernie's sister Marie and their cousin Angela were like two peas in a pod. All frilly skirts, hair ribbons and little bits of glass jewellery. They both liked cake rather more than would be good for them later if they kept on eating it and they made shy eyes at any boy who came near them. Becky stole a quick look at the ring under the glove that covered her left hand. A one-carat solitaire diamond. Marie and Angela would love it. She pulled her glove back on again.

William Street, Stratford was typical of the type of

accommodation rented by workers on the London and North Eastern Railway lines leading into and out of Stratford. Built in squat terraces, blackened by smoke from the trains and nearby factories, the houses were cramped, dark and didn't have running water. Though not a railwayman by birth, Bernie's uncle Derek had managed to get a job 'on the railway' through his father-in-law who had come to Britain from Italy in the 1900s. Now a guard on the Liverpool Street to Southend-on-Sea line, Derek was full of stories about how, in the not too distant future, the line would be electrified.

'Which means no more bloody great plumes of smoke like that!' he'd said when a steam train had pulled out of the nearby station.

But the men who drove those trains, many of whom were his neighbours, looked at him and frowned. It wasn't good manners to bring up their own fears about this modern trend on Coronation Day.

Down the middle of the road, the women had put up tables and brought out chairs. Each table was covered with a cloth so white it was almost as if snow had somehow come to earth in that dark, smoky place. But then good laundry, as Becky knew only too well, was important to East End women. It was a matter of pride. A woman whose whites were grey was a lazy slut.

'God in heaven, could you not think of anything but jam tarts, Kitty?' Bernie's nan said as she watched her daughter place her contribution on the nearest table.

'Oh, Mammy, give over! I've a Victoria sponge coming too and some sausage rolls!' Kitty shook her head in reproach. 'Marie and Angela have eaten all them marzipan hearts Sandra put out. Greedy mares!'

'And you couldn't even make a fruit cake!' Theresa Burke said.

'Oh, Mam, it's all right!' Derek said. 'There's loads of nosh.'

The old woman looked at Becky and said, 'What do you want, miss?'

But Bernie was rapidly at her friend's side, camera in hand. 'Hold still, Nan, while I take your photograph.'

'Ah, get away with you!'

The old woman pushed her way through a crowd of kids with sticky fingers and went and found a chair.

'That's got rid of her.' Bernie winked. 'She does the same thing whenever I try to draw her. Thinks I'm stealing her soul.'

'I think your nan believes I'm some sort of posh girl,' Becky said.

Bernie laughed. 'If you've got your own teeth, she thinks you're posh,' she said. 'Daddy always says she still acts as if she's straight off the boat from Ireland.' She scanned the street. 'Where's Rosie?'

'I think she's looking for your Dermot.'

Bernie shook her head. 'I thought he'd be here too,' she said. 'But Mammy said he and Joey have gone drinking with their workmates. He's been acting strange lately. Chrissy Dolan's hit hard times and Dermot would usually be there to help, but not a bit of it. I can't remember when they last saw each other. I think our Joey's involved somehow but I don't know in what way. Docks business, I suppose.'

'What?'

'Ah, it's another world down the docks,' Bernie said. 'When Daddy was up the West India there were things went on he wouldn't talk about. It's another country, trust me. The men who wait on the stones live by their own codes. Men outside and women can't even begin to fathom that country of theirs.'

A hard country, Becky thought. Full of hard men with hands callused and torn from hauling sugar or flour or rum. Not like 'her' Chaim's pale, soft hands. She hated that she'd finally agreed to be his wife. She wanted to say something. She wanted to tell her two best friends, but she wanted to tell them together.

'It was a good day's work how you managed to get Rose that position with the matchmaker,' Bernie said. 'Now she's out of that rancid flat maybe she can get going properly.'

'I think she misses her mum.'

'I'm sure she does. But she won't be missing Len Tobin,' Bernie said. 'And at least with the old woman, she won't get hurt.'

'No.'

Mrs Rabinowicz hadn't been sure about Rose when Becky had first spoken about her. Mrs Suss's dinner table probably hadn't been the best place to broach the subject. But she had and it had worked. Would the *shadchan* have taken Rose on if Becky hadn't said yes to Chaim Suss? She didn't know. Her papa still thought that Rose and Mrs Rabinowicz were not going to suit each other, but Becky wasn't so sure. Rose had been through a bad time, Mrs Rabinowicz's house would provide her with some security. And that was what life was all about, wasn't it?

With German help the Spanish fascists were winning the war against the Communists. No one had heard anything from Solly Adler, not a word. He'd disappeared in a country splitting apart and turning into something else. In Germany itself, so her papa said, if you were a Jew you couldn't get a place to live or a job. Security was disappearing there. While in the land of the new King . . . Becky looked around the very ordinary street all set for its Coronation party. She would have smiled had she not remembered Mosley and his Blackshirts. Had they really gone away for good? Or would they, emboldened by what was happening in Spain and Germany, be back one day soon?

Everything tasted bad. Roy's mum had even brought him some biscuits made with almonds, which he'd always loved, but they'd tasted of grit. Outside in the street, kids were hollering and whooping and it made him feel almost alive. Almost.

Roy's dad worked as a signalman on the London and North East and whenever he came in from work you could smell smoke.

'How's it going?' he said to his wife.

Roy's mum said, 'I don't know about all this, Sam. I know what Roy said ...'

'So give it another day then,' her husband said. 'One more day and then we'll get some help.'

Of course they thought he was asleep, but he wasn't. Sleeping was bad because of the dreams it brought with it. Dreams soaked in blood ...

'God save the King! God save the King!'

A group of old women who had been listening to the service from Westminster Abbey on the only wireless in William Street, came pouring out, holding their glasses of stout in the air.

'They've crowned him!'

'Just now!'

'Long Live King George VI!'

'God bless him!' some old railwayman boomed.

Where she was standing when the news came, Rose didn't know anyone. But a man gave her a drink and a woman she didn't know hugged her while a load of kids ran around the tables as if they were possessed.

'Cheers!'

It was port and lemon, which she didn't like very much, but Rose drank it anyway. The man who'd given it to her smiled.

'Happy day, ain't it, love?' he said.

'Yes.'

'After all that business with his brother and that woman from America. People say he, Edward, is a friend of that Herr Hitler in Germany – and if that's the way of it then good riddance to him!'

Rose didn't know what to say. She knew that King Edward VIII had abdicated over an American woman who was divorced but she didn't know anything about Hitler.

The woman who'd hugged Rose said to the man, 'Oh, for Christ's sake, Sam, poor girl don't want to listen to your politics!'

'Maybe not,' the man said, 'but we'll all know more'n we want to about Herr Hitler soon unless someone does something about him.'

'Well, if you mean war again, then I'm not for it,' the woman said. 'Not again.'

The man sniffed and said, 'Might come to it, though, love. Man's a bully. He has to be shown.'

A lad who'd had rather more booze than was good for him, shouted, 'Up the Irish!'

A woman sitting on her doorstep threw a rock cake at him. 'Shut up!'

And then the music started. A squeeze-box to begin with and then someone joined in on a piano inside a house. It was 'Underneath the Arches', Flanagan and Allen's song.

People began to sing.

Some little bastard had daubed the word 'Yid' underneath the parlour window in what looked like dung. It wasn't the welcome Mrs Rabinowicz had planned for her guests, but there was nothing she could do about it until Rose came back and cleaned it off, so she ignored it.

Of course the sister-in-law from Enfield had seen it, no doubt.

But there was no way she was going to mention it. The *shadchan* knew that her late brother's wife, Esther, looked down on her and where she lived. Not that she was any better than she should be. Born in a tenement in Bethnal Green, she'd been. One of twelve kids brought up in a basement bug-hutch by parents who couldn't speak a word of English. The only reason she lived in what she called a 'villa' out in Enfield was because of the *shadchan*'s brother who'd worked as a furrier until cancer took him off.

Once all her guests had arrived, Mrs Berger served tea and they all listened to the Coronation on the wireless. Or rather they talked while the wireless was on. The Rebbetzin Cohen, in spite of her loss, could talk for England and the Misses Lipmann, two spinsters who lived with their mother in Wentworth Street, kvetched professionally. Esther set herself grandly apart as usual, leaving only the poor men, Mr Shapiro and the ancient diamond merchant Mr Letterman, silently drinking their tea amid a hailstorm of gossip.

'Mama said she'd rather be dead than pay that!' the oldest Lipmann sister, Helga, said.

Her sister, in another conversation completely, said, 'They get inside your stockings! So you have to scratch wherever you are. In the street! No wonder you look like a *schlump*!'

Helga said, 'And at a time like this, to put the rent up?'

'Death isn't the worst. We're used to death,' the Rebbetzin said. 'I told him, "It's natural, don't fight it." But then it'll all turn out good in the end, won't it?'

'She always said serviette, I said napkin, what of it?'

'Oh!' the *shadchan* said. 'The King's just been crowned!'

They paused for a toast and, immediately afterwards, Mrs Rabinowicz attempted to stir all of her guests into what she hoped might be an actual conversation. A bit 'British' for

Jews who'd always had to fight to be heard – had to fight for everything – but if *she* couldn't have a nice, polite Coronation Party, then who could?

'Now Mr Shapiro here has some wonderful news, don't you, Mr Shapiro? About your daughter?'

'Oh, yes. But ...'

'She courting?' asked Helga.

Her sister Heidi said, 'Married, is she? I never heard. You should've said.'

'*Nu* ...'

'She's engaged to Chaim Suss the jeweller!' Mrs Rabinowicz yelled.

Moritz Shapiro's face reddened. 'Yes, well, it's not common knowledge ...'

'*Mazeltov!*'

'Oh, you must be so happy!' the Rebbetzin Cohen told him.

For the first time Esther put her oar in. 'The Susses live in Stamford Hill. Your daughter will be able to move out of the East End, Mr Shapiro.'

'Yes, but as I say, it's not common ...'

'Arranged by me,' Mrs Rabinowicz interrupted him. Where was the harm in a little bit of advertising? 'I saw the boy, I met the girl, and I thought, "Perfect, just perfect!"'

Heidi Lipmann put a hand on her knee and said, 'You have a gift, Ada. You have a gift.' And then she changed the subject. 'Dr Klein– have you seen him? Ill, we were told when we tried to get him out to Mama's chest, but then he was seen in the Ten Bells! You think a man's a *mensch* ...'

And so it continued with everyone happy in his or her own little bubble – except for Moritz Shapiro. Rebekah hadn't wanted a big announcement about her engagement and he'd promised her that wouldn't happen. She wanted to tell her friends herself and that was, though unusual, her prerogative. It was also the least that Moritz could do for his daughter.

He knew she didn't want to marry Chaim Suss. And, in a ideal world, he wouldn't want her to marry the young *frummer* either.

People celebrated in different ways. But some, men in particular, just did what they did irrespective of whether the King was being crowned or not.

Chrissy Dolan ripped the sheets off poor old Dilys' bed while she was in with mad Mary Isaacs who had a sink in her room. Bleeding again. Blokes just treated old girls like her like bits of meat. Christ knew what that last punter had made her do to make her bleed. Not that Mrs Smith-Brown gave a shit. All she cared about was her cut, which was considerable. Chrissy flung a half-decent sheet onto Dilys' bed and hoped she was sober enough to cover that disgusting mattress up with it herself. Then he ran downstairs and out into the back yard. Every sheet and pillowcase had to be accounted for so he couldn't just chuck the filthy thing away. All he could do was scrub it in one of the washing tubs and hope that Mrs SB didn't notice. Washing 'costs' came out of the girls' wages even though it was Chrissy who did all that, for not much more than a bug-infested bed beside the kitchen range.

Not that he was ungrateful to Mrs SB. Nobody else would have given him employment. Not after his dad had thrown him out when he lost his job.

Albert Lacy had started at Swan and Edgar five years before Chrissy. He too worked on the windows. Smart and clever, Albert liked a drink after work on a Friday and, one day, he invited Chrissy to join him. A kiss on Windmill Street had become something more as Albert introduced Chrissy

201

to a different kind of life amongst the dark streets of Soho. Chrissy was in love before he learned that Albert was married to the daughter of his manager, Mr Reynolds. Devastated, Chrissy began crying at work every day, he felt sick all the time and, worse than that even, Albert had begun to avoid him. He had found himself another, younger boy. It was then that Chrissy threatened to tell Reynolds if Albert didn't drop the new boy and come back to him. The next thing he knew he was out on his ear together with Albert's latest beau, accused of committing 'unnatural acts' in the staff toilets. Their accuser, Albert, had stood beside Mr Reynolds while he sacked them.

No references could be expected, of course, but Chrissy hadn't imagined that Reynolds would write a letter to his father. Or had that been Albert's idea? It didn't matter. Whoever it was told his dad, who told his brothers, who told everyone. Chrissy was a poof and there were no jobs for them. Well, there was one ...

He'd sold himself for a while, just so he could eat. He'd met Dermot once who didn't seem to know, or behaved as if he didn't, and had offered to buy him a pint. But Chrissy had refused. Like his brother, Dermot worked down the docks and so couldn't be seen with someone like Chrissy – or not without tongues wagging maliciously. Chrissy had even wondered when he'd met Dermot whether their friendship was responsible for his mate not getting called on. Unless of course Dermot had finally done something himself ...

Chrissy rubbed the sheet with Sunlight soap and then pushed it up and down the washboard. He liked Mrs SB's 'girls' even if he didn't like being called a 'prossie's maid'. Mrs SB wasn't bad exactly ...

Her shrill laughter ripped out into the yard from the kitchen and he heard her say, 'You know some mad people, don't you, Michael?'

A man's voice replied: 'Christ, Hannah, that from you?'

She laughed again. Then said, 'I thought it was all about catching them young with you?'

'It is,' he said, 'but sometimes we get a specific request. In this case, old, which is why I've come to you.'

'How nice.'

'You know what I mean!' he said. 'Not that you're old but that . . .'

'I'm a dealer in old whores, yes,' Mrs SB said. 'Our clients are poor. My girls fulfil a need. But, as I understand it, the customers you cater for . . .'

'Jaded palates, Mrs Smith-Brown, that's the truth of it,' the man said. 'The rich can have whatever they like and eventually that can, well, get a bit strange. Anyway it's only photographs. All money in the bank.'

Chrissy heard the back door open and so he hid himself and his washing tub behind the khazi. The sheet on its own could get him into trouble, but if she thought he'd been listening in on her conversation too . . .

Mrs Smith-Brown said, 'Well, if you're sure this is what you want, Michael, I'll arrange it.'

The man followed her out. He smiled and said, 'Handsome.'

And Chrissy Dolan had to stop himself from making an anguished noise as he looked at the bloke's face and recognised him.

Chapter Sixteen

There was smelling a mouse and then there was smelling a rat – and this was a big rat. They weren't on their way to the West India, they were walking away from the docks. Past noisy pubs, even noisier street parties and gangs of women sitting on doorsteps talking about how their nippers were sending them round the bend.

'Where we goin'?' Dermot whispered to Joey. 'I thought we was going down the West India to the rum warehouses?'

Joey laughed through his fag smoke. 'Yeah, well, bit of a change of plan, bruv,' he said.

'Where we going?'

'You'll see.'

It had been dark by the time Artie Cross and his mob left the Railway Tavern. Half out of his mind with tension, Dermot had wished his mum had insisted he go with the rest of the family out to Uncle Derek's. But he knew she'd never make him or Joey do anything if 'docks business' was involved. It had been the same with their dad, although Pat

Lynch was well known for being as straight as a die. This definitely wasn't.

They walked along the Whitechapel Road, past girls sashaying along in their best frocks watched by groups of Jewish lads in sharp suits and hats tilted at jaunty angles. Dermot heard Artie whisper 'Bleedin' Yids' under his breath. Joey laughed.

Dermot pulled his brother towards him. 'What's that about?' he said.

'What's what?'

Joey, like the rest of the mob, wasn't drunk but he'd had enough to put his temper, which wasn't good at the best of times, on a hair-trigger.

'Jewish lads are our comrades,' Dermot said.

Joey put his face close to his brother's and said, 'Where'd you get that idea from?'

'Religious divides are bourgeois constructs designed to keep the working classes weak,' Dermot said. 'We've no axe to grind with the Jews! They're poor like us.'

Joey frowned. 'You sound like Dad.'

'Who's a good man!'

'Who's a fucking idiot,' Joey said. 'Don't you get it, mate? These Jews are taking our jobs, our homes and our women. And we're gonna get a bit of our own back.'

'Didn't what we done at Cable Street mean nothing to you?' Dermot said. 'Class solidarity ... '

'Which you can stick up your arse,' Joey said. He pointed one finger in Dermot's face. 'We're gonna send the Jew-boys a message tonight and you, my little fairy brother, are going to give us a hand.'

She'd have to take her gloves off sometime. Unless she didn't want to eat anything. Of course, the good women of William

Street had put out their best cutlery, but most of that had gone into the hands of the kids who were playing 'war' in and out of their houses. Off their heads on beer they'd nicked from their dads' glasses and smothered in cake, the local nippers were going bonkers now night had fallen. But she was hungry ...

Becky heard a woman on a doorstep say, "Course now she's had her teeth took out, we can get her married off.'

The women sitting with her all nodded in agreement.

It wasn't often she thought about how marriage was conducted among the *goyim*. To Becky, as well as a lot of other young Jewish girls, gentile marriage rites looked so simple. You found a boy you liked, he asked your dad if you could get married, and the next thing you knew, you were in church. But it wasn't that simple, especially if you were poor. And there were people at this street party who were very poor. People she'd only heard about; people who had their daughters' teeth taken out as an incentive to prospective husbands unwilling or unable to pay for dental treatment in the future. And here was she, engaged to a man who not only had money and a good trade but was also nice-looking. What on earth did she have to complain about? Becky took her gloves off, but she didn't help herself to any food because she'd suddenly lost her appetite.

'No!'

Rose pushed the boy away. She knew where all that kissing business led and she didn't want any of it. Blond and tall, the boy, Reg something or other, had wooed her with ham sandwiches and lemonade and pulled her into an alleyway for 'afters'.

'Oh, come on, girl!' he said. 'I only want a little peck!'

Rose ran. She had no doubt that Reg hadn't meant to hurt

her like those men who'd brutalised her that night, men like her step-father ... But she wasn't having it! She knew where it led, which was to the doorways of women like Mrs Swan who charged ten bob to almost kill you.

Reg called out after her, 'Prick tease!'

But she ignored him. He could think what he liked, she wasn't doing *that* again whatever anyone said. Her employer Mrs Rabinowicz was a funny old lady but, so far, she was kind and Rose had a good position with her. And although she took most of her earnings home to her mum and Len, she had a decent place to live that was safe.

'Hello, gel!'

It was that nice man she'd met with his wife, who'd helped her toast the king. He was sitting drinking beer with Bernie's dad.

'You know each other?' Pat Lynch said to the man, Sam Oberman.

'We raised a glass to the King, God bless him,' Sam said. 'Me and Rita and this little girlie here.'

Rose smiled.

'Best mates with our Bernie, ain't you, Rose love?' Pat said.

'And Becky too.'

Her Uncle Pat smiled. 'Three of them, you know, Sam. Like sisters, they are.'

He was drunk and so was the other man.

'It's good for girls to be together – they can watch out for each other,' he said. 'Shouldn't be that way, but it is.'

'What Socialism's about,' Uncle Pat said. 'Equality.'

'Which'll come if we go to war,' Sam said. 'You know Hitler and Mussolini are armed to the teeth and they've millions ready to take up arms. We should be ready too, but we ain't, and Chamberlain won't do nothing about it.'

'He don't want another war.'

'Nobody does. I don't. Sod that! But he'll get a war whether he wants one or not unless he puts a crimp on the Germans.'

Rose didn't care for talk about war and so she went to where some of the women had cleared a space in the street for dancing. A piano had appeared underneath a street lamp and old women and their daughters waltzed drunkenly to 'Down at the Old Bull and Bush'. Rose smiled. It was funny the way so many men thought it was 'poofy' to dance and yet loads of women waltzing together just looked odd. They spent much of the time laughing and falling over. Rose looked around for more food. Because it was dark now, Becky's dad would be arriving soon to take the two girls back to Spitalfields, so she'd have to fill her belly before that happened. Mrs Rabinowicz's larder would be empty after her Coronation do and there'd be a ton of washing up to do before the morning.

There were only one or two Huguenot families left in Spitalfields. Most of the old French Protestants had moved out to more prosperous London suburbs decades ago. Fred Lamb was one of the exceptions. Still living in the house his ancestors had built back in the eighteenth century, Fred also plied their original trade and was one of a handful of silk weavers left in London.

A recent widower, he hadn't felt inclined to go to any of the Coronation street parties and so had stayed at home alone in his big house on Fournier Street, listening to the radio. He'd noticed that the furrier next door, Meyer Nadel, had taken the day off and had no doubt gone off cavorting with one or more of his many girlfriends. Fred liked Meyer, even though they were very different. The furrier was a bit of a show-off if the truth be told, but he was also kind. When Fred's beloved Doris had died, Meyer had opened his home and his heart to the Huguenot – something Fred would never forget.

Fournier Street hadn't had a street party for the Coronation, probably because too many other streets had 'dos'. Most people seemed to be elsewhere and so, come nightfall, with the exception of the pub, there was nobody about. Sitting behind his front parlour window, Fred wondered what he would have done had Doris still been alive. They would probably have gone over to their Jane's place in Barking. He could've gone on his own, his daughter had invited him, but he hadn't fancied it. Not without Doris.

Fred didn't know when he fell asleep, but when he woke up, it was with a start. There was a hell of a commotion coming from next door. Meyer must have got as drunk as a sack!

But as he listened, Fred realised that he could hear more than one voice coming from the furrier's – and none of them sounded like Meyer's. A few years before, the place had been broken into by one of Meyer's disgruntled former employees and the furrier had lost hundreds of pounds' worth of stock. Fred got out of his chair and went out the back of his house to see if he could see into Meyer's place. There was a warehouse where once the old weaving shed had been, where the furrier kept his stock.

At first Fred couldn't see anything, but then he saw a light . . .

'What's that?'

She'd only reached a couple of inches across the table towards the pickles, but it had been enough for Bernie's eagle eyes.

'What's that?' she repeated. 'Becky?'

Becky held up her left hand. The one-carat solitaire diamond glittered in the jaundiced light from the street lamps. Beautifully cut and perfectly clear, the stone was dazzling.

'It's my engagement ring,' she said.

Bernie grabbed her hand and looked at it, closely. Knowing Bernie, she wouldn't be impressed.

'This from that jeweller?' she said accusingly.

Becky tried to take her hand back, but Bernie was holding on fast.

'Yes.'

Bernie looked her in the eye. 'Why?'

'It's important to be married.'

'No, it isn't,' Bernie said. 'Who told you that?'

'For Jewish girls . . .'

'Yeah, and Christians too,' Bernie said. 'Parents always want us married so we behave ourselves, so we're "safe", so we're decent . . .'

'For us it's even more important!'

'How?'

Becky took a deep breath. 'Because as Jews we're not safe,' she said. 'You know about these stories that have come out of Germany.'

'I know Jews are no longer German citizens. Those attacks, bloody awful . . .'

'And so if we have to run, we need money,' Becky said. 'The Suss family have money.'

'Yeah, but that's Germany, not here!'

Becky looked down at the ground. The gutters were full of fag ends and beer bottles.

'We defeated the fascists, remember,' Bernie said. 'Cable Street? They won't win here.'

'It wasn't going to happen in Spain but it seems it has,' Becky said. 'The fascists are too strong. Good men like Solly Adler went out there to fight them and look what happened.'

'So all the more reason to live your life as you want to,' Bernie said. 'Don't let the fascists change you! Marry who you want to marry or don't marry at all. This is just selling yourself and you're better than that!'

210

Becky's eyes filled with tears. 'Oh, Bernie,' she said, 'you mean well, but you don't understand. You can't, you're not a Jew.'

'No, but I am a girl, and I know that if we don't fight to take control of our own lives, nobody's going to do it for us,' she said. 'Even male comrades like me dad can never do enough. They don't understand. We have to do it for ourselves!'

Becky pulled her hand away and put her gloves back on. 'I'm sorry, Bernie, but you're wrong,' she said. 'And anyway I've made up my mind. Chaim is a very nice boy and I like him a lot.'

'Do you? Really?' a deep voice said.

It was then that Becky saw her father. She dabbed her eyes and smiled at him. 'Yes, Papa,' she said. 'I do.'

Bernie turned away in case Mr Shapiro saw the fury on her face.

Joey Lynch held up a long fur coat and shone his torch over it.

'Oi, Artie,' he said, 'you think this is mink?'

Artie Cross pushed a handful of fur hats into his duffel bag. 'How the fuck should I know?'

One of the other blokes said, 'My missus has always wanted something in astrakhan.'

'Well, I don't know what that is either,' Artie said. 'Look, just help yourselves and let's get out of here. We ain't setting up a shop.'

Dermot Lynch stood in the middle of Meyer Nadel's warehouse rooted to the spot. He didn't want to rob Meyer! Why would he? The furrier wasn't exactly a mate or even that nice a bloke, he was a bit of a crook on the quiet, but he didn't deserve this.

'Oi,' his brother said to him, 'fill your bag!'

There'd never been an order for rum. This had been the

'job' all along. To rob a Jew, thereby giving him grief, and then fence the goods to put money in their own pockets. Artie Cross at his worst. In fact Artie Cross at worse than his worst. Dermot hadn't realised the foreman was a fascist. Joey too. How could that be?

''Ere, san fairy ann, if you ain't gonna help then fuck off!' a bloke called Harry Sims said. Harry was one of Artie's core followers, one of his 'royalty' who were always called on.

Dermot said, 'No.'

'No, you ain't gonna help? Or no, you ain't gonna fuck off?' asked Harry.

'Neither.'

Joey grabbed his brother by the scruff of the neck and thrust a fur coat into his hands.

'Put it in yer duffel bag!' he growled.

But Dermot threw the fur on the floor. 'No,' he said. 'I won't do it! What's Meyer Nadel ever done to you? To any of us?'

'He's a Yid,' Artie said. 'They take our jobs!'

'No, they don't,' Dermot said. 'They do their own jobs. We do ours. This is wrong.'

Joey hit him so hard he ended up on his arse.

Artie said, 'Little poof! Ain't you seen the lines of blokes outside the Labour Exchanges? Ain't you . . . '

A loud knock on the door stopped him in his tracks followed by a voice calling, 'Mr Nadel! Are you in there, sir? It's the police!'

Rose didn't see anyone settle the young man into the chair in the doorway of the Obermans' house, which was why, for a while, she thought he'd arrived there by magic. Covered in blankets, right up to his chin, all she could really make out about him was that his face was bone white. In the sick light

212

from the street lamps it looked a bit like a thin, silvery moon. It was scary, which was why Rose felt wary of approaching the man. But at the same time she felt as though she ought.

A lot of the kids who had been running around the tables and in and out of the houses had either gone home or fallen asleep in the street. But the music still went on even though the pianist had disappeared. A woman played a ukulele – like George Formby, but not so well – and another man tooted on a tin whistle. But only a few people sang. It was late and everyone was tired. Rose looked around to see if she could find Becky and her dad but she couldn't and so she went to have another look at the man in the doorway.

By the time she got close enough to realise that she'd seen him before, the man was asleep. Hair that had once been a glossy black was now dulled by streaks of grey. This matched his skin which, now she was close, Rose could see wasn't white at all but a blue- grey, like that of a dead person.

And yet he breathed . . .

'Rosie!'

She turned at the sound of her name. Becky and her dad stood on the other side of the street.

'We've got to go now,' Becky called.

And so Rose had a decision to make. She either told them or she didn't. Bernie had said that Becky was engaged to that jeweller she didn't like. But did that actually change anything? Bernie said that Becky was unhappy, which had to be bad. But if Rose told her . . .

She looked at the sleeping man and then waved at Becky and her dad.

'All right,' she said, 'but come over here first, I need to show you something!'

*

Constable Dean had been on his way back to the station on Bishopsgate when Fred Lamb had run up to him in the street. When he'd seen lights on in Meyer Nadel's warehouse, Fred had checked the furrier's front door, which had very obviously been jemmied open. Now, watching from his back yard, Fred saw men run out of the warehouse and begin to scale the wall that separated the furrier's house from Christ Church graveyard. He heard Dean blow his whistle to summon help and Fred yelled out, 'They're getting away out the back!'

Other whistles replied, which meant more coppers were on their way. But the robbers were getting over the back wall easily and, if no one turned up soon, they'd get away scot-free.

There wasn't a real fence between Fred's yard and Meyer's. It had blown down last winter and neither of them had bothered to replace it. Fred kicked what was left of it out of the way and stepped off his property. The oiks were gathered by the wall, helping each other over and throwing bags up in the air. No doubt full of stolen furs.

'Oi, you lot!' shouted Fred. 'Toe-rags!'

He couldn't see how they reacted, it was too dark, but he heard them.

'Quick! Get over!'

'Gi'us it here!'

'Police are coming,' Fred said. 'So I'd stay where you are if I was you!'

'If I was you? I don't fucking think so!'

Fred turned and instantly recognised the man who had replied. But then there was pain and blackness and he knew nothing more. .

Chapter Seventeen

Mrs Poster had never seen her floor quite so clean before. She said, 'Well, when little 'un comes at least he'll have somewhere you could eat your dinner off to play!'

Becky took the compliment and managed a smile, but her heart wasn't in it. When she went out to Mrs Poster's yard to fill the kettle she had to fight to keep herself from crying. That clean floor had been the result of pure, wild misery and confusion.

He was alive! Somehow Solly Adler was alive. Sitting on a chair in a doorway in a house in Stratford, he'd been so deeply asleep he'd looked almost dead. Almost ...

Papa had whisked her and Rose away quickly and had refused to let her friend say anything about it on the way home. All he'd commented was, 'Well, I'm happy for him. *Mazeltov* to him. He did a brave thing but a futile one and now the poor man's finished, by the look of him.'

And that was that.

But was Solly 'finished'? Becky didn't know, and although

Rose had whispered that she'd try to find out, how could she? At the *shadchan*'s? Even if Mrs Rabinowicz did know anything about Solly she wouldn't let on in front of Rose. And there'd been that burglary.

Five doors down from the Lynches' building, Mr Nadel's fur warehouse had been robbed by a load of men, one of whom had knocked out poor Mr Lamb who lived next door. Whoever had done it had hit him so badly he was still unconscious. Papa said whoever had burgled Nadel's had done so because the furrier was a Jew. This was how, he said, anti-Semitism started . . .

Becky set the kettle down on the ground and put her head in her hands. Solly had looked so ill! And yet he had also looked so much himself she had wanted to take him in her arms and kiss him. Even though she'd never so much as touched him before.

And then there was Bernie. As far as she knew Bernie didn't know about Solly, but she soon would. Word would go round. If Rose knew and Becky knew, others had to know too. The people who lived in the house where he'd been were called Oberman, so they were Jews. And if Becky knew anything, it was that if one East End Jew knew something, they all did. Including Solly's mother.

Sugar from the West Indies meant hard graft. Cranes and carts could only do so much. Once the sacks were in the warehouse, they had to be stacked by hand, which meant men lifting and carrying until their muscles burned.

But then to Dermot Lynch the pain was both to be expected and appreciated. A penance of sorts – as if any sort of penance would ever make up for what he'd done. Why hadn't he just run into the furrier's house and told the police? Why had he scrambled over that wall into the graveyard with the rest of them, holding a fur hat in one hand?

He hadn't even known he had it until he'd got home and thrown it at Joey. The rest of the family had still been out, thank God, because if they'd seen how pleased his brother had been with himself they would have been ashamed. His poor dad would have died.

Mr Lamb, nice, quiet, weaver Mr Lamb, might actually die. Dermot hefted one sack of sugar on top of another and then stopped for a moment to wipe his brow. He felt sick. The rumour was that Lamb was in the London Hospital and still unconscious. Nadel the furrier was going out of his mind with worry about him, it was said.

Dermot looked around the warehouse and watched his fellow thieves graft and laugh and joke, and wondered whether the fault lay with them or with him. If he wasn't something he didn't understand himself, would any of that even have happened? He cared about Chrissy, although he knew he didn't love him, but why did he care so much? And why did that matter so greatly to people like Artie Cross?

He went outside to the cart and hefted another sack of sugar. He'd have to do something, but what? Then he saw Artie Cross looking at him. Saw the foreman wink.

Bernie put the photographs side by side. The one that Wolfie Silverman had dropped in for framing, of Solly Adler, and the one she'd taken of Becky at the street party. They both looked so young and happy and beautiful. Now one of them was going to marry a man she didn't love while the other was probably dead. Life was wicked sometimes.

Bernie had left the party on William Street just after she'd seen Becky's engagement ring. Little Paddy and Aggie had been tired and so she'd offered to take them home. Becky's news had taken the shine off the party and she'd wanted to avoid talking to her about it any more. Then when she'd got in she'd found Dermot and Joey still not talking. Joey had been drunk. It was becoming a habit with him.

She'd come to work two hours early so that she could start to develop the photographs she'd taken at the street party as well as printing the shots Mr Devenish had taken at a wedding over in New Cross the previous Friday. The old man wasn't coming in – again – probably because he'd got drunk for the Coronation. So Bernie had the place to herself. She'd only printed up Becky's photo so far and was curious to see what the other pictures had come out like. Looking at the negatives, she'd seen one of Rose that looked promising. She'd been eating a bowl of jellied eels and her eyes had been darting around as she did so, as if she was afraid someone might take her food away. Thin and pale, wearing an old dress many times too big for her, she'd looked like a Dickensian orphan.

The shop doorbell rang and a very red-faced Wolfie Silverman entered. Bernie looked up at the clock on the wall. It was eleven o'clock and so he was probably popping in for his photo during his tea break.

'Hello, Wolfie,' she said. 'Do you want . . .'

'He's alive!' he gasped, out of breath.

'Who?' Bernie went over to him and pulled up a chair. 'Sit down before you fall over.'

Wolfie sat. Then, after breathing deeply for a few moments, said, 'Solly Adler's alive.'

Bernie felt her own legs wobble and clung on to the counter.

'Back from Spain three weeks ago. He's been staying with the family of some comrade he met out there. Come back months ago,' Wolfie said.

'So why didn't he come straight home?'

Bernie knew her face was dead white. Solly hadn't written

218

and she'd felt that acutely. But then maybe he hadn't had time . . .

'Didn't want his mum and his brother to see him like that,' Wolfie said.

'Like what?'

There'd been a rumour he'd lost a leg but was there anything else wrong with him? Bernie's heart began to pound.

'What?' She shook Wolfie's arm.

'I've heard, but it's only a rumour that he can't speak proper,' the big man said. 'But I dunno. I ain't seen him yet.'

'Has his mum?'

'I doubt it, she's gone to work. Thought I'd come and tell you and collect Solly's picture. I don't really know whether to give it to her now . . .'

Bernie glanced at the photograph, lying on the counter beside Becky's. They both looked like film stars. She said, 'Well, you take it anyway, Wolfie. You keep it until you're ready to give it up. And someone should tell his mum or his brother. Quickly!'

She handed the photograph over. Suddenly she couldn't bear having it near her. If Solly was back, what did that mean for her? And did Becky know?

'I'll see Fred Lamb right.'

'I know you will, mate.'

'If I can. If anyone can.'

Pat gave Meyer Nadel a fag and ordered him a pint. He couldn't afford it, but the furrier was, if not a friend, a valued neighbour. And Pat Lynch was a man with a heart of pure marshmallow.

Two pints in hand, Pat sat down beside Meyer and asked him what had happened.

'Coppers say there was a group of them.'

'What? Oiks?'

'Who knows? Could've been anyone – the way things are.'

Pat knew what he meant. With millions unemployed, crime was a continuing threat. Also because Meyer was Jewish there was possible anti-Semitism in the mix too. Pat feared, like a lot of people, that the Battle of Cable Street had only temporarily inconvenienced Mosley and his fascists. They would be back.

'You know me and mine'll stand firm, don't you, Meyer?' Pat told him.

The furrier smiled. 'You're a *mensch*.'

'So tell me what you know,' Pat said. 'I'll put some feelers out.'

Everyone knew the police stood no chance of catching a cold in the close Spitalfields streets. Fascists or no fascists, the East End would deal with its own.

'Poor old Fred Lamb raised the alarm just before midnight,' Meyer said. 'Heard some voices and saw lights moving about in me warehouse. So he run out, saw me front door was open and got the Peelers. Or rather poor old Constable Dean staggered along.'

Everyone knew Constable Dean. Since he was well beyond retirement age, the local kids ran rings round him.

'Dean sees my street door open and runs inside. Then Fred calls out from his yard that the bastards are getting over the back wall into the graveyard. Dean gets on the whistle to call up reinforcements. Meantime poor old Mr Lamb's tried to stop these toe-rags on his own and got his head smashed in for his pains.'

'His head's smashed in?'

'Well, not quite, but he's in a bad way,' Meyer said. 'He ain't conscious yet. Dean reckons if he does come round he might be able to give a description of who hit him. But then again he might not and Dean don't know nothing. I do, though.' He moved his head closer to Pat's. 'If you wasn't in the brotherhood yourself, Pat, I wouldn't say nothing. But when I had a look at my back wall this morning there was some deep gouges in the brickwork. And I may be wrong or I may be right, but them marks look very like the damage I've seen done to places where dockers fight.'

Pat said, 'Hooks.'

'Dockers' hooks, yes,' Meyer said. 'I've told the coppers nothing but if you ...'

'I'll ask around,' Pat said. 'Leave it to me.'

When he left the Ten Bells, Pat Lynch's face was set in a scowl. Dockers' hook marks on a Jewish furrier's wall wouldn't normally make sense. What use did hard men have for mink? But there was one exception ...

The little bird in the golden cage was clockwork. It 'sang' when you wound up a key. Disappointingly for Rose, it didn't sing a song but cheeped and squawked like a real bird. But at least the sound provided some background to her work today, which was endless dusting.

Mrs Rabinowicz had stuff. Some of it, like her three Dresden tea services, at least served a purpose, but most of her knick-knacks didn't.

These could be anything and come from anywhere. As well as some very beautiful hand-carved musical boxes Mrs Rabinowicz said came from Switzerland, there were plaster donkeys from Blackpool, baby dolls all dressed up in Brussels lace and a very scary-looking glass dome covering a group of stuffed mice having a picnic.

When Rose had first come to the house, the matchmaker had told her she 'collected'.

'I like to have nice things around me,' she'd said. 'I've worked all my life, like a dog I've worked, and so why not?'

Mainly, though, Mrs Rabinowicz liked to collect jewellery, much of which she wore all the time. Some of it she'd purchased from Becky's prospective in-laws' shop in Black Lion Yard. However none of her considerable number of diamonds matched Rose's mate Becky's engagement ring for brilliance or size. She'd shown it to her friends not long before they found Solly Adler at the street party. Then Becky seemed to have completely forgotten about it. But Rose hadn't and neither had Mrs Rabinowicz.

'Rebekah's a very lucky girl,' she said to Rose as she watched her dusting the legs of the chaise longue in the corner of the parlour. 'A ring like that! Those things only come about once in a lifetime! He must be impressed with her. But then of course I did do a very good job for the girl. She was so shy! I understand that, I was a shy bride myself. Which is why it's so important to have a woman of mature understanding to put in a word or two, smooth the ruffled brow of care over money . . . Not that it's about the money!'

Well, it certainly wasn't about love. Rose knew that much. Love was the fierce light in the eyes that Becky had shown the moment she'd seen Solly again. It was the joy mixed with so much sadness Rose had seen in those same eyes when Becky saw what was left of the man she loved.

'Mr Suss . . . that's Mr Menachim Suss, the bridegroom's father . . . he wants the happy couple to marry in September. But for once I'm with the bride's father who says he favours a spring wedding, next year,' Mrs Rabinowicz said. 'Of course, between you and me, Mr Shapiro hasn't been doing so well lately and so he needs time to make money for the celebrations. But he'd never admit to that!'

But was that the real reason Becky's dad was putting off the wedding? Or did he know that she didn't really love Chaim? What Rose did know was that Mr Shapiro always seemed ever so rich to her.

'And you need to have money to hire the La Bohème Ballrooms,' Mrs Rabinowicz continued. 'I don't suppose you know them, do you? On the Mile End Road. Only the best families have their weddings there.' She sighed. 'Flowers supplied by Bookshneer's and catered by Stern. And the dress? Well, it has to be a dream . . .'

But Rose wasn't listening. It had suddenly occurred to her that, as far as she knew, Bernie didn't know Solly was still alive. What would she do when she found out? He hadn't written to her, like he'd promised, and she'd been sad about that, even though she hadn't said anything. It was obvious she still had feelings for him. But Solly had changed. The man Rose had seen had no longer been the happy-go-lucky boy Bernie once danced with.

Waitressing was like being in the theatre. A bit. As if you were on the stage, you had to be someone you weren't and wear clothes you wouldn't normally be seen dead in. Not that the standard Lyons Corner House 'nippy' uniform with its crisp white apron and dear little white hat was unappealing. Indeed Dolly Adler had always rather liked it.

Across all its restaurants and cafés, Lyons Corner House, Coventry Street could feed upwards of three thousand people at any one time. And though it was the height of elegance, the place did that at prices ordinary people could afford. That was how it had achieved its great success.

Today, and to her delight, Dolly was working in the really elegant Mountview Café. Looking like a cross between a

223

Hollywood musical set and an Egyptian palace, the Mountview was an Art Deco masterpiece and, back in the days before Solly went missing, when she was happy, just being here had always made Dolly feel like a star. Today it still pleased her, albeit through a haze of melancholy.

A man, Yiddisher by the look of him, sitting opposite a blonde girl, beckoned Dolly over.

'Yes, sir?'

'We'd like tea, please,' the man said. 'And a chocolate éclair for the young lady.'

'Yes, sir.'

Dolly wrote the order down on her pad. Ben always liked an éclair whenever he came in.

At first when she heard her son's voice, Dolly thought that maybe it was just because she'd been thinking about him. But when she reached the tea urns, she saw him waving his hat at her.

'Ben?'

His face broke into the biggest smile she'd ever seen on it.

'Mum!' he shouted over the heads of the customers. 'Solly's alive!'

Dolly dropped her pad on the floor and, eyes filled with tears, ran across the restaurant and into Ben's arms.

Chrissy Dolan felt a heavy hand land on his shoulder. He flinched. People who put their hands on him like that tended to go on and beat him up.

'Hello, Chrissy,' Pat Lynch wheezed. 'What you up to?'

Dermot was often in the Railway Tavern these days. Chrissy had seen him go in with a bunch of other blokes, including his brother Joey. The boy had sidled in after them, careful not to be observed.

'Oh, just on me way home,' he said.

Did Mr Lynch know why he'd been chucked out of his dad's place? Chrissy would have been surprised if he didn't. Everyone else seemed to know.

'I'm trying to find my boys,' Mr Lynch said with a smile. 'It's like trying to get an audience with the Pope these days!'

'They're busy?'

'Thank Christ!' the older man said. 'Mind you, when they're not working they're always in here, spending money they ain't got.'

Chrissy looked down at the ground. 'Oh, well . . . '

It was pointless trying to have a word with Dermot under these circumstances. He'd have to try again another time. And yet, wasn't it urgent? He wondered for a moment about telling Mr Lynch, but then thought better of it. That would mean having to explain where he worked, and Chrissy couldn't bear to do that.

'See you, Mr Lynch,' he said as he began to walk away.

'See you, son. Oh, and Chrissy . . . '

He turned to face Pat.

'Anything you want me to pass on to our Dermot?'

He smiled gratefully. Of course he should tell a kind man like Mr Lynch, he would understand, but Chrissy found he couldn't. 'No . . . No, thanks.'

'Okey-dokey.' Pat Lynch waved to him. 'And remember, son, you're always welcome round our place. Kids and our Kitty'd love to see you.'

'Thanks.'

Then Chrissy turned away quickly before Pat Lynch saw him cry. Everyone, except Joey, at the Lynches' place would want to see him, he had no doubt. And Dermot, of course. He wouldn't want to see him and the thought broke his heart.

*

225

Artie Cross was just as Pat had always known him: s loud-mouthed bully, and even more so when he was on the booze. He wasn't pleased to see Pat. Never had been. But then, it wasn't surprising.

Pat had always had the measure of Artie and, while he'd never confronted the man while he worked in the West India, the foreman had known that Pat was taking careful note of everything that happened there. When the boys had started working in the docks, Pat had understood that their employment depended, in part, on his keeping his gob shut. Just as it used to do when Pat himself had been working – he kept quiet, work was forthcoming. And with Joey, Artie had kept his side of the bargain. But not with Dermot.

Pat knew why and it didn't make him happy. Unlike Kitty, he'd always known their middle boy was different. People like Artie smelled that out. So he'd decided to punish the boy and Pat could understand, if not like, that. When the boy couldn't get regular work at the docks, his father had hoped Dermot would eventually find work elsewhere. But when his son did start to get work, about the same time as he fell out with his brother, Pat had wondered what was going on. He should have acted then.

'What's your poison, Pat?' Artie called out. All fake bonhomie, he made Pat's skin crawl.

'A word, Artie mate, if you don't mind,' Pat said.

He could see Dermot, sitting on his own in a corner, face as white as a sheet, surrounded by glass domes filled with dead animals. Old Charlie Brown and his collection! A bit of a mad bastard, Pat had always felt. Briefly his eyes met Dermot's and he saw his son's face go taut.

Although it was getting late now, the Railway Tavern was still crowded. Groups of blokes too skint to buy a drink hung around in the hope of meeting a mate who was flush; kids whose dads were in the pub played in the gutters outside.

Pat lowered his voice. 'I've just come from my neighbour's gaff,' he said. 'Meyer Nadel.'

Artie pursed his lips as if thinking. 'He that furrier what got done over last night?'

'Yeah.'

Artie shook his head.

Pat took a deep breath and said, 'Reminded me of the time old Aaron Shaffer and his missus got beat up ...'

And there he let it hang, watching the other man closely.

Artie smiled. 'That was donkey's years ago.'

'Ten years.'

'Yeah. Down Flower and Dean Street, and you know what sorts live there.'

Although not as deprived and depraved as it had been while still a Victorian Rookery, the tenements of Flower and Dean Street, off the southern end of Brick Lane, still evoked fear in East Enders. The haunt of cut-throats, thieves and prostitutes, it was known as a place where people could easily get into trouble. And back in August 1926 an old Jewish couple, Aaron and Essie Shaffer, had been viciously attacked there.

Of course nobody had seen them get their heads and just about everything else kicked in and so no one had ever copped for the murders. But Pat Lynch remembered that time well. He also remembered Artie's daughter, Linda.

'I know she was your favourite kid and you know your Linda wouldn't have liked what you done,' Pat said. 'She was a decent girl.'

Artie's face creased and went red. 'Killed by a fucking Yid!'

'Your girl died in childbirth ...'

'With a Yid's kid!'

'I know what you done that night on Flower and Dean Street and you know I know it,' Pat said.

'You know nothing!' Artie spat. But he looked around to make sure no one else was listening. 'All that was just a coincidence.'

'Two days after Linda's death, her bloke's aunt and uncle are brutally beaten up?' Pat said. 'Coincidence, my eye!'

'You can't prove nothing!'

'Yes, I can, and you know it,' Pat said. 'We both do. It meant making a deal with the devil for me so I could keep on getting work and, later, my boys could too. I'm not proud of it, but that's life. Then you started ignoring our Dermot ...'

'Poof!'

Pat grabbed Artie by his collar. A couple of blokes in the group nearest to them shuffled their feet uneasily. Pat said, 'All right, gents?' then turned back to Artie. 'I should've sorted you out then. But I fooled meself it was gonna be all right. It ain't because now you've done it again, ain't you? Scum like you never learn!'

'Me? I ain't done nothing ... never have!'

'There was dockers' hook marks on Meyer Nadel's back wall!' Pat told him.

He saw Artie's face go pale.

'And I can't think of no one on the docks what hates Jews like you do! Jews are our comrades!'

The Public Bar door swung open and Joey, plus three of Artie's 'royals', stood watching Pat slowly release Artie's collar.

'Everything all right here?'

Pat knew Tony Norman of old. One of Artie's favourite sons.

'Yeah, we're fine, Tony,' he said.

He let go of Artie and smiled at his son. 'All right, Joey boy?'

But Joey didn't answer. He looked at Artie, as if waiting for permission to speak. Pat Lynch was a tough man whose life had always been hard. He'd never been defeated before but now, for the first time, he felt close to it. He looked at Joey and knew that he'd lost him.

Chapter Eighteen

Kitty had watched her daughter Bernie for any sign that she wasn't herself, but found nothing out of the ordinary. The girl went to work early, as she usually did, without a word about Solly Adler and his reappearance. Did she even know? She had to! It was all round the manor. When he'd got back from Spain, Solly hadn't gone home but instead had stayed with Sam Oberman's family in Stratford. Kitty hadn't realised that Sam's son Roy had gone to Spain too. The two young men had met over there.

It was said Solly was in a bad way. Lost a leg and that was why he hadn't been home. Didn't want his mum to see him like that. But word was that Dolly Adler had been out to Stratford and brought her son home with her. If Bernie didn't know anything about it yet, she soon would. And then what? She hadn't shown interest in any of the other young men who ogled her in the street, or even the rather nicer boys who attended Mass. Not that Bernie had been to Mass lately.

The girl hadn't exactly been stepping out with Solly but Kitty knew her daughter was sweet on him. As was Becky over the road and every other girl in Spitalfields. But Becky was marrying a jeweller and now that Solly was . . . well, hurt, would girls still go mad for him like they used to? Maybe, maybe not. But if anyone did, that would be her Bernie. Always a lover of lame ducks, it was she who'd brought poor little Rose into everyone's lives and ducks didn't get much lamer than that.

And, of course, Solly loved Bernie. Or so he'd said in his letter. The one Kitty had read and read and read and then burned in the range. How could the dopey boy love her daughter? He hardly knew her! And yet did that, even if it were true, excuse what Kitty had done? She knew the answer to that and it took her legs from under her. Kitty sat down on the stool outside the back door and put her head in her hands. She'd have to tell Bernie what she'd done. The guilt was making her ill, she was sure of it. Your sins always came and found you out in the end.

'There's a man lurking across the road looking at the house,' Mrs Rabinowicz said. 'I don't like the look of him. Who knows what goes on these days? What with Mr Nadel's place being robbed . . .'

Rose followed her gaze to a slumped, ragged figure leaning against the wall of the pub.

'Oh,' she said, 'it's me dad.'

She hadn't wanted to tell the matchmaker she didn't know who her real father was and so she'd called Len Tobin her dad. Rose knew that nobody the old woman knew, including Becky, would contradict her.

'What does he want?'

Rose had wondered that too. She couldn't imagine it would be anything good.

'I dunno.'

'Well, go out and tell him to move along,' Mrs Rabinowicz said. 'He looks most disreputable. I know you're his daughter, but that doesn't give him any excuse to hang about round here.'

'No, ma'am.'

Rose let herself out of the house and ran over to where Len Tobin slouched smoking a fag.

'What do you want?' she said. 'Mrs Rabinowicz don't like you hanging about. Says you make the place look disreputable.'

'So? Come to find out when you've got your afternoon off,' he said.

'Why?'

She didn't go home as a rule unless she had to and then only when she thought her mother was alone.

'Your mum needs to talk to you,' he said.

'About what?'

'How should I know?' He shrugged. 'So when you off?'

Rose didn't like him knowing anything about her but what choice did she have? If her mum needed to speak to her, she needed to speak to her.

'It's me afternoon off tomorrow,' she said. 'Tell me mum I'll see her then.'

'All right,' he said.

'Now go,' Rose said. 'Or you'll get me in trouble.'

Len Tobin smirked and then, slowly, pushed himself away from the wall and began to walk away.

Pat Lynch watched the police arrive. Mob-handed, they assembled outside the furrier's place. Pat feared the worst. And when Constable Dean strolled up to speak to him, he confirmed it.

'Fred Lamb died last night,' the copper said. 'So we're looking at murder.'

'Christ!'

'Just told poor old Meyer Nadel. He's in pieces.'

Pat shook his head. Was now the time to tell the coppers what the furrier had told him about the dockers' hook marks? If the coppers had eyes in their heads they'd see them for themselves.

'What now?' Pat said.

'We go looking for furs,' Dean said. 'Good job Meyer's a stickler for keeping records.'

'So you know what you're looking for?'

'Oh, yes,' he said. 'So if you get a whisper, Pat . . . '

'Fred was one of us,' Pat said. 'Goes without saying.'

And he knew that most of his neighbours would think the same way. The police weren't liked in Spitalfields. Generally in the East End they were considered the enemy. But when one of their own was murdered, that was different. Fred had once told Pat that his family had first come to London in 1710, which meant that he had been more of a Londoner than anyone else in the manor.

Dean walked back towards Fred Lamb's house. His colleagues, notebooks in hand, were spreading out and knocking on doors. Not everyone would open up to them but, once the news about Fred was out, people would help. Pat thought about Artie Cross and wondered, yet again, if he'd been involved. He also wondered whether he might have voiced that suspicion to the police if his own boys hadn't been working for the man.

He didn't have to think about it for too long.

Thank Christ for Ben! Dolly Adler had one of the biggest hearts in the East End, but she could also jaw for Britain. She'd started the moment Solly had opened his eyes and she hadn't stopped until Ben had told her they'd run out of *beigels*. Then she'd taken her apron off, put on her hat and immediately headed for Brick Lane.

Ben sat down on Solly's bed and gave him a fag and a glass

of whisky. Solly smiled for the first time since he'd got home. His brother knew him well.

After a few minutes' companionable silence, Ben said, 'Wanna talk about it?'

'What – the war? No,' Solly said.

Ben had studied the situation in Spain closely before his brother had gone to fight.

'I heard there was infighting between the Commies and the Anarchists.'

Solly shook his head. 'They're all Republicans. All want to kick out Franco's fascists. Fighting among themselves is stupid. I can't ...'

His voice trailed off. He put out his fag and immediately lit up another. He said, 'Only good thing to come out of the whole mess, for me, was the Basques.'

'The who?' Ben said.

'The Basques. They're a separate group up in the North,' Solly explained. 'Not Spanish or French. Got their own language. They helped me get across the border into France. One old boy made me my peg-leg. Without him I would've died.'

Ever since she'd seen her son in Stratford, Dolly Adler hadn't stopped talking about how they had to get him a new, proper wooden leg to replace the peg: 'Like the one Mr Rich the baker's got'. It had given Solly a headache. The old leg looked horrible, but he was used to it. And anyway, what did it matter if it did look bad? It wasn't as if anyone he cared about romantically was waiting for him. Not a whisper from Miss Bernie Lynch, which had to mean she'd met someone else. And why not? Good-looking, girl like her!

'I was in a town called Guernica,' he said. 'Pretty place.'

Ben felt himself turn pale. 'Christ, Solly, I know that name! Weren't that place bombed to the ground a few weeks ago?'

Solly's eyes glazed over. 'The Germans done it,' he said. 'They'll kill us all. I tell you, Ben, if they get any more power, they'll come after us. You mark my words.'

The two young men fell quiet for a while. Solly watched as a group of hungry sparrows gathered hopefully outside his window, while Ben looked at his brother and wondered at how old he suddenly appeared.

In an effort to lighten the mood, he eventually broke the silence with, 'So what do you wanna do then, Sol? Go out for a pint? Go to the flicks? War hero like you'll be right bait for girls ... '

'No!'

Ben almost jumped. Solly didn't usually shout, it wasn't like him.

'No, no girls,' Solly said, his voice softer and his face averted. 'A pint maybe but ... '

'Wasn't there that blonde Irish girl ... '

But Ben stopped well before he finished his sentence because he saw Solly's eyes on him. They were full of pain and also hatred – although for what or whom Ben didn't know.

'Sol ... '

'There is no girl in my life, now or in the future,' he said. 'I know the one you mean. I wrote to her, she never wrote back. Anyway, I wouldn't want her or any other woman in my life now I'm like this. Not when I'm someone to be pitied. Would you?'

'Well, it's striking,' Mr Devenish said as he looked at the picture Bernie had carefully displayed in his shop window. 'Not sure it'll bring people in like a nice wedding photograph, though. It's a bit, well, artistic ... '

'Which could mean we'll get customers who want to buy photographs as works of art,' Bernie said.

Her employer looked at her disdainfully. 'And who around here does that?'

Bernie shrugged. It had taken a lot of persuasion to get Mr Devenish even to look at the pictures she'd taken at the Coronation street party. But he had and then, grudgingly, said he thought they were 'all right'. Bernie knew they were better than that. What's more, she knew that shots like this one, of a young girl dancing in front of a candle- and cake-strewn table, with a look of absolute bliss on her face, was the sort of photography she wanted to devote her talent to. Real images of real people in situations that were both ordinary yet amazing.

'Oh, let's see how it goes,' Mr Devenish said dismissively. 'You may as well have your lunch now, Bernadette.'

'Thank you, sir.'

He went back inside the shop while Bernie continued to gaze at her photograph. It had been the best she'd taken that day, and maybe any other day too. She'd even shown it to Mr Katz who had been, as he put it, 'more than impressed'. He'd gone on to tell her he thought she had a big career ahead of her, although he hadn't said how that might happen. Taking wedding photos alone couldn't build a big career, could it? And anyway, Bernie wasn't that keen on weddings. Or so she told herself. Becky had already asked her to take the photographs at her wedding, though as far as Bernie knew, no date had yet been set for it. Thoughts of Becky's wedding made her look across the road at Suss the Jeweller's.

She could see Chaim Suss, Becky's intended, serving a man who wore the big black furry hat that distinguished him as a very Orthodox Jew. Most of Suss's customers were. They came from that world. Becky's father was a religious man but not like *that*. Bernie wondered what sort of life her friend would lead around such people. She also wondered whether Becky had heard about Solly Adler.

Did Solly even mean anything to Becky any more? The girls saw so little of each other these days, Bernie didn't really know. But what she did know was that Solly still meant a lot to her. If only he had written to her as he'd said he would, she knew she would have walked over blazing coals to get to him. But he hadn't written and so that was that.

Kitty hung up the last of the Misses Lipmanns' bed sheets and bloomers in the yard and then sat down on the back step so she could catch her breath. It was horrible to think that Mr Lamb was dead. Her Pat hadn't been close to Fred Lamb, but they'd known each other and the weaver had been a respected member of the community. Kitty mused on the notion that there weren't many of those to the pound. Lamb's death also meant that someone else they might all know had been prepared to kill, to feather his own nest. The coppers were looking for Meyer Nadel's furs because they could lead them to the murderer.

Kitty knew a few fences. Her cousin Brendan had been put away for dealing in stolen goods. There were two on Brick Lane – Tommo Roth the rag dealer and Mr Leopold who worked in the Russian Vapour Baths. Pat had said that Constable Dean had gone straight down to Tommo's. With one hand on her aching back, Kitty got to her feet. No rest for the wicked. She still had the boys' blankets to do while the weather was halfway decent. All she had to do was get them out of the copper, put them through the mangle and then hang them out. Work so heavy even a donkey would have been hard pressed! And she'd left the alcove the three boys slept in like a tip when she'd stripped their beds . . .

If she left the blankets a while maybe Pat would be home

from his dad's and she could get him to help her. Although it pained her to admit it, Kitty didn't feel as strong as she once had. She tired much more quickly these days too. And she hadn't even thought about what they could have for tea! She went into the boys' alcove and began picking pillows and socks off the floor. Little Paddy was probably the tidiest of the three and Joey the most messy. Dermot was the only one who had books, which he did tend to scatter. Today was no exception.

It was while she was stacking a copy of *Dracula* on top of *Das Kapital* that one of Kitty's hands brushed against something that made her blood freeze.

Off shift and down the pub: that was a docker's life, or so men like Artie Cross always said. But Dermot Lynch wasn't like Artie or any of the other men he worked with and that included his brother Joey.

'A coupla pints'll make you feel better,' Joey said when he saw Dermot walk away from the rest of the mob going into the Railway.

Dermot didn't answer him. The West India had been swamped with rumours about Mr Lamb. Some said he was dying, others that he was already dead. One bloke had even told them that the coppers had caught whoever had done him in. But Dermot knew that wasn't true. Artie had spoken to all of them. He'd said, 'Just keep schtum and everything'll be all right.'

But Dermot knew it wouldn't. Walking with his cap pulled down and his hands in his pockets, he hoped he might somehow disappear into the filthy pavements of Limehouse. Anything to stop the events of that terrible night forever playing themselves over and over in his mind.

Dermot hadn't seen who exactly had hit the weaver over the

head. There'd been several blokes round him, one of whom had been Joey. But Dermot had been halfway over the wall at the time. And just because, when he'd seen Joey in the graveyard he'd had blood on his face, that didn't mean that he'd done it. Did it?

It might. Joey had been beside himself that night and, when he'd stuffed his cut of the furs into his old rucksack underneath the bed, he'd acted like the cock of the walk. Until the family had got back from the street party, he'd done nothing but go on about what he was going to buy once he'd sold his share. Dermot hadn't even wanted to touch the furs. As far as he was concerned Joey could do what he wanted as long as he shut up about it. When the rucksack had gone, Dermot had breathed a sigh of relief. But the guilt remained ...

Up ahead he saw Chrissy Dolan come out of a doorway and pour a bucket of water into the gutter. He didn't want to talk to anyone, but Chrissy had seen him.

'Chris,' Dermot greeted him.

As ever, he was clean and relatively smart but Chrissy looked careworn and dark around the eyes, as if he wasn't sleeping. He smiled but looked over his shoulder as if expecting someone to be behind him. Then he took Dermot's arm and pulled him into an alleyway. Dermot felt his heart begin to pound.

Chrissy whispered, 'Look, I can't be long because I'll be missed but I have to tell you something.'

'What?'

Dermot felt his face colour and hoped that Chrissy didn't notice.

'I don't know if you've heard where I work ... '

Of course Dermot had. A knocking shop full of old whores, although he didn't know what Chrissy did there.

'Yeah.'

'I can imagine what you must think of me for that but I can't worry about it. I had to find work and it was all I could get. But, Dermot, I have to tell you . . . I saw someone come and speak to Madam – Mrs Smith-Brown – about photographs. It was your Bernie's boss.'

'Devenish? Yeah, well, he's a photographer,' Dermot said. 'So what?'

'People only come to our place for . . . you know. And so then he turns up with some little girls and his camera, and our old girls – they put on dresses like the kids'. They looked horrible! And then they all went into a room together.' Chrissy shook his head. 'Dilys . . . she's one of our oldest ladies . . . she told me what happened next.'

'What do you mean?' Dermot asked, with a sick feeling in his stomach.

Chrissy closed his eyes momentarily. 'They made them do things to the little girls,' he said. 'Sex things. Dilys didn't like it. But she said Devenish threatened them . . . said he'd cut them, and the kids, if they didn't do as they were told. He don't look it, I know, but that man's violent. He's also mixed up in some horrible things.' Chrissy put his hand on Dermot's shoulder. 'I thought I should tell you, for Bernie's sake. She should know she's working for a pervert. Dilys told me after he took the photos Devenish joined in.'

All Dermot could think of to say was, 'But she loves that job.'

Chrissy shook his head again. 'I'm just saying what I know, Dermot. Been trying to tell you for days. I couldn't live with myself if Bernie got involved in anything bad.'

Chrissy was such a good friend. Dermot had never had one like him. For just a moment he slid his arms around the smaller boy and hugged him.

*

240

The little girls who tap-danced on a board outside the Jolly Butchers knew all about the murder of Fred Lamb even though they could barely speak English.

'The veaver is dead!' they shouted. 'Horrible murder!'

Mrs Diamond the *mikvah* attendant told them to, 'Shut up with the murder talk!'

Men in Homburgs whispered together in tight-knit huddles, while drunks looked nervously over their shoulders for policemen.

And, for once, 'the law' was visible everywhere in and around Brick Lane. In the pubs, on the streets, in kosher butchers, vapour baths and the brewery. Even Baruch Zilberman the street singer stopped his warbling to say to Becky, 'The poor weaver has died. A *goy*, trying to help his Yiddisher neighbour! They say Meyer Nadel will pay for his funeral. Imagine ... '

Becky had always liked Mr Lamb the weaver. He had been like a visitor from a previous era. Polite and meticulous, he had always raised his hat to her even when she'd been a small child. But, to her shame, Becky wasn't as fixated on Mr Lamb's death as most people were. There was another story on Brick Lane which, though less dramatic, was no less gripping to her.

How had Solly Adler managed to get home from Spain when he'd been so badly hurt? It was said he'd been hidden in a haycart and brought across the border into France by anarchists. That he'd married a French Communist woman who had driven him home, and, the one people claimed to have heard from his mother, that he had walked from the Pyrenees to Paris on a peg-leg made by a gypsy.

The people of the East End loved a good story, but Becky doubted whether any of these were completely true. Solly, because of his politics and his good looks, had been a local legend since well before the Civil War in Spain. Why shouldn't

241

that continue now he was home? Not that it should concern her. Solly wasn't going to be her husband, that was Chaim, which was only right and proper. Chaim had money, he was polite and socially acceptable. Most importantly, her papa wanted the match. So that was that.

She knew she should really talk to Bernie. But, even though they were like sisters, Becky knew she couldn't start such a conversation. Solly hadn't written to her, which had hurt Bernie. But because she was a strong girl, she'd accepted it. She'd said she wasn't even thinking about him any more even though she'd told Becky that she had to declare *her* feelings for him. At the time, they hadn't known whether he was alive or dead. But Bernie had been adamant. Becky loved Solly and so she shouldn't marry Chaim. And Becky knew that was true.

He'd been able to see all the coppers gathered around the end of his road when he was on Commercial Street so Dermot walked down Brick Lane instead. He saw Becky Shapiro and they waved to each other, but the Lane was packed and anyway he didn't want to talk. Not to anyone.

Even as he walked down the area steps, Dermot knew that something was wrong. There was no noise coming from inside. His mum had been hard at work washing for the Misses Lipmann when he'd left that morning. She couldn't be finished yet. And where were the kids?

He opened the front door and saw his dad sitting in his chair beside the range.

'Hello, son.'

Pat Lynch was a smiling man. He always smiled when he saw his kids. He usually shuffled over and hugged them too. But not this time. Dermot felt his heart begin to pound.

'Dad.' He looked around. 'Where is everybody?'

Pat cleared his throat and said, 'Your mum and the kids have gone down your nana's.'

'Why?' Dermot put his hook up on the nail on the wall.

His dad reached behind him and pulled out something that made Dermot gasp.

'Because your mum found this,' Pat said as he held up the mink coat. 'Under your mattress.'

Dermot had taken nothing. Everyone else had, but he had refused. Even the hat someone had thrust into his hand, he'd thrown away.

His father put the coat down on the floor beside his chair and said, 'Don't waste your breath telling me you don't know where it come from. We both know.'

'It's not mine.'

'No, it's Meyer Nadel's,' Pat said. 'What I want to know is how it come to be under your bed.'

Joey. He'd taken two coats. This had to be one of them. Why had he put it under his brother's bed if not to incriminate him? Bastard!

'I never took anything from Meyer's, Dad,' Dermot said. 'Nothing!'

'Maybe not, but you was there, you little shit!'

Pat Lynch didn't roar like other people's dads. He didn't use his belt as a weapon and his eyes had never blazed with fury. Until now

'Dad . . .'

'There are marks from a hook on Meyer's back wall,' Pat said. 'And don't think I don't know Artie Cross hates the Jews. I know it better'n most. What did he do? Threaten never to call you on again if you didn't help at the warehouse? Why didn't you come to me? I'd've sorted him!'

'Dad, you're sick.'

243

'Not too sick to give that piece of scum the hiding of his life ...'

'You know that ain't true!'

Pat stood up, shakily. 'And what about your brother?'

'He's still down the pub.'

'I'm not asking where he is! I know! Artie's little prince is Joey. Was he with you the night you done Meyer Nadel's place? Don't answer that ... of course he was.'

Dermot didn't say anything.

Pat picked up the mink. 'So is this his or yours?'

Dermot wanted to confess – to all of it – but the words wouldn't come. Especially the words that would incriminate his brother. Joey had become someone else since he'd been in deep with Artie and his mob, but he was still Dermot's brother.

'You know I know it's his, don't ya?' Pat said. 'Because we both know what Joey's become. And I admire your loyalty to your brother. I do, boy. But what do we do now, eh? Fred Lamb's dead. You heard that?'

'I heard a rumour ...'

'Well, it's true,' Pat said. 'Why'd'ya think the manor's full of coppers today? They're looking for the murderer. They're looking for the bloke as needs to swing for Fred's murder and that man does need to swing ...'

'I never saw who done it!' Dermot said. 'On my life!'

'Yeah, but you're gonna tell me what you do know,' Pat said. 'You'll sit in your mother's chair and you'll tell me or I'll kill you meself.'

His whole body shaking, Dermot sat down in his mother's chair on the other side of the range.

His father said, 'Start from the beginning and tell me all of it. Leave nothing out because I'll know if you do and then there'll be hell to pay.'

*

The little girl's family sat behind the camera and, even if Bernie hadn't been able to hear them, she'd have been able to smell them. The Collinses were poor even by East End standards. The old man, who liked a drink more than he should, was in and out of work while it was said that his wife had come from the workhouse. Eleven children later and Mrs Collins pregnant with her twelfth, they'd come to have photographs taken of eight-year-old Concepta in her first Communion dress. Where they'd got the dress from and how they were going to pay for the photographs was anyone's guess. But they would. A child's First Holy Communion was important. Bernie had created a tasteful backdrop for the little girl who, she could tell, was pleased with the way she looked in her pretty white dress.

It was while Bernie was framing the shot that she saw smudges of what was probably coal dust on the hem of the dress. She got some soap and was attempting to wipe it off when Mrs Collins said, 'You've a picture of a young girl in your window. Did you take that yourself, Miss Lynch?'

'I did, Mrs Collins,' Bernie said.

'I love it.'

Bernie looked behind her. Mrs Collins' thin face was full of tension. 'The child is poor, your picture tells the truth about her,' she said.

Bernie smiled. 'Thank you.'

'Ah, Communist nonsense!' Mr Collins said.

He wasn't drunk but he was in need of a drink and therefore belligerent. Mrs Collins didn't contradict him, probably because she didn't want to suffer a beating later on. But Bernie knew that she'd made a connection with her. And if someone as poor as this woman understood her photographs, Bernie knew that others would too.

*

245

'I was halfway over the wall,' Dermot said. 'But I could see there was a group gathered around Mr Lamb. Joey was one of them but I don't know whether he or one of the others hit him. I swear to you, Dad, I don't know!'

'But it could have been?'

'I s'pose ...'

'Whoever done it'll hang.'

Had it been Joey? Dermot had thought about that moment a thousand times since. He hadn't slept properly at night for thinking about it. But he still didn't know.

Pat got out of his chair and walked over to his son. He raised his fist.

'Tell me now, boy, or I'll knock your block off.'

Every part of Dermot shook. If his dad hit him it could change everything between them. Pat Lynch wasn't a violent man. But he was angry, so angry ...

'What did Artie say about it after?'

He couldn't speak. If he told, he and Joey would never work again! Not just in the docks, but anywhere. Grasses were never trusted, they were cast out and so were their families. His dad had to know that.

Pat punched him square in the face. Dermot felt his nose crack and watched as blood ran down onto his shirt.

'Tell me!'

'Aggie?'

Bernie had just said goodnight to Mr Devenish when she saw her youngest sister walking towards her.

'You've gotta come down Wapping, we're at Nan's,' the ten year old said.

'At Nan's? Why?'

Bernie knew that her mammy hated going to Wapping to see

her mother. Nana Burke was so bitter and twisted, being with her was depressing.

'Dunno. But we're all down there,' Aggie said. 'Except for Dad.'

'Where's he?'

'At home.'

'Are Dermot and Joey down Nan's?'

'No.'

Bernie frowned. That didn't sound right.

'What's going on?'

Aggie shrugged. 'Mum told me to come and get you. She said you're not to go home.'

There were police all over the place because of Mr Lamb's murder. Maybe her dad had wanted them all to get away from that? But nobody they knew could've had anything to do with it. Her mammy and dad knew some dodgy people, true, but murder was something different. Or was it?

Bernie couldn't not know. She just couldn't. She said, 'Look, Aggie, you go back to Nan's and I'll see you there later. I've got something to do first.'

Chapter Nineteen

Joey Lynch looked at his brother's bloodied face and then at his father.

'What's going on here?' he said. 'You two had a barney?'

Then he saw the fur coat and his face dropped.

His father said, 'Yes, the coat you stole from Nadel's.'

'No, I never, that was him!'

He pointed at his brother. Had the stupid little poof told their dad everything? Artie'd have something to say about it if he had!

'I took nothing!' Dermot yelled.

'Oh, and you think I did?'

Joey was blind drunk. Artie had bought all the rounds and no one even commented on it. But then everyone knew what they had to do. If they all kept together and stayed schtum they'd be all right. Artie wouldn't lie to them.

'Well, no one else in this family would have done something like that!' Pat said.

'The coppers know it was someone on the docks,' Dermot said. 'They'll find out in the end!'

Joey lifted his chin in defiance. The two of them were barmy! 'So what's all the fuss about some rich Jew's coats?' he said. 'Jews who steal our jobs and our houses ...'

'Oh, listen to yourself!' Pat gasped. He sat down again, he could barely stand. 'I never brought you up to think like that! That's fucking Artie Cross ...'

'Artie's done more for me ...'

'Than your own family? Yeah, yeah, that's how he gets a hold on people and makes them do what he wants,' Pat said. 'Years ago when his Linda married a Jewish boy he was completely against it. Good comrade that kid ...'

'Yeah, but ...'

'Shut up and listen!' Pat said. 'Poor Linda died in childbirth. Nobody's fault. But from then on Artie's been dead set against the Jews. And he's a tea-leaf. Always was. I kept me gob shut about that because I needed the work and because it's what we do. Then he beat up that poor boy's auntie and uncle, and still I kept it shut, God forgive me. But I won't this time. I know without you even telling me that it was Artie as thumped Fred Lamb and killed him. The man's a fucking bully ...'

'Oh, well, that's where you're wrong,' Joey said.

Pat shook his head. 'Nah.'

'Artie never killed him,' Joey said.

'So who did?'

'I'm not grassing anyone up. And I won't let you grass either.'

'Oh, yeah? What you gonna do about it?' Dermot said.

Joey turned towards his brother, just in time to see his sister Bernie walk into the flat.

'Do about it?' Joey said. 'Nothing, bruv. Because none of you'll say anything to anyone.'

Bernie said, 'Say anything about what?'

'How you gonna stop us, Joey?' Pat Lynch said.

'By telling you the truth.'

And then he smiled.

'And what is the truth Joey?' Pat asked, with a feeling of dread.

'Truth is, Dad, I killed Fred Lamb. I never meant to. But I ain't gonna hang for it because all you lot are going to *keep your gobs shut.*'

Mrs Rabinowicz always went to bed early. She liked to get what she called her 'beauty sleep'. But what she actually did, for hours on end, was read magazines. Rose didn't know what any of them were because she still couldn't make her letters into words. Luckily, because of Mrs Rabinowicz's many, many 'knick-knacks' there was always dusting to be done, otherwise she would just have laid on her bed looking at the ceiling.

It hadn't been a bad day although seeing Len standing about outside had been a shock. Rose wondered why her mum had sent him to see her and not come herself. She hoped Nell wasn't ill. Maybe when she went round the next day she'd take her some kaolin and morphine from the pharmacist's. Her mum sometimes suffered with her stomach but that stuff usually put her right. If Rose could afford it, she'd get some.

Mrs Rabinowicz had looked down her nose at Len, as well she might, but she and Rose's step-father were quite alike in one respect. Like Len, Mrs Rabinowicz couldn't look at anything without either saying what it was worth or speculating about it. Whenever she took her jewellery off at night she'd tell Rose, 'My engagement ring, solitaire, very good-quality diamond, worth at least four hundred, if not five. Those earrings, Hatton Garden, made for me, emeralds and diamonds, two hundred and fifty pounds at the very least . . . '

Rose knew that the matchmaker had been poor in her youth and that was how not being poor any more affected some people. Or so she'd observed. The poor who remained poor, like her mum, either gave up thinking about such things or else like Len they lusted after stuff they couldn't have, all the time. Rose was like her mum. She didn't want much. The main thing was to have someone to love and who loved you too. But life didn't often work out like that. Both Bernie and Becky loved Solly Adler and that wasn't right. Especially now Becky was going to marry somebody else. And what about Rose herself?

The only boy she'd ever really liked was Dermot Lynch, but she had no idea what he thought about her. They'd been to the pictures together that once, but he hadn't tried to kiss her. Then again, that had been a relief. Because everyone knew where kissing could lead and Rose was determined she'd never do *that* again. Now she was away from Len she didn't have to. And she never would.

Nobody moved until Pat rose from his chair and said, 'Well, you won't silence me.'

Although not quite as tall as Joey, when he stood up straight Pat's eyes were nearly on a level with his son's.

Fearing a fight her father would lose, Bernie put herself between the two men.

'Joey, Dad, we have to talk about this . . . '

'We have,' Joey said, and balled his fists. He stank of beer and sweat and his eyes were bulging with anger.

'Stop protecting that toe-rag!' Pat said. 'He's a killer!'

'We don't know that, Dad!'

'Joey said *he* killed Fred Lamb! You heard him!'

'He's boasting! He wants to be a big man! It was an accident!' Bernie gabbled.

She was desperate. Joey might have become a different person in the last year, but he was still her brother and she loved him. Everybody stood without moving until Dermot said, 'I was there and I'll hold my hands up to it. But I won't grass up Joey nor anyone else.'

'Then you'll hang,' Pat said. 'For something you say you never done!' He breathed deeply to calm himself. 'Dermot, did your brother have blood on him when he finished at the furrier's? Do you remember seeing blood?'

Dermot knew that he had. But he said nothing. Joey had taken that shirt to work with him the morning after and thrown it into the dock.

Joey raised his chin. 'Yes, I did,' he said. 'And I'd do it again. We're fighting for our lives here, Dad. These Yids'll finish us!'

Pat, suddenly exhausted, sank down and put his head in his hands. 'God help me, what did I do wrong to raise something like you?'

Dermot went to his father and knelt down beside him. 'Dad, it's not your fault,' he said. 'It's Artie Cross and his mob. They're bullies and he, if not the rest of them, is a fascist. It's too hard not to go along with him. He hands out the work. He got me too, remember? I was at Meyer Nadel's ...'

'Yes, but you never killed no one.'

'He's too much of a poof!'

Bernie punched Joey in the ribs and he doubled over.

'You fucking ...'

'Shut your filthy mouth!' Pat roared. 'Don't speak to your sister like that!'

Amazed at the force she'd put behind that punch, and at how much her fist hurt, Bernie shook with rage and misery. Her brother was a self-confessed murderer! How would she ever be able to look anyone in the eye again? How could the family go on living here?

When he spoke again, Pat Lynch sounded exhausted. He

said, 'Seems to me all of this rests at Artie's door, so I should go and see him. Sort it out.'

Joey went white. 'You . . . '

'Yes, I fucking can, and yes, I fucking will!' Pat said. 'That man's as guilty as sin and what he's made of you, well, you shame everyone in this family. So you take that coat you nicked and you lay it on Meyer's front doorstep and then you leave here and never come back.' He looked up at his eldest son for the last time. 'You're dead to me, understand? Dead.'

'He wants to stay in with his old mum,' Dolly Adler said as she stroked the side of Solly's face. 'As usual.'

She was driving him mad.

His brother said, 'Mum, why don't you and Mr Green go down the pub while I stay with Solly? Give you a break?'

Another irritation was their mum's beau, Stanley Green. Solly had never met such a buttoned-up old bore in his life! Going on all the time about his house and his car and his this, that and the other! And since when had Dolly become a gold-digger?

'Oh, I'm happy with me cuppa,' the old man said as he held up one of Dolly's best teacups.

Too bloody mean to pay for a sherry and a pint, more like it! He might have money but he wasn't often seen spending it. As far as Solly could tell, Mr Green was taking more from the Adler household than he was giving.

'Well, I'm going down the pub then,' Ben said.

As he passed Solly on his way out, he said, 'Fuck this.'

When his brother had gone, Solly knew he should have gone with him. But then he knew he didn't want to be seen out anywhere until he'd had a decent leg made for himself. The peg he'd got in Guernica had meant he'd made it home, it was comfortable, but he didn't want anyone seeing it now. He especially didn't want Bernie Lynch to see it. If he ever saw her again.

Solly would have been happier staying with Roy Oberman's parents. He'd not really wanted to come home. He knew Dolly would fuss and that people would want to talk to him about Spain. But he didn't want to talk about it. Even though people needed to know what fascists could and had done, he wasn't the man to tell them. He was in too much pain, both physically and in his mind. All he wanted to do was be quiet and try not to think about it.

Dolly, still fussing, said, 'Here, Solomon, I've got some milk stout in the pantry. You fancy a bottle, don't you? You always liked a drop of milk stout ...'

'No, thanks, Mum.'

Solly pushed himself up out of his chair.

'Think I'll turn in, if it's all the same to you.'

'Oh, yes,' Mr Green said. 'Can't beat plenty of shut-eye.'

In the bedroom he shared with Ben, Solly sat beside the window and looked down into the street. What a grim, dark dump this place was! If nothing else, Spain had opened his eyes to the beauty of sunlight. Even when they were fighting for every street in Madrid, with blood on the pavements, the fact that the sun still shone had given Solly hope. Probably misplaced but it had kept him going.

And now what? Back to the ghetto for him and, in spite of Cable Street, there were still anti-Semitic daubs on every other wall. The people here didn't have a clue about the wider world and he didn't have the strength to change that. Christ, what a hollow 'hero' he was!

Down in the street, a group sitting on the pavement inspected their disintegrating shoes while sharing a fag. Even the lowest prostitutes lurking in shop doorways ignored the unemployed. What was the point in accosting them? They didn't have anything. Suddenly there was noise below. Two men and a girl walking quickly in the direction of the river. The girl, whose long blonde hair streamed out behind her like a scarf, was crying.

'Dad, no!' Solly heard her say, over and over again. 'Dad, no!'

And Solly wondered what Bernie Lynch was so upset about and what her father was about to do. He wanted to shout out to her but she didn't want him, did she? What was the point? A girl like that would have someone else by this time. A real man.

That had been a good night. The Jew's furs had bought a lot of rounds, a few bunk-ups with some girls, and there were still two more coats left in Artie's coal cellar. So far his old woman hadn't twigged and probably never would, the thick cow. He'd get himself a suit from one of the Jews on the Lane and then go up West and treat himself to a real classy woman.

When he left the Railway, Artie was on top of the world.

But it didn't last.

He was on Watney Street, almost at his front door, when he was pushed up against the window of the grocer's, a hand squeezing his throat.

'Now you open your lug'oles and listen to me,' Pat Lynch wheezed into his face. He was a sick man, his breath smelled like death. 'I know what you done at Meyer Nadel's.'

So that fucking little iron Dermot had grassed! Standing beside his father, holding Artie's arms, pretending to be a hard man. But then he remembered that Dermot Lynch hadn't actually seen what had been done to the weaver . . .

'Oh, fuck off, Lynch!' Artie snarled.

'And my son Joey's paying the price for it,' Pat said.

Christ! Had Lynch gone to the coppers with Joey? Artie felt his heart begin to pound.

'Homeless my boy is now,' Pat wheezed. ''Cause of you.'

'Me?'

'Our Joey tells me he killed Fred Lamb the night you stupid bastards robbed Meyer Nadel. So you done a right good job on him, didn't you?'

'What do you mean?'

'All that loyalty pony you used to pedal at me, you used on him,' Pat said. 'See, I know he never done Fred Lamb. That ain't what Joey's like. Easy led he may be, but he's no killer. But I know who is.'

How could he? Dermot Lynch hadn't seen what happened because he was on the wall and Joey hadn't blabbed. Maybe someone else had. But who?

'So here's the deal,' Pat said. 'Now our Joey's gone ... '

'Where?'

'Never you mind. He ain't your business,' Pat said. 'But our Dermot is. You call my boy on for as long as he needs and you and your mob don't give him no grief and we'll say no more about it. And you don't get him involved in no more of your scams, you hear me?'

Artie heard the girl, Bernadette, say, 'Dad, they killed a man! You can't ... '

'And if this family don't work, we'll all die too!' he said.

Fucking Irish bastards! Artie felt the drink course defiantly through his veins. 'And what if I don't agree?'

'Then I'll go to the law,' Pat said.

'What? With your own boys involved?'

'Yes.'

And Artie believed him. Just one look in the man's blazing eyes was enough to convince him.

'And if that don't work, I'll kill ya,' Pat said. 'Don't think I won't. And don't forget, I know all about your other little scams too. For years I watched you and your mob and did nothing because you left me alone. But that's changed now. You made my boy something that he weren't until he started working for you, and I will never forgive you for that.'

Christ knew where a sick man like Pat Lynch got the strength from but the next thing Artie knew he'd been punched in the stomach – and it hurt like hell.

Holding her ring under the light from the gas lamp made its facets reflect rainbows across the walls of her bedroom. Everyone liked that ring. It was beautiful. A lot of people were jealous of her and not just because of the ring. Becky's intended was going to take her on honeymoon. She couldn't remember hearing about anyone else who'd been on one of those, except for the *shadchan* who'd gone to Devon. Most of the ladies she worked for had been lucky to have a day out in Southend. And here Becky was, going to Amsterdam! She should be happy ...

Becky walked over to her bedroom window and looked outside. As usual kids were still playing in the street while women gossiped on their doorsteps. Fournier Street was poor and dirty and it made her sad that so many of the kids here were so thin, but she knew she didn't want to leave this place.

She'd been to Chaim's house in Stamford Hill three times now and familiarity didn't make it any better. It was much quieter there, the people were fatter and they had more money, but it wasn't her home and it never would be. The way things were now, she rarely saw her friends; she'd never see them again if she moved to Stamford Hill. And what about her ambition to become a nurse? Her work as a mother's help had been intended to give her an advantage when she applied to train as a nurse ...

if she ever did apply now. As Chaim's wife, Becky knew that she wouldn't.

He and his family were Orthodox and Orthodox women didn't work. They stayed at home and had lots of children and looked after their husbands. They also wore wigs and, though many of them were wealthy, their everyday clothes were deliberately dowdy. Jewish Communists hated them. There'd once been a story that had gone around about Commie boys throwing bacon at *frummers* as they came out of Synagogue. Her papa, she knew, had believed it. But then he always thought badly of the Communists. He thought badly of Solly Adler.

Down in the street, mad Hyman Salzedo swung around a lamp-post singing tunelessly while Bernie's oldest brother Joey ran past with a large bundle underneath his arm. Sitting on her area steps was Rose's mother Nell, smoking a cigarette and looking up and down the street, clocking the other women, who felt they were a cut above her, and occasionally laughing at them.

Night-time in Spitalfields had a strange, edgy magic all its own. With its towering church on Commercial Street, its Huguenot houses with their huge weaving windows and elegant Georgian doorways, the many Synagogues, vapour baths and markets that could have been lifted straight from Poland or Lithuania, it was a place set apart with its own unique culture, haunted by diaspora and yet vibrantly alive. Just the thought of leaving it made Becky want to weep.

Chapter Twenty

She'd had no sleep, but then neither had Dermot. While their father had collapsed onto his bed as soon as they'd got home, Bernie and her brother hadn't been able to. They'd talked and she'd done her best to patch up Dermot's nose, but it was broken and so all she'd done was stuff it up with rags.

He hadn't said why he'd got involved in Artie Cross's plan to rob Nadel the furrier. But she knew. Dermot had always been a bit of a square peg. As a kid he'd stood up to people who tried to bully the small, soft ones like Chrissy Dolan. Since he wasn't loud like Joey, people often got the wrong idea about Dermot, which meant he got into trouble. Dermot had acted as he had because he'd feared for his job.

Once her brother had left for work, the flat became strangely quiet except for the sound of her dad, snuffling and snorting in the bedroom. While she waited to go to work, Bernie wondered where Joey had gone and what he was doing now. He'd left with almost nothing; even his docker's hook still hung on its nail by the door. What was he going to do? All Bernie knew was that her dad would never have him home again. How could he?

Her dad would tell her mum when she came home but Bernie doubted whether the kids would be told the truth. They blabbed and so some story would have to be made up for their benefit – and everyone else's. There were things that went wrong in families and then there were things that were too shameful to tell. This was one of them.

Whatever her dad said, Bernie couldn't help wondering whether Joey really was a murderer. She'd heard him own up to it, and it had sounded convincing to her. But was it? Her dad said he 'knew' that Artie Cross was the real murderer, but was he? Would any of them ever know? And even if they did, what good would it do?

Bernie knew that her father would suffer for not having grassed up Artie, Joey and the rest of them. He'd probably never be able to look Meyer Nadel or Fred Lamb's daughter in the face again. But she understood why he'd had no choice but to act as he had. Grasses didn't get work in the East End, and if you didn't work, you died. The shop doorways of Spitalfields were full of the homeless, dead or dying. Some people laughed at the Communists for always going on about 'class war' but Bernie could see it coming if things didn't change. Only so many poor people could die ...

Before she left for work, she woke Pat up.

'Dad, what do I say if anyone asks where Joey's gone?'

Her dad thought about this while he coughed and then said, 'Tell 'em he's gone to the Irish Free State. Tell 'em he's gone to reclaim his homeland.'

Then he laughed, joylessly.

The Salzedo family lived on the top floor of the Rothschild Buildings in Flower and Dean Street. There were a lot of them. As well as Hyman, the mad boy of Spitalfields, there were his parents,

Rosa and Reuben the *mohel*, his sister Marie, brother Irving, his wife Anna and their three–year-old twins Robert and Doris. Now Anna Salzedo was pregnant for a second time their numbers were about to increase. And so, in spite of having a sister-in-law and a mother-in-law to help her with the housework and the nippers, Anna had asked for a mother's help, which was why Becky had just schlepped up so many flights of stairs. When she arrived she was greeted by the sight of Rosa and her daughter watching helplessly as the twins ran up and down the landing, screaming. Marie, their aunt, put her fingers in her ears as she dragged hard on a cigarette and said, 'They're driving us all bonkers!'

Becky introduced herself and then grabbed the twins' hands and took them inside the flat. They both tried to squirm out of her grasp but Becky held on tight. She heard Rosa say, 'Thank Gawd they've gone!'

The expectant mother, when Becky found her, was hanging over the kitchen sink.

'Sorry, love,' she said once she saw her helper, 'I've got the sickness with this one. Never had it with the twins. Feel like I'm bloody dying!'

Then she was sick again.

Becky said, 'There's not a problem, Mrs Salzedo.' Even though the smell made her want to heave. 'You just ... er ...'

'Just keep them little buggers away from me,' Anna Salzedo said. 'If you can take them out or something, I'd be obliged.'

Becky had wondered whether she might do some drawing with the kids or perhaps read them a story, but there wasn't a pencil or a book in the place. The Salzedos did have a pushchair though, a vast home-made thing that was kept underneath the stairs on the ground floor. She had to tie them in with string, which Robert and Doris didn't like, but where restraint didn't work, Becky used bribery.

'If you keep still and behave yourselves we can go and see the Tower of London,' she said. 'And, if you're VERY good maybe we'll get some sweets.'

The twins squeaked with delight.

'Sherbet dab!'

'Lollipop!'

'Gobstopper!'

'What a Tower of London?'

Becky showed them. Only from the outside. Doris kept on asking whether there was a princess inside, while Robert went on and on about sweets until she got them a sherbet dab each. Then, squashed together in the pushchair, they both went to sleep.

She was pushing them along Commercial Street when she saw Solly Adler, leaning up against the wall beside the kosher butcher's, his eyes closed against the sun. He looked weather-beaten and thin but he was still handsome and Becky really wanted to say hello. But, even though every part of her ached to talk to him, she didn't. That part of her life ... the Commie boys, Cable Street, a new world where women could do what they wanted ... that was all over. As her papa never tired of saying, there was a war coming and Jews needed to be safe and that meant having money. The Suss family had relatives in Holland and so if things got really bad they could always go there. She'd see what she thought about it when she went there on honeymoon.

Later, when she got the twins home, a grateful Anna Salzedo made her a cup of tea. Becky noticed that the other two women were still sitting outside the flat smoking and gossiping. No wonder the poor woman needed help.

'Me mother-in-law's got nerves,' Anna said by way of explan-ation, 'and course she's always worried about Hyman. With him not being right.'

Becky smiled. Everyone knew Hyman Salzedo and most people looked out for him. But she could also appreciate the family's concern.

'Then there's Marie,' Anna confided. 'Thirty and still not married! Won't happen now. Going about with a face like a sour lemon.' Then she brightened. 'But you're engaged, aren't you?'

'Yes.'

'*Mazeltov*. Mr Suss the jeweller's son.' Anna smiled. 'You're a pretty girl though, and young. Of course you'll get a good man. Don't think Marie was ever young and she's far from pretty.'

Life was cruel, Becky thought. The way her mum had died young, her papa had been left alone, Marie Salzedo was on the shelf and she herself entering into a marriage she knew would be without love. Chaim was polite and apparently kind, and he was very complimentary about her looks, but whether he liked her or not, Becky didn't know. Was it even important to him?

'I can't work, see, lovey. Not like this,' Nell said to her daughter. 'No one'll come near. Not when I've got these ulcers.'

Rose had never seen her mother's 'ulcers', she didn't even know where they were. But she did remember when Nell had them before. Then, as now, she couldn't 'work' and she experienced a lot of pain.

'But they went, didn't they?' Rose said. 'Last time you had them?'

'Oh, yes,' Nell said. 'But I had some money then.'

'Have you bought some medicine?'

'I went to the doctor,' Nell said. 'Len took us. Doctor give me a piece a paper to take to the pharmacy.'

'What was the medicine?'

She shrugged. 'I dunno, girl. Can't read any more'n you can. But I know you need the paper to get the stuff.'

'You need to pay for it an' all.'

'Yeah.'

Len always managed to get money when he needed to, Rose knew that, and she also knew her mum did too. So if Len wasn't paying for medicine, the only conclusion Rose ecould come to was that she was expected to cough up herself.

'But, Mum, I give you most of me money as it is! Where's that gone?'

'Rent. Some of it.'

The rest went on booze. And if her mum wasn't working that made sense. It was pointless asking whether Len was working or not.

'I can't ask Mrs Rabinowicz for no more wages.'

'Not on tick?'

'No, Mum! She's a proper lady, she don't do no tick like some bookie's runner!'

'Yeah, but chavvie, if I can't work ... '

'I know, Mum, I know,' Rose said. 'Shut up a bit and let me think, will you!'

Nell folded her legs up beneath her as she leaned back in the one easy chair beside the fireplace.

Rose's brain whirled. The last time her mum had had these ulcers she'd not been able to work for a month and they'd nearly been chucked out of the flat. In spite of that Len had not offered to help; he never did. Rose had always suspected that he made money from somewhere other than her mum, but she didn't know where. Whatever was going on, he kept it to himself. And he'd do the same this time too. What was more, she knew she was being used – by her mum and by Len Tobin. Not that her mum would have wanted to ask her unless she'd been desperate.

Mrs Rabinowicz wouldn't give her maid any more money

and she certainly wouldn't give her any on tick. If Rose had anything to pawn she'd do it, but she didn't.

'Mum, couldn't you borrow ... '

'Oh, no, no, no!' Nell waved her arms as if repelling a curse. 'No, I can't go to them people ... Jews and the like!'

'Mum!'

'No, you has to do it, Rosie,' Nell said. 'You know Jews. You get it for me. Then, when I'm well, I can pay you back.'

But Rose knew that she wouldn't. Still she said, 'Yes, Mum.'

Nell smiled then and Rose saw something that might have been an ulcer break open on her lip and bleed.

How on earth was Rose going to deal with a moneylender? She was just a maid! She couldn't do it. But she still had to find some way to help her mum.

'Feter Walter?'

Walter Katz looked up. His hands stopped balling string, then he smiled and said, 'Ah, Heinrich! *Shalom Aleichem*!'

The man smiled back. *'Aleichem Shalom,'* he said. 'But let us speak English, my dear uncle. We are in London! We are both English now!'

The two men embraced.

'Ah, Heinrich Suskind!' Walter Katz said. 'Let me look at you! I remember when you were in short trousers. I remember when you went to university. Now you're ... what is it? Thirty-five? Forty?'

The man laughed. 'Oh, Uncle, I'm fifty,' he said. 'Last week!'

'Fifty!' The old man waved the notion away. 'How can that be?'

Heinrich shrugged. 'I got old. Where's your brother? Where's Uncle Herman?'

'Out,' Walter said. Then whispered, 'He goes to see his

runner, you know, for betting on the horses. He thinks I don't know, but ...'

Heinrich laughed. Although he had a German name his accent was entirely 'London' as were his clothes, which were very smart. Tall and slim, he looked every inch the successful English businessman.

'So what have you been doing?' the old man asked. 'I've not seen you since we left Berlin. Since then I was in Hamburg, then Frankfurt, now here. How long have you been in London? What are you doing here? Why haven't I seen you before this?'

The younger man laughed. 'So many questions!'

'*Nu*?'

'So we came ten years ago. Abba saw the writing on the wall. We're British now, changed our name and everything.'

'To?'

'We're called Simpson.'

'So why didn't I see you? Herman and I are here a long time too. All Yiddisher people come here.' Then Walter smiled and said, 'Ah, but your abba had good connections, I know. So where'd you live now then, eh? Somewhere up West? Somewhere smart?'

His visitor nodded.

'And you still write? Tell me you still write!'

Heinrich smiled. 'Reporter,' he said. 'On the *London Evening News*.'

'*Oy vey*!'

'German affairs,' he added.

'German!'

'Yes. I speak the language. Why not?' He took the old man's hand. 'I am British now. I can enter Germany and come back. I can tell people here what it's like for Jews over there. What it's really like.'

266

Walter Katz shook his head. 'And is it . . . '

'Hitler gets stronger all the time. Jews walk in the shadows. I do what I can, Uncle. I do what I can.' Then his face brightened. 'I'm glad I've found you at last. God forgive me, it's taken me all this time to come here, now you can show me where the real Yiddisher people live. You can be the guide and I can be the tourist!'

'Tourist in a slum?' Walter shook his head again. 'Ah, Heinrich, you are, I think, working on a story for that paper of yours, aren't you?'

He smiled. 'You have me,' he said. 'But again, it's all to the good. It's important to find out what German refugees think of their new home.'

'What they think? They came here,' Walter said, 'from nice apartments in Berlin to *this*. What do you imagine they think?

The only time any of the other men spoke to him was when they needed him to do something. But Dermot had expected that. Of course Artie had told them and of course they hated him. But with his nose stuffed with rags and a pain like a hammer in his head, Dermot didn't need their chat. What he needed was for things to be back to normal again, but that was never going to happen.

Every so often he heard them speaking about him, sometimes between themselves and sometimes with Artie in amongst them. Words like 'grass' and 'bastard' peppered their speech. Artie, holding on to his guts, as if still in pain from Pat's punch, looked at him with undisguised fury.

When the shift finished, Dermot went up to the foreman and said, 'If you're gonna come for me then I'll meet you, man to man.' But Artie didn't reply. What could he do? If he came at Dermot he'd have Pat to deal with and there could be no doubt the Irishman would blow the gaff on the whole affair if he didn't get what he wanted.

But as Dermot walked home, he couldn't help but keep glancing back over his shoulder. If they could, the mob would get to him some other way and he knew it. And even though he'd seen them all go in the Railway together after work, he was still wary. He also found he was on the look-out for his brother. Wherever Joey had gone, he'd taken that mink coat with him and not put it on Meyer Nadel's doorstep as his dad had said. But then why would he? As far as Dermot knew Joey was skint. He'd have to fence the coat and quick, but then what would he do? Would he leave the East End? Leave London?

Bernie had reckoned he'd go to Artie's but there was no reason to believe that had happened. There was also no reason to think he hadn't either. Had he really killed Fred Lamb? Or had it been, as his dad said, Artie Cross who'd done the deed? Pat had no evidence against Artie except his belief that the man was a wrong 'un. Bernie has been more suspicious but then that was her all over. His sister rarely took anything or anyone at face value. She was, their father always said, too clever for that.

And then suddenly Dermot remembered something Chrissy had told him about Mr Devenish the photographer, Bernie's boss. Something about mucky photos ...

'Becky!'

Rose had just come out of her old flat when she saw her friend. 'Rosie!'

And then there were three as Bernie appeared on the steps of the house opposite!

Bernie, Becky and Rose ran into each other's arms. They met so infrequently nowadays it was a real treat for them all to be together at the same time.

Although Becky knew her papa didn't like it, the three girls sat on the Shapiros' big, wide doorstep and Bernie lit a fag.

Rosie, of course, just came out with what she knew Becky must be thinking, which was, 'Bernie, do you know about Solly Adler?'

'That he's back? Yes,' she said. 'I'm glad.' Then she looked at Becky. 'I've not seen him.'

Becky smiled but said nothing. What was there to say? But at least now she knew that Bernie knew. She touched her friend's arm.

Then she said, 'So how's it going at Mrs Rabinowicz's, Rosie?'

'She's kind,' Rose said. She was, in a harsh sort of a way. A bit like a school teacher really. 'She talks about your wedding all the time.'

Becky looked down at the ground. 'That's not going to happen any time soon,' she said.

Bernie, Rose noticed, didn't say anything to this.

'I think your ring is lovely.'

Becky smiled at her. 'Thank you, Rosie. So, Bernie ...'

She shrugged. 'Got one of me photographs in the shop window.'

'That girl who danced at the street party? Yes, I saw it,' Becky told her. 'It's really, well, it's unusual.'

'It's not posed. But then people want poses. I expect Mr Devenish'll take it out the window soon.'

Bernie was upset about something besides Solly Adler. Rose didn't know what. Maybe about the murder that had happened on the street? She liked her new life with the matchmaker but did feel a bit out of things over on Folgate Street.

'Becky,' she said, 'do you know any moneylenders?'

She hadn't known how to go about introducing the subject and so she just said it. It had seemed to her to be the best way. But Bernie looked shocked.

'Rosie!'

She looked back at Bernie. 'What?'

'Well, you don't just . . .'

'Yes, I do know a few moneylenders,' Becky cut in. 'But they're no friends of mine and Papa has always said we have to keep away from them. Mr King the rag man lends and so does Minnie Berger, who lives next door to the coal merchant's on Wentworth Street. But if you don't pay on time, it's bad, with both of them. They know people, you see . . .'

'Gangsters?'

Becky laughed. 'Where'd you get that word from?'

'Thinks she's in America,' Bernie said.

Rose didn't understand. 'No, I don't.'

Becky put a hand on her shoulder. 'Rosie, don't borrow from moneylenders, you'll get in all sorts of trouble.'

'Oh, it's not me,' Rose said, 'it's me mum.'

'Well, then, tell her not to borrow from them. And don't give her all your money either. It's yours, not hers.'

Rose knew that her friends didn't really like her mum and so it was pointless telling them she was ill because they wouldn't care. She could understand it. Nell hadn't been the best mum but Rose loved her. She'd have to find another way.

A tangle of voices at the top of the road signalled the arrival of Bernie's mum and her little brother and sisters. Rose called out, 'Hello, Auntie Kitty.'

But Kitty Lynch didn't answer. Like Bernie, she looked tired and strained and she didn't smile.

Bernie got up and said, 'Gotta go.'

She went and joined her mum who hugged her tightly. They looked like people who had just been bereaved. When the family had gone indoors, Rose said to Becky, 'Do you think Bernie's all right?'

'I don't know,' she said. 'Seems a bit upset to me. Maybe it's because she thought that more people would like her photo.'

But Becky didn't actually believe that for a second. Bernie, and her mum especially, had looked strained in a way they'd never looked before. It was worrying.

The Suss family had come to Britain from Holland but the patriarch, Menachim, had lived for a time in Berlin back in the 1920s.

'It was really rather immoral then,' he told Heinrich Simpson. 'Living among the *goyim*. Sex of all sorts, drugs, too much drink, jazz.'

Speaking in German the two men, plus Walter Katz, sat at the back of the jeweller's shop in Black Lion Yard, reminiscing about Berlin after the Great War. A period known as the Weimar Republic, it had been a time of great decadence.

'It went too far,' the jeweller continued. 'So when the Nazis came with their public morality drive and their doctrine of racial purity, a lot of people listened. I listened! To begin with. Only afterwards came the anti-Semitism. Then I had to leave. First back to Amsterdam, but Father was already here and so it was we settled in England. You know in Berlin in 1922 they had shows with lesbian women? Kissing on-stage and ... all kinds of things!'

Did his eyes shine a little as he recounted the more salacious details of life in the Weimar Republic? There were better people Walter could have introduced Heinrich to but the jeweller had seen them together out in the Yard and insisted they come in. He didn't even live in the East End and he wasn't German, but what he was, was nosy. So now he probably knew more about Heinrich than the reporter knew about him. But such was life.

Then a rat ran over Heinrich's shiny, black shoes and Walter put a hand to his head. God!

Strangely, Heinrich didn't seem to notice. His eyes were fixed, or seemed to be fixed, on something across the road.

'That's an amazing picture,' he said.

'Picture?'

Then Menachim realised that the younger man was looking at his friend Mr Devenish's photography shop.

'Ah, yes, Mr Devenish. But he's not Jewish ...'

'This picture ...'

Walter peered at an image he recognised. Ah, yes, Bernadette's photograph of a girl dancing at a Coronation street party. It was good. A work of art. He'd told her so when she'd shown him. Wasted on the East End, of course.

'God, that's a talent,' Heinrich said. 'I wish I could have a photographer like this accompanying me when I go to Germany. I can describe what I see in words, but something like this has real impact.'

Chapter Twenty-One

4 June 1937

Bernie and Becky had tried to help, and Auntie Kitty. But Rose's mum just wouldn't let anyone into the flat. Len, the bastard, had taken up with some old prossie from down Shadwell and left Nell with nothing. Sick and needing drink, she was crying all the time. And now it was Friday, rent day. Come lunchtime Nell Larkin would be out on the street.

Rose was polishing the mirror over the parlour fireplace when Mrs Rabinowicz told her she was going out.

'The Rebbetzin Cohen's youngest girl is seventeen today and I need to go and pay my respects,' she said. 'Lovely girl like that can't be seen to be unattached for long. People'll think she's got something wrong with her.'

She rammed a red felt cloche hat on her head, picked up her handbag and left.

Rose finished cleaning the mirror and refilled the coal scuttle before she went upstairs to Mrs Rabinowicz's bedroom and, with shaking hands, opened her dressing-table drawer.

'Where you off to?'

Kitty put her hat on. 'Where'd you think?'

'Oh, Kit, not again!' her husband said. 'Girl, I'm telling you, how he was weren't nothing to do with you. It was all that Artie Cross!'

'Yes, but we know about it, don't we?' Kitty said. 'We know what Joey done. We're hiding it and making Dermot and Bernadette hide it too!'

Pat put his newspaper down. 'And you know why, don't you? Grasses don't get work round here. You know that! What choice did we have, eh?'

'Mr Lamb was a good man and now he's dead and we know who did it!' Kitty protested.

'Yeah, Artie Cross ...'

'You don't know that! Joey said he did it. A confession out of his own mouth!' She began to cry. 'And now he's gone!'

'Would you rather he hanged?' Pat said.

'No!'

'Well ...' He shrugged. 'We keep schtum and there's an end to it.'

'But where is he? Where's my son?'

Pat shook his head. Joey had disappeared and, although he still loved his eldest, he was glad. With any luck he'd make a new life for himself somewhere and be happy. Maybe one day he'd even come home a new and better man.

Kitty picked up her gloves and walked towards the front door.

Pat said, 'If you think that old drunk can get God to forgive you then good on ya.'

274

'Father Reynolds . . . '

'Is on the whiskey from the time he gets up until the time he goes to bed,' Pat said. 'You know it and I know it. You're wasting your time.'

Kitty left, slamming the door behind her. She'd never been a religious woman but what else could she do? She'd committed so many sins! Not just with regard to Joey but over Bernadette too. She still hadn't told her daughter about Solly Adler's letter. Kitty was a coward and she knew it. And so if there was a God and there was any chance of Him forgiving her, surely she should go to Confession and ask Him? And keep on asking until He gave her an answer.

Mr Devenish put a framed photograph of a bride and groom he'd taken the previous weekend upright on the shop counter. They looked as if they'd been cast in plaster. But Bernie smiled when he showed her. 'Wooden' was the look most people seemed to want to go for.

The bell over the shop door tinkled and Walter Katz walked in. Both the photographer and his assistant were pleased to see an old friend.

'Ah, Mr Katz . . . '

'Good morning.'

And he wasn't alone. A smartly dressed middle-aged man with very neat black Brylcreemed hair stood beside him. Bernie thought he looked like a doctor or a brief.

'To what do we owe the pleasure?' Mr Devenish asked in his best 'posh' voice. He was about as posh as she was, Bernie thought. And, if little Chrissy Dolan was right, he had a nasty hobby taking dirty pictures of women. She could believe it, even if it was only a rumour. Not that he'd ever done anything improper to her, because he hadn't and thanks to Chrissy's tip-off she would never put herself in a position where he might try.

'Well, Mr Devenish, this gentleman here is an old friend of mine ... Mr Simpson.'

The two men shook hands.

'But to be honest with you,' Mr Katz continued, 'it is Miss Lynch we have come to see today. Could you possibly spare her for a few minutes? Maybe an early lunch even, if it's not inconvenient?'

What had she done? Was this Simpson bloke really a lawyer? Had the coppers found out about Joey? And what did Mr Katz have to do with any of it?

'Mr Simpson is a reporter for the *London Evening News*,' Mr Katz said proudly. 'He's working on an article about the East End and he'd like to speak to a young person. I thought that a young lady of Miss Lynch's calibre would give a very good impression.'

'Oh, indeed,' Devenish said. 'And, er, well, if you can mention where this estimable young lady works, Mr Simpson ... '

'That would be up to my editor, but I take your point.'

Now *he* was posh. And Bernie felt, for a man who was really quite old, a bit of a looker too. She made herself glance down at the floor in case her face had gone red.

'Well, then, yes,' Devenish said, 'take an early lunch by all means, Miss Lynch, and don't worry about hurrying back. You take your time.'

Then he smiled at Simpson. He didn't smile often but lately, whenever he did, Bernie couldn't help being reminded of a lizard.

The landlord had already arrived. Half the street was out watching as he threw Nell's clothes into the street.

Some of the women shouted, 'Bloody shame on you, Mr Brown!'

But nothing more, because he was their landlord too. The only exception to this was Rose's 'uncle' Pat Lynch. Wheezing and coughing on the area steps, Rose heard him say, 'Look, just give her the weekend. She's not well. Can't you see?'

Her mum stood beside Uncle Pat, white-faced and shaking.

'That's what happens when you sell yourself for twenty years,' the landlord said as he threw a pile of her mum's knickers into the gutter.

Nell screamed.

Uncle Pat said, 'Don't worry, love, you can stay with us.'

'No, she can't,' Brown told him. 'I've had enough prossies and pikeys in my properties. More trouble than they're worth. You take her in and you and your tribe can get out too!'

Rose could see that Uncle Pat was about to square up to the landlord, who was, it had to be said, built like a bull.

She ran over and took her mum's arm.

The landlord said, 'Oh, Christ, the daughter now! That's all we bleedin' need!'

Rose put the rent money into his hands and smiled at him. 'It's all there, I think,' she said. 'And that's for next week too.'

She knew she shouldn't have done it in front of everyone like this, but she had to stop him throwing her mum's smalls about, didn't she? It was embarrassing.

For a moment Mr Brown did nothing. Then, watched by at least half the street, the landlord counted out the money and said, 'S'right. I s'pose . . . '

'So Mum can stay then, can she?'

He couldn't hide his disappointment but he did manage to mumble, 'Yus.'

Money in hand, he started to walk away. Pat yelled after him,

'Oi, you wanna pick up Mrs Larkin's clothes that you threw into the street?'

Mr Brown snarled back, 'Fuck off, Lynch! She'll be behind again soon. You know it and I know it.'

And while Uncle Pat didn't say anything to her about the money, as Rose picked up her mother's clothes she saw the other neighbours looking at her and wondering where she'd got it from.

Things hadn't worked out the way Rose had hoped they would and now she didn't know what to do next.

This was the second time she'd seen Solly and so it had to be fate throwing them together. Admittedly Becky had pushed the Salzedo twins along Commercial Street where she knew he lived several times, but that didn't mean she'd know he'd be out of the house at the time. People said that he didn't leave his mum's flat unless he had to. But there he was, leaning against the wall where she'd seen him last time.

Becky's voice trembled slightly when she spoke, which irritated her.

'Hello, Comrade Adler,' she said. 'I don't suppose you remember me, do you?'

Unsmiling, he looked her up and down. 'You're Mr Shapiro's daughter,' he said.

She smiled. 'We stood up to Mosley together,' she said. 'On Cable Street.'

'You and your mates,' he said. 'I remember. The little gypsy girl and Miss Lynch who sat on top of the barricade. Good times. Times when we had hope.'

The girl twin, Doris, squirmed as if she might want to go to the toilet.

'We have hope now,' Becky said.

'Do we? You might, but I can't see much to be hopeful about when Hitler's fascist air force are bombing innocent Spaniards. And I can't see that all the anti-Jewish rubbish written on walls round here has gone away, can you?'

He sounded liked Bernie's dad. A lot of the Communists were disillusioned now. Fascism was growing stronger in Germany, Spain and Italy and a lot of the Commie boys were beginning to lean towards anarchy as the only solution. In a world with no rules except the will of the people, no one could oppress anyone else. That was the theory at least.

Becky said, 'Things will pick up.' And instantly regretted it. It was the sort of thing silly old women on the markets said!

'You think so, do you?' Solly Adler retorted. 'Well let me ask you this, Miss Shapiro: if things are picking up, why did Hitler execute a Jewish activist this morning, eh?'

Becky hadn't heard about that. She didn't know what to say.

'Don't you read the papers?' he said.

Again, she stayed silent.

Solly shook his head. 'It's over,' he said. 'The "Comrades" have failed and now all we do is wait to get picked off by the vultures.'

Not only did he look much older, he sounded older too. Becky wanted to cry. Had the Spanish War broken this man completely? Less than a year ago he'd been so full of life, hope and joy . . .

Doris said, 'Want to go pee.'

Becky said, 'All right darling.'

Solly Adler turned his face away and shut his eyes. Becky took the brake off the pushchair and began to move away. But just before she was out of earshot she heard him say, 'Give my regards to Miss Lynch if you see her.'

And it was all too much for her then. Becky began to cry. She ran away so that he wouldn't see. Not even so much as a smile for her, but he still had words for Bernie. That was because he must really love her.

They took Bernie to the kosher restaurant on the opposite side of the road then asked her if she minded.

'I mean it is Friday and so you can have fish,' Walter Katz told her. 'We know that's important to you. Do you mind having it in *matzoh* meal?'

Bernie didn't. This Mr Simpson was paying so what did she care? In the end they all had cod and chips and pickles and it was really nice.

Mr Simpson said, 'Firstly, may I call you Bernadette?'

'Yes,' she said. 'Mr Katz does.'

The paper and string man smiled.

'Well, Bernadette, I have to say first of all that we've got you here under false pretences,' the smart man said.

'What? You don't work for a paper or ...'

'Oh I work for the *London Evening News*, that's completely true,' Mr Simpson said. 'But I don't want to interview you about living in the East End. I want to talk to you about your photographs.'

'Heinrich ... Mr Simpson ... saw your photograph of the girl at the Coronation party and was very impressed,' Mr Katz said.

'It was real,' Simpson said. 'Not posed or set-up. It's a bold shot but it's also got warmth. I can tell you love what you do.'

'So I showed him the pictures you took on Cable Street,' the old man told her.

'They remind me of the work of Cartier-Bresson ...'

'Who?'

'A young Frenchman,' Simpson said. 'He takes photographs for a Parisian magazine called *Regards*. He photographed the

Coronation. But his coverage was nothing like the work of other photographers. His shots are candid, they are of the crowd … the emotions felt by those watching the spectacle. Like your girl and your pictures of Cable Street, they portray what is happening through the faces of people we can all relate to.'

'Oh.'

Bernie thought that, yes, that was the sort of thing she'd wanted to do, but she wouldn't have been able to put it the way he had.

'You have an eye for the drama of the ordinary man and woman, Bernadette.'

'Comes from a good Socialist family too,' Mr Katz said.

Bernie frowned. 'Yeah, but me dad won't get the *Evening News* because it's pro-Hitler and the fascists.'

Mr Simpson put down his knife and fork and rested his chin on his fists. 'The *News* is owned by Lord Rothermere,' he said. 'Who has, well, certain sympathies …'

'Yeah.'

'But our editor is more concerned with good stories. His job is to sell newspapers and so, as well as running copy that might be sympathetic to some of the Nazis' ideals, he also employs people like me, for a balanced approach,' Simpson explained.

'What do you do, Mr Simpson?'

'I report what goes on in Germany.'

'Heinrich comes from Berlin originally,' Mr Katz explained.

'A Berlin Jew, now an Englishman.' He smiled. 'I try to convey what I see there in ways that will make people take notice. Hitler is dangerous and not just to Jews. People outside his country need to see that. I do that through words, but I also take a photographer with me who does the same job with pictures. We should be in Germany today, God knows we should!'

'Why aren't you?'

Heinrich shook his head sorrowfully. 'Mike got sick last week. It's his chest. I couldn't make him do that journey, not the way he is. It's not the first time he's been ill. But this time it's – well, it's bad.'

A lot of people, as Bernie's mammy put it, 'suffered with their chests'. It was worse in the winter cold and fog, but even in the summer the smog that always hung over the city made people wheeze and cough and die. Bernie tried not to think about her dad.

'Mike will come back to work, God willing, but he admits himself that his days of travelling are over,' Simpson said. 'Which means we have to replace him.' He looked Bernie straight in the eye. 'Which means we need someone young and fearless and talented who understands people. A tall order.'

Bernie looked down at her fish and said nothing. Surely he couldn't mean her? She had no experience.

He continued, 'Germany gets more dangerous by the week. As a Jew, it is only my British passport that keeps me alive sometimes. And just today we heard that an anti-Nazi activist called Helmut Hirsch has been executed for so-called plots against the State. That's the story I was meant to be covering. Hirsch was a Jew like me. They cut his head off.'

Bernie felt her eyes bulge out of her head. 'Jesus, Mary and Joseph!'

'The Nazis are barbarians, Miss Lynch,' Simpson said. 'I can't put it any other way. And I also can't quite believe that I'm asking you to go to that hellish country with me, but I am. Bernadette, subject to the approval of my editor, I'd like to engage you to take photographs in Germany for me. I can offer you no guarantee that you will come out alive or that you won't be deeply shocked by what you see, but I can give you a good salary and, if we make it through whatever we have to face in the next few years, a career with a reputable Fleet Street newspaper. Also, you'll be helping to tell the truth about Hitler and his evil henchmen.'

Bernie could hardly breathe for surprise and excitement.

They'd all known where the money had come from. Rose had been able to see it on the faces of the women of Ten Bells Street – as her mum called it. She'd also seen it on the face of Pat Lynch. He hadn't said anything, but he *knew*.

Rose hadn't taken all the money that Mrs Rabinowicz kept in her dressing-table drawer. Only some of it . . . just a little really. She probably wouldn't even notice, at least not for a while.

Rose knew she was fooling herself. Nothing got past the matchmaker and that included the rumours that were seeping like blood across Spitalfields. How could a girl like Rose Larkin have got hold of that much money?

And yet she'd had no choice! Rent day had come and her mum was out on the street. What else could a good daughter do but settle the debt and give her mother something extra to pay for food and medicine until she could work again?

Rose walked down Commercial Street, past Spitalfields Market and its gangs of thin, ragged costers until she came to Folgate Street.

At first Rose didn't think there was anybody but kids about. But then she saw the coppers patrolling at the end of the street, almost outside Mrs Rabinowicz's front door, and her heart hammered.

With her head down and her hat pulled close in to the collar of her jacket, Rose walked past and kept on going.

Chapter Twenty-Two

'You know the girl,' her papa said. 'You must know where she goes.'

'I don't,' Becky said. 'And anyway, Papa, if I go to the police I'll be breaking the *Shabbos.*'

Her father shook his head and walked back into the parlour. Rose had gone missing and the *shadchan* was going mad. It was said she'd pulled some woman out of the pub opposite her house to be her *Shabbos goy* and this woman was now telling people that Rose had stolen from her mistress. If only Becky could talk to Bernie! But she was at work and now it was *Shabbos* and no one Jewish could go anywhere and it was all hopeless!

And that was without the added horror of what Mrs Rabinowicz was going to say to her about Rose. Becky had recommended her after all.

There would be hell to pay.

'You have to get the men to, er, protect themselves, Mrs Larkin,' the doctor told her.

Nell had asked Dr Klein to come out to her. What did she want to go sitting in some surgery for with everyone staring at her? Thanks to Rosie's money she didn't have to do that.

'I tried that, doctor, but they won't,' she said as she put her skirt back on. 'Ain't the same for 'em.'

He handed her a prescription. 'Then this infection will spread.'

'I won't work for a little while,' Nell said. 'This the same stuff as last time?'

'Yes,' he said. 'And, remember, one of the constituents is arsenic so follow my instructions to the letter.'

She smiled at him. 'Yes, doctor.'

He was a good sort but Nell still didn't want Dr Klein to know she couldn't read or write. Last time she'd taken the arsenic medication three times a day, because that was what Len had said. She'd do that again.

The doctor put his hat on. 'And remember, Mrs Larkin,' he said, 'there is no actual cure for syphilis. This will make you feel better but it won't actually kill the infection. That will still be in your system. I would strongly suggest you seek a different kind of employment. I'll let myself out.'

He touched his hat and opened the front door. Outside, her face red with what could be fear or exertion, was Kitty Lynch.

'Oh, Dr Klein,' she said. 'Is Mrs Larkin . . . '

'I'm in here, missus,' Nell said.

'Good day to you, Mrs Lynch,' the doctor said, and walked past her up the area stairs and into the street.

When he'd gone Nell said, 'What you want, Kitty Lynch? I have to get down that pharmacy, have this prescription thing made up.'

Kitty sat down without asking and said, 'Nelly, now don't panic, but your Rosie has gone missing.'

'Missing? She was only here yesterday. She come, give me some money because she knows I been hard up these . . . '

'She stole that money,' Kitty said.

'Who says?' People were always accusing Nell and her daughter of something. 'I'll lamp whoever says it!'

'The lady she worked for – Mrs Rabinowicz,' Kitty explained.

'Well, she's lying.'

'Fifty quid she found missing from where she keeps her cash when she got home yesterday,' Kitty said. 'Only your Rosie had been in the house. How much did she give you, Nelly?'

Nell looked down. 'Dunno.'

She did. Fifty pounds.

'Well, Rose never went back to work after she left here and Mrs Rabinowicz is doing her nut. Going on about going to the coppers apparently. Do you know where Rose is?'

'No . . . '

Nell felt sick. That job with the Jewish lady had been a right good thing for Rosie and Nell had hated asking her for more money when she got ill, but what else could she have done? Len had said that now Rose was working she could go to a money-lender. Wasn't her fault the girl wouldn't go.

But if she were truthful with herself, Nell would admit she'd half expected Rose to steal from Mrs Rabinowicz, to help her out. She just hadn't expected the girl to take that much. Not that she'd said anything of the sort to Rosie. She'd just taken the money – in front of the whole street.

'Will the Jewish lady expect me to pay her back?' Nell asked.

'How should I know?' Kitty Lynch got up and grabbed Nell by the shoulders. 'First off we have to find Rosie. So get your coat and hat and let's start looking. We have to find her before the coppers do.' Then her face darkened. 'Ain't right not to have your nippers where you can find them.'

Mr Devenish kept on digging, but Bernie gave him nothing.

They were both working on the Carrier/Richardson wedding, photographing the happy couple on the steps outside Christ Church.

'Yes, but what did he want to know?' Devenish pressed her.

Bernie focussed the lens. The newly married couple froze. Perfect!

'Nothing important,' she said. 'What I do with me spare time, what I want to do in life . . . '

'I hope you told him I'm helping you with that,' the photographer said.

Bernie moved the bride and groom to one side and assembled the bridesmaids: three little girls with their hair in ringlets and a woman of about forty who looked permanently disappointed. One of the kids smiled, the rest complained about how their petticoats were itching them.

'Why didn't he want to speak to me?' Devenish persisted.

'I don't know, Mr Devenish,' Bernie said. 'Maybe Mr Simpson only wanted to talk to young people, just like he told you.'

'Don't you be sarcastic with me, young lady!'

'I wasn't.'

'I think you were.'

Bernie couldn't take much more of this. Mr Simpson was going to meet her at Mr Katz's shop after work and then go and ask her dad if he'd agree to let her take the job with the *Evening News*. She was only seventeen and if she did go abroad she'd need her dad's permission. She expected he'd give it. Not just because of the money but because her dad had always wanted her to live her dreams. Then it was up to Mr Simpson's editor,

Mr Fitzhugh. It was difficult not to get excited. But she had to calm down. She had a job to do – and also a problem.

'Can we have the parents with the bride and groom now?' Bernie said to the wedding party.

Two clearly middle-class, sensibly dressed people and a coster and his wife joined the bride and groom on the steps. The middle-class parents were for the groom, the costers the bride. It was clear from their facial expressions that there was no love lost between these two families. But then Bernie, who knew about such things, could see that the bride was in the early stages of pregnancy and so this whole thing had probably been organised in about five minutes.

She framed the shot and took the picture. Just like waxworks. Brilliant!

'Now everyone, please.'

And as Cousin Graham refused to stand next to Auntie Rita (because she was an old slapper) and kids in tight clothes fought against other kids in tight clothes, Bernie considered her problem. Rose was missing and was said to have taken a load of money from her employer. Dermot said the story was she'd given it to her mum for rent, which was possible. Nelly had been looking ill for some time and, since Len Tobin had left her, she didn't seem to be working.

People were out looking for Rose and Bernie wanted to be there too if she could. But that wasn't possible. Not with the Carrier/Richardson wedding to record for posterity.

One of the bride's little sisters fell over in the churchyard, pulled her ankle and said 'shit'. The groom's father first frowned and then laughed out loud. Both mothers smiled through gritted teeth, and the bride's father started patting his pockets for the bottle he'd concealed earlier.

*

Nell tripped over outside the doss house on Crispin Street. They'd just passed the men's entrance and the smell had been enough to knock anyone flat. Even in the cold, hundreds of starving men, some of them the worse for drink, standing on the pavement for hours on end, brought their own health hazards.

'Blimey, rivers of piss!' Nell said as she tried to get up without touching the ground.

Kitty gave her a hand. Then she yelled, 'Anyone see a small black-haired girl in a short grey coat and purple hat?'

Nobody said a word. But then why would they? These were the desperate, diminished men her husband and her sons would become if no one in the family could work. Kitty looked for her Joey's face, but didn't find it. She didn't know whether to be relieved or frightened.

'What was Rosie doing wearing a purple hat?' Nell said as she got to her feet. 'That's for widows, ain't it?'

'It was one of Mrs Rabinowicz's old ones,' Kitty said. 'You must've seen it.'

Nell gripped her stomach.

Kitty said, 'What's the matter?'

'Ah, just me sickness,' Nell said. 'I need to get me paper to the pharmacy for me medicine.'

Kitty got her to produce the prescription. She wasn't surprised to see what it was for. Her own Uncle Ernest had caught the pox in South Africa during the Boer War, probably from a prostitute like Nellie.

The doss-house doors opened and men began to file in, hoping for a bed for the night. The sky was darkening now and Kitty knew that with Nell's face the colour of chalk, they needed to get home.

'Come on,' she said as she took the woman's arm. 'We'll start looking again tomorrow. Let's get your medicine. You look right queer, so you do.'

And, for once, Nell Larkin didn't put up a fight.

'It won't look good that you vouched for the girl,' said Moritz. 'When Mr Suss finds out it could be a problem. They might call off the wedding.'

Becky said nothing.

'If they think you're mixing with the wrong sort they could get nasty,' he continued. 'Families like to know that brides who are marrying their boys are good girls.'

'I am a good girl,' Becky muttered.

'I know that! But they don't. Why are you friends with such a person anyway? A gypsy! All they know is how to steal and play tricks on people ...'

'Papa, that's unfair,' Becky protested. 'Rose and her mum are just poor.'

'The mother's a ...'

'I like Rose,' Becky said. 'And so does Bernie.'

'Huh,' he said, 'another one!'

'Another what?'

He waved a hand in the air. 'You know!'

'No, I don't!'

'Another street urchin! Another uneducated cockney with air between her ears ...'

'Bernie's really clever!' Becky yelled.

'Don't shout at me!'

'But she is, Papa. She'd the cleverest of all of us.'

'Pah! That's your problem, isn't it?' he said. 'Wasting yourself on such people!'

'This from the refugee!'

His face drained of colour. But Becky stood her ground. Her

290

papa was a good man but he looked down on everyone – *goyim* and Yiddisher alike, to be fair. She hated it.

'Don't speak to your father like that,' he said.

'I'm sorry but ...'

'Yesterday the German government executed a Yiddisher. They called him a traitor and chopped off his head. The world is going mad again and all I want is for you to be safe,' he said. 'And safe means being with those who have money, who can take you to America, Australia, anywhere.'

'Papa, they have relatives in Holland.'

'Or Holland! Although soon maybe, if Hitler decides to spread his poison all across Europe, that won't be possible. Who knows? But, Rebekah, you must see that a good match like this gives you advantages! I am struggling to make a living now. I do what I can, but ...'

Becky had never really talked to her father about her betrothal. She'd just agreed to it.

'And Chaim Suss is a pleasant young man ...'

'If only I loved him,' she sighed.

'Love?' Her papa smiled. 'You think that your mother loved me when we were married? Love grows, Rebekah-*leh*. It's not like you read about in books. Jane Austen, is it that you like?'

'Papa, I know I'm no Elizabeth Bennet! It's not just about love. I want to do things with my life. The mother's help work I do was meant to give me a start towards being a nurse.'

'Which is no life for a girl.'

'No? What's wrong with serving the sick, Papa? It's a noble thing, a good thing, a job that can both break your heart and make you sing with joy!'

He crossed his arms over his chest. 'Romantic nonsense. It's about blood and sickness. That's it.'

'Yes, it is,' she said. 'That too. But I want to do it, Papa. I don't know why. I just do.'

'When you were a child you wanted to be a doctor.'

'But you couldn't afford that, Papa, and I understand.'

The black marble clock on the black marble mantelpiece chimed to tell them that another hour of the Sabbath had been and gone. Rebekah could just about remember her mother, Chani. Had the house been less gloomy when she'd been alive or was it just her daughter's imagination? And yet . . .

'Papa,' she said, 'the truth is, I don't want to leave you. I don't want to leave the East End. Everything and everyone I love is here. Being part of a *frum* family in Stamford Hill, walking behind my husband, being told what to do by my mother-in-law, wearing wigs . . . You've brought me up to be observant, but you've not brought me up like that! To be part of a living death!' Tears started to roll down her face. 'I only agreed to make you happy. Now I wish I was dead!'

Moritz Shapiro had seen many things that made him sad in his long and difficult life, but nothing had made him sadder than witnessing his child's tears now. Listening to gossip, he had become obsessed by the idea that his daughter was in love with that Communist Adler. But she hadn't said his name once in this discussion and that was because there was so much more at stake for her here. Familiar surroundings, her ambition, her close link to her father . . .

She would be shielded by the wealth that the Suss family could provide, it was true. But that was Moritz's priority, clearly not Rebekah's. And yet he'd only been trying to do his best for her. Keep her safe.

The two boys looked at each other, but neither of them spoke. Dermot was looking for Rose while Chrissy emptied chamber pots into the gutter. One of the old girls he cleaned up after sat drunkenly on the doorstep of the knocking shop, laughing.

Chrissy had always been happier around women, even as a kid. People used to wonder how and why he became friends with Dermot who had always explained it as 'we just clicked.' But he knew there was more to it than that. Something unspoken had always held them together.

He looked in the steamed-up window of a Chinese restaurant and, when he saw only old Chinamen inside, moved on. Chrissy went back inside the knocking shop.

Dermot had never found out what had happened at Swan and Edgar to make his friend lose his job, though he suspected it was something Chrissy could go to prison for. 'Unnatural acts' was how such things were classed by the law. Words like 'lewd' and 'sinful' came to mind. That was because they were meant to come to mind, because such behaviour was wrong. But who decided that?

Everyone in the world, it seemed. Even some who hid their own tendencies that way behind a pretence of respectability. Married and often fathers, these men would hang about in alleyways and round public toilets on dark, foggy nights. But come daylight they'd loudly condemn 'such people' and want them all hanged. Staying alive by crawling over the bodies of their own kind.

Dermot kicked the body of a dead rat into the gutter and carried on looking in doorways and alleyways. Rosie was a strange little thing and it made him sad to think that she was in trouble. She was a bit like Chrissy in her vulnerability: he always wanted to take care of her too.

Kitty could hear Aggie and little Paddy having a blazing row in the street but she ignored it. Knowing them it was probably over who'd had the most chips from the fish shop. Staying out all day looking for little Rosie Larkin meant that she'd been too tired to cook and so Marie, who worked on and off at the chippie, had come home with burned chips and dodgy-looking saveloys for them all. Now she was out making doe eyes at Judah, the son of Mrs Diamond who worked at the Jewish baths on Brick Lane. But Kitty couldn't think about that now. Mr Katz had come to visit and had brought some smart bloke from the *Evening News* with him. Apparently he wanted to take their Bernie away.

'Bernadette will earn twice what she's earning now,' the man had told them.

'It ain't about the money,' Pat said. He'd hardly smiled once since Joey had gone and today was no exception.

'Dad, it means I'll travel,' Bernie said. 'Remember when I was little and I wanted to go to Egypt?'

'Mr Simpson here is talking about Germany,' Pat replied. 'No Pyramids there, only fascists. How you gonna keep a seventeen-year-old girl safe while she works for you, Mr Simpson?'

'As part of the international Press Corps we have protected status, Mr Lynch.'

Simpson was a smart man, dark and affluent-looking. Whenever he glanced at Bernie, he smiled. Most men did.

'Yes, but how you gonna keep my daughter safe?'

'I don't know what you mean?'

'He means,' Kitty said, 'how're you gonna make sure our Bernie don't get shot? And how're you gonna make sure men don't take advantage of her?'

'Mammy!'

Kitty raised a finger to silence her daughter. 'Well?'

'What can I say?' Heinrich shrugged expressively. 'As a family man myself, I understand your fears, Mr Lynch. If my daughter wanted to leave home to go abroad, I too would be concerned.

But I give you my word that I will protect Bernadette's honour as closely as that of my own child. As for either of us getting shot ... At the moment, as foreigners, the worst that can happen to us is that we may be deported by the German authorities. I know there are all sorts of stories about the regime there these days, but if you're not an opponent of the Nazis then they do tend to leave you alone. We are merely reporting.'

'Working for Beaverbrook's paper?' Pat shook his head. 'You must think I'm silly, Mr Simpson. Lord Beaverbrook, the owner of your paper, is pro-Hitler.'

'I don't know about that,' Simpson said. 'But I do know I'm not. I'll be honest with you, Mr Lynch, I'm a Jew.'

'Came here from Berlin long ago,' Mr Katz told them.

'I want the British public to see the truth about Hitler. His persecution of Jews, Communists and dissidents. And if I can do that and sell newspapers, then that is all my editor cares about. I can't tell you how passionately I feel about this. Mr Lynch, if Bernadette comes to Germany and takes her wonderful pictures, she will be helping so many people. Your daughter is brilliant. She captures people's souls ... '

Kitty looked into her daughter's earnest eyes and knew that her father wouldn't be able to deny her this chance, even if her mother could.

Kitty said, 'One of our sons has gone away, to the Irish Free State, and we miss him.' She felt herself start to cry. 'I don't know if I can bear to lose another child.' She turned her head away.

Pat said, 'There, there, my old love.'

'Mrs Lynch, I feel for you, I do, but Bernadette could play a part in making sure these fascists don't win,' Simpson said. 'Men and women from all over the world went off to Spain to fight them, remember, and they're still going.'

'And come back with legs missing!' Kitty said. 'Bombed and shot at. Like those poor buggers from the Great War who sit outside railway stations playing music for ha'pennies! Blinded and with their arms and legs gone . . .'

Everyone had seen the Great War veterans, wounded and penniless, playing tin whistles at Liverpool Street and Paddington stations, all but begging for money to fund their pitiful old age.

'It's a disgrace!' Kitty fumed.

'Yes, it is,' Simpson said. 'And if we don't do something about Hitler – now – it'll happen again. Your daughter can be part of the fight to stop that. And she will be one of the great photographers of our time, that I can promise you. I know you're people who care. I know you were at Cable Street. You're good people . . .'

Kitty wept. He was pressing every button he could to get them to do what he wanted.

'But she's my daughter!'

'And I want you to be proud of me, Mammy!' Bernie said. She looked at her father in appeal. 'I want this, Dad. God knows, I don't want to leave you, but what started for me on Cable Street can't just end now. We're in a fight to the death here, Dad, and we have to win. I want to make sure we do.'

Pat held out his hand to his daughter and Kitty knew what he was going to say next. She howled like a wounded dog.

Rose didn't know where she was. She'd seen St Paul's Cathedral yesterday, but she'd moved on from there when a copper told her she couldn't sleep on the steps. She hadn't slept at all the first night. Just walked round and round, in and out of places she didn't know or looking in shop windows. If you had money there were beautiful clothes for sale. Elegant gowns in every colour imaginable ... and hats! Styles with feathers and bows, silk flowers and little clusters of jewels. Not that such things would look any good on her. But on tall, slim Bernie they'd be just right.

Rose knew what Trafalgar Square looked like and she'd spent some time there watching children feed the pigeons. Then she'd walked towards Buckingham Palace, where the King lived with the Queen and the little Princesses. In front of the palace she'd found a park with a big pond where people fed bread to ducks and geese and other birds. Sometimes bits landed on the grass and so, when the people went, Rose helped herself to it. She was hungry and thirsty but knew she couldn't go back to Mrs Rabinowicz's and felt bad about that. She'd let her mistress down, and Becky too. They'd all be angry with her. But she couldn't have her mum chucked out on the street, not when she was sick. Rose just hoped that the matchmaker didn't ask for the money back. But she couldn't think about that now.

When it got dark, she started to feel frightened. Park-keepers in uniform went around telling people to leave the area and so she had to hide. At some point the park would, she thought, be empty so maybe she could sleep on the grass or in a bush. It was a bit creepy, but she didn't know what else to do.

Luckily it was warm and she was tired and so she found it easy to sleep on the grass using just her coat as a blanket. But some time later, when the park was really dark and totally quiet, she woke up with a jolt. In front of her, his face illuminated by a cigarette, was a man. Rose knew enough about life to realise what someone like this might want and so she pulled her coat up to her chin and said, 'Don't you touch me! I know what men like you want. Don't you dare!'

But then the man smiled and said, 'Oh, I don't want to touch you, darling. But I do want to help you.'

Rose, unconvinced, said, 'How do I know that? I ain't gonna let you do nothing!'

The man reached out his hand to her. 'Okey-dokey, sweetheart,' he said. 'We ain't gonna do nothing you do not like. I promise.'

And then he smiled. He had a nice smile. A bit like her Uncle Pat's. Slowly at first, and against her better judgement, Rose reached out and took his hand.

Chapter Twenty-Three

Christmas Eve 1937

'Have you never been to Harrods?'

'No.'

Bernie couldn't stop staring. It was like being in a palace. A vast glass atrium soared above her head. The walls were studded with huge, colourful mosaics and her surroundings lit by enormous crystal chandeliers. Everything about this place was giant-sized.

'Well, this is Berlin's version of Harrods,' Heinrich Simpson explained. 'It's called Wertheim's. When I was a child, my mother used to bring my brother and me here all the time. Of course, it was mainly so's she could buy clothes for herself, but if we were good and didn't make nuisances of ourselves we got to go to Café Kranzler afterwards for coffee and cake. Although there is a grand tea room here as well as a garden, would you believe?'

'It's amazing!'

Last-minute shoppers thronged the floor of the huge atrium that dominated the department store's lush interior. In the middle stood an enormous Christmas tree covered in candles.

'It's beautiful!' Bernie said.

'Maybe.' Heinrich moved his head closer to her ear and said, 'But look more closely at the Christmas tree and tell me what you see.'

It was without doubt the biggest Christmas tree Bernie had ever seen and completely covered in candles. There were huge piles of gaily wrapped boxes around its base that she assumed were either real or pretend presents. The smell of pine that came off it was intoxicating.

'Look at the top,' Heinrich said.

And so she did. And felt her face lose its colour.

'Oh my God,' she said. 'Is that what I think it is?'

Dolly threw another packet of fags into her handbag and then stood by the front door.

'I do wish you'd come with us, Solly, I really do,' she said. 'It's your first Christmas home ... '

'We're Jews, Mum, we don't celebrate Christmas,' he said.

Dolly waved his comment away. 'Ach, so what? We always have in the past. When Mrs Llewellyn was still alive, God rest her soul. It's a party, ain't it?'

'Not at *Stanley's* it won't be.'

Dolly shook her head. Neither of her sons liked her gentleman friend. But then even she had to admit that Stanley Green had about as much go in him as a flounder. But he was kind, he treated her nicely and wasn't too demanding in the bedroom stakes.

'Ben's coming,' she said. 'You'll be all on your tod.'

'Ben's only going to please you.'

'So why can't you do the same?'

Solly shrugged. 'Because I can't bear the small talk, Mum. I just can't. The world is a nightmare at present and I can't stand people like your bloke making light of that.'

She put a hand on his shoulder and then stroked his face. She had some idea of what he'd been through in Spain. He'd not, of course, told her everything. His mum didn't need to know about people being blown apart by bombs, or women being raped by Nationalist mercenaries.

'You need a job now, you know, Solly,' she said as she opened the front door of the flat. 'It's not good for you sitting here in the flat all day long.'

She left and he was relieved. The more time he spent with his mother and Mr Green, the more guilty he felt about the fact that she'd borrowed money from the old man to buy him his new wooden leg. Solly didn't even like it. It was uncomfortable. As soon as his family were out of the way, he always went back to his old Spanish peg. He'd walked across long stretches of the Pyrenees on that. It was, like the Spanish War, part of him. What he had seen could never be unseen even though he hoped never to witness such sights again.

He'd heard that Bernie Lynch was working as a photographer for the *London Evening News* and was pleased for her. He'd seen passion in her eyes for the first time on Cable Street, then he'd seen it again when she'd kissed him outside her flat. He wished she'd answered his letter. Maybe she had and he'd never got it? But he accepted now that they were never to be. Bernie was talented and ambitious and he was a bloke who'd lost his way, both politically and deep down in his soul. He was broken and had no idea how he might be fixed.

But his mum was right about him getting a job. He had to work or he'd end up on the street. He couldn't expect Dolly and Ben to carry on keeping him. But what could he do? What was there to do in a country where so many were out of work already? And how was he going to manage to hold down a job with a broken body and mind?

Solly put his head back and closed his eyes. Tomorrow, on Christmas Day, he'd eat the chicken soup his mum had made him and then drink the whisky Ben had bought him. With any luck he wouldn't come up for air until Boxing Day.

'Why is there a swastika on top of the Christmas tree?' Bernie whispered.

'Because it's said that Hitler wants to make Christmas a Nationalist rather than a Christian festival,' Heinrich said. 'He doesn't like the idea that Jesus was a Jew.'

Bernie said, 'He's a nutcase.'

'This store is Jewish-owned,' Heinrich continued. 'Georg Wertheim is a prominent member of the community. But his wife is a gentile and there are rumours that ownership has now been transferred to her, for political reasons.'

'That's terrible.'

And yet all around them people were laughing, smiling and spending freely, which made the world look normal apart from that Nazi symbol on top of the massive Christmas tree.

'So why are we here?' Bernie asked.

'Because, if we can get away with it, I'd like you to take a photograph of that Nazi tree,' Heinrich instructed her.

The Caravan Club didn't usually open in the afternoon, but because it was Christmas Eve, people had just turned up. And because it was Christmas the following day, most of them didn't have anywhere else to be until the festival was over. This included Rose.

'Well, fancy seeing you here, my little *bona palone*,' a deep, Cockney voice boomed.

Rose smiled and ran into the arms of a tall middle-aged man wearing a silver sheath dress and false eyelashes. 'Happy Christmas Eve, Tilly,' she said.

The silver dress-wearer, one Herbert Lewis to those who didn't *really* know him, said, 'So, not taking your kit off for the eager men of Soho today, little Rosie Red?'

'I need a rest, Tilly,' she said. 'It's not easy standing completely still when you're naked, you know.'

'But you're so good at it!'

Rose laughed. Once she'd got over the first flush of fear when Tilly/Herbert had originally found her in St James's Park, she'd found almost every word he said irresistibly funny. Office clerk and part-time drag-queen, Herbert had a friend at the Windmill Theatre, a man he knew would take to Rose as soon as he saw her. Pretty, small and a little bit plump, Herbert knew she'd make a wonderful addition to his friend Vivian van Damm's 'tableau vivant' show.

'That's naked standing still to you,' Herbert had told her.

The only thing Rose had worried about was whether she'd have to have sex with the people who came to see the show, but Vivian, who was the manager of the Windmill, had assured her that 'wasn't obligatory'.

'Although what I can't stop is blokes hanging about outside afterwards,' he'd said. 'But the other girls'll teach you how to deal with them.'

And they had. Especially a girl called Sarah who came from up North, with whom Rose ended up sharing a bedsit in Greek Street. It was Sarah who knew all what she called the 'gay' types, the drag queens, appreciators of boys and all things male. Rose loved them. They spoke a weird language called

Polari that she didn't always completely understand, but they had to do that, they said, so the police, or 'Lilly Law', didn't know what they were saying.

Gay boys, Rose had learned, met in certain pubs, at the theatre and in clubs like the Caravan, which was, so she'd been told, sometimes raided by 'Lilly Law'. What these men and boys did together was considered an 'unnatural act' and just being gay meant that they could end up in prison. But they were kind to Rose and that was all she cared about. In fact, ever since she'd fetched up in this place called Soho, she'd been happier than she'd ever been in her life.

Here no old women made her clean their houses, her mum didn't worry the life out of her all the time, she had money of her own and, best of all, there was no Len Tobin. The only thing that really made her sad was that she couldn't see Bernie and Becky any more. She missed her friends, but knew she'd never be able to go back home, not after what she'd done.

Decorated in a way Herbert, or rather Tilly, described as 'Moroccan', the Caravan was a low dive with colourful cushions, a ceiling people said looked like a tent, and the smell of gin and fags hanging in the air thick as a blanket. Rose smiled. This was her home now and no one was ever going to take her away from it. She picked up a piece of mistletoe she'd nicked from the foyer at the Windmill and held it over Tilly's head.

'Kiss for Christmas, Tilly?'

Tilly wrinkled up her nose and then kissed Rose hard and firm on the lips.

'There you go, you naughty girl,' she said. 'Big smacker from your Auntie Till.'

'All right ... now!' Heinrich said.

The tune playing throughout the store was 'Stille Nacht'.

Bernie, although unable to speak German, recognised it. As she raised the camera to frame the shot, she hummed it to herself. Nobody was watching her. All too busy with their Christmas shopping ...

She took one shot, then two. Then she decided to take the tree from a different angle. Heinrich put a hand on her arm. 'Bernie ... '

'Just one more.'

What happened next was so fast she didn't even have time to breathe. One moment the camera was in her hands, the next it was lying on the floor in front of her. And, although Heinrich was clearly trying to reason with him, the man in the black uniform shouting into her face had his foot raised above the camera, ready to destroy it. A member of the feared SS, judging from his black uniform and insignia, his brilliant blue eyes were those of a fanatic.

'Happy Christmas Eve, Auntie Kitty!'

As soon as Bernie's mum had opened the door, Becky put the brisket into her hands. Kitty Lynch looked tired and strained, but when she saw the meat she smiled.

'Oh, Rebekah!'

'From Papa,' she said. 'A Christmas present.'

It was Marie who had told her that Uncle Pat was bed-bound. His chest, she'd said, rattled like an old door in the wind. Auntie Kitty had had to all but give up work to look after him. The family had nothing.

All the remaining Lynch kids crowded around the meat with big, hungry eyes.

'Blimey, Becky,' Dermot said, 'that's bloody huge!'

'I know you'd rather I was Bernie home for Christmas but ... '

Auntie Kitty threw her arms around her and cried, 'Oh,

Jesus, Mary and Joseph! You are the most darling girl and your father is a saint.'

While Marie, Little Paddy and Aggie fired up the range, Dermot took Becky to see Uncle Pat. Lying in bed, pale and thin, he looked twenty years older than his real age. Seeing this made Becky sad. But she smiled in spite of herself because he was smiling.

'Bit of brisket'll do us all good,' Uncle Pat said. 'You tell your dad he's a *mensch*, Becky love. You tell him that from me.'

'I will.'

Ever since she'd admitted to her father how much she didn't want to get married, Moritz Shapiro had changed. She'd thought he'd go through the roof, but in the end he'd taken it calmly. He'd gone to see the *shadchan* and told her that the match was now at an end and he didn't want to hear any more about it. Mrs Rabinowicz, it was said, had needed to lie down for a week to recover. And of course Mr Suss and Chaim were hurt and offended and made it known that they would never speak to the Shapiros again. But it had been worth it.

'I'm going to train as a nurse in January,' Becky told Pat.

'At the London Hospital?'

'Yes.'

'You can come and look after Dad,' Dermot said.

Becky squeezed Pat's hand. 'You'll be better by then, Uncle Pat.'

"Course I will!'

But she saw Dermot frown and knew in her heart that Uncle Pat was never going to get better, even though Bernie sent money every month for the ephedrine injections. Becky was sure that was, at least in part, why she'd taken the job with the *Evening News*.

Uncle Pat coughed. 'Pity ... er ... pity Bernie ain't ... '

'Oh, Bernie's doing what she's always wanted to do,' Becky said. 'Exploring the world. I'm so happy for her. We're very lucky, Bernie and me, we've both got what we wanted out of life.'

'In spite of everything, eh, girl?'

She kissed his forehead.

'In spite of everything, yes. Although we've both been equally lucky to have such good parents' she said. 'I only wish I knew that Rosie was happy too. I just wish ...'

'Oh, little Rose'll be all right,' Uncle Pat said. 'You mark my words, that kid's a survivor. Wouldn't be surprised if one day we saw her ride past in a big old Rolls-Royce.'

Becky laughed, even though she doubted whether that would ever happen.

Auntie Kitty put her head around the door and said, 'Rebekah love, there's so much meat there, would you mind if I invited Nell Larkin over to share it with us tomorrow? What with her being all on her own ...'

'I think that's a good idea,' Becky said. 'If she'll come.'

Nell had hardly been seen since Rose had disappeared. She was still 'working' but, as far as anyone knew, Len Tobin was no longer on the horizon.

Kitty hovered in the doorway. 'And you and your dad?'

'Oh, it's the Sabbath tomorrow, so no thanks,' Becky said. 'But that's as it should be, Auntie Kitty. Papa and me, we're all right now, we understand each other and we're happy together. And as Uncle Pat said about Rosie, everything's going to be all right.'

''Course it will.'

But Becky saw the sadness behind Auntie Kitty's smile and knew that she was still grieving over Joey's absence. There were fewer of them than there had been the previous Christmas, true. But those who remained were alive and as well as they could be, and in spite of the ever-worsening news from Germany life in the East End went on as usual. And, of course, Solly Adler was alive. And for Becky, even though she hadn't seen him for a while, that was everything.

Love, even when it wasn't reciprocated, would pull her and all the rest of them through whatever lay ahead.

Acknowledgments

This book would not have been possible without the great archive of stories handed down to me by my family. I'd also like to thank my agent, Juliet Burton, for believing in the project and for Dominic Wakeford at Piatkus for all his hard work.

Author Q & A

You've previously written crime novels as Barbara Nadel, what inspired you to start writing saga novels as well?

I thought it was a good medium through which to explore recent East End history. Much has been and will continue to be written about East End crime, but I wanted to look at family stories, which abound in the East End. I grew up with these family 'sagas' and was always fascinated by the variety of characters involved in these tales. It always annoys me when people refer to 'a typical East Ender', there is no such thing! Part of my 'mission' for this book is to, hopefully, explode that myth.

Why did you set *Ten Bells Street* in Spitalfields?

Spitalfields is one of my (many) favourite parts of the East End. It has a fascinating history involving refugee weavers from France, Irish in-comers escaping from the Potato Famine, a vibrant Jewish community and an Asian community that actually goes back a very long way. It is also where Jack the Ripper stalked his victims in the 1890s and where many of the 'troops' involved in the Battle of Cable Street came from in the 1930s. It's a place filled with amazing historic buildings and many, many stories. I sometimes act as a guide for tourists to the area and it is always magical.

Do you have more stories planned for these characters?

Absolutely! *Ten Bells Street* is set in the 1930s and I have already written the next book which is set in the 1940s. I want to see how the lives of Bernie, Becky, Rose and their families change over time and, believe me, I'm just as curious about it as any reader!

Do you have a favourite character to write about?

I have several favourites if I'm honest. I've a real soft spot for Bernie's father, Pat Lynch, because he is very like my own late father. Tough, but kind and interested in learning and bettering himself, Pat has much in common with my old dad. I also love writing about Rose. Her life is pure chaos and she could so easily give up, but she doesn't. Illiterate and almost unimaginably poor by today's standards, she nevertheless knows what she wants and I get a feeling that, in part at least, she may get it.

What kind of research did you do to write the book?

I spent a lot of time in Spitalfields and a lot of time talking to relatives and friends about the many stories they knew and had inherited. I also did a lot of reading around subjects like the Battle of Cable Street and the British Communist movement.

If you could travel back to any period in time, what would you most like to see and why?

I guess it would be late 19th century Spitalfields. Poor and filthy yes, but also alive with cooking smells, customs, sounds and sights from all over the world. Back then it was a place of noisy commerce and of new and exciting ideas brought to the UK by people like Karl Marx and Friedrich Engels. Change was in the air back then as people realised that they could control their own destinies. Also, I would love to have seen the old music halls and Yiddish Theatres back in their heyday as well as, possibly, sneak a peek at some of my own ancestors!

Do you love historical fiction?

Want the chance to hear news about your favourite authors (and the chance to win free books)?

Mary Balogh
Lenora Bell
Charlotte Betts
Jessica Blair
Frances Brody
Grace Burrowes
Gaelen Foley
Pamela Hart
Elizabeth Hoyt
Eloisa James
Lisa Kleypas
Stephanie Laurens
Sarah MacLean
Amanda Quick
Julia Quinn

Then visit the Piatkus website
www.piatkusentice.co.uk

And follow us on Facebook and Twitter
www.facebook.com/piatkusfiction | @piatkusentice

piatkus